W9-AQT-117

LARGE PRINT

RANDOM HOUSE

LARGE PRINT

after the end

Also by Clare Mackintosh
Available from Random House Large Print

I See You

Let Me Lie

after

the end

Clare Mackintosh

RANDOM HOUSE
LARGE PRINT

Copyright © 2019 by Clare Mackintosh

Published in the United States of America by Random House Large Print in association with G. P. Putnam's Sons, an imprint of Penguin Random House LLC, New York.

Cover design and art: Ploy Siripant
Cover images: (background texture) Dragana Jokmanovic / Shutterstock; (feather) Arcady / Shutterstock

The Library of Congress has established a Cataloging-in-Publication record for this title.

ISBN: 978-0-593-10420-0

www.penguinrandomhouse.com/large-print-format-books

FIRST LARGE PRINT EDITION

Printed in the United States of America

10 9 8 7 6 5 4 3 2 1

This Large Print edition published in accord with the standards of the N.A.V.H.

To the NICU team at the John Radcliffe Hospital, Oxford.
Thank you.

after

the end

prologue

Leila looks around the courtroom. Only the handful of press given permission to attend are moving, their pens making swift marks in shorthand, recording every word the judge speaks. Everyone else is quite still—watching, waiting—and Leila has the strange sensation of being frozen in time, that they might all wake, a year from now, and they will still be here in this courtroom, waiting for the ruling that will change so many lives.

Leila swallows. If it is this hard for her, how impossible must it be for Pip and Max to listen to the judge's words? To know that in a few moments they will hear their son's fate?

Before the break, Max and Pip Adams were sitting at opposite ends of the long bench seat behind their legal teams. They are still on the bench, but the distance between them has contracted, and now they are sitting close enough to touch each other.

In fact, as Leila watches, and as the judge draws

clare mackintosh

closer to his ruling, she sees movement. She could not say if Max moved first, or Pip. She can't be certain they even know they are doing it. But as she watches, two hands venture slowly across the no-man's-land between them, and find each other.

Dylan's parents hold hands.

The judge speaks.

And a courtroom holds its breath.

2

before

one

Pip

Dylan was six hours old when I noticed a mark behind his left ear the size of a thumbprint. I lay on one side, watching him, my free arm curled protectively across his body. I watched his perfect lips quiver a breath, and I traced my gaze across his cheeks and round the whorls of ears still too new to have found their shape. And then I saw a thumbprint the colour of milky tea, and I smiled because here was something totally new and yet completely familiar.

"He's got your birthmark."

I showed Max, who said **He's definitely mine, then**, and tiredness and euphoria made us laugh so much the nurse popped her head round the curtains to ask what was the commotion. And when Max had to leave, and the lights were turned low, I touched the tip of my finger to the milky-tea mark that linked the two people I loved more than anything else in the world, and thought that life could never get more perfect.

There's a low keening from somewhere on the ward; an accompanying murmur from a parent up as late as I am. I hear the squeak of rubber shoes in the corridor, and the bubble of the water cooler releasing a dose, before the shoes take it back to the ward.

I rest a hand gently on Dylan's forehead, and stroke it upwards. His hair is growing back in fair wisps, like when he was a baby, and I wonder if it'll still be curly. I wonder if it'll turn brown again, like it did when he hit two. I trace a finger down his nose, careful not to touch the narrow tube that snakes into one nostril and into his stomach.

The endotracheal tube is wider than the feeding one. It pushes between Dylan's lips, held in place by two wide strips of tape, one across his chin, and one above his lips. At Christmas we brought in the sticky moustaches that fell from our novelty crackers, and chose the curliest, most extravagant for Dylan. And for a few days, until the tape grew grubby and needed changing, our almost-three-year-old boy made everyone around him smile again.

"Is it OK to touch him?"

I look across the room, to where the new boy is; to where his mother, anxious and uncertain, hovers by her son's bed.

"Of course." The charge nurse, Cheryl, smiles

encouragingly. "Hold his hand, give him a cuddle. Talk to him." There are always at least two nurses in here, and they change all the time, but Cheryl is my favourite. She has such a calming manner I'm convinced her patients get better just from being in her presence. There are three children in this room: eight-month-old Darcy Bradford, my Dylan, and the new boy.

The name **Liam Slater** is written in marker pen on the card stuck to the end of his bed. If the children are well enough when they're admitted to intensive care, they get to choose an animal sticker. They do the same on the nameplates above the pegs at Dylan's daycare. I chose a cat for him. Dylan loves cats. He'll stroke them oh so gently, and widen his eyes like it's the first time he's felt something so soft. Once a big ginger tom scratched him, and Dylan's mouth formed a perfect circle of shock and dismay, before his face crumpled into tears. I felt a wave of sadness that he would forever now be wary of something that had brought him so much joy.

"I don't know what to say," whispers Liam's mum. Butterfly breaths flutter her throat. Her son is bigger than Dylan—he must be at school already—with a snub nose and freckles, and hair left long on top. Two thin lines are shaved into the side, above his ear.

"Pretty cool haircut," I say.

"Apparently everyone else's parents let them." She rolls her eyes but it's a pale imitation of a mother's frustration. I play along, giving a mock grimace.

"Oh dear—I've got all this to come." I smile. "I'm Pip, and this is Dylan."

"Nikki. And Liam." Her voice wobbles on his name. "I wish Connor was here."

"Your husband? Will he be back tomorrow?"

"He's getting the train. They get picked up, you see, on a Monday morning, and brought back on Friday. They stay on-site during the week."

"Builder?"

"Plasterer. Big job at Gatwick airport." She stares at Liam, her face ashen. I know that feeling: that fear, made a hundred times worse by the stillness of the ward. There's a different atmosphere on the cancer ward. Kids up and down the corridors, in the playroom, toys all over the place. The older ones doing maths with the education team, physios helping reluctant limbs behave. You're still worried, of course you are—Christ, you're terrified—but . . . it's different, that's all. Noisier, brighter. More **hopeful**.

"Back again?" the nurses would say when they saw us. Soft eyes would meet mine, carrying a second conversation above the lighthearted banter. **I'm sorry this is happening. You're doing so well. It'll be OK.** "You must like it here, Dylan!"

And the funny thing was, he really did. His face would light up at the familiar faces, and if his legs were working he'd run down the corridor to the playroom and seek out the big box of Duplo, and if you saw him from a distance, intent on his tower, you'd never know he had a brain tumour.

Up close, you'd know. Up close you'd see a curve like the hook of a coat hanger, across the left side of his head, where the surgeons cut him open and removed a piece of bone so they could get at the tumour. Up close you'd see the hollows around his eyes and the waxy tone of skin starved of red blood cells. Up close, if you passed us in the street, you'd flinch before you could stop yourself.

No one flinched in the children's ward. Dylan was one of dozens of children bearing the wounds of a war not yet won. Maybe that's why he liked it there: he fitted in.

I liked it, too. I liked my pull-out bed, right next to Dylan's, where I slept better than I did at home, because here, all I had to do was press a button, and someone would come running. Someone who wouldn't panic if Dylan pulled out his Hickman line; someone to reassure me that the sores in his mouth would heal with time; to smile gently and say that bruising was quite normal following chemo.

No one panicked when I pressed the button that last time, but they didn't smile, either.

"Pneumonitis," the doctor said. She'd been there for the first chemo cycle, when Max and I fought tears and told each other to **be brave for Dylan**, and we'd seen her on each cycle since; a constant over the four months

9

we'd spent in and out of hospital. "Chemotherapy can cause inflammation in the lungs—that's what's making it hard for him to breathe."

"But the last cycle was September." It was the end of October. What was left of the tumour after surgery wasn't getting any bigger; we'd finished the chemo; Dylan should have been getting better, not worse.

"Symptoms can develop months afterwards, in some cases. Oxygen, please." This last was directed to the nurse, who was already unwrapping a mask.

Two days later Dylan was transferred to paediatric intensive care on a ventilator.

The atmosphere in PICU is different. Everything's quiet. Serious. You get used to it. You can get used to anything. But it's still hard.

Nikki looks up. I follow her gaze to where it rests on Dylan, and for a second I see my boy through her eyes. I see his pale, clammy skin, the cannulas in both arms, and the wires that snake across his bare chest. I see his hair, thin and uneven. Dylan's eyes flicker beneath their lids, like the tremor of a moth within your cupped hands. Nikki stares. I know what she's thinking, although she'd never admit to it. None of us would.

She's thinking: **Let that boy be sicker than mine.**

She sees me watching her and colours, dropping her gaze to the floor. "What are you knitting?" she says. A pair of needles pokes from a ball of sunny yellow yarn in the bag by my feet.

"A blanket. For Dylan's room." I hold up a completed square. "It was this or a scarf. I can only do straight lines." There must be thirty or so squares in my bag, in different shades of yellow, waiting to be stitched together once I have enough to cover a bed. There are a lot of hours to fill when you're a PICU parent. I brought books in from home at first, only to read the same page a dozen times, and still have no idea what was happening.

"What year's Liam in?" I never ask why kids are in hospital. You pick things up, and often the parents will tell you, but I'd never ask. I ask about school instead, or what team they support. I ask about who they were before they got sick.

"Year one. He's the youngest in his class." Nikki's bottom lip trembles. There's a blue school sweater stuffed into a carrier bag at her feet. Liam's wearing a hospital gown they'll have put on when he was admitted.

"You can bring in pyjamas. They let you bring clothes in, but make sure you label them, because they tend to go walkabout."

Cheryl gives a wry smile.

"You've got enough on your plate without chasing after a lost T-shirt, isn't that right?" I raise my voice to include Aaron and Yin, the other two nurses on duty, in the conversation.

"We're busy enough, certainly." Yin smiles at Nikki. "Pip's right, though, please do bring in clothes from home, and perhaps a favourite toy? Something wash-able is ideal, because of infection, but if there's a teddy he particularly loves, of course that's fine."

"I'll bring Boo." Nikki turns to Liam. "I'll bring Boo, shall I? You'd like that, wouldn't you?" Her voice is high and unnatural. It takes practice, speaking to a sedated child. It's not like they're sleeping, not like when you creep into their room on your way to bed, to whisper **I love you** in their ear. When you stand for a moment, looking down at the mess of hair poking out from beneath the duvet, and tell them **Good night, sleep tight, don't let the bedbugs bite**. There's no soft sigh as they hear your voice in their sleep; no echo as they half-wake and mumble a reply.

An alarm sounds, a light flashing next to Darcy's cot. Yin crosses the room, reattaches the oximeter to the baby's foot, and the alarm stops, Darcy's oxygen levels reading normal again. I glance at Nikki and see the panic in her eyes. "Darcy's a wriggler," I explain. It's a while before you stop jumping at every buzzer, every alarm. "Her parents are normally here in the evenings, but it's their wedding anniversary today. They've gone to see a musical."

"Ooh, what are they seeing?" Yin has seen **West Side Story** eleven times. Pinned to the lanyard around her neck are badges from **Phantom, Les Mis, Matilda** . . .

"**Wicked**, I think."

"Oh, that's brilliant! I saw it with Imogen Sinclair as Glinda. They'll love it."

Eight-month-old Darcy has meningitis. **Had** meningitis: another reason why her parents are having a rare evening away from PICU. They're finally through the worst.

"My husband's away, too," I tell Nikki. "He travels a lot, with work." I turn to Dylan. "Daddy's missing your big day, isn't he?"

"His birthday?"

"Better than a birthday." I touch the wooden arm of my chair, an instinctive gesture I must do a hundred times a day. I think of all the parents who have sat in this chair before me; of the surreptitious strokes from superstitious fingers. "Dylan's coming off the ventilator tomorrow." I look at Cheryl. "We've tried a few times, haven't we, but this little monkey . . . Fingers crossed, eh?"

"Fingers crossed," Cheryl says.

"Is that a big step forward?" Nikki asks.

I grin. "The biggest." I stand up. "Right, my darling, I'll be off." It feels odd, at first, talking like this, with other families all around you. You're self-conscious. Like making phone calls in an open-plan office, or when you go to the gym for the first time and you think everyone's looking at you. They're not, of course, they're too busy thinking about their own phone call, their own workout, their own sick child.

So, you start talking, and three months later you're like me—unable to stop.

"Nanny's coming to see you at the weekend— that'll be nice, won't it? She's missed you terribly, but she didn't want to come anywhere near you, not with that horrible cold she had. Poor Nanny."

It's become a habit now, this prattling on. I'll catch myself talking out loud in the car, at the shops, at home; filling the space where **See the tractor?** and **Time for bed** and **Look with your eyes, Dylan, not your hands** should be. They tell you it's good to talk to the kids. That they find it reassuring to hear Mum and Dad's voices. I think it's us who find it reassuring. It's a reminder of who we were before we were PICU parents.

I drop the side of Dylan's cot, so I can lean over him, my forearms resting either side of him, and our noses touching. "Eskimo kiss," I say softly. He never let us forget that final good-night kiss, no matter how many cuddles had been given, how many raspberries blown.

"Keemo!" he'd insist, and I'd drop the cot side once more, and lean for a final good night, and he'd press his nose against mine and wrap his fingers around my hair.

"Love you, baby boy," I tell him now. I close my eyes, imagining warm breath on my face, sweet from bedtime milk. **Tomorrow**, I think. **Tomorrow they'll take out the tube, and this time it won't go back in.** I kiss his forehead and raise the cot side, making sure it clicks safely into place so he can't fall out. "Night, Cheryl. Bye, Aaron, Yin. See you tomorrow?"

"Off for three days," Yin says, holding up both hands in a **hallelujah**.

"Oh, so you are—you're going to visit your sister, aren't you? Have a lovely time." I look at Nikki Slater, who has pulled her chair a little closer to her son, so she can rest her head beside his. "Get some rest if you can," I say gently. "It's a long road we're all on."

I say good night to the girls at the nurses' station, and to Paul, the porter who brought Dylan from the cancer ward to PICU, and who always asks after him. I collect my coat, find my keys, and walk to the car park, where I feed another ten pounds into the ticket machine.

You can buy season tickets, if you're visiting someone in intensive care. I always make sure new parents know about it, because it all adds up, doesn't it? Especially when you have to bring two cars here, like Max and I often do. It's ten pounds to park for twenty-four hours, but they'll give you a week for twenty quid, or a whole month for forty. I bought the month ticket in November, and again in December, but when January came and I stood by the office with my purse in my hand, I couldn't bear to ask for another month's parking. It felt so . . . **defeatist**. We wouldn't be here for another four weeks, surely? Not when Dylan was so much more stable.

Frost glitters the tarmac. I scrape the ice off the windscreen with an Aretha Franklin CD case, and put the heating on full blast till the glass clears of mist. By the time I can see, it's so hot I have to open the window to stop myself from falling asleep.

The drive home takes a little over an hour. The hospital has accommodation for parents—three bedsits with tiny kitchens as new as the day they were installed, because who thinks about cooking when your schild's in intensive care? We stayed there for most of November, and then Max had to work, and Dylan was **critical but stable**, and it felt right to give up the flat for someone who needed it more. I don't mind the drive. I stick on one of my programmes and before I know it I'm pulling up on the drive.

I'm listening to **Bringing Up B**, a podcast recorded by a mum who sounds about my age. I don't know B's name, only that she has two siblings, she likes piano music and velvet cushions, and she's profoundly disabled.

We've known for a few weeks now that Dylan has brain damage, not just from the tumour, but from the surgery required to remove as much of it as possible. Thinking about it makes my chest tighten until I feel as though I'm the one who needs help to breathe, and so listening to **Bringing Up B** helps me find perspective.

B can't walk. She spends most of her time lying flat on her back, watching the CDs her sisters have strung into a shiny mobile to make rainbows on the ceiling. They collected the CDs from friends, and B's mum found them ribbon and buttons, and they chattered to

B as they argued gently over what should go where. There was laughter in her mum's voice as she told the story for the thousands of listeners she won't ever meet, and I wondered how many of them were like me. How many were listening with tears in their eyes but fire in their hearts, thinking, **I can do that. I can be that mum.**

The house is dark and unloved, the answerphone blinking. A neat pile of post on the table in the hall tells me Mum's been here, and sure enough, there's a Tupperware in the fridge marked **lasagne** and a note by the kettle saying **Love you, M & D x**. I feel suddenly tearful. My parents live in Kidderminster, where I grew up—more than an hour across Birmingham from the house Max and I bought just outside of Leamington. They visit Dylan at least twice a week, but Mum's caught one cold after another, and they both decided it would be best to steer clear of PICU for a while. Nevertheless, every few days one or both of them still makes the two-hour round trip to Leamington to make sure their daughter and beloved son-in-law are eating.

My parents fell for Max almost as quickly as I had. Mum was charmed by his accent; Dad by the earnest way he promised to take care of their only daughter. With Max's relatives all in America, my mum made it her duty to fuss over us both.

It's too late to eat, so I put the lasagne in the freezer with the others, and make a cup of tea to take to bed.

I pause in the hall and look around in the shadowy light thrown down from the landing. It had seemed extravagant, buying a four-bedroom house when we only needed two. Future-proofing, Max called it.

"We might have a whole football team of children."

"One will do for now!" I'd laughed, finding it hard to visualise Dylan as anything other than an enormous bump that meant I hadn't seen my feet in weeks.

One will do. My breath catches.

I open the door to the dining room and lean in the doorway. This will be Dylan's new room. The little blue-and-white nursery upstairs was already too baby-ish for a two-year-old more interested in football than Peter Rabbit; this time last year we were talking about redecorating. **This time last year.** It feels like another world, and I screw up my eyes against the what-ifs that jab at me with accusing fingers. **What if you'd noticed sooner? What if you'd trusted your instincts? What if you hadn't listened to Max?**

I open my eyes and distract myself with practicalities. Dylan's almost three now. He's easy to carry, but in a few years he'll be too heavy to take upstairs to bed. In the dining room, there's space for a wheelchair, a special bed, a hoist if we need one. I imagine a mobile of shiny CDs above Dylan's bed, dancing rainbows across the ceiling. I close the door, and take my tea to bed.

I message Max.

Good day today—sats stable and no sign of
infection. Our boy's a fighter! Fingers
crossed for tomorrow x

I'm too tired to work out the time difference, or whether Max will already have left Chicago for New York—the last leg of this trip before he comes home. There was a period in my life when I could have told you what time it was anywhere in the world. New York, Tokyo, Helsinki, Sydney. I could have recommended somewhere to eat, told you the exchange rate, suggested a good hotel. The cabin crew in business class aren't just there to pour drinks and recite the safety briefing. We're PAs, chefs, tourist guides. Concierges in a five-star hotel. And when the work stopped, the party started. Dancing, drinking, singing . . .

Whenever I miss the good old days, I remember why I left. I couldn't do the hours on long-haul once Dylan arrived, not with Max away so much with work, so I swapped my stylish blue uniform for garish polyester, and luxury layovers for budget trips to Benidorm. Full-time for part-time. I didn't love it, but it didn't matter. It worked for Dylan. For our family. And then, when Dylan got ill, I stopped. Everything stopped.

Now, PICU is my job. I'm there by seven, before the winter sun makes it across the car park, and I leave long after it's dark, long after the night staff have come on duty. I take a turn around the hospital grounds midmorning, and again in the afternoon, and I eat my sandwiches in the parents' room, and the rest of the time I sit with Dylan. Every day, every week the same.

Upstairs, I switch on the television. When Max is away the house is too silent, my head too full of the beeps and whirs of intensive care. I find a black-and-white movie and turn down the volume until it's almost inaudible, and pull my pillow into a Max-shaped lump beside me.

Three times they've tried to extubate Dylan. Three times he's crashed and they've had to put him back on the ventilator. Tomorrow they'll try again, and if he can manage on his own—if he can just keep taking breaths . . . then he'll be one step closer to coming home.

two

Max

Something to drink, sir?"

The flight attendant has bright white teeth and shiny hair. We've barely left Chicago, but I'm exhausted. The client I was summoned to see is new—an Illinois start-up with academic funding—and I'm expected to not just keep their business but double it. I spent the first day presenting quick-wins to justify their choice; the evening impressing them with a reservation at Schwa. When we finally left—**One more for the road?**—I sat up till three getting set for the next day. And repeat.

"Sounds like we're in good hands," the client said as I left, but we both know it's results that count. The proof of the pudding is in the eating, as the Brits say.

I yawn. Those three a.m. finishes have taken their toll. I'd give anything to sleep now. Dylan was sleeping through the night around ten months old, but you never sleep the same when you have kids, do you? You're always listening for a noise, half ready to wake. I'd be convinced Dylan was lost somewhere, and I'd wake with a start and my legs would be out of bed before my brain kicked in and told me I'd been dreaming. Even then, I'd have to cross the hall and stand in his doorway to check that he really was in his crib.

But in hotels, when I knew Dylan was safe at home? Boy, could I sleep . . . Sure, the jet lag was tough, but nothing beats a soundproof hotel room with black-out blinds, a minibar, and a room service breakfast.

"How was the trip?" Pip would ask when I got back from Phoenix, or New York, or Toronto. "Nice hotel?"

"Not bad," I'd say. "I was hardly there." And I never am—our clients pay big bucks and my God do they make every cent count—but those hours that I was . . . I swear I'd never slept so well.

Those deep hotel room sleeps stopped when Dylan got sick. I started having the dreams again, only this time Dylan wasn't just lost in the house, or in the park, he was underwater, and if I didn't find him he would drown. I would lie awake in my pitch-black room and wish I was at the hospital, or home making sure Pip was OK. I watched CNN and felt numb to other people's grief.

I order a vodka and Coke, then open my laptop. If I can finish my report in the air, I can "work from home" once I get back to the UK, and spend the time at the hospital with Pip and Dylan instead. If I can get this report done. I stare at the screen, my eyes gritty and my head someplace else, then I move my finger across the trackpad and open Photos.

When Dylan was born Pip started a shared album. She posted a new photo every day, and invited the family to join. It was a neat way of bringing everyone together, despite the distance between them. Scrolling through the photos fast is like flipping through one of those animated books, only instead of a stick man it's my son, growing from baby to toddler, with hints of the man he'll one day become.

The blond hair he was born with—as fair as Pip's—began darkening last year, and by the time chemo started, the strands left on his pillow were as dark as mine. But he was still the spit of Pip. Big, brown eyes, with long lashes and round cheeks. **Hamster cheeks**, Pip calls them, puffing them out and making me laugh.

Beneath the photos are comments. **So adorable! He likes his food, then? He looks so much like you in this one, Pip! I have a picture of Max on the beach just like this. Oh do please share—we'd love to see it!** Grandparents who have only met once, at our wedding, united across an ocean by their only grandson.

Each photo triggers a memory. Dylan's first flight, to visit Granny Adams in Chicago. The farm park with the postpartum gang. Birthday parties, Thanksgiving, Dylan's baptism.

"He'll break some hearts when he's older." The flight attendant takes my empty glass. "Have you chosen your meal?"

"The salmon appetizer, please. And then the beef."

She smiles at the screen. "Cute kid."

The photo on the screen was taken last summer. Dylan's wearing a pirate outfit and a pink tutu he refused to take off.

"Just while you sleep," Pip tried, but no one ever negotiated successfully with a toddler, and for three weeks Dylan slept with a circle of pink net around his dinosaur pajamas.

"He looks like some of the women on my Ibiza flight yesterday," Pip said. We were walking through the grounds of Packwood House, Dylan's tutu at odds with the T-shirt and shorts underneath.

"Hen party?" I said, the English term for a bachelorette party still foreign to my ear, even after ten years in the UK. My American colleagues tell me I sound British; the English ones say I'm Yank through and through. Pip says she can't tell anymore.

"All I hear is Max," she always says.

We turned into the topiary garden, where centuries-old yew trees covered the lawn like giant chess pieces, and Dylan ran between them with his arms outstretched, like an airplane.

"Yup, hen party. Tutus and wings, and drunk before the seat belt signs went off. Too tight to pay for prebooked seats, so they spent the whole flight running up and down the aisle, and sitting on each other's laps."

"Bit different from yours." Dylan ran to hide behind a huge tree, and I ran the opposite way, shouting **Boo!** and making him squeal.

Pip and I had borrowed from both sides of the Atlantic for our prewedding celebrations, hosting a party in the pub down the road in something that was part wedding shower, part bachelor party, part rehearsal dinner. No presents, we'd said, but people brought them regardless, or sent them after the wedding via an endless stream of delivery drivers.

"It's an etiquette thing," Pip had said, as our kitchen table wobbled beneath the weight of more carefully wrapped boxes. "People feel rude not giving us something."

"Surely it's ruder to ignore a request from the happy couple not to bring presents."

"Maybe it's all for my benefit," Pip said, with a sideways glance and a mischievous glint in her eye. "They think a nice crystal vase might make up for the fact I married this horrible American, who tries to stop people giving me presents and wouldn't let me wear a nice pair of fluffy wings at my hen party—"

I'd grabbed her and tickled her till tickling had become kissing and kissing had become something we had to push the boxes to one side for.

The flight attendant is smiling at the photo of Dylan. "How old is he?"

"He turns three in May. That was taken last summer."

"They change so fast, right?" she says. "I bet he's completely different now."

I manage a tight smile and the attendant goes to fetch my meal. She leaves a trace of something floral in the air. Pip would know what it was. She knows perfume the way some people know cars, or music.

"Jo Malone, Pomegranate Noir?" she'll say to someone in the elevator. And they say Americans are direct.

I liked her straightaway. I was flying home to Chicago after a trip to a client in London—pretty much the reverse of what I do now. She had the longest eyelashes I'd ever seen in my life, and I was so busy wondering how women got eyelashes to grow like that, that it was several seconds before I took the hot towel she was patiently holding out.

Afterward—when we found ourselves in the same bar in River North and were three cocktails down— I complimented her on them.

She laughed. "I have them stuck on."

It was like being sixteen again, and realizing girls padded their bras and tanned their skin, except I wasn't sixteen, I was twenty-eight and hardly inexperienced. I knew what false eyelashes were, I just didn't know they looked so . . . The truth of it, of course, is that I'd been blown away by how gorgeous she was.

Pip put both her hands on her head. "And then of course, there's my wig." She moved her hands and her scalp shifted forward and back, and I'll admit that for a second . . .

"Your face!" Another burst of laughter. When Pip laughs, her whole face lights up. Her cheeks dimple, and her nose screws up, and it's impossible not to laugh too.

"I wouldn't care," I said recklessly.

"You wouldn't care if I was bald?"

I'd kissed her, then, right there in the middle of the bar, and she'd kissed me back.

I wasn't even supposed to be on that flight. I'd booked with American, then the flight got canceled, and the office switched me to British Airways.

"Imagine," I said to Pip once, after we got engaged. "If my flight hadn't been canceled, we never would have met."

"We'd have met," she said, right away. "If something's meant to be, it's meant to be. No matter what."

We saw each other again, the next time she flew into Chicago, and again when I found myself in London with a few hours before my flight, and she had just finished work. I started to miss her, and she said she missed me.

"Couldn't you get a transfer?" she said.

"Move to **England**?" I said, in a tone that was only half joking. But I was already in love with her, and I figured I could just as easily work from the UK office as the Chicago one, and the rest, as they say, is history.

I tap the keypad and move the images forward, one by one. Dylan with a football, Dylan with his balance bike, Dylan with the goldfish we won at the fair. Each photo is different, each one freezing a moment in time we'll never get back.

The daily photos stopped in October. Pip continued, for a while, after Dylan got sick. The photos show him losing weight, losing his hair, making a double thumbs-up by the door of the oncology ward. They show him helping out on hospital radio, and playing with his buddies in the room at the end of the hall. But then he got pneumonitis, and they transferred him to PICU, and as one day bled into the next, the photos weren't marking change, but instead reminding us all how little progress he'd made.

I look instead at the WhatsApp message Pip sent last night. Our boy's a fighter!

My message history is a cross-section of our lives, in texts and images. Flight times, airport photos, tired selfies, and silly gifs. Photos, too. Ones that the grandparents don't see. Photos that speak for us, when we can't find the words. A glass of wine; an empty pillow; the car radio playing "our" song. Dylan's blood test results, his feeding tube, the labels from new drugs. When I can't sleep I hit up Google and look up the drugs, search for success rates.

At dinner, homesick and jet-lagged in some forgettable hotel bar, I'll scroll back through our conversations until I get dizzy; until I hit last summer, before we knew Dylan was sick. I read our messages, and it's like listening to a conversation between two people you once knew, but have long since lost touch with.

Back by 8. Take-out, bottle of wine, and some sexy time once D's asleep?

Dude, not if you call it sexy time.

I smile, carry on scrolling. That bloody dog has been barking for an hour!

Did we really care about next-door's dog? About an hour's disruption to our otherwise perfect lives? The last six months have brought life into sharp, painful focus.

"Your appetizer, sir."

I put away my phone and move my laptop to the empty seat beside me. The flight attendant waits for me to make room. "Sorry."

"No problem. Would you like some wine with your meal?"

"Red, thanks."

If we hadn't had Dylan, Pip would still be working transatlantic flights. It's funny to think of her here, pouring wine for tired business execs, and touching up her makeup midflight. She missed it, when she left—missed the big planes, the big destinations—but she never complained.

"Short-haul fits far better around Dylan," she always

said, when I asked. Now it's as though she's never worked, as though she's always spent her days in a hospital ward.

I envy Pip the time she spends with Dylan, but at the same time, I don't know if I could do it. Time away from the hospital gives me strength for when I come back. Eating proper food fuels me for when I don't eat at all. Seeing healthy, happy people around me reminds me that's the life we once had. The life we'll have again.

"How's the family?" my New York client asked as he shook my hand in reception last month.

"Great!" I said, not just to spare him the awkwardness, but because for that moment I could pretend that it was.

I watch the flight attendant as she walks back down the aisle, stopping to fill someone's glass. In the galley kitchen at the end, she leans against the counter and lifts one foot out of her shoe to rub the heel. She's talking to someone I can't see, and I see her laugh at something they've said. I feel a wave of homesickness, and for a second, I miss Pip so much it physically hurts.

When Dylan got sick I stopped giving a shit about work. My inbox filled up, my phone blinked with unplayed voicemails. We spent all day and all night at the hospital, we didn't eat, we didn't sleep. And then the consultant took us to one side.

"Go home. Eat. Get some rest."

"But Dylan—"

The doctor was firm. "You can't help him if you're sick yourselves." It was advice we'd hear a lot over the coming weeks; advice we quickly began to give ourselves, to new parents arriving on the unit. **Get some rest. You have to stay strong for your son, your daughter, each other. It's a marathon, not a sprint.**

Neither of us had been to work in weeks. Pip's boss couldn't have been more supportive. He put her on open-ended compassionate leave; paid for the first six weeks, and with an open door whenever she's ready to come back. **Exceptional circumstances. We're all so sorry. If there's anything we can do, just ask.**

My firm, Kucher Consulting, holds family days twice a year, where middle managers are photographed handing out candy and shooting hoops with starched teens briefed to look like they're enjoying themselves. Last year **Forbes** listed us in the top twenty-five US companies nailing work-life balance.

When I told Chester my son had a brain tumor, he gave me three days. I used all my vacation allowance, took a week off with fictitious flu, and then I simply went AWOL. When I finally listened to my voicemails they were all from Chester, each terser than the last. **What am I supposed to say to the clients, Max? Schulman are threatening to go to Accenture. For fuck's sake, Max, where are you?**

I wanted to quit, but Pip stopped me.

"How will we live?"

"I'll get another job." But even as I said it, I knew I

31

couldn't quit. I was good at my job. I was respected—to a point. I had flexibility—within reason. I was well paid.

I went back to work.

None of us knows what Dylan will need when he comes home. He might need a wheelchair. Special equipment. A live-in nurse. We don't know, and that unknown could be expensive. The bottom line is, I need this job. And, if I'm honest, I couldn't do what Pip does. I couldn't be at the hospital, day in, day out. I don't know how she does it.

The flight attendant takes away my salmon and replaces it with roast beef, complete with tender vegetables and a tiny jug of glossy gravy. I'm not hungry but I eat it anyway, twisting my head toward my laptop between bites, to remind myself what I've written so far. The attendant takes it away; offers me cheese, dessert, coffee, more wine. I take the coffee. Around me, people are finishing their meals and sliding their seats into beds. The attendants hand out extra pillows, unfold blankets, lay out snacks. The lights dim.

I fight tiredness. **Get this report done**, I remind myself, **and you get to see your boy**. The boy who—God willing—is going to breathe on his own tomorrow.

I look at my watch. It's already tomorrow in the UK. I sit up straighter, focus harder. Today. Dylan comes off the ventilator today.

three

Leila

Leila Khalili's alarm goes off at five thirty. Frost from the windows ices the air above her bed, despite the central heating, which she is resigned to keeping on overnight until her mother acclimatizes. It is only ten degrees colder here than it is in Tehran, but seventy-two-year-old Habibeh Khalili feels each one of them in her bones.

When Leila goes downstairs Habibeh is already there, dressed in the mint-green velour tracksuit she wears in the house.

"Maman! How many times have I told you? You don't need to get up when I do." On the television in the sitting room, an immaculately made-up woman in a lemon-colored suit is demonstrating the nonstick qualities of a saucepan set. Shopping channels are

Habibeh's guilty pleasure, and QVC her drug of choice. In the last two weeks Leila's kitchen has acquired a spiralizer, a pineapple corer, and twenty microfiber cleaning cloths.

Habibeh kisses her daughter. "I've made you a lunch. What do you want for breakfast?"

"Just tea. But I'll make it. You go back to bed."

"Sit!" She presses Leila into a chair and boils the kettle, rinsing the teapot Leila only uses for visitors.

"Maman, I don't have time for breakfast." Leila doesn't tell her it's unlikely she'll have time for lunch, either, and that the **kotlet** and pickles Habibeh has lovingly packed into boxes will stay in Leila's bag until the end of the day, when she might find time to eat them as she walks to her bike.

Leila drinks her tea, accepts a slice of flatbread with her mother's famous strawberry jam. "I need to go. Will you take a walk today?"

"Maybe. I have a lot to do here. Your windows are a disgrace."

"Don't clean my windows, Maman, please. Go for a walk."

Beneath the porch, Leila's bike is silver with frost. Her neighbor Wilma Donnachie waves from her bedroom window. It is half past six—why does no one want to be in bed today? When Leila is retired, she thinks, she will sleep in every day. She waves back, but Wilma points down at the pavement, then disappears. She's coming down. Leila checks her watch. It takes twenty minutes to cycle to work, and she has only a little more than that before her shift starts.

"Morning, love. I just wanted to see how Mum was settling in." Wilma is fully dressed, a thick cardigan buttoned over a roll-necked sweater. "I didn't see her at the bake sale in the end."

"Sorry." Habibeh has been here for two weeks, and has not yet left the house. Leila spent a long time persuading her mother to visit the UK. She spent an even longer time persuading the authorities to allow her. Leila worries Habibeh will now spend the six months permitted by her visa shut inside Leila's two-bedroom terraced house in the suburbs of Birmingham.

"I'll pop round to see her, later, shall I? For a cuppa?"

"You're very kind, thank you."

Leila takes off the flowery shower cap keeping the seat of her bike dry, and drops it in the old-fashioned basket at the front. "If she doesn't open the door . . ."

Wilma smiles. "I won't take it personally."

Leila likes cycling to work. She likes the subtle change in landscape as the suburbs become city; the freedom of sailing past a queue of cars, their occupants drumming impatient fingers on static steering wheels. She likes the fresh air that bookends a working day without daylight, and the exercise she would otherwise have no time to take. There are days when it is a joy to cycle through Birmingham; through

Highbury Park, and past the Central Mosque, with its crescent-topped minarets. Then there are days like today.

The rain seems to come at her horizontally, regardless of which direction she's traveling in. Icy water trickles past her sodden scarf and down inside her T-shirt, and despite her waterproofs her trousers are sticking to her legs. Her trainers are soaked; her feet numb. Lack of sleep makes Leila's limbs heavy; makes each turn of the pedals an effort.

There's a flash of silver in the corner of her eye; the brush of a wing mirror against the fabric of her sleeve. A car slices past, far too close, and she feels the clutch of fear that comes with a near miss. This stretch of road isn't quite wide enough for passing when there's oncoming traffic, but that doesn't stop people trying.

Another car passes her, and another, and as Leila looks over her shoulder to see what else is coming, she feels her front wheel sliding away from her, derailed by this break in concentration. There's the harsh sound of a horn, then two, three cars whipping past, keen to move on before an accident happens that might force them to stop.

Leila's shoulder hits the ground first, with a bang that instinct tells her will bruise, but not break. Her head, next, then her body, concertinaing the air from her lungs in an involuntary curse. "La'nati!"

She hears a clatter of metal, the skid of rubber on

tarmac. Her head wants her to sit up, but her body won't comply. Someone is holding her down.

"Lie still, that's it. Can someone call an ambulance?"

"I'm OK—I don't need an ambulance."

There's a woman in a blue cagoule kneeling over Leila, looking up at a knot of passersby who have gathered to gape.

"My bike—"

"Never mind your bike," the woman says bossily, "don't move your head—you might have broken your neck. Ambulance!" she shouts again.

"I haven't broken my neck." A dull ache radiates from Leila's shoulder. She wiggles her fingers and toes, to check they still work, then unclips her helmet and pushes it off, suddenly claustrophobic.

"Never take off a helmet!" the woman shrieks, and for a second Leila thinks she might try to ram it back onto her head. She tries again to get up, but she's still winded.

"Can I help?"

There's a man standing on the other side of Leila. She moves her head to get a better look at him, and cagoule woman shouts at her to stay still.

"I'm a trained first aider, and an ambulance has been called."

"I'm a paramedic," the man says. "I'll take a look, then I can update the crew."

"You're not in uniform."

"I'm on my way to work." He shows his identification, and above Leila's head she sees the familiar colors of the hospital ID card.

"She took her helmet off—I did tell her."

"I'll take it from here." He walks around Leila and kneels, leaving the other woman no choice but to move out of his way. Leila hears her muttering to someone she can't see.

"You're not supposed to take helmets off. I did tell her . . ."

The man smiles. "Hi, I'm Jim. What's your name?"

"Leila Khalili. I'm a doctor. And I'm fine."

Jim rolls his eyes. "Ugh, you lot make the worst patients. Dentists are a close second. Always know best. Mind you, the general public aren't much better—they'd rather put their trust in Dr. Google than in someone actually trained to do their job . . ." While he talks, he's examining Leila; gently checking her skull, the back of her neck, her ears and nose. He loosens Leila's scarf and runs his fingers over her collarbone. Leila gasps.

"Painful?"

"No, your hands are bloody freezing."

He laughs, a rich sound that matches the warmth in his face. "Sorry." His brown eyes are flecked with gold. A smattering of freckles covers the bridge of his nose.

"I landed on my left shoulder. It's just bruised." The throng of people has broken up now, the level of drama insufficient to merit getting soaked through. Jim continues with his methodical examination. He isn't wearing a coat, and the rain has darkened his blond hair.

Finally, he sits back on his heels. "It's only bruising."

"I know," Leila says, exasperated, but she's smiling because he is, and because she knows that, in his shoes, she'd have done exactly the same. She takes the hand he holds out, and gets gingerly to her feet. Cagoule lady has retrieved Leila's bicycle, which—apart from a dented mudguard and a bashed basket—has escaped unharmed. "Thanks for your help," Leila says to them both.

"I'll cancel the ambulance," Jim says. "My car's over there. Sling the bike in the boot and I'll give you a lift to work."

"Thanks, but I'm—" Leila stops herself. The ache in her shoulder has intensified, she's soaked and freezing, and late for work. "That would be great."

With the back seats down, there is just enough space in Jim's Passat for Leila's bike.

"Sorry about the mess." He sweeps an armful of clothes from the passenger seat and dumps them behind them. The footwell is a thick soup of empty water bottles, sandwich packets and McDonald's wrappers, and something that crunches beneath Leila's feet. "I had to move out of my flat a couple of weeks ago and I haven't found a new one. I'm kipping at friends', but it means I'm kind of living out of my car, and . . . well, it's hard to keep tidy."

"I should lend you my mum."

"Does she like tidying?"

"I daren't put a mug of tea down till it's finished—she'll have it washed and back in the cupboard in ten seconds flat."

Jim laughs. "She sounds like the perfect flatmate. Will you be all right here?" He pulls into the bus stop by the children's building, gets out, and sets down Leila's bike, bending the mudguard so it no longer fouls the wheel. "Might be worth taking it somewhere to be checked over, to be on the safe side."

"I will. Thanks again."

O n her way to the ward, Leila stops by Neurology, poking her head round the open door of a large office lined with shelves. Her mentor, Nick Armstrong, is reading a file, leaning back on a chair balanced on two legs. He rocks forward when he sees Leila, the chair landing squarely on all four legs with a thud.

"What happened to you?"

Leila looks down at her waterproofs, which are smeared with mud. "Fell off my bike." She sits, and roots in her rucksack for fifty milligrams of codeine; puts it on her tongue and swallows it dry. "I'm fine."

"I don't suppose you've got anything to eat in there?"

Leila takes the two Tupperware containers from her bag and slides them across the desk. "**Kotlets.** My mother's finest."

"How is she?"

"Driving me nuts. She won't leave the house."

"You'll miss her when she goes back."

Leila looks around Nick's office; at the shelves crammed with reference books, the walls covered with pictures of his wife and their four grown-up children. On the windowsill behind Nick is a photo of him with the queen, when he received his MBE in 2005. He has a few more lines now—his hair starts perhaps a little further back—but otherwise he hasn't changed. His suits are permanently creased, his tie always crooked. Today he looks particularly crumpled.

"How long have you been here?"

Nick looks at his watch. "Five and a half hours. Subarachnoid hemorrhage on the stroke ward."

"Have you slept?"

"I managed a couple of hours under my desk." He rubs his neck. "I wouldn't recommend it."

"And the patient?"

"Died." He takes a mouthful of **kotlet.** "This is amazing. What is it?"

"Beef mince and potatoes, covered in eggs and bread crumbs, then deep-fried. Very fattening." Leila grins, because Nick is tall and skinny, with the enviable ability to eat whatever he fancies without ever putting on weight. Leila is the opposite. Not quite as

41

diminutive as Habibeh, or as comfortably built, but curvy and able to absorb kilos simply by looking at a pastry.

"Busy day ahead?"

"Isn't it always? We're extubating Dylan Adams this morning."

Nick wrinkles his forehead. "Remind me."

"Three-year-old medulloblastoma."

"Pneumonitis?"

"That's the one. We've attempted three times and each time he's been back on the ventilator within twenty-four hours."

"Airway reflexes?"

"Intact."

"Secretions?"

"Manageable. He's definitely ready. We've weaned with SIMV and pressure support over the last forty-eight hours—all the signs are good."

"Happy days, then," Nick says, through a mouthful of **kotlet**. Leila says nothing. She can't shift the feeling that something bad is about to happen.

She hears the raised voice before she gets to the ward, and she quickens her pace until she reaches Room 1, where Cheryl is speaking calmly to the source of the shouting: a thick-necked man, with an England football shirt stretched across a barrel stomach.

"Like I said, I can't do that."

"Then find a fucking doctor who can!"

"Good morning, everyone," Leila says brightly, as though she hasn't noticed anything is amiss. A second nurse, Aaron, stands next to Cheryl, fists clenched, like the men on the fringes of a pub brawl.

Pip Adams has one arm across her son's pillow. In her free hand is a small hairbrush with soft bristles— the sort you'd use on a baby. She strokes the sparse fluff on the boy's head; a far cry from the soft brown halo of curls in the photo on the wall by his bed.

Dylan Adams, almost three. Medulloblastoma. The details pass through Leila's thoughts almost subconsciously, like the caption of a photograph flashing on-screen.

On the other side of Dylan's cot are Alistair and Tom Bradford, Darcy's parents.

Darcy Bradford, eight months old. Bacterial meningitis.

"How was the theater?" Leila asks them, partly through politeness, and partly to defuse the atmosphere.

Alistair smiles. "Very nice, thank you."

"Happy anniversary for yesterday."

There's a derisive snort from the other side of the room, and suddenly Leila both realizes what's going on, and at the same time hopes she is wrong. She walks over to Liam Slater's bed, to where mum Nikki is standing with the barrel-stomached man Leila assumes must be her husband. She extends her right hand. "Dr.

Leila Khalili. I'm one of the consultants looking after Liam."

The man stares at Leila, who resists the urge to flinch. She holds his gaze and keeps her hand outstretched until it is clear he isn't going to take it.

"This is Connor," Nikki says, her voice shaking as though she isn't certain. "Liam's dad."

There's a vein throbbing in Connor's neck. Leila can smell fresh sweat and the faint trace of stale beer. Finally, he speaks. "I want Liam moved."

Liam Slater, five years old. Asthma attack. Critical but stable.

"Moved? Mr. Slater, your son is very sick. Pediatric Intensive Care is the best possible place for—"

"Don't patronize me, **Doctor**." He makes it an insult. "I want him moved to a different bed. Away from these people." He spits the words in the direction of Tom and Alistair Bradford.

Leila lets her face show confusion she doesn't feel. "I'm sorry—away from who?" She hopes Connor Slater will balk at spelling it out, but Tom Bradford doesn't give them the chance to find out.

"Away from the **gays**, he means." There's amusement—real or manufactured, Leila can't be sure—in the exaggerated way Tom says it, and Connor's top lip tightens.

"Really, Mr. Slater?" Leila is a doctor, not a guardian of social morals, but judgment colors her question nevertheless. She thinks of the night Darcy came in, her temperature sky-high, and a telltale rash covering her little body. Alistair and Tom, white knuckles intertwined. Parents, like all the others, frightened for their child.

"I want him moved." Connor Slater's voice is harsh and angry, his fists clenched by his sides, but his eyes are swollen and red rimmed. There are parents who cry openly on the ward, others who would rather die than be seen crying. Connor Slater, Leila suspects, falls into the latter category.

"I'm afraid that's not possible."

"I think it's incredible Tom and Alistair are being so calm when you're talking about them in such a revolting manner," Pip says. "It just shows what lovely people they are."

"Thank you, darling, you're pretty lovely yourself." Tom adopts a camp voice Leila has never before heard him use. He raises one hand and lets it dangle limply from the wrist.

Alistair rolls his eyes. "Not helpful, Tom."

"I'm not having my son exposed to"—Connor's face is turning puce, so screwed up in rage he's struggling to get the words out—"to **that**."

Aaron takes a step toward Connor. "Come on, mate, you can't—"

"I'm not your fucking mate!"

A visiting parent, walking past the open door, stares openly. Leila holds up both hands, palms raised. "That's enough! This is a hospital, Mr. Slater, there are critically ill children and their terrified parents within earshot and your behavior is not acceptable."

"I pay my taxes—"

"—for which the NHS is truly grateful. There are no other beds, Mr. Slater. Liam is here because this is where he needs to be. If he's moved, it will be because of a medical need, not because of personal preference. Particularly when that personal preference appears to be at best unpleasant, and at worst homophobic." Leila stops abruptly, before she oversteps the mark. Perhaps she already has.

An ugly red flush creeps over Connor's neck as he continues to stare at Leila. He gives a twisted smile and furrows his brow, before looking at his wife and shrugging. "I can't make out a word she's saying, can you?"

Leila looks again at Connor Slater's red-rimmed eyes. She reminds herself that he is teetering on the brink of losing a child, that it is the world he is angry with, not her. She speaks slowly and clearly. "I will not be moving Liam, Mr. Slater."

He holds her gaze. "Sorry, I can't . . . it's the accent, love."

There is a sharp intake of breath from somewhere behind Leila. Pip, perhaps. Leila does not react. Connor Slater isn't the first, and he won't be the last. "Would you like me to find another doctor to speak to you?"

"Yes." Ill-disguised triumph floods Connor's face. "Yes, I would."

No issue with her accent that time. "That's no problem at all. I believe Dr. Tomasz Lazowski is on duty. Or perhaps Dr. Rehan Quereshi?" There's a beat, as Leila and Connor Slater lock eyes, and then Connor breaks away.

"Going for something to eat," he tells his wife. She scurries after him, and as the door swings shut—a safety mechanism preventing the slam Connor no doubt would have liked—there's a slow handclap.

"Bravo, Dr. Khalili."

Leila picks up Liam's chart and scrutinizes it, embarrassed by the Bradfords' applause. "He's scared, that's all."

"We're all scared," Pip says quietly.

"You were magnificent," Tom says, effusive in his praise. Leila wonders if he and Alistair care more about Connor Slater's words than they appear to. She wonders if it hurts them, or if—like her—they are immune to it.

"I don't know about that. I'm only sorry it happened at all."

Alistair puts an arm around Tom. "We've been through worse, I can assure you."

"Even so. Would you like me to try and find another space for Darcy?"

"And let him win? Not a chance." Tom grins. "Besides, we won't be here much longer, will we?"

"Not too much longer." Leila is unwilling to commit to a timeframe. "We'll get you into High

Dependency as soon as a bed's free, then I want to see Darcy's sats a little more stable before we start talking about her going home."

"Hear that, princess? Home!" Alistair reaches into Darcy's cot and picks her up as gently as if she were made of glass, careful not to dislodge the oximeter wrapped around her foot, the sticky electrodes keeping tabs on her heart rate. Tom puts his arms around them both, and the two of them gaze at their daughter.

"Gorgeous family," Pip says, and on her face is a smile you'd swear was genuine, had you not glimpsed—as Leila did—the pain in its place a moment ago. "You'll have to have a big party to make up for spending her first Christmas here."

"Now there's an idea," Tom says, but Alistair is looking at Pip, who has picked up her knitting again, the smile still fixed to her face.

"Sorry, Pip. We don't mean to rub it in."

"Don't be daft. I'm happy for you. It'll be our turn before too long." She looks at Leila. "Dylan's coming off the ventilator today, isn't he?"

Leila nods. "After ward round's finished. I'd like to do it here, to minimize stress for Dylan, so . . ." She looks at Alistair and Tom.

"We'll make ourselves scarce," Tom says.

The door to Room 1 is closed. The Slaters are in the canteen, and the Bradfords at work. Leila has tried to persuade Pip to go for a walk, for her own sake as much as for Leila's and her team's, but Dylan's mother has insisted on staying with her son. She is sitting in a chair in the corner of the room, in a small concession to Leila's plea for space.

Beside Leila, on a metal trolley, are endotracheal and tracheostomy tubes, as well as a sterilized scalpel and lidocaine, in the unlikely event that Leila might be required to establish an emergency airway. On one side of Dylan is Cheryl; on the other, Aaron, who is pulling the sticky tape away from Dylan's face with such care, such tenderness, that Dylan might have been his own child.

"OK?" Leila nods to each of her colleagues in turn. Aaron suctions the ET tube, then deflates the cuff of air that keeps it in place. Leila checks the monitors, looking for a steady heart rate, a steady saturation level. Slowly, millimeter by millimeter, she withdraws the tube. She hears Pip's rapid breathing behind her; Cheryl's calm voice as she talks to Dylan, despite his sedation.

"Almost there, love, that's it. You're doing so well."

They didn't make it this far, last time. Leila had thought Dylan was ready, they'd prepped everything just the same, but his vitals had dropped so fast and so hard that they'd stopped and waited for him to stabilize, and when he didn't Leila had had no alternative but to reverse the process.

This time, she thinks. But there is still the ghost of a doubt that shivers down her spine. Something bad is going to happen.

Only then it's out, with a bark of a cough that makes Pip jump up from her chair. "What's happening? Is he OK? Is he breathing?"

"It's a reflex," Leila tells her gently. "We'll give Dylan a little bit of help with his breathing to begin with, then we'll gradually reduce the pressure and see how he copes." Aaron suctions Dylan's airways, and Leila slips a BiPAP mask over his face, and adjusts the pressure. "If he gets on well with this," she says to Pip, "we'll try a high-flow nasal cannula. But one step at a time."

Pip nods meekly. She waits until Aaron and Cheryl take the trolley away, and until Leila steps away from Dylan's bed, and then she crosses the room and presses her lips to the boy's forehead. She runs her fingers across the sticky residue left by the tape.

"I'll get someone to bring you some rubbing alcohol."

Pip starts, as though she forgot Leila was there. Then she gives a tentative smile, her eyes darting across Leila's face as though she might be able to read her thoughts. "He's doing well, isn't he? Isn't he? What do you think?" And her face is so pleading, and her voice so desperate, that all Leila wants to say is **Yes, he's great, he's doing fine, he's going to be fine.**

But Leila can't lie. And so instead she says, "We'll see how he goes over the next twenty-four hours," and she leaves. Because the feeling she's had in the pit of her stomach all day—the feeling she had in Nick's office, that something bad was on its way—is stronger than ever.

four

Pip

On the opposite side of the corridor to PICU is the parents' room, a communal space with comfortable chairs, a kettle, and a fridge stocked with milk and a variety of labelled plastic containers. **Anna Roberts. Beckinsale. Noah's cheese strings. Please don't touch—it's all he'll eat!** I take out my sandwiches and sit at the table to eat them.

The room is furnished like the nursing home my grandma was in: high-backed chairs with wooden arms and wipe-clean covers, pale varnished coffee tables with piles of out-of-date magazines. There's a rack of leaflets headed **Your child is in paediatric intensive care—what now?** and a television mounted on the wall, too high for comfort. The sound is always muted, subtitles coming a moment after the action moves on, like a badly dubbed film. I watch an ITV newsreader silently speaking above the script for a carpet-cleaner commercial, before her own words catch up. I'm reminded of Mothering Sunday, last March, when Max got up to let me sleep. Dylan was going through a phase of waking at five, and when I emerged at seven thirty—quite the lie-in, comparatively speaking—I found the two of them watching an episode of **Peppa Pig** with the volume turned off.

"We didn't want to wake you," Max says. "Happy Mother's Day, sweetie."

"Why have you got the subtitles on?" I asked him, scooping up Dylan for a cuddle. He burrowed into my neck, one hand snaking down the back of my T-shirt. "I mean, our son is obviously exceptionally gifted, but I don't think he can read yet."

Max rubbed the back of his neck. He gave a casual shrug. "It's the one where Dr. Hamster picks her own pet to win first prize—it's pretty funny."

"You're telling me the subtitles are for **you?**" I laughed so loud Dylan touched my face in astonishment, then he laughed too, and the pair of us howled while Max pretended to be affronted.

"Shh, this is the bit," he said, and he turned up the volume and moved over so Dylan and I could squash in next to him. And long after Dylan had slid off the sofa to play with his dinosaurs, Max and I were still cuddled on the sofa, watching **Peppa Pig**.

It's too early for lunch but I didn't eat breakfast and hunger has made me nauseous. My sandwiches—in the fridge from yesterday—are dry in my mouth, and I gulp water from the tap to chase them down. I feel flat—the anticlimactic aftermath of this morning's stress. There's so much riding on Dylan's coming off the ventilator successfully, and yet there was no **ta-da!** moment, no definitive verdict. **Hurry up and wait**, my mum used to call it, when we had to rush rush rush to get somewhere, only to hang about when we got there.

Forty-eight hours, Dr. Khalili says. She'll have a good idea in the next twenty-four of how Dylan's responding, but if he stays off for two days, she'll call it a success. He's still sleepy. It's hardly surprising, after the length of time he's been sedated, I remind myself, determined not to let this flat feeling sink any lower. I pull out my phone.

ET tube removal went v v well. BiPAP mask for now, but looking good so far. Safe trip home tonight. We miss you! x

Almost immediately, my phone buzzes with a reply.

Miss you too. Not long till I'm back xxx

Three kisses.

"One for you," Max said, all those years ago, in the first note he wrote me after I told him I was pregnant, "one for me, and one for our baby. A family of kisses."

I feel a prickle of tears and blink them away. I stand

up, screwing the rest of my sandwich up in its tinfoil packaging, and putting it in the bin. I flick on the kettle, then walk around the room, stretching my neck from side to side and feeling it crack in complaint or relief, I'm not sure which.

On the coffee table is an A4 book Cheryl gave me when I asked if I could start a suggestions book.

"Not for you guys," I explained, "but for other parents. New ones. Somewhere to share tips on how to cope."

"What a brilliant idea. I'll get you a notebook."

I thought there'd be a stationery cupboard or something, but when she gave me a spiral-bound book the next day I spotted the price sticker half-peeled off the back. I tried to give her the money, but she wouldn't hear of it. I open it now, twiddling the pen between my fingers. The last entry is mine.

Domino's Pizza will deliver! Give them the postcode for the children's hospital, and meet them at reception. It was one of the porters who told me that, when he found me staring at an empty vending machine, late one Sunday night. Max and I ordered pepperoni, and fell on the greasy slices like they were Michelin-starred.

Above my entry someone has written in careful cursive: **If you turn left out of PICU and cross the car park by the nurse's block there is a bench underneath a huge oak tree. It's a lovely quiet place to sit and think.**

I know that bench, and they're right—it **is** a lovely quiet place. I take the lid off the pen, trying to think of a tip I haven't shared, something that will make a difference to exhausted, anxious parents. Parents who aren't coping, who don't know what to do, what to say, where to go.

I put the lid back on the pen.

Blood sings in my ears as a wave of fear and grief washes over me, and I stand and walk to the sink. I think of the swans we take Dylan to feed on the Stratford canals, and I wonder if they ever give up—if all that furious paddling beneath the surface one day just gets too much, if it builds and builds, like it's building in me, until they can't be serene anymore, can't glide across the surface, pretending everything's OK. And then . . . what?

I feel myself sinking, my knees buckling, and I lean on the draining board, my face distorted in its stainless-steel reflection. I open my mouth in the silent howl of **Why me why us why my boy** that is never far from the surface and I think of the swans, paddling paddling, seeming so calm, so in control. **Why me, why us, why my boy?**

Behind me, the door opens. I take a deep breath. Blink hard. **Paddle.** "Kettle's on!" I paste a smile on my face. In the draining board a warped reflection smiles back. **Paddle, paddle, paddle.** Nikki Slater, perhaps, or her husband, or a brand-new parent still wide-eyed with the strangeness of it all, and needing a friendly face, needing reassurance.

And then an arm wraps around my waist, and rough stubble scratches the side of my neck.

"Hi, honey, I'm home."

I drop the mug I'd picked up, and it clatters into the metal sink. Max. He smells of coffee and travel.

"Surprised?"

I twist round to face him. My heart bursts. "How did you know?"

"Know what?"

I start crying, the weight of everything suddenly too much to bear. "That I needed you right this very second."

He takes his arm from my waist and puts his hands on either side of my face. Dark shadows ring his eyes. "Because I needed you right this second too."

Over the last few months we have learned that hope is one side of a seesaw balanced by despair; too quickly tipped from one to the other. We have learned to be cautious, to ask rather than assume, to take each day—each hour—as it comes.

And so even as the sedation leaves Dylan's body, we are cautious. Even as Dr. Khalili comes by and says **OK, now let's switch to a nasal cannula**, we are cautious. We share a surge of delight as we see our son's face free from a mask or ET tube for the first time in weeks, then immediately temper each other's enthusiasm.

"There's colour in his cheeks—look!"

"He's not out of the woods yet."

"So good to see his sats stable."

"Early days, though."

We take turns to throw cold water on each other's sparks of hope, not letting them catch fire. And yet, as twenty-four hours become thirty-six become forty-eight, and Dylan's extubation is officially declared a success, it is impossible not to hope.

"He's breathing," Max says, in a voice little more than a breath itself. He stares at our boy, the nasal cannula now lying on the pillow beside him, just in case. I look at the saturation monitor, see the oxygen levels flirt around 93 percent. A healthy child's sats range from 96 to 100, but for Dylan, 93 is good. Ninety-three is great.

"He's breathing," I say. We look at each other, neither of us wanting to be the first one to say what we're both thinking. **He's going to be OK.**

Max nods. "He is." And Dylan moves his head and looks at his dad as if to say **Of course I am—did you ever doubt it?**

"How's he doing?" Nikki and Connor come back from the canteen. Liam's on BiPAP, too, but the nurses have said nothing that suggests they're trying to wean him, and I wonder if it's hard for them to see Dylan off oxygen completely now.

"OK, I think." I make my voice sound neutral, just in case.

"Fingers crossed," Nikki says. They sit next to Liam's bed, and Connor says something in a low voice I can't hear. I was nervous, when he came back to PICU the day after his outburst, but he's hardly said a word ever since. I'd like to think he's embarrassed, but you wouldn't say so from his face, which is permanently screwed up in silent fury. Liam has school-age siblings, and the Slaters only have one car, so by two thirty each afternoon they pack up and go home. The routine means they miss Tom and Alistair, who arrive at seven in the morning to give Darcy breakfast, then return after work to spend all evening with her. **Like daycare**, Tom said once, although we all know it isn't. I'm relieved the Slaters' weekday routines mean they won't be in PICU at the same time as Tom and Alistair, but I'm nervous for the weekend, when they might be.

When the Bradfords do arrive, Alistair does a double take on seeing Dylan. "Way to go, little man!"

"Ninety-four percent," Max says proudly.

Alistair shakes Max's hand and Tom gives me a hug, like it was us who put breath in Dylan's body, although it's all down to him—my little fighter.

"You'll be beating us home, at this rate," Tom says, even though Darcy is sitting up in her cot and babbling, and it's clear that despite the IV line drip-feeding her antibiotics, she is almost ready to be back where she belongs.

"Still a way to go, I think," I say, but dates flip in my head like the calendar on Max's desk, and I wonder if Dylan will be home this month, next month, by Mothering Sunday. I won't want a lie-in this year. I won't ever want another lie-in. I think of all the times I complained about being too tired, about never getting to go to the loo by myself, or drink a cup of tea while it was hot. I think of all the times I moaned that I **just want five minutes to myself is that too much to ask?** Bile rises in my throat. Why couldn't I see what I had? How lucky I was? When Dylan comes home I will sleep when he sleeps and get up when he wakes, and I won't miss another second of our time together.

"Let's go out for dinner," Max says later, when Dylan is sleeping again. He looks at his watch. "If we leave now we can be at Bistro Pierre by eight thirty."

"We haven't been there for ages. Not since before." I hesitate. Dylan's eyelashes rest on his cheeks; a tiny flutter of movement beneath his eyelids. "I don't know."

Max takes my hand. "He'll be fine." He raises his voice, turning to where Cheryl and a nurse I don't know are checking meds. "He'll be fine, won't he?"

"Course he will. Go and have dinner. Ring if you want to see how things are, but if anything changes, I'll call you."

"It doesn't feel right—going out for dinner when Dylan's stuck here."

"Put your own oxygen mask on before helping

others," Cheryl says. She smiles and raises an eyebrow. "Isn't that what you lot always say?"

Bistro Pierre is where we got engaged, in this dimly lit restaurant only two tables wide, with a labyrinth of narrow corridors and tiny rooms that make it feel like you're the only ones there. Pierre himself is actually Larry—Birmingham born and bred, but with a flair for French cooking you'd never guess from his accent.

"All right, strangers!"

"Hey, Larry, how's it going?"

He shows us to our favourite table—in a room of its own, off the landing at the top of a flight of stairs—and gives us the menu, a single printed A4 sheet, run off that morning. There are no specials, no vast array of dishes, just three options for each course, based on whatever Larry buys fresh from the market each morning.

"So, what time does the babysitter clock off tonight?"

We came here the first time we left Dylan with a babysitter, and I spent the whole evening checking my phone and wondering if I should call home. We bolted our mains and skipped dessert to be back by ten, only to find the babysitter happily watching TV—Dylan fast asleep in his cot.

"Back already?" she said. "I thought you'd be hours."

"No babysitter," I tell Larry now. I hesitate. "Actually, Dylan's been in hospital for a while." I feel Max tense. "He has cancer." Max wouldn't have told him. Max doesn't tell anyone.

"Shit . . ." Larry's floundering. He doesn't know what to do, what to say. No one does. I rush to reassure him.

"It's OK, though, we're through the worst. Dylan's had six lots of chemo and they've managed to remove most of the tumour, so it's all looking good. In fact, we're here to celebrate him coming off oxygen!" I feel Max's eyes on me. I'm talking too fast, telling Larry things he doesn't need to know. But Larry's eyes light up.

"Well, that's bostin'! And listen, you bring the little fella for tea once he's home, all right? On me."

"Thanks, Larry."

We eat onion soup with a thick crust of melted cheese, and cassoulet with duck that falls off the bone and has to be chased with a spoon. We talk about Connor Slater, and how quiet he's been since Dr. Khalili put him in his place. We talk about Tom and Alistair, and how I'd like to have them for dinner sometime.

"Do we have anything in common, though?" Max says. "Besides PICU?"

"That's how it starts, though, isn't it?" I tear off a piece of bread and dip it into my cassoulet. "Friendship, I mean. You have one thing in common—children, or dog-walking, or being in intensive care—and it grows from there. There aren't very many people who can relate to what we're going through."

"They can't, though. Not really. Tom and Alistair's experience is different to ours, is different to Nikki's and her Neanderthal husband's. It's like . . ." Max grapples for the words. "Like we're all travelling the same country, but to different destinations. On different roads. You know? We're the only ones who know what our particular journey is like, how it feels to travel it." He reaches for my hand. "Just us."

After the warmth of the restaurant, the cold night air makes me shiver, and I wrap my scarf around my neck twice, three times. Our breath ices the air a second before we step through it, so that we walk home enveloped in a mist of our own making. I slide my fingers into Max's and he takes my hand and puts it in his pocket.

By tacit agreement, when we reach the house we don't linger in the hall, in the kitchen. We don't stand at the dining room door and discuss how we might convert it to a bedroom. We don't talk at all. We go upstairs, and we make love for the first time in the longest while.

five

Max

W hen do you think he'll be able to come home?"
We're in the sort of bar you never go to until
you have kids, when high chairs and an outdoor play
area are suddenly more important than its range of
botanical gins. Alison and her husband, Rupert, got
here early, claiming two large tables by the door to the
beer garden. The kids demand constantly to be taken
outside, then—almost immediately—want to come
back inside, their parents held hostage by three-foot ter-
rorists needing coats and gloves they'll shed a minute
later.

"Hard to say."

"Are we talking weeks or months?" Rupert is a GP,
which apparently gives him the authority to ask questions the others might think, but wouldn't ask.

I look at my watch. "We don't know." **An hour**, Pip

said. They won't expect us to stay long, not with Dylan the way he is.

"I mean, he's been in PICU now for—what—six weeks?"

Three months, I reply silently.

"Weeks, I'd think." Pip looks at me. "Don't you?" She doesn't wait for an answer. "Weeks. A month, at most." I tune out. I don't want to talk about Dylan in front of all these people, leaning forward in case they miss a single word of the awful, terrible story they're desperately relieved isn't happening to them.

"We can't bail," Pip said, when I suggested crying off. "Imagine how you'd feel if they didn't come to Dylan's birthday."

"I'd understand, given the circumstances."

But Pip was adamant, and so instead of being with Dylan we're spending Sunday afternoon in a chain pub with someone else's children. Someone else's **healthy** children. Not that I'd wish what we're going through on them—on anyone—but . . . it's tough, that's all.

Pip is still filling them in. "We had a couple of blips after he came off the ventilator, but he's been stable for a couple of days, now. He's got a scan on Monday to make sure the tumor hasn't got any bigger, and then we'll see the consultant when Max is back from Chicago. Won't we, Max?" She tries to make me join in.

"That's great," one of the other women says. Phoebe?

I get the women mixed up. I have to mentally put them with their husbands to remember which is which. Phoebe and Craig; Fiona and Will. It **is** Phoebe, then. She has her head tilted on one side. **How dreadful.**

"We're all thinking of you so much," Fiona chips in. "All the time."

"And praying," adds Phoebe.

Thoughts and prayers, I think. I catch Pip's eye, but she seems genuinely moved by the platitudes. "Thanks, girls. That means a lot."

It means nothing. It **does** nothing. I stand up and go to the door. Outside, a toddler is trying to climb over the bottom of the slide. He's gripping the edges in pudgy gloved fists, but he can't step high enough, and every time, his trainers catch the slide, and knock him back. A man runs into the play area and grabs the kid around the waist, swooping him high over the slide like an airplane. Something tightens in my throat. I look away.

A waitress arrives with two bowls of fries— **Something to nibble on**, Alison said—and everyone's gathering children onto their knees, and tearing fries in half to blow on and dip in ketchup. **I know it's full of sugar, but I don't let her have it at home.** Will's little girl is crying because she didn't want to stop playing but now she doesn't want to get down, and **If she doesn't want anything don't force her—she'll eat when she's hungry.**

66

Only Pip is still. Only Pip is sitting alone, her lap empty, her arms empty. She's smiling and talking to Craig about car seats, and you'd think she was having a nice time, but I know my wife. I **know** her.

We'd been together a year or so when I took her to a drinks reception hosted by the UK office. We got separated—Chester had wanted me to network, and Pip had been swept away by Janice from accounts—and every time I tried to get back to her there was someone else I had to meet. I watched Pip smile and laugh with Janice, then smile and laugh with Janice's friends, then with Brian from IT, and if you didn't know her you'd have thought she was having the best time. But I knew her.

"Wanna go someplace nicer?" I whispered in her ear when I finally managed to cross the room.

"Yes. So much yes."

I watch now, as she laughs at something Craig is saying, and passes the vinegar to Fiona for their little girl—**She has it on everything; mad, isn't it?**—and I leave my spot by the door and move round to where Pip is sitting. I bend down until her hair is brushing my lips.

"Wanna go someplace nicer?"

"So much yes."

In the long corridor on our way to PICU we stand to one side to let a porter and a kid in a wheelchair through. The kid's about fourteen, jaundiced and steroid swollen. He pushes his wheeled drip stand in an outstretched hand bruised from its cannula.

PICU is busy, and we wait several minutes before we're buzzed in. We hang up our coats, wash our hands, do the things we've done every day for so long. **Weeks or months?** Rupert had asked. Please let it be weeks.

Pip nudges me as we reach Room 1 and find both the Slaters and the Bradfords there. They are separated by Liam's bed, and by Dylan's and Darcy's cots, both families studiously ignoring each other. Three older kids are with the Slaters, plugged into iPods and looking bored.

I don't spend too long considering the dynamics of the room, because the sides of Dylan's cot have been lowered to halfway, and instead of lying on his back he is leaning against a large foam wedge. A physiotherapist is tapping his chest with a cupped hand.

"He's sitting up!" Pip rushes to his side. She grins at the physio. "It's so good to see him like this."

"Almost finished. This'll loosen the secretions and hopefully he'll give us a good cough." The physio has a nose ring and a South African accent. A rainbow-colored lanyard is covered in bright badges. She taps again and Dylan splutters, thick mucus filling his mouth. The physio tips him forward, a tissue-covered hand holding his chin and clearing his mouth in one well-practiced move. "There's a good boy." She taps his

68

chest again, moving her cupped hand across his thin body. Dylan's arms fall like two sticks by his sides.

He was nine pounds ten ounces at birth. Two weeks overdue, and so low Pip couldn't walk without clasping both hands beneath her bump, like that was the only thing stopping him from falling out. Arms and legs like the Michelin Man, with cheeks so fat his eyes looked closed even when they weren't.

"Maybe he'll be a wrestler," Pip said, when he was six months old. She was changing his diaper, and she squeezed his chunky thighs and blew a raspberry on his belly.

"Or a pizza tester."

Pip threw a burp cloth at my head.

He lost it all when he started moving, of course. Almost overnight the bracelets of fat melted from his arms, and gradually I watched him morph from baby to toddler to child.

And then he got sick, and he got thin. And now I'd give anything to see those Michelin Man legs again.

"How's it going, champ?"

Dylan coughs up more phlegm.

"Good job, Dyl!" The physio wipes his mouth, then rests his head gently back on the foam wedge. "He can stay sitting up for a bit, if you like?"

It's good, seeing him sitting up, and even though he drifts in and out of sleep (no surprise, given the cocktail of drugs he's on) you can tell that he knows we're here. After a while the physio comes back and takes away the foam wedge, and lies Dylan down on one side—a smaller cushion holding him in place. Pip gets out her knitting, and I pick up my iPad and tap on the menu of articles saved in my reading list.

Dylan wasn't talking much even before he got sick. He knew fifty-some words—we wrote them down on a piece of paper stuck to the fridge—but he'd only just started stringing them together. **Want milk. No toast. Daddy book.**

I swallow hard. Frown at a feature about Bitcoins, then close the tab and tap on the menu of bookmarked links. **Survival rates for medulloblastoma**, reads the first headline. I don't need to open the link. **If the disease has not spread, survival rates are around 70 to 80 percent.**

"Eighty percent," Pip repeated, when I told her. "That's good. That's really good." She kept saying it, as though she wasn't quite convinced. I didn't tell her what the next line said.

The disease tends to be more aggressive in children under three, for whom the survival rate is lower.

I look at my son, pale and weak beneath his blanket, the scar from his surgery visible through his thin hair. He was in theater for six hours, and every minute felt like a year. I brought my laptop; sat in the canteen replying to emails I barely read, and compiling a presentation I couldn't bring myself to care about.

Pip stared at me. "How can you think about work at a time like this?"

"Someone's got to pay the mortgage," I snapped, hurt by the look in her eyes, and unable to put into words what I really wanted to say, which was that thinking about work was easier than thinking about what was happening in the operating theater.

They got most of it. A **subtotal resection**, they said. I looked it up while we waited to see Dylan. **Fifty to ninety percent removal**, Google told me.

"There's a big difference between fifty and ninety." We were sitting on either side of Dylan's crib, the surgeon standing at the end, clipboard in hand. "Can you be more specific?"

"I removed as much as I could without causing more damage to the healthy cells around the tumor." He slid away from the question, replacing one worry with another.

Brain damage.

Dylan is brain damaged. First from the tumor, then—in some cruel irony—from the surgery to remove it. Some parts of the brain will recover, others won't, and despite all their knowledge, all their study, the doctors cannot be certain about the split. We have to **wait and see**.

"I'm going to get some air," I tell Pip. She tips her head up for a kiss.

I walk across the car park and past the nurses' accommodation to the bench beneath the oak tree. I sit down and lean my elbows on my knees, rubbing the heels of my palms into my eyes. Pressure fills my head like I'm underwater, like the weight of an ocean is pressing against me. I think of the tumor at the base of Dylan's brain, and wonder if this is how it felt before they took it away. I think of the scan he'll have on Monday. I try to visualize what's left of the tumor—imagine it shriveled and shrunken from radiotherapy—but all I can see is the shadow on that first scan we were shown after Dylan was admitted.

"I'm sorry," the consultant said, like it was his fault.

The tumor had been there awhile. Months. Months of headaches. Months of nausea. Months of blurred vision and loss of balance and a dozen other symptoms an older kid could have vocalized, but Dylan . . . I screw my palms harder into the sockets of my eyes. I think back to last summer, I try to think if there's any way I could have known, any way I **should** have known . . .

"Oops-a-daisy!" Pip said, when Dylan ran head-long into the wall, fell over, then fell over again when he tried to get up. We all laughed. Remembered the game we played as freshmen where you spin in a cir-cle, then try to run in a straight line.

We laughed at him.

Was it then? Was that when it started? Not clumsy, not a toddler finding his feet, but sick. I let out a low moan.

Someone coughs.

I sit up, embarrassed to discover I'm not alone, and see Connor Slater on the bench beside me. I give a curt nod, and make to stand, and then I realize it wasn't a cough.

Connor Slater is crying.

He's gripping the edge of the bench with hands that are rough and reddened. On the inside of his forearm is a tattoo—Liam's name in black swirls. Despite the time of year, he's wearing baggy shorts, his legs tan and freckled. On his feet, sandy-colored boots, worn across the toe to show shiny steel caps.

I don't know anyone like Connor Slater, I don't know how to help him.

I don't know him.

And yet.

I know what it's like to leave my family on a Monday and be away until Friday. I know what it's like to get a call from my wife saying **I'm at the hospital—you have to come. You have to come now.** I know what it's like to be so scared of losing my son that nothing and no one else matters.

That, I know.

"It's tough, huh?"

Connor nods slowly. He's staring at the ground between his feet, his hands braced on his knees.

"It's a good hospital. One of the best in the country. Liam's in good hands." Platitudes, I realize, even as I utter them, but Connor rubs his face and nods more vigorously and I guess sometimes platitudes are what we need to hear.

"I'm trying to be there for Nik, you know? And I

don't want the other boys to be worrying, so I'm telling them it's all OK, and I'm making sure all the time that they're OK, and Nik's OK, and—" He breaks off, but not before I hear my own thoughts in his.

"And no one ever asks if **you're** OK?"

Connor's lips tighten.

"And you're not."

"No." He looks at me, and his eyes are red and swollen. "Because it's my fault Liam's here."

six

Pip

"He forgot the inhaler." Nikki is changing Liam's pyjamas. Max is in the office today, so it's just the two of us. There are screens you can wheel across for privacy, but none of the other parents are here, and neither of us is bothered, and there's something comforting about us both looking after our boys.

Ages ago, Alison and I talked about going away sometime—about all us mums renting a place for a few days with the kids. Everyone mucking in. Cooking, looking after the kids.

"Like a commune," she laughed. I wonder if we'll ever do it now.

Nikki lifts her son's T-shirt over his head. "Liam got a new rucksack for his birthday. He'd put all his things in it for school, but he hadn't taken the inhaler out of the little pocket of the front of his old one."

I'm cleaning Dylan's teeth. He has fourteen of them, and right at the back, at the bottom, I can feel a set of molars pushing their way through the gums. Dylan looks at me, his eyes big and glassy.

"Are your teeth hurting, baby?" I wish he would say something. I wish he'd make a sound—any sound.

"He hadn't had an attack in ages," Nikki says. "But when they got to breakfast club Liam suddenly remembered he didn't have it, and he got quite upset."

"Poor thing." I move the soft bristles gently across Dylan's teeth. He's been tube-fed for months, but his teeth are still cleaned three times a day to make sure bacteria doesn't build up that might make him ill. I wonder how long it will be before I'll be making food for him again; I wonder if he'll still love banana porridge when he comes home, or if it'll be something else. Pancakes, maybe, or French toast.

"Connor was late, and—well, I guess he didn't think it was a big deal . . . like I said, Liam hadn't had an attack for months." Nikki's tone is defensive. "And then . . ."—her voice wobbles—"the school rang to say they'd called an ambulance."

"You must have been beside yourself." I finish Dylan's teeth and put his toothbrush in the drawer, crossing the room to tip out the water I used.

"They're supposed to have an emergency inhaler, but it hadn't been replaced. I keep thinking: if only Liam hadn't had that new rucksack, if only Connor had gone back . . ."

If only. The mantra of the PICU parent. **If only we'd gone to the doctor sooner, if only we'd listened, if only we'd thought, if only . . .**

"I knew." I take the clean pyjamas I've brought from home, and put them in Dylan's cupboard for tomorrow. "I knew there was something wrong with Dylan. I just knew." We went on holiday, the three of us, in May last year. A little apartment in Gran Canaria, where we ate chorizo and goats' cheese and sticky honey, and swam in a sea so blue it hurt our eyes. Dylan had found the flight hard. The cabin pressure hurt his ears and he cried the whole way there, and even the following day he was out of sorts.

"Look at this place," I said, waving an arm across the bay. "I thought he'd be racing around, wildly over-excited." Dylan was in the buggy, dozy and grizzling. Later, I watched him fall over as he explored our apartment. "He falls over a lot, doesn't he?"

"He's two."

"But more than an average two-year-old, don't you think?"

Max gave me the same look he gave me before Dylan was crawling, when I'd convinced myself he had developmental delays; the same look he gave when I wondered aloud if Dylan might be lactose intolerant, because he'd twice vomited up his bedtime milk.

"OK, OK!" I held up my hands. "So I'm a paranoid mum. Guilty as charged."

"We found out later that the brain tumour had

caused hydrocephalus," I tell Nikki now. "A buildup of fluid on the brain. It causes headaches, blurred vision, clumsiness. The cabin pressure on takeoff would have been twice as bad for Dylan as for a child without hydrocephalus." I swallow. **If only.**

"You couldn't have known," Nikki says.

Only I **did** know. A little bit of me knew. A mother always knows.

We're silent for a while, lost in our own thoughts, our own **if only**s. It was a whole month before I took Dylan to the doctor. **If only . . .** I scrutinise my son's face, looking for the child he was, for the child he will become. He looks the same and yet . . . there is a vacancy about his face, a blankness in his eyes that scares me. He lies meekly where he is put, occasionally moving an arm or leg, but mostly remaining still. Staring.

"He's not a bad man, you know. My Connor." It comes out of nowhere.

"I'm sure he isn't," I say automatically, although I can still hear the venom in his voice as Connor turned on Tom and Alistair, on Dr. Khalili.

"I don't even think he meant all that stuff he said. He was frightened, and ashamed that he never went back for Liam's inhaler." Nikki rests her hands on the edge of Liam's bed. "He looks after us all really well. They're not his, the other kids—only Liam is—but you'd never know. He loves them all so much, and he's much stronger than I am—he's a coper, you know? Not like me."

"He was **crying**," Max said, when he told me about meeting Connor on the bench. We'd driven home and Max was packing for another work trip. "There he was, this big, angry man, with tears running down his face." I tried to picture it, then I tried to imagine the situation reversed—Max crying, Connor reaching out to him—and found that I couldn't see Max that way.

"I know," I say now to Nikki. If Connor doesn't want his wife to know he's struggling, it's not my place to tell her.

"When's Dylan's scan?"

I'm glad of the change of subject. I'm glad to be married to a Max, not a Connor. Relieved my husband focuses on solutions, not problems; on the future, not the past. We couldn't afford for both of us to crumble. "Sometime this afternoon. Isn't it, Aaron?"

The nurse nods. "I'll see if I can pin them down, but you know what it's like."

I was self-conscious at first, holding conversations when there were always staff in earshot. I'd whisper to Max, like we were the only ones in a silent restaurant, even though everything I said was mundane. But what was I going to do—keep quiet for six months? And so Aaron, and Yin, and Cheryl, and all the other nurses have listened to Max's strife with clients and with Chester; to my rants about badger culling, and my guilt trips over Mum and Dad. They've been privy to arguments induced by stress and tiredness, and to make-up kisses when it's all blown over.

"You tune out," Cheryl said, when I asked her about it. "You might think I'm listening, but the reality is I'm probably wondering where my relief's got to, or I'm hanging meds or adjusting drip rates, or prepping a feed, or turning a patient . . ."

"Are you worried about the scan?" Nikki says now.

"Aren't we mums always worried?" I smile. "But everything looks positive. He's off the ventilator, breathing well, his temperature's down . . . Fingers crossed," I add, and wonder if there is anywhere else in the world where that phrase is used as often, where it means so much. "Then we meet with Dr. Khalili on Wednesday to talk about getting him home."

"Wow." The envy on Nikki's face is clear, and I immediately feel bad. The Slaters are right at the start of their PICU journey, just as we're coming to an end. I temper my statement. "That won't be for a while, though. You're stuck with us for a bit longer."

I remember the bitter jealousy that seized me in the early days, whenever a child left PICU for the standard wards. Why them and not us? When would it be our turn?

Now, I think, looking at Dylan. **It's our turn now.**

seven

Max

It's strange, returning to a house you grew up in. The street is the same, but different; the trees taller, the cars newer. Dozens of lots have been cleared, and new developments approved. When my parents bought 912 North Wolcott Avenue in the midseventies, it was one of a whole line of houses built the same way. Gable-fronted, with steps up to the porch and a neat square of grass out front. Narrow but long, with rooms one behind the other leading out to the backyard. By the time I was old enough to ride my bike up and down the street, these family homes were already being knocked down to make room for hulking brick blocks of condos. Now my mom's house is dwarfed by its neighbors, one of only three like it left on the block.

I lock my rental and stand looking at the house.

clare mackintosh

The brickwork needs painting—the rich red is peeling, and the siding has yellowed—and sagging drapes
hang at the windows of the basement where my friends
and I would pretend to be spies.

I knock on the door and hear Mom shout "Coming!"
like whoever it is might not want to wait even a second, and I lean against the porch and grin to myself.
Three, two, one . . .

"Oh!" Astonishment turns to delight, and she holds
out her arms. She's in slacks and a patterned blouse,
her dark hair in a ponytail. "You didn't tell me you
were in town!"

"I didn't know if I'd have time to stop by." I bend
down to kiss her, struck as always by how much
smaller she seems. When I was in college I told myself
it was because I was getting taller, but I sure as hell
haven't grown that much in the last twenty years. Dad
died two years after Pip and I got married, and Mom
shrunk an inch overnight. I worried about her—tried
to get her to come live with us—but she had her
friends here, had a life here.

"Are you staying the night?"

"I've got a ten o'clock flight." I see Mom's face fall,
and feel bad it's been so long since I last saw her. When
I moved to the UK I'd always tack a day on to my
Chicago trips, or meet Mom downtown for lunch
between meetings. When Dylan was born, it got a
little trickier. I guess when you become a parent
yourself you have to work harder at being a child to

82

your own parents. "I thought I could take you out for an early dinner?"

"It's a date. Give me ten minutes to put my face on."

I check my cell while I wait. **Really looking forward to working with you**, reads the follow-up email from today's prospect, and it isn't till I feel the relief in my stomach that I realize how apprehensive I was.

"I feel like your head's not been in the game," Chester said yesterday.

I spoke evenly, not wanting to sound like I was rattled. "I'm getting results."

He waved a hand in the air as though that were an irrelevance, even though Kucher Consulting is all about the results. Even though Chester is all about the results.

"They missed you at the golf day. Bob asked after you."

Bob Matthews. Head honcho at Send It Packing, a London courier start-up expanding faster than it can handle. They brought us in to improve the efficiency of their internal processes, to free up their middle managers to focus on the new markets.

"I had family commitments."

Bob Matthews has kids too, although you'd never know it. Like Chester, he likes doing business over dinner, or on the golf course. Like Chester, he measures commitment by the time his team puts in after hours.

Chester leaned back in his chair, pressing his fingers together. "When you moved to the UK the deal was that you'd handle the UK clients. Be 'me,' only with a 'British' spin." He puts air quotes around each word. "Entertain with that charming wife of yours." I balled my fingers into fists.

"My son's in hospital."

"Still?" Like it was news. "I'm sorry." Like he wasn't. "Will he be in for much longer?" Like he cared.

I was about to say **We don't know, yes, possibly, it's going to be a long road**, but I took in Chester's pen, tapping against his desk, and the concerned smile that only reached as far as his top lip.

"No, he'll be home soon, and everything will be back to normal." A lie, whichever way you look at it.

Mom comes downstairs. "How do I look?" She gives a twirl. She's changed into a green dress with a wide belt the same color as her shoes.

"Beautiful, Mom." I smile.

We eat at the Rookery, on West Chicago, where I have poutine and Mom chooses shrimp salad with a mixed-greens side.

"So," she says, her eyes serious. "How's our little boy?"

I take a sip of water before I answer. "He's good. He had a scan today. Pip said it went well." She sent me a photo afterward, of her face pressed against Dylan's. Both facing the camera, both unsmiling, both beautiful. I show Mom the photo. "We'll know more tomorrow."

"I miss the pictures Pip used to share."

"I know. It's hard. She finds it hard."

"How is she?" She doesn't wait for my answer. "Stupid question. But you're looking after her, right?"

"Of course I'm looking after her." I feel a pang of guilt that I'm not with her right now, that she's at home, or at the hospital, worrying about the scan, knowing that Dr. Khalili will have already seen the results, already be thinking about the next steps . . .

"I'd like to come over. I haven't seen Dylan since his last birthday." **Before he got sick**, I think. **Back when everything was still OK.**

"I could give Pip some support, look after the house, give her a break from being at the hospital all day—"

I cut in. "Come when Dylan's home, Mom. It won't be much longer, and you'll be able to spend some quality time with him then." I don't tell her that I'm worried the intense atmosphere in PICU will be too much for her; that the buzzers and bells and alarms will stress her out. I don't tell her that—however much she tries to help—her presence will be another thing for us—for Pip—to think about; that we don't have space right now to think about anyone but Dylan.

She nods, and says **Whatever you think's best**, and I think about the summer, and meeting Mom at the airport with Dylan by my side. I think about the pair of them lying on a blanket on the grass with a tray of strawberries.

"And how's **my** boy doing?" she asks, holding my gaze like she can see right through me.

"Me?" I smile. "I'm good." Another lie, whichever way you look at it.

eight

Leila

Leila looks out of the window. "What if there's something I'm missing?"

"There isn't." Nick is firm.

They sit in silence. Outside, a tiny robin flits to the windowsill, then flies away.

"Are they expecting it?"

"They asked us to be straight with them right from the start. I've never thrown any punches." Leila looks for the bird, but the sky is empty.

"Pulled."

Leila looks at Nick, confused.

"You haven't **pulled** any punches. Pull, not throw."

"Oh. Thank you." The correction is unsettling. Leila's English is fluent. She thinks in English, she even dreams in English, has done for years. But sometimes the subtleties of the language escape her, and she worries she will cause offense, or that something she says will be misunderstood.

When she walks back to the ward her head is full to bursting. She is thinking about the patients in her care; about her clinical responsibilities. She thinks about the report she is expected to submit to the Child Death Review board, and the minutes from the last governance meeting still unopened in her inbox. She thinks about the request from the clinical lead, that she become involved in the teaching program, and wonders where she might find the extra hours that will enable her to do that. She thinks about her bed, and how long it's been since she was in it. She thinks about her mother, and how she can persuade her out of the house.

Habibeh was waiting in the kitchen when Leila got home last night. A shiny SodaStream machine sat on the counter next to the microwave.

"When did you get that?"

"It arrived today." Habibeh recited the marketing blurb. "'Delicious carbonated drinks at the touch of a button!'" She filled a bowl with **ash reshteh** from the pot that never leaves the hob, flat noodles slithering from ladle to bowl. "**Bokhor, azizam.**" Eat.

Leila's stomach rumbles now at the thought of food. In her locker, another of Habibeh's packed lunches waits for a window when Leila might have time to take a mouthful, still chewing as she returns to the ward. Her mother was wearing her house clothes again last night, shrugging when Leila asked her if she'd been outside.

"I've been busy. Say hello to the bottom of your ironing basket—you can't have seen it for some time."

"You don't have to do my ironing."

"Someone has to."

"I worry about you, Maman."

"Me? Huh! Worry about yourself, Leila **joon**, working all hours of the day. When are you going to find time to meet a nice man?"

"There's plenty of time to meet someone."

"You're thirty-four, Leila."

"You think I should settle for someone mediocre?"

"I settled for your father."

Leila smiles now, as she remembers Habibeh's attempt to deliver it deadpan, before her mouth twitched, and her eyes sparkled. Leila's parents loved each other so intensely that when Leila's father was killed she thought her mother would die too—that the life would simply drain out of her without him at her side. Habibeh didn't die, but she withered. She stopped going out. Stopped seeing people. Leila worries about her, alone in her apartment in Tehran.

"If I could find a man like Bâbâ, I'd settle."

Habibeh's eyes softened, the joking over. "There aren't many like him."

"Well, then."

Leila is still thinking about all these things when it is time to brief the incoming team. She tries to focus.

"Luke Shepherd, eleven years old. Successful living-donor kidney transplant three days ago, neckline and NG tube removed yesterday." Leila pictures Luke, a cheerful boy and an ardent Birmingham City FC fan, who regularly begs to be allowed to the family room to watch the game, and—if he continues to make progress—will soon be allowed to do so. "Wound draining well and no infection markers."

Cheryl interrupts to tell Leila she has a visitor. She gives Leila a look she can't quite decipher.

"Go for it." Jo Beresford—the consultant taking over from Leila, and the only woman she knows who can look glamorous in flat shoes and a white coat—consults her notes. "We're pretty much done, I think. Only Liam Slater left. Room one. Male, five years old, acute asthma? IVI salbutamol. Tachycardiac. Monitoring for hypokalemia." Jo has blond, almost white hair, cut in a neat crop that would make her look boyish, were it not for her lips, which are full and red, their color enhanced only by a slick of clear balm.

"Spot-on."

"That's the lot, then. Go do what you need to do."

In the corridor outside PICU, leaning against the wall with his hands thrust deep in his pockets, is Jim, the paramedic who picked Leila up off the road after her accident.

"Thought I'd see how the patient was doing."

Leila smiles. "I've got some impressive bruises, but

the prognosis is good. Thanks again for coming to my rescue."

"Need any meds?"

Leila looks around, then feigns disappointment. "You didn't bring the Entonox?"

"More than my job's worth." He scuffs the toe of his boot against the floor, leaving a black rubber mark. "But if you're free one evening next week I could write you a prescription for vitamin B."

"Vitamin B?" Leila is confused. She is mentally scrolling through a list of supplements and their benefits, when Jim raises his right hand and mimes a drinking action.

Leila laughs. **Vitamin B.** Beer. She reflects for a moment. Thinks of the hundred and one things she has to do. Then she thinks of her mother's insistence that she make time to meet someone. She takes a scrap of paper from her breast pocket, checks that there is nothing important on it, and scribbles her mobile number.

"Make it a vitamin L and S, and you're on."

And now it is Jim's turn to look confused, as Leila returns to work, wondering how long it will take him to work it out.

Leila waits until the end of her shift to speak to Pip and Max Adams. She wants to be sure that she will not be called away; that there are enough people on duty to deal with the day-to-day running of the ward. She wants to give Dylan's parents all of her attention.

"Would you like anything? Tea? Water?" Cheryl is here, too. She will take notes, so that there can be no doubt at all about what was said, and by whom. Like Leila, she is quiet. Subdued.

"No, thank you," Pip says.

"I'm fine." Max Adams is as dark as Pip is fair, with thick hair that would curl if it wasn't cut so short. He has the type of facial hair that is more stubble than beard, with a neat line beneath his chin confirming he hasn't simply forgotten to shave. He's tall—almost six foot—and in a suit he looks quite imposing. He has an air of confidence that has on occasion resulted in a new parent mistaking him for a consultant.

Max's fingers are laced through his wife's, their hands buried in the sofa between them. The room is simply furnished. A sofa for parents, two chairs for staff. A coffee table, and a basket of toys for siblings. A box of tissues. Plastic flowers, dusty on the windowsill.

The sign on the door says THE QUIET ROOM, and anyone can ask to use it, either for a moment of contemplation, or for a conversation away from the ward.

A difficult conversation.

Leila has never once brought parents in here to tell them their child is in remission, clear of infection, ready to go home. She has only ever delivered bad news in the quiet room, and already she can feel the air pressing down on her, heavy and expectant. The crying room, she's heard it called.

Leila cannot sugarcoat what she is about to tell Dylan's parents, and so she doesn't try.

"The tumor has grown."

There is a silent gasp from Pip, an openmouthed intake of breath she holds and then releases oh so slowly. Leila explains that the centimeter of tumor left behind after surgery—because removing it completely was impossible—has become one point three centimeters. It is growing slowly, but it is growing.

"Does he need more surgery?" Max asks. He is frowning; Pip bites the inside of her lower lip. Both are leaning forward, listening, waiting. They want Leila to suggest something new—something they haven't yet tried.

Something that will work.

"The tumor is close to the brain stem." Leila speaks softly, knowing the impact each of her words will have. "Further surgery would carry significant risk."

"More chemo, then?"

Leila looks at them both in turn. "Mr. and Mrs. Adams, the damage to Dylan's brain is global and extensive. His condition—ultimately—is terminal, and although further treatment might buy him some time, we have to balance that against his quality of life."

There's a burst of muffled laughter from the corridor as footsteps pass the door to the quiet room.

"What are you saying?" Pip's voice is a whisper.

A hard lump forms in Leila's throat. When she was at medical school one of her fellow students worried that she would never be able to break bad news without crying herself. She was emotional, she said—always had been. The tutor advised her to focus on a spot on the bridge of the nose of whoever she was talking to.

"From their point of view, you're still looking directly at them," he explained. "But you won't see their eyes—you won't experience the same emotional response." To Leila, it had felt like cheating. She looks into Pip's eyes. Her head moves from side to side; the tiniest motion, but it doesn't stop. **No, no, no, no, no . . .**

"I'm asking you to make a decision about Dylan's future."

Pip lets out a moan. It comes from deep inside her and escapes from between barely parted lips, going on and on until there can be no breath left in her body.

"I know this is everything you've been dreading since Dylan was admitted, and I can't tell you how much I wish there was something else we could do."

"How long?" Max says. His voice is too loud for the space, and Leila sees Pip flinch. "Without more treatment. How long would we have?"

The one thing every relative wants to know, and the one thing no doctor can answer. "There's no way of knowing for sure," Leila says. "We'd make Dylan comfortable, manage his pain, possibly give him more chemo, but it would be palliative—purely to alleviate symptoms and ensure he didn't suffer."

"How long?"

"Weeks. Three months, at most." Leila's eyes sting. She can't lose it now. She has to be the one in charge, the one in control. She swallows.

"And if we keep going," Pip says, her voice choked with tears. "More surgery. Chemo. Radiotherapy. What then?"

Leila hesitates. "It is possible you could have several months. Perhaps a year—even longer. Even with aggressive treatment it is extremely unlikely that Dylan would live beyond another two or three years, and the extent of the neurological impairment means he would be severely disabled." Pip closes her eyes, her face contorted into silent pain as she curls forward over her clenched fists.

"Many people with disabilities lead contented and fulfilling lives," Max says abruptly, as though he's quoting from a public service announcement.

He is right. Of course he is right.

"Dylan is paralyzed from the neck down," Leila says. "He is unlikely to ever walk or talk or swallow, or have control over his bladder or bowels. Without medication he will be in constant pain. It is unlikely that he will have any awareness of his surroundings. He will depend on you for all his needs."

Slowly, Pip looks up. Her forehead creases. "We're his parents," she says. "That's what we're here for."

"More research is carried out into cancer than any other disease," Max says. "There are new drugs, new treatments being trialed all the time."

"Yes," Leila says.

"There are miracle cures **all the time**."

Leila says nothing. She does not believe in miracles. She believes in science, and drugs, and MRI scans. She believes Dylan has suffered enough. But it is not her decision.

"People write books by blinking, paint pictures with their feet."

"Yes."

"Disabled people do incredible things every single day."

"Yes."

Max leans forward, searching Leila's face. "You said Dylan is **unlikely** to walk—you don't know that for certain, do you?"

Leila hesitates. She is as sure as it is possible to be that Dylan Adams will never regain voluntary movement. But can she—can anyone—be completely certain?

"No."

Max stands, and Pip follows, leaving Leila no alternative but to stand, too. He holds her gaze. "Then we keep trying."

⁓

"How did you leave it?" Nick and Leila walk toward the car park, Leila's steps twice as fast as Nick's long strides.

"I told them to take a few days to think about it, to ask me as many questions as they want, and to consider what's best for their son."

A man emerges from Maternity with a laden car seat in each hand, biceps flexed as he tries to stop them banging against his legs. Behind him a petite blond woman walks with the careful gait of the recent mother. Leila smiles at the new parents, and they beam back. They have a mix of pride and fear on their faces; the responsibility of solo parenthood settling further onto their shoulders with each step away from the midwives. He'll drive slower home, now, than he's ever driven. She'll sit in the back, between her babies, because if she can't see their faces, something terrible might happen and she won't know.

Leila and Nick duck between Maternity and Research, toward the narrow gap in the hedge that acts as an unofficial entrance to the hospital, saving the five-minute walk around to the main road. They go to the King's Arms, close to the hospital, and consequently always occupied by medics grabbing a pint after work, or an exhausted on-call coffee. Leila should be somewhere else—she is late, very late, for her friend

Ruby's birthday dinner—but she needs to decompress before she surfaces into the real world.

Neither of them is drinking alcohol. Leila doesn't, and Nick is on call, and so they order two coffees and carry them to a free table, where Nick looks at Leila thoughtfully. "What do you want them to decide?"

Leila's heart is heavy. **Want** is the wrong word. She does not **want** to put Dylan's parents in this predicament at all. But Leila's job is full of difficult conversations.

"I think they should let him go," she says eventually.

A gaggle of women burst through the door, talking all at once. **Perianal abscess . . . wouldn't bloody lie still . . . Both of us, covered in pus!** They order wine—**Large or small, ladies? Oh, large, definitely!**—and stand at the bar until they've all been served.

"And if they don't think that?" Nick pauses, giving weight to what follows. "Have you thought about your next steps?"

Leila's mother struggles to understand Nick's role in Leila's working life. "He's a teacher?" Habibeh said. "You're studying again?"

"I'm always studying, Maman, but no, he's not a teacher. He's a mentor."

Have you thought about your next steps?

In all the times Leila has known Nick, he has never once given her the answer. Instead, he has asked questions. Asked for her thoughts, then reassured her. **See,**

you know what to do. You know what you're doing.
In all the years Leila has gone to Nick for advice, she
has always already known the answer.

Until now.

Her silence speaks for her, and she looks down
at her coffee. When Nick speaks, it's gentle but
insistent.

"Maybe you should."

Leila thinks that perhaps she won't go to Ruby's
birthday dinner. She is, after all, embarrassingly late
anyway, and she would not be good company. "Are
you hungry?" she asks, before she can decide not to.
"We could get something to eat?"

There is an awkward silence, then Nick smiles
kindly, which is worse than the silence because it is
clear that Nick doesn't want to upset or offend, and
now Leila wants to crawl under the table and disappear. "I need to get back," he says. "Family stuff."

Family stuff. His wife.

"Sure." Leila's cheeks are on fire. She hadn't
meant . . .

Or had she?

"Another time."

"Sure." She stands up, knocking against the table
in her rush to be gone. "I'm supposed to be at a party
anyway—I guess I should show my face, at least."
She's glad of the text message that pings her phone as
she walks away, giving her something to do with her
hands. The number isn't saved in her phone.

Lime and soda! reads the text. Jim the paramedic has finally worked out Leila's drink of choice. He would like to take her for a drink. Next week?

Sure, she texts. Why not?

T he restaurant is busy, and Leila scours the tables for her friend. "I'm so sorry, Ruby. Work."

"No worries," Ruby says, but this has happened too often for the smile she gives to reach her eyes. There is a reason why doctors and nurses socialize together, why they date, why they marry. There are fewer explanations needed, fewer apologies.

Ruby moves up so Leila can squeeze onto the bench seat next to her. Leila leans across to kiss Ruby's husband, waves to Scott and Danni, who are midconversation on the other side of the table, and looks around to see who else she knows. There are a dozen of them, here for a belated fortieth-birthday dinner for Ruby, the first person Leila met when she moved to the UK to do her MA. Ruby was embarking on a PGCE, following what she called a midlife-crisis decision to leave her nice safe accountancy job and become a science teacher. Eight years on, she's the deputy head of a school the local paper refers to as "challenging," with a social life restricted to half-terms and holidays.

"We're on dessert," Ruby says. Everyone has finished their main courses, the tables cleared away and the once-white tablecloth marked by half-moon wine stains and oil-slicked olive dishes. Leila orders a virgin mojito, and dips a piece of leftover bread in balsamic vinegar. The air is filled with the clink of cutlery; the chatter of conversation punctuated with laughter. So much laughter. She looks around the room. On the central tables, beneath the vast chandeliers, it's mostly groups—the odd hen party, and perhaps a delayed Christmas do or two. On the outskirts of the restaurant are smaller tables, where low lighting casts shadows over courting couples. An older couple, dressed for the theater, check watches and rush the bill. Lives full of celebration, love, happiness. Leila's throat constricts and she forces down a mouthful of bread. She wonders what Max and Pip are doing now. Whether they've decided.

"Are you OK?" Kirsty is a teacher friend of Ruby's, and now, by proxy, of Leila's.

"Rough day at work."

"Tell me about it! I think my A-level history class expect me to sit their mocks for them, if the amount of revision they've done is anything to go by."

"How will they do?"

There's a glimpse of grudging pride on Kirsty's face. "They'll be all right. The straight passes and the straight fails will get what they deserve, and the ones in the middle will get a kick up the arse to revise properly for the real thing. That's if they haven't blown their chances of a uni place." She takes a deep slug of wine, then grimaces. "Stressful!"

Leila's phone vibrates. She checks the screen in case it's work, but it's a message from Jim, confirming a time.

"Ooh." Ruby is looking at Leila's phone. "Date?"

Leila turns the screen to the table. "It's nothing."

"Come on, don't be like that." She grabs at the phone, and something snaps in Leila—a breaking point brought on by too many hours at work and too much in her head and—

"For fuck's sake, Ruby!" There is a split second's silence around the table, before the hubbub of conversation resumes. "Sorry." Leila touches her friend's arm. "I'm sorry, Rubes."

"Tough day?"

Leila nods. She wants to talk about it, but Ruby's husband has put down his fork and is leaning across the table.

"Did you hear about the biology resits? Apparently the papers were 'compromised.'" He makes quote marks in the air. There's a break in conversation around the table; a collective "ooh" as everyone tunes in. Leila exchanges a glance of solidarity with Danni, a journalist and the only other non-teacher here.

"I wish my GCSE French paper had been compromised," someone is saying. "My **espèces de merde** might stand a chance of passing, then." There is raucous laughter at this, and Leila leans back against plush red velvet and thinks about Dylan. As Leila left work, delayed by a febrile seizure, she paused in the open doorway of Room 1. Keeley Jacobs, fresh from general pediatrics, was cradling Darcy in one arm, rocking her gently as the baby sucked hungrily on a bottle. As Leila watched, Darcy's monitor began bleeping insistently, and Keeley deftly removed the bottle and waited for the baby's breathing to stabilize before allowing her to continue. She caught Leila's eye and smiled.

"Eyes bigger than her stomach, this one."

In the middle bed, Dylan lay asleep, amid a tangle of tubes and wires. A thin feeding tube snaked from one nostril, and cannulas in both arms meant swift access when it was needed. Pip and Max sat next to him, their chairs pulled close together so that Pip could lean into her husband, his arm tight around her. They didn't look up. They didn't see Leila, or the tears that filled her eyes before she could blink them away.

"Did something happen today?"

Leila looks up, confused. Around the table, everyone's desserts have arrived.

"At work," Ruby says, scanning Leila's face. "Did something happen?"

Leila shakes her head, not trusting herself to speak.

"Did you lose someone?"

Leila takes a sip of her drink to clear her throat. "No," she says. "We didn't lose anyone."

Not yet.

nine

Pip

Max drives us home. I sit with my hands clasped in my lap, envying him the distraction of driving—the focus of gaze, the pattern of movement with his hands and feet—that means he has something to do. Something to think about other than Dylan.

Max's car is less frequently used than mine—it spends as much time in airport car parks as on our drive—and so it bears fewer traces of car picnics and muddy walks, but nevertheless I know that if I got down on my knees and felt beneath the seats I'd find a raisin, a bread stick, an empty packet of the organic puffs that pass for crisps. Beside me, in the pocket of the door, is a CD of nursery rhymes. Behind me, Dylan's car seat waits patiently for his next trip.

How can my son be a breath away from death, when evidence of his life is all around me? When I **feel** him in my heart, as surely as when I carried him in my womb?

I turn, and lay my cheek against the headrest, watching the buildings give way to hedgerows. I have made this journey two hundred and forty-two times. How many more times will I make it? How many more times before we leave PICU without saying **See you tomorrow?** Without kissing our child good night?

I have been thinking about death since the day Dylan was diagnosed with a brain tumour. Every out-patient appointment, every consultant review. Every round of chemo. And then, after he got pneumonitis and went to PICU, and he stayed there first for days and then for weeks. Bracing myself for a phone call at three a.m.: **I'm sorry . . . we did everything we could . . . he just slipped away.** I have imagined the crash team, the defibrillator, running feet, a racing trolley. **Prepare for the worst, hope for the best,** Cheryl said once. **That's how you cope.** I told myself I was a realist, imagining that call from the hospital, but the truth is I was dancing with the devil. A staring contest; a game of chicken. **If I think it, it won't happen.**

Only it **is** happening.

"It isn't fair," I say quietly. I mean that it isn't fair to ask us—ordinary people with no medical knowledge—to decide whether someone lives or dies, but as I say it I realise that I mean it isn't fair this happened at all, that Dylan was healthy, and we were happy, and then someone threw a grenade into our life.

What did we do wrong?

"No." Max's jaw is tight, his knuckles white on the steering wheel. His eyes flick to the rearview mirror and I wonder if he's seeing our son in his car seat, the way I'm imagining him right now. Jabbering nonstop in a barely intelligible stream of real words and made-up ones. Pointing out tractors, horses, lorries. Kicking the back of my seat and finding it funny. I have a sudden picture of snapping at him one day to stop talking, and the memory is like an uppercut to the gut. If I'd only known . . . I picture the curls flopping over his eyes because I couldn't bear to take him for a haircut yet. It seemed so grown-up— I wasn't ready to let go of my baby yet. And then all his hair fell out, in a matter of days.

"When it grows back," I told him, "I'll take you to that posh barber's in town. You'll lie back in the big chair, and they'll wash your hair. They'll get out their sharp scissors, and they'll be ever so careful, and perhaps they'll use the clippers on your neck, and it'll tickle a bit."

I close my eyes. "What are we going to do?"

He shakes his head, and I don't know if that's his answer, or if he doesn't know, or if he doesn't want to talk about it. So instead I look out of the window and try not to make a sound. But tears fill my eyes, and seconds later they're streaming down my cheeks and I'm catching my breath and feeling like I'm choking. I take a breath in but then it doesn't want to leave, and I hear Max's concern like it's coming to me through water, and I can't breathe I can't breathe I can't breathe.

"Pip! Calm down. Calm down!" Only he doesn't sound calm, and he's got one hand on my knee and the other on the steering wheel and I can't breathe I can't breathe . . .

"Pip!"

And then he's stopped, and we're in a lay-by, with the engine off and the handbrake on, and he pulls against his seat belt to take me into awkward arms. And oncoming cars light us brightly but fleetingly, and everything I feel is mirrored in his face.

"I can't do it, Max."

"You can. You have to. We both will."

He's crying.

I have never seen Max cry. On our wedding day his eyes shone with emotion; when Dylan was born I could hear the lump in his throat. But I have never seen him cry.

My own floodgates opened with motherhood and have never since closed. Adverts, charity appeals, Richard Curtis films. Hellos, goodbyes, I-love-yous. Max laughs at my tears, although not unkindly.

"It's sweet," he says, when I bawl at **that** bit in **Four Weddings**. "Endearing."

It made him feel protective, I decided. Like a proper alpha male.

Now, tears push their way from beneath closed lids to stream across his cheeks, and it's all wrong—it's all wrong that Max is crying, when he's always been the strong one. This isn't happening, it isn't happening. I want to go back to last year, when everything was still OK, to when Dylan was playing in the garden, swimming in the sea in Gran Canaria. I want to go to the doctor and have him check over Dylan, and tell me everything's fine, **all toddlers are clumsy**. I want to go home feeling foolish, have Max say **I told you so**.

This isn't my Max. My Max is strong. Capable. In control. Dry-eyed and levelheaded, when I'm sobbing and emotional. This Max is as lost as I am, as helpless as I am.

"I can't—" I start, and Max shakes his head again and again and again.

"No. We can't. We won't." The words—or perhaps the act of speaking, moving—seem to galvanise him, and he rubs his face violently with both hands, sits up straight, clears his throat. "We won't," he says again, with even more certainty, even more vigour.

He puts his arms around me and holds me, and I shut my eyes tight against the decision that has to be made, and against this Max who looks as lost as I am, as broken as I am. I can't see him like this. I need Max to be strong, because I don't think I can be.

We're home for less than a minute before Max opens the laptop. He sits at the kitchen table, his coat still zipped up, and the car keys still in one hand. I go through the motions of coming home: I shut the front door, take off my shoes and put on my slippers, turn on the main lights. I read the note Mum's left by the kettle, move the plastic dish of **chilli—quite spicy!** from the fridge to the freezer.

There is no reason why the house should feel emptier than it did this morning—than it does on any day I come home without my boy—and yet it feels that way today. Today it feels as though we've already lost him.

I stand uselessly in the middle of the kitchen, searching for something to do, then pick up a cloth from the sink and squeeze it dry.

"What are you doing?"

"Cleaning the kitchen."

"Why?"

I spray the surfaces with antiseptic, and rub it away in a circular, rhythmic motion I find oddly soothing.

"Pip."

There's a smear of sauce—ketchup probably—on one of the chrome handles. I hear Fiona's voice in my head. **I know it's full of sugar, but I don't let her have it at home . . .** I think of that horrible chain pub, with

Alison and Fiona and Phoebe and their braying husbands and their perfect healthy children . . . I scrub at the ketchup. **Fuck you, Fiona. Fuck you and your sanctimonious sugar sermon.** If Dylan comes home, **when** Dylan comes home, I will give him ketchup every fucking day if he wants it, I will give him as much chocolate and sweets and crisps as he wants, I will give him the moon if he asks for it.

I move on to the cupboard doors, which we've surely not cleaned since before I was pregnant. Nesting, isn't that what they call it? I was forty weeks pregnant—due any day—and adamant I would clean the house and paint the skirting boards in the hall before the baby arrived. That must have been the last time the larder cupboard was cleared out, too—there are things in here well past their sell-by date.

I drop my cloth and sit on the floor, pulling out tins and jars and packets of flour that sigh as I put them on the floor, tiny white clouds spelling out their displeasure at being moved.

"Pip!"

Dylan was overdue by two weeks. I was the size of a whale, a building, a country. My ankles were swollen and he'd dropped so low I waddled, ducklike, into the health centre for my sweep. Max wouldn't come.

"It's . . ." He searched for the word. "Icky."

I rolled my eyes. "Don't be ridiculous. What about when he's born? Is that going to be icky, too?" The look on Max's face suggested it might be.

110

In the event, he didn't seem to find the birth icky. Nor did I. And I know that we're genetically programmed to forget the terrible bits, and remember only the wondrous, beautiful feeling of holding a child that you've made—you've actually **made**—but I swear to God, that's the only bit I do remember. That, and looking up at Max to see his eyes shining.

"Our son," he said. "We have a son."

"Pip!" A shout, this time, filtering through the memories. I look around, dazed, at the pile of tinned foods and the packets of pasta and rice.

"It needs cleaning out."

"It doesn't."

"It does! Look at this tuna—it's from . . ." I search for a date but can't read it. I brandish it regardless. "Ages ago. And these beans—"

"Stop it."

"No, I want to—"

"Pip, stop it!"

"So it's OK for you to get on the laptop and start doing heaven knows what, but I can't clean the kitchen when it's filthy and—"

"I'm trying to find a cure for our son!"

He bellows the words, and had I not already been sitting, they might have felled me. As it is, I freeze, a tin of baked beans in one hand. What am I doing?

"There has to be something," Max says. "A treatment they've missed. Something they don't even know about."

"They're doctors, Max."

He looks at me. "What—you think that makes them better than us?"

"No, but . . ." I stand, staring at the food I don't remember taking out. "They're the experts."

"They can't be experts in everything, though, can they? In every type of cancer, every blood group, every nervous system?" He carries on talking, but his eyes flit across his screen as fast as his fingers move across the keyboard. "Do you remember what the GP said, that first time we took Dylan?"

You know your son.

"He just doesn't seem quite right," I'd said, expecting—no, **wanting**—the doctor to send us home with a benevolent smile and a private reflection on overprotective parents. We'd been talking about this for weeks, after all—ever since that holiday in Gran Canaria. **Is it normal to sleep this much? Alison's twins aren't nearly this clumsy. He's pale—don't you think he's pale?** "Not quite himself," I told the doctor. "It's probably nothing."

"You know your son" was the response from the doctor, as he wrote the referral, and there was a flash of our future in the grave expression on his face, although I didn't recognise it then.

"We know our son," Max says now. "There must be a hundred patients on that unit, and Dr. Khalili will oversee—what?—thirty of those? Maybe she sees each of them for a few minutes each, three times a day—that's ten, twelve minutes a day with each patient. **Twelve minutes.**" Fleetingly, he meets my eye. "How can she possibly know more about what's best for a child than a parent who spends twelve **hours** by his bedside? A parent who's spent nearly three years holding his hand?"

Dizziness makes me wish I'd stayed seated. I try to remember when I last ate something.

"We need to research it." Max looks at me, making sure I'm listening. "With the right treatment, Dylan could live for another five years. He could be cured completely—you read about it all the time." There's an energy about him I know I don't have; an energy he's only found since we arrived home, since he started searching online. "Think about it: How can doctors treat every case perfectly? Research every single condition to the nth degree? How can they afford to?" This is Max in problem-solving mode. Analysing, searching, testing. He looks at his watch. "Eight here, so . . . two in Chicago, three in Washington, DC . . ." He stands and takes the phone from the cradle on the side.

"At least take off your coat."

He shrugs it off, and it slides off the back of his chair and puddles on the floor.

"I'm going to put the fire on." Weeks ago, we took the central heating off the timer that would have switched it on at four p.m. and kept us warm till ten. What was the point, when we wouldn't be there?

When we fell through the door each night only to go straight to bed?

I walk into the sitting room and light the gas fire. I half expect Max to stay at the kitchen table, but he walks through too and sits heavily on the sofa, the laptop on his knees and the phone beside him. I sit next to him. Dylan's toys are in the corner of the room, neatly piled into cream hampers. I tidied the house the day he was admitted to hospital. There seemed to be toys and newspapers everywhere. I let Dylan watch **Paw Patrol**, and I whizzed around the house, restoring order before we left for the hospital, never for a moment considering that Dylan might not be back. Now I wish I'd left everything the way it was; left his toys out like he'd only stopped playing for a moment.

"I should phone my mum."

Max doesn't acknowledge me. I don't even know if he heard. I pick up the phone and dial the number of my childhood; picture Mum looking at Dad, saying, "Who could that be?" because no one would ever call past nine o'clock, then putting down whatever it is that she's knitting, and picking up the—

"It's me."

I hear a sharp intake of air. "What's happened?"

My family don't use the phone. When we call, there's something wrong.

I open my mouth but the words are strangling me and I make a tiny sound that makes Max look up from his screen and reach out a hand.

"It's Dylan," I manage, as if it could be anything else. And then it leaves my body in a great wordless wail and I double over, and wrap myself in my arms, and Max takes the phone from me because I can't speak for sobbing.

"Karen? No, he isn't—it's not . . ." He falls silent, although I don't know if it's because she's talking or because he needs to compose himself. "But we have had some bad news, I'm afraid."

From within my self-made cocoon, I'm dimly aware of his voice; of the soothing ups and downs as he explains to my mum what Dr. Khalili told us this morning. He is every bit as calm as she was, every bit as dispassionate. How can he switch off his emotions like that? Doesn't it hurt him, here, in the chest? In the heart? Doesn't he have the same pain I have right now—a pain that squeezes every bit of air from my lungs? Isn't it killing him, like it's killing me?

"We're not giving up," I hear my husband say. "Not while there's still a chance."

A chance. That's all we need. Just one tiny chance that Dylan might live.

If there's a chance, we'll take it.

Two hours later my head is fuzzy from lack of sleep, and from the jags of crying that erupt even when it feels like there can be no more tears left in me. I take a sip from the mug of coffee in my hand and find it cold. I lean against Max's shoulder. We're both look-ing at his laptop, at a research paper he's found, but

115

the words are swimming before my eyes. **Overall survival was significantly poorer for recurrent disease (P = 0:001; Fig. 2A) and significantly better for patients who had not received previous irradiation (P = 0:001; Fig. 2B).** Max highlights a phrase, copies it, and drops it into a Word document open on the screen. It is full of similar phrases, their meanings clear only after I have read each one a dozen times.

"Do you want another coffee?"

Max makes a noncommittal sound I take as a yes. I stand and walk into the kitchen, feeling the room sway as though I've been drinking. I stare at the kettle for a full minute after it's boiled, unable to remember what I'm doing here, then I spoon coffee granules into two mugs and splash milk into mine.

"Do you think Dr. Khalili will agree?" I say, as I walk back into the sitting room, my eyes on the mugs in my hand. "The oncologist said he couldn't have radiotherapy because of his age." I've overfilled the coffee and it slops against the inside of the cup, a few drops spilling on the carpet. I press my sock into the stain.

"Proton beam therapy is different. It uses particle accelerators to go directly to the cancerous cells, without damaging the healthy tissue around them." Max speaks confidently, without referring to the copious notes he's made on his laptop; the way he can scan a corporate brochure over breakfast, then give a presentation about oil refinery before lunch. I present Max with his coffee and he looks at it for a second, like he's not sure what I'm handing him, before taking it and setting it down beside him. "The five-year survival rate for patients under the age of eighteen is **seventy-nine percent**." He stresses the figure, then frowns at his screen. His fingers fly across the keyboard.

"He isn't yet three," I say quietly. "What are the survival rates for patients under three?" Max doesn't answer. His notes are filled with percentages found on an internet that gives us whatever answer we're looking for. The numbers are convincing. Dylan could live another two years, another three. We could have another Christmas together, more birthdays, holidays. Unbidden, the images form in my head—running along the beach, jumping through waves, blowing out candles—and then reality bites.

"We need to talk about the damage to his brain."

"I've bookmarked this article." He clicks a link and spins the screen around to show me. A teenage girl smiles lopsidedly at me. "She had the same surgery as Dylan, and it left her mute and paralysed, but she's learning to speak again, and she's just done a 5K sponsored walk!"

"What if that doesn't happen, Max?"

There's a long pause, and then he looks at me, his eyes shining but his jaw set hard. "Then we'll have a disabled son. And we'll be grateful every single day for him." He reaches for my hand and squeezes it, then returns to his laptop.

Suddenly cold, I pull my feet onto the sofa beneath me, and cradle my coffee. I think about Dr. Khalili's words, about a boy who cannot walk or talk, who cannot eat food, or use the toilet, or ask for comfort. I pick up my phone and find the **Bringing Up B** podcast that has kept me company on the long drives home from the hospital, and I click on "contact us."

You don't know me, I write, **but I need your help.**

ten

Max

Dylan looks at the ball, concentration etched on his face. He runs toward it and kicks with all his might, almost falling over in his effort to make the ball reach its target, all of five feet away from him. In front of the white plastic goal—so small I can place my outstretched arms around both posts—I kneel on grass still damp from the night before.

The goal was a present for Dylan's second birthday, and every morning since, he's dragged me out at first light to play. I've been in the UK office for the last two weeks, with my next trip not for another week, and I'm soaking up this time with my boy. He changes so much, even in a day, that a trip away means coming home to a completely different child.

The ball's slowing down. The grass was only cut a few days ago, but it grows fast at this time of year, and

Dylan's blow-up ball is no match for a clump of daisies. I edge forward and lunge at it in a slow-motion dive designed to fail. As I overshoot the ball, I nudge it in the right direction, rolling on the wet grass and clutching at my head in mock dismay.

"Go!" shouts Dylan, in the abbreviated version of "goal" Pip and I love so much we've adopted it for our own.

"How was the match?" she'll ask me, after the five-a-side I join when I can.

"Not bad," I'll say. "Nil-nil, then Johnno scored a go just before the whistle."

Dylan jumps on me and I lie on the grass, looking up at my son, silhouetted against the morning light.

"Good go," I tell him. "Great go!" Despite the warmth of the sun, damp is seeping through my clothes, and my neck feels stiff and uncomfortable. "Off you get, champ." I sit up and let him slide off my chest, and he makes a crash far too loud for a boy dropping onto grass . . .

I blink hard, my body dragged reluctantly from sleep. The open laptop is on the floor by my feet. The fire is still on, but daylight streams between the drapes we didn't bother to close last night, and the air in the room is stale and hot. Pip is curled, catlike, on the sofa beside me, both hands folded beneath her head. I touch her shoulder and she murmurs but doesn't stir.

"Sweetie, it's gone nine."

She opens her eyes and pushes herself upright.

"What? Oh no!" She stands, and almost falls, groggy with tiredness and stiff from sleeping on the sofa.

"It's OK."

"But I'm always there at seven. Always!"

"It's OK."

She rounds on me. "It's not OK. Stop saying it's OK! We have a routine. I'm at the hospital by seven. Every day. Every. Single." She dissolves into tears before she finishes her sentence, and although I stand up and put my arms around her, she's stiff and unyielding.

"Why don't you go and have a shower, and I'll call PICU and tell them—"

"I don't want a shower, I just want to be with Dylan." She wriggles away from my attempts to comfort her, and I wish I hadn't tried.

I walk out of the room. "Well, I'm having one. I've been in these clothes for twenty-four hours and I stink."

Fifteen minutes later I'm clean and awake. I put on a suit, but leave off the tie. Armor, Pip used to call it, when I was packing for a trip. She'd sit on the bed and I'd tell her who I was meeting, and what I'd be doing, and she'd pick out shirts and tell me it was like going into battle.

"If you were a woman you'd have makeup too," she said once. "That's why we call it war paint. Something to hide behind—to make us look stronger than we really are."

Pip's waiting in the hall for me. She's picked up her bag, but her hair is matted on one side, and a half-moon crease runs from her left ear to her nose. The front door's open before I'm on the bottom step, the engine running before I'm out of the house. If she notices my suit, or wonders why I'm wearing one when I'm not going into work, she doesn't say anything.

She drives angrily, snatching the steering wheel and snapping at anyone who dares to pause at a junction, or hesitate on a roundabout. Traffic's bad, and from the tension in Pip's ramrod arms that's my fault too. At the lights, she rocks on the clutch, even though she knows it bugs me, and tuts under her breath when the lights turn red again before it's our turn.

We don't speak. I close my eyes.

The speed bumps at the entrance to the hospital wake me up. Pip looks at me.

"I don't know how you can sleep . . ." She lets her sentence trail away as she gets out of the car.

"I'm used to it, I guess," I say, thinking of the jet-lagged power naps I grab in taxis between airports and hotels, then I see the stiffness in her back as she walks away, and I realize what she means is **How can you sleep at a time like this? How can you sleep when our son's dying?** Frustration churns inside me. It's wrong to sleep, is it? To take a shower, to get dressed, to brush my hair? It's wrong to function normally, because our son's in hospital—is that it? Wrong to cope?

We walk in angry single file through parked cars toward PICU. Pip hasn't brought a coat, and I see the white tips of her fingers as she hugs her arms around her. As we draw near to PICU I see a couple I recognize. Between them is a child—a teenager. The mum catches my eye and lifts an arm in greeting. The teenager was in PICU when Dylan was admitted. A car accident, I think. He was transferred onto the general wards just after Christmas. Dad's carrying a bag; there's a pillow stuffed under his arm. I guess they're going home. Unjust, uncontrollable jealousy floods my heart. I look straight ahead and pretend I haven't recognized them.

Pip's seen them, too. She turns her head in the opposite direction, and I see the tightness around her jaw that means she's trying not to cry. She stops and lets me catch up with her.

"I'm sorry."

"I am, too." I take her hand and squeeze it.

"I keep reading about couples who split up." She turns to face me. "Interviews with people whose children had accidents, or got cancer, or died, and they always say the same thing. They always say how it **took its toll on our marriage**, or how **our relationship wasn't strong enough to withstand**—"

"That isn't us." I make her look at me. "We're the strongest couple I know. Whatever happens, we will get through this."

Her voice is a whisper. "I'm so scared of losing him, Max."

I wrap my arms round her and we stand that way for a while, until Pip's breathing slows and she pulls away. She's exhausted. She's spent every day at the hospital since Dylan was admitted. No wonder she's breaking.

I hold Pip's hand for the rest of the way to PICU, only dropping it to press the doorbell. One of the nurses leans over the desk to look up the hallway. I smile through the glass door and she buzzes us in. Silently, we stand side by side at the narrow, trough-like sink in the corridor outside of Room 1, and roll up our sleeves. We scrub up like doctors, rubbing foaming soap across our hands and into the creases of our fingers; digging the tips of our fingers into the palm of the opposite hand. Rinse. Dry. Sanitize.

"Ready?"

Pip nods. She doesn't look ready.

"He's **our** son," I whisper. "They can't do anything we don't want them to do."

She nods again, but there's uncertainty in her eyes and I know she's scared. We're all brought up to believe doctors know best, and every appointment, every diagnosis, every spell in hospital disempowers us still further.

You know your son, the GP said.

We know Dylan. We know what's best for him.

"Oh!" As we walk into Room 1, Pip stops short. The crib next to Dylan's is empty.

"Darcy's fine," Cheryl says quickly. "She's graduated. They moved her to High Dependency last night."

124

"Oh, thank God. I couldn't bear it if . . ." Pip doesn't finish her sentence, but she doesn't need to. I don't say anything. Darcy has her own parents to worry about her. Liam has his. There's only one child in the room I'm interested in, and it's the beautiful boy asleep in the middle crib.

"How's he doing?"

"He's comfortable. Sats stable, fluids fine, and no temp."

"That's great."

"I was about to give him a wash, but as you're here . . ." Cheryl holds out a cloth.

Pip rolls up her sleeves and takes the cloth, and I get a bowl from the counter and fill it with warm water. "Have you checked the temperature?" she says, when I return. I feel a burst of irritation.

"No, I thought I'd just wing it. I have done this before, you know." I look across at Cheryl and try for some solidarity, but my raised eyebrows aren't returned. She looks away.

"Women don't trust us, mate." Connor comes in like he works here, loud and swaggering. "They treat us like kids ourselves, half the time." He claps a hand on my back and peers over my shoulder, like we're in the pub and he's looking to get served. I shift slightly, seized by an overwhelming desire to hide Dylan from his gaze. From everyone's gaze.

"Hey," I manage. I want to ask how he's doing today, but the face I saw on the bench beneath the oak tree isn't the face I'm seeing now. Now he's loud and cocky again—no sign of the broken man who cried into his hands.

"Nik's at home." Connor carries on to his own son's bed. "School boiler's broken down, so they've sent all the kids home. Bunch of pansies. They never heard of putting a coat on?"

"How many do you have?" Pip talks over her shoulder. She's taken off Dylan's onesie, careful not to dislodge the sticky pads that hold the wires to his chest. I take a ball of cotton wool and dampen it, cleaning his face and behind his ears.

"Four. Liam here's the youngest."

Pip squeezes the cloth out and begins gently wiping Dylan's arms. "And how's he doing?"

"All right, I think. They don't tell you anything, do they?"

I wonder if Cheryl will say something, but either she isn't listening or she's choosing not to comment. Pip doesn't answer, and I don't want to, and so we talk instead to Dylan, telling him we'll **just clean this bit here**, and **I expect this tickles a bit**.

At home, Dylan had a bath every night. It was part of his bedtime routine. Story, bath, milk, bed. Every single night. He must have had—what—seven hundred baths? Eight hundred? How many of those did I give him?

It was hard, with work. I'm gone for a week at a time, sometimes, and when I'm in the UK I'm not back till late, making up for the time spent out of the office. Most evenings I'd come home to find Dylan already in the tub, Pip kneeling beside him, soap suds to her elbows. I'd kiss them both, then go back downstairs to fix us a drink; be ready with a warm lap to read my boy a story when he came back down.

Why didn't I take over? Why didn't I get home earlier? Why didn't I take every opportunity I had to kneel by that tub while my boy—my healthy, happy boy—splashed in the water? Why didn't I realize one day I might not be able to? All those times I wished Dylan was bigger, imagined taking him fishing, teaching him to drive . . . Wishing away the future, when the present was right there. The present was perfect.

I take a clean ball of cotton and rub it across the palm of Dylan's left hand. As I do, it tenses, curling around my finger in an echo of when he was a baby. My heart swells, with love and hope and excitement, and I stop thinking. I stop moving. I just stand there while Pip washes our boy, holding his hand, and feeling him hold mine.

Everything changes when you become a father. I didn't know it at the time, but before Dylan came along I was treading water, taking each day as it came, and rarely thinking about the future; beyond what vacation we might take the following year, or whether I should trade in the car before it needed expensive work done on it.

Sure, I'd felt a responsibility toward Pip when it was just the two of us, but nothing like the way I felt when I drove her and our infant son home from the hospital. I stuck to five miles under the speed limit, my palms sweating on the steering wheel, convinced that, after driving for sixteen years without a wreck, today would be my first. I cursed at someone who pulled out in front of us—didn't they know we had a baby on board?—then panicked I'd give my kid a potty mouth. What were we thinking, getting pregnant? I wasn't ready to be a father. I didn't know enough, I wasn't old enough, wise enough.

I carried the car seat inside, then came back to help Pip, who was walking like she just got off a horse. I settled them both on the sofa, fetched the nursing cushion, a magazine, a snack, a drink. I hovered nearby as Pip tried to feed, trying to remember what the midwife had said about latching on, and wincing when Pip screwed up her face in pain. And as they finally got it, and Pip closed her eyes and Dylan fed, I looked at my wife and my son, and thought how it was down to me to look after them, and I felt a mix of macho pride and blind terror.

It was a steep learning curve. We had always shared the chores equally, always lived side by side like the two adults we were. Now Pip was home with the baby, and fitting in housework while he napped, and I was bringing home the bacon, like we were June and Ward Cleaver. I'd never worried about losing my job before—there were always other jobs, other opportunities—but now I worked twice as hard, twice as long, because what would we do without my monthly paycheck? I stopped goofing around at weekends and looked at repairs I needed to do around the house. I leapt to Pip's defense, even though I knew she was more than capable of looking after herself. I turned into my father.

And now my family needs me more than ever. I look at my boy, pale and listless in his crib. I look at my wife, singing nursery rhymes under her breath as she gently washes the dried saliva from around his mouth. I force my fears down into my chest, where they sit in a hard knot. Pip and Dylan depend on me, and all over again, it's just like that day when I drove them home from the hospital, and I feel just as out of control, just as scared.

All I know is that this is my world, and I can't lose it.

eleven

Pip

My mother puts a large glass of wine in my hand. I shake my head. "I can't."

"It's medicinal."

"But if something happens—"

"Then your father will drive you." Mum pulls my chin up till I'm looking at her. "You need to switch off, Pip." She strokes my cheek gently and my eyes fill with tears. I'm bone-tired, my body aching like I have the flu. Max is at a dinner. He told Chester he'd be working from home for a few days, but he couldn't get out of tonight.

"Surely if you explained?" I said, finding it hard to comprehend how Max could think about anything except Dylan.

Max's response was curt. "He knows."

I'm not running a charity, Chester said once, when

Max had asked to cut down on the travelling while Dylan was in PICU. **I sympathise**, he'd said, **I really do, but we've all got families, Max, we've all got baggage**.

That's how he saw Dylan. Baggage.

So I went to my parents' house, slipping off my shoes and sinking into the warm embrace of my childhood. After supper, Dad retired to the sitting room to fall asleep over the newspaper, and Mum and I cleared up, and talked about whether the wisteria might flower this year, and if St. Giles Blue would be too garish for the spare bedroom. I thought of Max, at his work dinner, and wondered if there was a bit of him that needed the distraction of work, the same way I felt better for my mother's inconsequential chatter.

"So." Mum pulls up a chair next to me. "What's the latest?"

"Max has found a doctor in Houston who thinks he can help." I look at the pictures of Dylan on the kitchen wall, and the high chair wiped clean and waiting in the corner. I think of the cot upstairs, for when he stays overnight, and of the box of my toys Mum kept in the loft all this time.

"That's wonderful!"

"The next step is to ask Dr. Khalili if the trust will send Dylan there for proton beam therapy." I skirt over the issue of funding, but a leaden, sick feeling builds in my stomach at the thought.

"If we had insurance," Max said, "we wouldn't even

have to ask. We'd just take Dylan to the best doctor in the States—wherever they were."

It wasn't what he **said**, but what he didn't say. He didn't say that he'd **had** insurance, back when he lived in the States. He didn't remind me that it was me who wanted him to live here, who persuaded him to transfer to the UK office, who scoffed at the changes in employment terms because what did that matter, when you were in love? He didn't remind me that I'd dismissed his musings over whether he should extend his cover to include his newborn son; that I'd told him the practicalities made it pointless.

"It would mean flying to the States if he got ill," I'd said. "And besides, the UK has the best health care system in the world—everyone knows that." And somehow it had turned into one of those jokey conversations like why Brits couldn't make proper sandwiches, and why Americans don't use kettles. Because who ever thinks they're going to need insurance anyway?

Mum is full of questions. "And does he think—this doctor—does he think he can remove the tumour completely? Are there any side effects? Would he come here, or would you have to take Dylan to America?"

"America," I say, because that one, I can answer. "We'd be out there for ten weeks."

"Ten weeks . . . Goodness." Mum rallies. "Still. Whatever it takes, right? Getting him better, that's all that matters."

I chew the inside of my lip. I look at the determination in Mum's face, at the love in her eyes. Love not just for her grandson, but for me, and for Max. "Mum?"

She waits.

"What did I like doing, when I was Dylan's age?"

She hesitates, not wanting to indulge me because she knows where this is going, why I'm asking. She sighs. "You liked feeding the ducks. We went every day after your lunchtime nap, and I had to hold on to your hood to stop you jumping in with them." She smiles at the memory.

"What else?"

"Books. You'd climb onto my lap and turn the pages faster than I could read the story." Her voice cracks on the last word.

"What else," I say fiercely, even though it's hurting us both.

"Dancing," she says softly, her eyes filling with tears. "You loved to dance."

I swallow hard. I picture my three-year-old self, twirling in pale pink ballet shoes, throwing bread in my yellow hooded rain mac, turning the pages of book after book, pointing at the pictures, laughing at the voices my mother was so brilliant at. I picture Dylan the way he was; the way he is now; the way he might be, if he lives.

Mum knows me too well. "It's a different sort of

life," she whispers, pulling me close. "But it's still a life, Pip. It's still **his** life."

And I sob in her arms and wish I was still that twirling three-year-old, and that she still had hold of my raincoat to stop me from falling.

B's real name is Bridget. Her mother—the woman responsible for all those hours of **Bringing Up B**—is Eileen Pearce, and they live in a small terraced house on the outskirts of Bath. She replied to my email with her phone number, and when I called, her voice was so warm, and so familiar, it was like speaking to a friend.

"If it would be easier to talk over a coffee," she said, "we live outside Bath, not far from—" She interrupted herself. "Although you might not be able to leave the hospital—I understand."

I've never missed a day with Dylan. I've taken Dylan to all his appointments, all his blood tests and chemo sessions and follow-ups. When he moved to PICU, after we left the parents' flat and drove in each day, I fell into a new routine. Up at five thirty; in the car by ten to six; with Dylan from seven in the morning till ten at night. Max came with me, if he was working from home, or joined me after work, if he was at the UK office. We would drive back in convoy, Max insisting on my going first, as though he could keep me safe simply by keeping me in view. At the lights by the retail park I'd look in my rearview mirror, and he'd be there, blowing me a kiss, or pulling a face to make me laugh.

"I'd love to meet you," I told Eileen.

Max promised he'd be there at seven on the dot, and Mum said she'd do the afternoon, so Max could show his face at the office. And then I drove the two hours to the quiet street where Eileen and her family live in a terraced house with a paved front garden, fighting the urge to turn around and drive back to my boy.

Objectively, I note the concrete ramp replacing the steps to the door, and the silver van with the sticker on the back: **Please leave room for my wheelchair!** I tell myself what I told Max: that I'm on a reconnaissance mission.

"I thought it would be useful to get a picture of what equipment we'll need when Dylan comes home."

"It's a good idea. She might be able to let you have supplier details, that sort of thing."

I've never lied to Max before.

"You must be Pip." Eileen is tall and strong, with salt-and-pepper hair in a long plait down the middle of her back. She wears jeans and a rugby shirt, with the sleeves rolled up. "Phil's at work and the twins are at school, but Bridget's here—come on through."

The house is cluttered, with a pile of shoes by the front door, and PE kits hanging on pegs coming away from the wall. I follow Eileen and see an open doorway leading to what must be B's bedroom.

Eileen stops. "That used to be the sitting room. Now it's Bridget's room, and her wet room is the old kitchen, and our kitchen is the dining room, and our sitting room is upstairs." She laughs. "It was cheaper than moving, but my God, what a year that was!"

The room is dominated by a hospital bed and hoist. There's an oxygen tank, and a metal cabinet on the wall. "Drug safe," Eileen says, following my gaze. "Essential, with two other kids in the house."

Cheerful curtains hang at the windows, and I smile to see the CDs above the bed, spinning rainbows around the room. "That was such a beautiful episode," I say, pointing at the mobile.

"The twins would do anything for her." Eileen smiles. "Sadly, Bridget's sight's been failing for some time now, so I don't know how much longer she'll be able to see it. Come on—I'll put the kettle on, and you can meet her."

Bridget is fourteen. Her limbs are so thin I could close my thumb and forefinger around them, and they are secured to her chair with strong black straps. A foam rest circles her head.

"It looks barbaric, I know," Eileen says quickly, "but it's much more comfortable for Bridget if she's in the right position. You're lucky—she's having a good day today, aren't you, Bridget?" She drops a kiss on her daughter's head. I look for a reaction from Bridget— a movement, a flicker of acknowledgement on her face—but there is nothing.

"Hi, Bridget, I'm Pip." I smile at the girl. It's strange, meeting someone you know so much about. I think of the funny stories Eileen tells on her podcast, and the places she and her husband have taken B over the years. "No school today?" I know Bridget's deaf, and that she cannot lip-read, but it would feel rude to talk to Eileen as though Bridget isn't here.

"Ah," Eileen says, with a roll of her eyes. "There's a story." She hands me a mug of tea. "Sorry, I didn't even ask if you take milk—is that OK?"

"Perfect, thank you."

"Bridget's school closed last week. We got a letter on Monday, and they shut the doors on Friday." Eileen sits at the kitchen table, which is piled with books and pens and the remains of breakfast. I sit too.

"Can they do that?"

"Apparently so. They've offered us a place in a school two hours away, or a residential placement in Sussex—thanks but no thanks."

"What are you going to do?"

For the first time since I arrived, Eileen's no-nonsense tone falters. She shrugs. "I honestly don't know. I work part-time during school hours—we can't cover the bills without it—and although Bridget has carers, they're not supposed to be here without one of us." She smiles. "It'll work out. It always does."

We drink our tea, and then Eileen excuses herself to put Bridget to bed for a rest, and I insist on doing

137

the washing up. Afterwards I take a deep breath, and I ask the question I know she's been waiting for.

"Did you know Bridget was going to be disabled?"

"We knew from the twenty-week scan she had spina bifida." Eileen gives a wry smile. "The rest was a surprise."

"And you—" Eileen said I could ask her anything. But I can't. I can't.

"Still had her?"

I nod, ashamed of what my question implies. "I'm not saying I'd—"

"It's OK. These are important things to talk about." She leans forward and clasps her hands together on the table, staring at her thumbs. "There was never any question of my having a termination. It was a huge shock, but we'd named her, we were excited about her. We already loved her. I would walk through fire for that girl—and some days it feels like I do."

"So you've never regretted it?"

Eileen looks up. "I didn't say that." She gazes through the doorway towards Bridget's room, speaking quietly, as though she hasn't ever voiced the words before. "People say we're selfless, putting Bridget's needs ahead of ours; giving her a life, even though sometimes it makes it difficult for anyone else to have one. But it's the other way around. I had my daughter because I wanted a baby." She pauses, and I hold my breath, willing her to continue, needing this insight into her thoughts.

"Bridget has enriched my life—and the lives of everyone who knows her—in a million and one ways," she says. "But if I'd known how hard her own life would be, if I'd known that the moments of pleasure would be so few and so fleeting, amid the drugs and the seizures, and the operations . . ." Eileen straightens, her eyes refocusing on the room around us. "Well," she says, her voice still soft, "I don't know if I would have been so selfish."

twelve

Leila

It has been five days since Leila asked Max and Pip Adams to make a decision no parent should ever have to face. She has checked in with them each day, answered their questions and made herself available whenever they have needed. She has not pushed them for a decision, but she knows that the time will come—and soon—when she will have to do so, and so she is relieved when Max Adams asks for a meeting.

"We've made a decision." He is wearing a suit, and the formality is at odds with his wife's shapeless jumper, stretched over restless fingers that scrunch the cuffs into balls.

Leila knows what it is without asking—she can see it in the fix of his jaw and the steeliness in his eyes—but she waits for Max to voice it.

"We're not prepared to give up on our son." He is holding his wife's hand, and he rubs his thumb over her knuckles as if she needs this physical reassurance that he is there. "We've researched Dylan's condition and we understand that he will have life-limiting disabilities, but we feel that if there is a chance of prolonging his life, we should pursue that option."

Leila has rarely heard a parent speak so confidently and so fluently in the midst of tragedy. Max Adams doesn't sound like a parent at all, she thinks. His speech is slick. Rehearsed. It is, she realizes, a pitch. Because that, she supposes, is the world that Max Adams knows. It does not mean that he isn't falling apart on the inside. And in fact, when she looks a little closer, she sees that his tie is not quite straight; his shirt is a little crumpled. A muscle ticks at the side of his jaw. And behind the confident, self-assured eyes is pure fear.

"I understand." Leila is not a mother, but her arms have held many infants. She has delivered babies, both kicking and still. She has lost children; seen the pain in parents' eyes as part of them dies, too. Leila would not give up on her child, either.

"We want Dylan to have proton beam therapy."

Leila has not expected such specifics, but she is not surprised. She imagined the Adamses would suggest another course of chemotherapy, but they are not the first parents to suggest proton beam therapy.

"The NHS has agreements with centers in the US,"

Max says. A casual observer might find his tone abrasive. Condescending, even.

"So I understand." Leila is not a casual observer. Leila knows that Max Adams is close to breaking point, as so many PICU parents are. He is fighting for control in a situation where he has none, and Leila will let him have it. "There are treatment centers planned for London and Manchester, but for now it isn't something we can offer here."

She notices that Pip has taken back her hand, wrapping her arms around herself. She is letting her husband take the lead, and Leila wonders if this, too, is contributing to the pain etched in Max's face.

"But you can send patients to the States."

"I'll need to talk to the oncologist team about whether Dylan's case is right for proton beam therapy."

"It is." Max is bullish, and Leila feels her spine straighten in response. **His son is dying**, she reminds herself. Leila has forgiven many parents many transgressions over the years. Spat-out insults, angry diatribes—even, once, a hard shove of the shoulder from a mother whose heart she had hewn in two with her words. **I'm so sorry—we did everything we could.**

"Now that I know you want to explore more treatment options—"

"We want to explore proton beam therapy."

"—we can look at the most appropriate course of

action." Leila looks at Pip, still curled into her own embrace. She will need to document this conversation, and she would like to record both parents' views. "Mrs. Adams, do you have anything you want to add?"

Pip Adams glances at her husband. She says a single word, but so quietly Leila has to lean forward to catch it.

"No."

"OK, then," Leila says, but there is something about the stricken look on Pip's face that makes her stop, makes her question what she heard. "Do you mean," she says quietly, keeping her eyes on Pip's, "**No, I don't have anything to add?**"

A single tear makes its way down Pip Adams's cheek. She gives another nervous glance at her husband, then swallows. "I mean, no. I mean, I've changed my mind. I don't want to put Dylan through any more treatment."

Max Adams stares at her, openmouthed. "What?"

"I can't do it." Pip starts to cry, and Leila's heart clenches.

"Can't what?" Max says, his voice too loud for this room, for the people inside it. The color has drained from his face, and although he's still seated, every muscle is tense, like he's on a starting block. He looks at his wife and his voice cracks as he speaks again, more quietly, this time. "Can't save Dylan's life?"

Pip's eyes fill with pain, and Leila's heart drums double-time in a chest suddenly too small for its contents.

"I can't," Pip begins, hard-fought breaths every few words. "I can't make him live a life I wouldn't want to live myself." And she looks up at Leila, with a jaw just as fixed, just as determined as her husband's.

"I want to let him go."

thirteen

Max

The first time I stayed over at Pip's she had me rescue a spider from the bathtub.

"Careful of his legs," she said, as I carried it downstairs in cupped hands and released it into the garden. "Don't hurt him."

I stare at her now, incredulous. Pip cries at dog rescue adverts, donates to disaster relief, moves rainy-day snails off the sidewalk so they don't get crushed. She cannot bear to see a living thing suffer. What is she saying?

"But we decided—"

"No. You decided." She turns to look at me. "He's been through so much, Max—I can't bear to see him suffer anymore."

"The proton beam therapy could take the cancer away completely. It could save his life!"

"What life?" She's crying, and I feel cleaved in two, wanting to comfort her, yet appalled by what I'm hearing. "Tube-feeding, catheters, cannula, mouth suctioning . . . that's not living, Max, that's existing."

Dr. Khalili clears her throat. "Perhaps it would be best if you took some more time to discuss—"

"There's nothing to discuss," I say. "I'm not giving up on my son."

"Take as much time as you need." She leaves, and I stand and walk to the window, my back to Pip.

"I can't believe you're doing this."

"It's breaking my heart."

"Then—" I spin round, my outstretched arms speaking for me. But she shakes her head.

"If he was an animal—a horse who couldn't walk, couldn't graze—you wouldn't hesitate. You'd say it was the kindest thing to do. One final act of compassion."

"Our son isn't an animal!" I spit out the words, appalled by the comparison, but Pip doesn't flinch.

"Please, Max. Don't let him suffer anymore. This isn't about us, it isn't about how we'll feel if we lose him. This is about Dylan, and accepting that we've reached the end of the road."

"No." I cross the room and open the door. I am no longer torn in two. I no longer feel the urge to wipe away her tears. "I will never, ever give up on my son." However long you spend with someone, however well you think you know them, they can still be a stranger to you.

In Room 1, I stand for a moment at Dylan's side, holding his hand and silently vowing to do everything in my power to protect him. I'm seized by the urge to gather him up in my arms and take him; to bundle him into the car and drive to the airport and take the first plane home.

Home. America hasn't been my home for more than a decade, yet I am suddenly overwhelmingly homesick. **We'll be there soon**, I promise Dylan. **We'll get you the best doctors, and the best treatment, and then you'll come home. You** will.

I leave the car keys by Dylan's crib, and go to the taxi rank by the main hospital entrance.

"Kenilworth? That's going to be seventy, eighty quid, you know that, right?"

I bite back a response that he's a cabdriver, not my financial adviser, and mumble a **That's fine**. He makes a halfhearted attempt at conversation, then gives up, and we travel home in silence.

I'm not used to being in the house on my own. Since October I've hardly been here at all. My time is split between hotels, airplanes and cars, and the sterile hallways and wards of the hospital. If I'm here, it's to sleep, or to rush in to shower and change after a long flight.

Upstairs the door to Dylan's room is open, and I

pull it closed without looking, without checking. I know Pip goes in there. Sits in the nursing chair and turns on his mobile, looks at the empty crib and imagines it full.

Occasionally Pip asks me to get something from his room. A clean onesie, a toy, a favorite book. I have to steel myself to walk in, and when I do I go straight to the bureau, the toy box, the bookcase. I don't look around. I can't.

There are two other bedrooms on Dylan's floor: the office, for when I work from home, and the guest room, for when my mom is over. Pip and I have the master suite on the top floor. There's a separate dressing room, lined with closets, and a bathroom with two basins, and low sliding doors where the sloping roof meets the ceiling. I open one of these now and pull out a suitcase from the crawl space.

I put it on the bed and start to fill it. Shorts, sweaters, pants, suits. I don't let myself think about what I'm doing; about whether I'm packing for a night, for a month, forever. I don't let myself think at all. I only know I can't be here right now.

fourteen

Pip

Sometimes you only know for certain if you've made the right decision once you've made it. Either it slides smoothly into place as though it were always meant to be there, or it sits, spiky and misshapen, in the corners of your mind. **This isn't right—you've made the wrong choice.**

That's how I felt when Max told Dr. Khalili we wanted Dylan to have more treatment.

This isn't right.

While Max talked, I thought about Bridget, and her mother. I thought about what makes a life a life. I thought how much I loved Dylan, and how I would take on his suffering in a heartbeat if I could.

And I realised that I could. I could do that one thing for him.

If Dylan dies, it will hurt me for an eternity. But for

him, it will be over. No more pain, no drugs, no more poison seeping through his frail body. None of the indignities of being dependent on others for every need, every movement.

I knew Max would leave PICU. I can count on two hands the number of arguments we've had, but they've all ended up with Max walking out, coming back when he's cooled off and had a chance to think things through.

"It's infuriating," I said once. "You're so bloody determined to have the last word."

Max was taken aback. "That's not it at all—it's because I'm scared I'll say something I'll regret—something you don't deserve."

So I'm not surprised to see the car keys by Dylan's cot, and in the midst of the awfulness of today, it makes me feel a little better to know that Max cares enough not to leave me stranded. In the quiet room he looked at me like he hated me. He needs space, that's all.

Automatically, I put on **Bringing Up B** for the drive home, but I can't listen to Eileen's voice without seeing her face as she talked about an alternative life— one in which she hadn't gone through with the pregnancy—so I switch off the radio.

When I reach the house, the driveway is empty. Max has taken my car. Misgiving roots itself in the pit of my stomach, growing so fast and so firmly that by the time I get inside I don't call his name, or look in the kitchen, I run up the stairs and into our bedroom and see the empty space on his bedside table where his book lives, his reading glasses, the silver alarm clock he never takes on business trips. Hangers rattle on his side of the wardrobe.

I call his mobile. It's switched off. I text him, my fingers hesitant over the keys as I work out what to say. What I want to say is Have you left me? but the question is redundant. I settle for Please call me.

He doesn't call. He sends a text, an hour later, when I'm standing in the kitchen watching the microwave warm a bowl of soup I know I should eat.

I've checked into a hotel.

Are you coming back? I ask. I watch the little dots that tell me he's typing a message, and realise that whatever he's about to say is longer than "yes." I look at the artwork stuck to the fridge. Painted finger-print petals in a field of sunflowers; autumn leaves on a paper plate shaped like a pumpkin; a cotton-wool snowman with a tissue-paper scarf. All carried reverently from daycare by a boy bursting with pride. **Look, Mummy! Dylan paint! Dylan draw!** Pain screws into my chest as my phone pings with Max's reply.

Only if you've changed your mind.

How did this happen? A year ago we were a happy family. This time last week Max and I were united,

celebrating the fact that Dylan was breathing inde-
pendently again, feeling hopeful for the future. And
now . . . Am I really having to choose between my
husband and my son?

There are five pieces of artwork on the fridge. Just
five. Another handful sent to Max's mum, the same
again to my parents. A box file of them in Max's office,
a stray painting left in the boot of my car. Forty?
Fifty? And the rest, pushed carelessly into the recycling box at the end of the week.

"It's not exactly Van Gogh, after all," I said to Max,
assuaging my guilt with a grin and a glass of Pinot
Noir. I held up that day's masterpiece—a spattering of
colours blown by a straw.

"You're right." Max gave the painting an appraising
eye. "It's more Jackson Pollock."

I dropped it into the bin, pushed a newspaper on top
so Dylan wouldn't see. "We can't keep everything."

I swallow a moan. Something builds inside me,
slow and insistent and then faster and harder. Guilt and
anger and shame and grief. Why didn't I keep everything? All Dylan's paintings. Every feather he picked up
on every walk, every shell, every stone he ran a finger over
and examined with eyes wide, looking at something I
had long forgotten how to see. Why didn't I keep them?

I type another message to Max. I just want what's
best for Dylan. The response is instant.

So do I.

I sleep fitfully, plagued by dreams of Dylan in a boat, a storm taking him further and further out to sea. I wake crying, reaching for the empty space on Max's side of the bed. At the hospital I scan the car park for my blue Zafira, and I'm not sure whether I'm relieved or disappointed not to see it. I spend longer than usual washing my hands, unsure whether Max might be here after all, wondering if the nurses have been talking about us.

"Morning!" Cheryl is as cheerful as ever. It's all I can do to stop myself from asking if she's seen Max. "I've popped a nasal cannula on—his sats have been all over the place overnight, so it's only to give him a bit of help."

A narrow tube of clear plastic loops around Dylan's head, two tiny openings delivering a light flow of oxygen through both nostrils.

"You look tired," Nikki says. "Rough night?"

I nod and sit by Dylan's bed. I want to pull the curtains around us, but it feels rude. I don't know why I care, but I do.

"Max away again?"

"Yes." I pull my knitting out of the bag beneath my chair, even though I haven't touched it in a week, and don't want to do it now.

"It must be lovely, travelling so much." There's no sign of the nervous woman who came in with Liam

153

that day. She's used to PICU now; she puts her lunch in the family room fridge, and writes down suggestions in the notebook for other parents.

"Mind you, they say you're just seeing the inside of hotel rooms and airports, don't they? Where is he this time?"

"Boston." I say it without thinking, and my pulse quickens as I think what will happen if Max comes in now. **How stupid I am**, I'll have to say, **I must have been looking at the wrong week . . .** My train of thought stops abruptly when Liam makes a noise. A soft sound, not quite a moan, but decidedly more than a breath.

"Did you hear that?" Nikki's voice is sharp with hope. She stands up, her chair legs scraping against the floor. Cheryl has already taken swift strides across the room, and is leaning over Liam. They took him off the ventilator the day before yesterday, his body gradually ridding itself of the drugs used to keep him sedated. **A waiting game**, Nikki told me, trying to be brave, and I'd squeezed her arm and said **Been there, got the T-shirt**.

Liam moans again—the unmistakable sound of a child waking up—and Nikki stifles a cry.

"I'm here, baby, Mum's here."

I stand and pull the curtain between Liam's bed and Dylan's, and mutter **Give you some privacy**, but no one hears because on that side of the curtain it's all **He's waking up, he's really waking up!** and Liam coughing and Cheryl calling for Yin to give him some water, **just tiny sips—not too fast**, and here on this side of the curtain my boy is quiet and still and pale, and I can't, I just can't.

Outside the hospital I lean against the wall, my breath ragged and painful, like I've been running. I haven't got my coat but I start walking regardless, needing to clear my head before I go back in. I head for the parade of shops two streets away, and walk aimlessly around the small supermarket, filling my basket with treats for the family room. The checkout queue snakes back through tinned goods, so I head for the self-service tills.

"It's **there**!" I mutter, passing a bottle of water across the scanner for a third time, a fourth time. "You're literally looking at it!"

A woman at the next till chuckles. "I'm glad I'm not the only one who talks to these things." I smile, continuing to scan my shopping and drop it into the bag on the right.

"Please place the item in the bag," says the machine, a second after I've loaded a packet of chocolate chip cookies.

"It **is** in the bag."

There's another chuckle of solidarity from the woman next to me, who has almost finished her shopping and is tapping in her PIN.

"Please place the item in the bag."

I think about Liam, and wonder if he's sitting up,

if he's alert enough to speak yet. I pick up the cookies and drop them again.

"Please place the item in the bag."

I wonder if Dylan noticed me leave, if he's confused, if he misses me. Guilt washes over me. "It's in the bloody bag!" I slam the cookies down so hard I hear them crack.

The woman next to me doesn't chuckle this time.

"Please place the item in the bag."

Sweat breaks out across my forehead, tears of frustration pricking at my eyes and making my nose run. I pick up the cookies and keep them in my fist and I raise my arm high and smash them onto my shopping bag again and again and again as I shout each word louder and louder and louder. "It. Is. In. The. Fucking. Bag." I'm vaguely aware of people around me, of the crackle of a radio, and an **Are you all right, love?** and of a firm hand on my arm.

I shake it off and take a step back. The air fizzes with whispers and stares, the queue for the till misshapen with onlookers stepping out to see. The no-longer-chuckling woman looks away as I catch her staring.

The hand belonged to a man in a black suit and a neon jacket, a radio clipped to his belt. He looks uncertain, and I think he must be more accustomed to dealing with shoplifters and underage wannabes than thirty-five-year-old women having breakdowns over automated tills. I pull the strap of my handbag more firmly onto my shoulder, jerk my chin upwards, and leave. I'm back at the hospital before I realise I'm still holding the cookies.

Is your husband coming in today?" Dr. Khalili can't know that my husband spent the night at a hotel, but her voice is as kind as if she did. It's after lunch, and I've heard nothing from Max. After the initial flurry of excitement, Liam is still again, Nikki glued to his side. Waiting, waiting.

"I—I'm not sure." I hesitate. "What will happen if he . . . if we can't agree?"

"You're not the first parents to have a difference of opinion on a course of treatment," Dr. Khalili says. "We can offer mediation—someone independent who can help you reach a decision you're both happy with, and then—"

"That isn't going to happen." I don't mean to be short with her, but she doesn't know Max, she doesn't know how deeply he has researched this, how deeply he feels about it. "So what are the next steps?" I speak with more authority than I feel.

Dr. Khalili hesitates. Two lines appear briefly above the bridge of her nose, before she assembles her features into something more neutral. "In the unlikely event that we can't reach agreement, it would be down to the trust to make a recommendation, and—if it came to it—to seek authority from the courts to go ahead with that treatment path."

I look at this doctor who has known my son for five months, yet never once seen him run or hear him talk. She knows so much more than me about the surgery Dylan's had, the drugs he's on, the damage to his brain that to my untrained eye is a whirl of dark space on a scan. I saw her sit up a little straighter when Max talked about proton beam therapy; I saw the flicker of respect in her eyes. He impressed her—he impresses everyone. I have Max's strength of conviction, but I don't have his powers of persuasion. I can't back up my decision with facts and figures, only with heart and instinct and the painful, absolute certainty that this is the kindest thing I can do for my son.

Can I trust this doctor to make the right decision? And what will happen to Max and me if she does?

fifteen

Leila

"I can't thank you enough, Dr. Khalili."

Leila smiles at Darcy, who babbles happily and reaches out chubby arms to grab Alistair's glasses. She is sporting a onesie bearing the slogan **Two dads are better than one**. It has been two days since I sat in the quiet room with Dylan's parents, two days where the atmosphere on the ward has been thick with tension. Today's good news is welcome.

"We'd love to show our appreciation," Tom says. "We have a house in Antigua—"

"Air con," Alistair chips in, "infinity pool, views overlooking the ocean . . ."

"—and we'd love you to use it. Take a friend—or your lovely mum, maybe?"

Leila thinks about switching gray, rainy Birmingham for a fortnight in the Caribbean sun; thinks about Habibeh, shivering in her thick fleece.

"It's really generous of you, thank you. But I can't."

"Of course you—"

"Hospital policy," Leila says gently. "To make sure we treat everyone the same." They look downhearted, and Leila feels churlish. "There's a charity called PICU Friends," she says. "I'm sure they'd be over the moon with a holiday for their next raffle, if you'd consider . . . ?" Before she's even finished speaking, both men are nodding enthusiastically.

"We'd love to."

Leila smiles. "Thank you so much. They're raising money for a new defibrillator. The trust doesn't have the budget to replace it till the new financial year."

"That's terrible."

"There's one in theater and another in HDU, but it certainly isn't ideal. Supporting the Friends would be the best possible thanks you could give us."

Leila walks with the Bradfords to the end of the corridor. On impulse, she gives them both a hug as they say goodbye. As she walks back to the ward, she sees Pip Adams watching from Room 1. It hurts, Leila knows, to watch someone else's child arrive and then leave, all while your own lies silent and sick. Max Adams is here, too, but something has happened— some shift in their relationship—that has infused the whole ward with unease.

Pip—or Max—has moved the two chairs by Dylan's bedside so that, instead of sitting side by side, they are separated by his cot, meaning any conversation must be had through bars.

"They're hardly talking, anyway," Cheryl said this morning. "This morning he said **I've got to go to the house later**." When Leila didn't bite, Cheryl raised her eyebrows. "**The house**. Not home, **the house**. I think they've split up."

Leila feels sad. She wishes she could tell the Adamses that it will be OK, that this is the most horrific, the most terrible thing that will ever happen to them, but that—one day—they will be able to laugh again. That the mountain that has formed between them and feels so insurmountable might not recede, but they will learn to climb it. They will meet again, at the summit, and look back at what they have climbed, and it will feel impossible, and yet somehow they will be there.

She cannot tell them that. It is not her place. She has a job to do, and today she must do the hardest thing she has had to do since qualifying as a doctor. She looks at the wall behind the nurse's desk, where a vast corkboard is covered with pictures and letters of thanks. School photographs, holiday snaps, graduation shots. Professional shoots—the whole family lying on their stomachs in a bright white studio, laughing. Kids skiing, kicking footballs, riding horses. Kids playing basketball in wheelchairs; running on prosthetic legs. Kids who have beaten the odds, whose lives hung in the balance in this very hospital, whose parents sat in this very room and listened to a doctor tell them their child might not live. And yet they did.

Today, Leila must tell Pip and Max Adams that the hospital has made a formal recommendation regarding their son's treatment path. She must give them the opportunity to agree with the recommendations, and then—if either parent dissents—she must inform them that the trust will be instigating legal action.

There is a break before her meeting, a rare twenty minutes in which she would have time only to walk to the canteen and back, with no time to buy anything in the middle. She goes instead to Nick's office, where she gulps down tea made with the kettle he hides in a cupboard.

"They might agree," he says.

"They won't."

"Then you have the backing of the trust." Nick looks at her. "You're not on your own with this."

But it feels that way. Among the many foodstuffs that Habibeh has optimistically packed for Leila, there is a flat, foil-wrapped package. Leila smiles. **Tahdig**. The cooking of Persian rice leaves behind a crisp disc at the bottom of the pan—a delicacy Leila was reminded to share with guests when she was a child. She tears the **tahdig** in half and hands some to Nick.

"You need to hide your mum's passport—this is incredible."

"It's pretty good." Leila feels fortified by her mother's love and by the reassurance from Nick. She calls Ruby as she walks back to the ward.

"I meant to ring sooner. I'm sorry I was late for your birthday meal. I'm sorry I was snappy."

Ruby has never held a grudge. "You looked stressed—I was worried about you."

"I'm always stressed." Leila tries to make a joke of it.

"Not like this. What's going on?"

Leila tells Ruby a little of what is happening, and Ruby listens silently and then says **Jesus, that's awful** and **I'd be in bits** and **I don't know how you do it**, and then Leila is standing by the entrance to PICU, and—

"I have to go."

"I'm here if you need me, OK?"

There are so many people there to catch her if she falls. It helps, a little, to know that, but as she puts her head around the door to Room 1, and says **Whenever you're ready** to Max and Pip, and as she walks a few steps ahead of them, down the long corridor to sit once again in the quiet room, she has never felt more alone.

No." A tremor runs through Max Adams, so that he appears to be moving, even though he is sitting still. "I won't let you do it."

"I know this is the worst possible news for you,"

Leila says. "We have reviewed Dylan's case at length, and although we accept that proton beam therapy could reduce the tumor, we do not believe it will eradicate it completely."

"So you'd let it grow?" Max says. "Until it kills him!"

"We would put in place a palliative care plan that managed Dylan's condition and pain, and—"

"This is your fault." Max turns on Pip, who has listened in silence to Leila's summary of this morning's meeting with the medical director. "The decision was ours. **Ours.** And then you changed your mind, and now—" He breaks off, scrubbing at his face with both hands.

"CAFCASS—the Children and Family Court Advisory and Support Service—will allocate an independent guardian for Dylan," Leila says. "The guardian will appoint a barrister for him." She looks between Max and Pip. "You will both be party to proceedings, and entitled to prepare a case."

"We'll have to go to court?" Pip says, looking stricken. "Against each other?"

Leila chooses her words carefully. "The hospital has applied for a court order to prevent Dylan from leaving St. Elizabeth's and receiving any treatment other than palliative care. At any point, that application can be withdrawn—"

"So—" Max tries to speak, but Leila is insistent.

"—should consent for this plan be given by you both," she finishes. Silence falls upon the room, as all three of them consider what this means for Dylan. For them.

"Then I will see you in court." Max flashes a glance at his wife, and Leila wonders if Pip can see the sorrow in his eyes, or whether it is hidden by the anger in his voice. "Both of you."

L eila's head is pounding. She has arranged to meet Jim at eight thirty, and she thinks about canceling, but it is already eight p.m., and she cannot bring herself to be that person.

They meet at the King's Arms.

"One lime and soda coming up." Jim gives a theatrical bow, and disappears to the bar. Leila sees the table she sat at with Nick, the night of Ruby's party, and feels a flush of embarrassment as she remembers how gently he sidestepped her suggestion they spend the evening together.

Jim reappears with a pint of lager and Leila's soft drink. "So, Khalili, give me the highlights of your day. Best bit, worst bit. Shoot."

He speaks as though he's entertaining a crowd—energetic and played for laughs—and Leila wonders if it would become wearing, in time. If he ever turns it off. Nevertheless, she can't help but smile. "Best bit?" she raises her glass. "A drink after work."

"That's the best bit? Wow, you must have had a really shit day." He grins, but his voice softens as he reads Leila's face. "Oh. You've had a really shit day, haven't you?"

Leila nods.

"Want to talk about it?"

"It's no worse than anything else, I mean . . ." She struggles to find the right words, and fixes her gaze on his. "Patients die, right? We lose people. All the time. But"—she shrugs unconvincingly—"that's the job."

"That doesn't stop it being hard."

They sip their drinks. Leila wonders what will happen to Pip and Max. "The parents of a patient disagree on their son's treatment."

Jim nods thoughtfully. "It happens. More often than people think."

He's thinking about the front-line quarrels he must deal with all the time. **He's not going to hospital . . . Yes he is! I'll go with him . . . No, I will! Don't touch him . . . Do something!** Leila questions her assumption that the arguments Jim finds himself caught up in are any less serious because they're played out in the street, in a pub, in someone's front room. He deals with life-and-death situations every day— perhaps more often than Leila does. If anyone understands what Leila is dealing with, it's him.

"The patient's terminally ill." There's no one at the tables next to them, but Leila speaks quietly anyway. Jim frowns into his pint as he listens.

"We're recommending end-of-life care. Mum agrees. Dad doesn't."

Jim looks up. "So, what happens now?"

"We go to court," Leila tells him, with a professionalism she doesn't feel. "And we let the judge decide."

There's a pause, then Jim leans back against the faded fabric of the bench seat. "I had a DNR last week. Old chap. Cardiac arrest. Riddled with cancer, in and out of hospital, and I guess he'd just had enough. He'd made it clear, the last time he'd been admitted, that he didn't want to be resuscitated if it happened again, and his wife knew all about it." He takes a sip of his drink, then sets the glass carefully back down. "Only, when it came down to it, she wanted us to save his life."

"What did you do?"

"We made him comfortable, and we let him die." Jim pauses. "And his wife called me a murderer, and even though I was looking at a DNR order signed by the man whose hand I was holding, there was a bit of me that felt like one."

"I'm so sorry."

He shrugs. "Like you said, it's part of the job, isn't it?"

They move on to easier topics—to where they grew up, and what brought them to Birmingham. Jim has a talent for mimicry, and Leila laughs so hard at his impressions of their mutual colleagues that she gets a pain in her side. They have another drink, and then another, and when Leila looks at her watch she is shocked to discover an entire evening has passed.

"We should do this again," Jim says, as they leave the pub.

It has been good for Leila, this evening. For three hours she has laughed and talked and thought about life outside PICU, outside her own world. But as she cycles home a weight descends on her once again, and she thinks of Pip and Max, and Dylan, and her chest grows tight once more.

Like most Iranians, Leila has two sets of curtains at her front windows. Heavy, patterned ones, for drawing against cold, dark evenings, and a gossamer-thin pair, with scalloped edges picked out in gold thread, for privacy. Both are closed, but as Leila leans her bike against the railings, and puts the flowery shower cap over her seat, she can hear the strains of the shopping channel, and the tinny sound of a female presenter waxing lyrical about something with attachments. A vacuum cleaner? Food processor? She goes inside.

"Leila **joon**! I made **torshi**."

Leila doesn't need to look to know that her cupboards will be lined with jars filled with vegetables—cauliflower, carrots, celery—preserved in sharp, spicy vinegar. "Did Wilma come round? She said she keeps missing you." Leila knows, of course, that Wilma cannot **miss** Habibeh, because Habibeh still hasn't left the house. Her mother looks away, apparently engrossed by what Leila now sees is some sort of DIY face-lift device.

"So that's just four minutes, for firm skin,

super-enhanced elasticity, and visibly younger-looking appearance. Where do I sign up?" The presenter gives a trilling laugh. Leila feels a surge of frustration. At her mother, for ignoring Wilma's attempts at friendship. At the shopping channel, for its superficial seductions.

"She might have done. I think I heard the door go, but my scarf was upstairs, and by the time I got there . . ." Habibeh holds up both hands and shrugs.

"Maman!" Leila picks up the remote and turns off the television.

Habibeh tuts. "I'm sure she's a nice lady, but does she speak Farsi? No, she does not. Do I speak English? No, I do not. I've told you, Leila, I'm happy here. Cooking, watching my channel." She pauses. Softens. Because she is, after all, a mother. "What's wrong, Leila **joon**?"

Leila tells her about Dylan Adams. About the court case that will tear his parents' lives apart even more than their son's illness already has.

Habibeh holds Leila's face in her hands, her thumbs circling Leila's temples. "You are a good girl, Leila, and a good doctor. You can only do what you think is right." And Leila lets her mother hold her, like she is a child again.

sixteen

Max

Gray sun loungers parade in neat rows on either side of the hotel pool, a tightly rolled towel on each mesh seat. Steam rises from a hot tub in the corner. For the past two weeks I've been first in the pool at six each morning, relieved to put an end to the pretense of sleep, and to fill these redundant hours before the rest of the world wakes up. I swim, and I run, and I do enough work to keep Chester off my back; biding my time till I can focus on the only thing that matters: Dylan.

I stand with my toes gripping the edge of the pool. The tiles lining the bottom are black, giving the water a dark mirror finish. I lean forward, and for a second I feel the clutch of imbalance, the point of no return. I couldn't change my mind now, even if I wanted to. I cut through the water in a swallow dive that takes me so close to the bottom my stomach skims the floor.

I'm not allowed to visit Dylan till three, a restriction that riles me anew each time I recall it.

"I have to think of the other patients," Dr. Khalili said.

It hadn't been an argument. A heated conversation, that's all, when Pip had dared to say that I was **dragging Dylan through the courts**, and I'd reminded her that she was the one who started all of this, that she'd gone back on what we'd agreed and forced the hospital to take sides, and we'd stared at each other, wondering who we were—how we'd got to this point.

"Please, Mr. Adams." Dr. Khalili offered us the quiet room, but I wouldn't move. I kept my eyes fixed on the corridor outside, where an engineer was fitting a new defibrillator to the wall, and I forced back the tears I wouldn't let myself shed in front of her. I hate the quiet room. I hate the scattering of counseling leaflets on the coffee table, and the box of Kleenex, judiciously placed to catch your grief. I hate the fact that someone made a conscious decision that brightly colored throw cushions might somehow make a grieving parent feel better. I hate the thick, textured glass in the window of the door, blurring the gateway between good news and bad. I hate it all.

"Perhaps if you and Mrs. Adams visited Dylan separately it would be easier for the staff," she said. I opened my mouth to argue, but she hadn't finished. "And for Dylan."

I accepted the restriction—how could I not?—and

171

from three p.m. until midnight my time with Dylan is broken only by the need to return a call or reply to an email as I build the case that will keep him alive.

The goggles I borrowed from the yawning girl on reception are scratched and misted with age. I follow the blurred line of the tiles on the pool floor, and as the thrust of my dive fades away, I take a stroke, then another. I don't take a breath.

Aged ten I could hold my breath for a fifty-yard length. Swim club was every Saturday, and after we finished training we'd get to goof around. Holding our breath was a thing for a while. There were only two of us who could do the full fifty yards: me, and a girl called Blair, who lived next door back then, and who won butterfly at the junior nationals.

Now, I feel my lungs contract even before my fingertips get within striking distance of the wall. I haven't counted my strokes but this pool can't be more than twenty-five yards long. I tuck in my chin and pull it into my chest as I flip into a roll, then kick off in a movement that should be fluid and smooth. Only my chest is burning and I fumble the contact, pushing with just one foot, twisting out of my imaginary lane. I'm thrown, and out of breath, and I surface and stand at the same time, gasping for air and coughing.

"You OK?" It's the girl from reception. She's standing by the locker rooms with a pile of towels.

"I'm good." Embarrassed to have had an audience, I start swimming again, slicing clean, clear strokes through the still water, rolling my body to the side every third stroke to take a breath. My lungs are still burning. I guess a lot's happened since I was ten years old.

I started Dylan swimming at three months. Pip thought he was too young, but he loved it. A real little water baby. We've got a photo of him underwater, eyes wide open, arms reaching for me. I take him on Saturday mornings, and then we sit in the café at the leisure center and dip buttery pastries into hot chocolate. **Took him.** I feel a pressure in my chest that has nothing to do with my breathing, and then an unbearable pain that makes me wonder for a second if I'm having a heart attack. My vision blurs, but it isn't the scratches on the goggles, it's the tears that are filling them. **Dylan.** Hidden beneath the water, I allow the remaining breath in my body to leave in thick, noisy sobs, and because the pressure eases a little I let it carry on.

I swim another twenty lengths like that, bawling into the water. I tear off my goggles when it feels like the water's more in than out, and swim faster and harder, chlorine stinging my eyes. Twenty strokes a length. Eighteen. Fifteen. When I'm done, I hold on to the edge and hang from my aching arms for a moment, feeling the muscles stretch, and then I haul myself out and go get dressed. I have a train to catch.

My barrister, Laura King, has chambers in London and charges two hundred and ten pounds an hour. On her fourth finger is a single square-set diamond, and I wonder how many hours' work it represents. A whole day? Two? Her office is large, with a curved walnut desk, and two sofas, set opposite each other, where we are currently sitting. A man with a hipster bun serves us coffee, and sets a tray of bite-size croissants on the table.

"I wasn't sure if you'd have had breakfast," Laura says. She wears a black trouser suit with a crisp white shirt. When she leans back, the jacket falls open to reveal a bright red lining that makes me think of a Dracula outfit Pip once wore to a costume party. "Right, let's crack on, shall we?"

I'm grateful for her businesslike tone, for the lack of sympathy she showed me when I arrived. It enables me to talk about Dylan without stuttering, without tearing up. I have to approach this like a case study—it's the only way I'll get through it.

"The hospital has applied for a declaration that the provisions of life-sustaining treatment are no longer in the child's best interests." Laura reads from a file on her lap. "Specifically, they seek declarations that (a) the child lacks capacity to consent or refuse treatment, by reason of his minority, and (b) that it is in his best interests to receive no further form of life-sustaining treatment, instead receiving palliative care at the discretion of his treating clinicians. OK so far?" She looks up, and I nod, although I am far from OK. My head wants to turn to look at Pip, my hand wants to seek out hers. This is something we should be facing together, and it feels every shade of wrong to be here alone.

"How can it be in his best interests to refuse him potentially lifesaving treatment?"

"That's precisely what we'll need to demonstrate to the judge." She checks off the points on slim fingers. "One, that the proton beam therapy you have identified has a strong chance of success; two, that the potential benefits to Dylan outweigh the negatives."

"What negatives?"

"The impact on him of a transatlantic flight, moving hospitals, more radiotherapy . . ." She gives a little shrug, as if to suggest the risks are endless, and I feel a sharp stab of anger. I reach for a croissant and use a napkin as a plate, tearing the pastry in half, so I don't have to make eye contact. Yes, there are risks. Yes, taking my son halfway across the world is going to be tough on him, even before the side effects of the proton beam therapy kick in.

But the alternative . . . the alternative is worse.

"The hospital argue that the quality of life expected by your son following proton beam therapy is significantly below what would be considered reasonable."

"Considered reasonable by whom?"

"An excellent point. The term is subjective—we'll look to demonstrate the various ways Dylan could enjoy life despite his disabilities."

"What do I need to do?" I consciously mirror the

crisp tone my barrister has used throughout our conversation.

"Help me build a case. Dr. . . . ."—she checks her notes for the name—"Sanders will be allowed to give evidence via video link, but he'll be expected to have examined Dylan in order to report his findings and support your case."

I've lost track of how many doctors I've spoken to in the last two weeks, how many I've emailed with the subject heading **Toddler with medulloblastoma**. Who knew there were so many proton beam therapy centers in the US? I found Dr. Gregory Sanders, from Houston, Texas, when I stopped searching for "proton beam oncologist" and instead searched for "proton beam court case."

Mr. and Mrs. Howes gave an emotional thanks to Dr. Gregory Sanders, whose "compelling" evidence undoubtedly contributed to this morning's ruling.

I had found our doctor.

I might not have done this before, but he has. And he won.

"I'd also suggest speaking to independent physios, play therapists," Laura is saying, "anyone who can give a view of Dylan's condition without being swayed by the trust."

"What if their findings are the same as Dr. Khalili's?"

"Then we don't use that evidence." She rifles through the file before looking up again. "My understanding is that proton beam therapy may prolong your son's life, but it's unlikely to remove the tumor completely. You might go through all this for a very short amount of time. Is that something you're prepared for?"

"Dylan is almost three years old. A month represents almost three percent of his life. Three percent. Even if proton beam therapy gives us only nine more months, it's adding twenty-five percent to his life expectancy. That's the equivalent of you or me living for another ten years." I look at her. "Wouldn't you take that?"

Laura avoids the question. "I understand," she says instead.

"What's stopping me taking Dylan out of hospital?"

If she's alarmed by the suggestion, she doesn't show it. "Right now? Nothing. But the law can move quickly when it needs to, Mr. Adams. The police could apply for an emergency protection order, Dylan could be made ward of the court, or subject of a prohibited steps order carrying a power of arrest." Laura pauses. "And, more importantly, without the correct medication, the right equipment, your son's welfare might suffer."

I'm silent, and she holds my gaze. "Mr. Adams, are you one hundred percent certain you want this to go to court? Whatever the outcome, this is going to have a lasting impact on you and your family."

I see a flicker of sympathy in her eyes, and I answer before the quiet voice of doubt has a chance to creep in. "I'm certain, Ms. King. I want to give my son a chance to live."

There's a pause before she answers. "Then that's what we'll do."

I check the time as I leave her chambers, mentally adding four hundred and twenty pounds to the rolling tally in my head. We have savings, thank God, but the legal fees will eat through them in no time, and that's before the treatment bills start coming. Dr. Sanders has agreed to treat Dylan—treatment that could run to a hundred thousand dollars—pro bono. **Charity**, he said, and I'm sure that's a part of it. Publicity for the clinic, that's the main reason. Another court case won, another line on his résumé. It doesn't matter why, it only matters that he's doing it. The flights, though—he won't pay for those. Living costs for the weeks we're in Houston, the hotel I'm staying in right now. I feel a surge of bitterness that I ever moved to this goddamn country with its archaic laws, that Pip dismissed the need for health insurance, that I even met her . . .

Except, of course, if I hadn't met Pip, I wouldn't have Dylan.

I can't pay Dylan's expenses myself, and I can't borrow that amount, either. I think of the many times

I've clicked on a link shared on Facebook, or forwarded from a work colleague. **Could you spare a few pounds to help?** How often have I done just that? Perhaps not every time, but often. Perhaps not a large donation, but a donation, nonetheless. And if that action is replicated again and again and again . . .

On the train back to Birmingham I find GoFundMe and open an account. I create a page, add Dylan's story, a few photographs. I scroll through Pip's album of daily Dylan photos, lingering on one of the three of us together. It's a selfie; we're squashed together, our cheeks touching, our grins wide. The shot is close on our faces; nothing in the background. It makes my chest tight. That's how I used to feel, being with Pip and Dylan. I'd get home on a Friday, and work would disappear, and the world would shrink, and it would just be Pip, Dylan, and me.

What will happen after the court case?

Will Pip come to Houston? I know the answer before I've even formed the question. Of course she'll come. Dylan will need her. I blink hard, looking out of the window at the barren fields until I'm sure I'm not going to cry. **I'll** need her. Turns out you can hate what someone's doing, yet still love them so much it hurts.

I send the crowdfunding link to everyone in my address book, then I open Twitter and paste the GoFundMe link into a tweet. I attach two photos of Dylan. In one, he's running down the sand dunes in

Woolacombe, laughing into the sun. In the other, he's in PICU, his eyes closed, and his skin translucent.

Prevented from taking my own son for
lifesaving treatment. Where are my rights
as a father? Please help raise money for
#DylanAdams's legal battle, and to pay
for living costs while he has treatment
in America.

I add some hashtags—#righttolife #prolife #parenting—then post it, sharing the message with every celebrity I can think of. **Could you please RT this for your followers?** I spend the rest of the journey retweeting, refreshing, and searching for celebrities.

So sad! a woman called Alexa Papadakis has tweeted. Her bio claims three reality TV shows and a link to her manager. **Come on tweeps—do your thing!** A sad-face emoji completes the post, which has already been shared forty-eight times. Alexa's fans follow her example, and my feed is soon a stream of crying emojis and hashtags. I click on the GoFundMe link and see that the big fat zero is now thirty pounds. We're on our way.

It's gone four before I get to PICU. My Twitter feed is a barrage of supportive messages, but answering them all has left me exhausted rather than invigorated, and it's a relief to switch off my cell and pull the screen around Dylan's cot, shutting out the rest of the room.

I tune out the sound of the Slaters, and the murmured conversation between Cheryl and Aaron. I lower the bars of the crib and lift Dylan gently out. His eyes are open, but he weighs heavy as a sleeping child. "The whole world's on your side, champ," I whisper.

When Dylan was born, the midwife encouraged Pip to lay him against her bare chest, a blanket around them both.

"We recommend as much skin-to-skin as possible when they're tiny," she told Pip. "It'll stabilize the wee man's heart and respiratory rates, regulate his temperature—even increase the amount of oxygen in his blood."

I sit Dylan on my lap. He is unwieldy, his head too heavy for his neck, and his back inflexible. One-handed, I undo the snap fasteners on his onesie, then unbutton my shirt. I move Dylan so his legs fall either side of mine, his head tucked into the crook of my neck, and his bare chest against mine. I pull the fleece blanket from the side of the crib and wrap it around his back. Emotion surges inside me and I fight it back down because this isn't the time. That isn't how I want my boy to see me.

I feel the flutter of his heart in its bony rib cage. I watch the readings on the monitor, see Dylan's oxygen saturation level rise from 93 percent to 95, 96. I see his pulse slow. And then I close my eyes, and ignore the machines. Instead I listen to what Dylan is telling me. I listen to the warmth of his body against mine, to the regular thump thump of his heart. I listen to his breathing, moist on my neck. I listen for life—and I find it.

seventeen

Pip

I switch off my alarm before it goes off, and lie in the darkness. Max has been gone for three weeks, and in that time I haven't slept for longer than a few fitful hours, before waking again with a leaden feeling in my chest, like someone is pressing me into the bed. This morning the weight is even heavier, my eyes sticky with yesterday's grief. The afternoon was spent reviewing Dylan's medical situation with my barrister and his team. Holding it together for three hours cost me a night's sleep—phrases from the doctors' reports swirling in the blackness around me. **No prospect of any quality of life . . . distressing seizures . . . permanent reliance on pain relief.**

Everyone party to proceedings must produce independent evidence in support of their case, and key to that, I was told, are the doctors' reports.

"The judge will expect a second opinion." My barrister, Robin Shane, is improbably young, with a beard that looks as though he has borrowed it from someone older. His eyes crinkle kindly when he speaks, making our conversations a little less overwhelming. My father engaged him, coming with me for that first meeting, and passing his card to Robin with the instruction to **send the bill to me**. I am not allowed to argue.

"You've got enough to worry about, without stressing about money," Dad said.

I searched his face for confirmation that I was doing the right thing, but he was as inscrutable as ever.

"No one else can decide this for you, Pip" is all he would say. "Not us, not Max."

"Would you pay the legal fees if you thought I was wrong?"

"Yes," Dad said simply. "Because that isn't about doing what's best for our grandchild, it's about doing what's best for our daughter."

The requirement for a "second opinion" means that Dylan has been examined by four different doctors, including one engaged by his state-funded legal team. The reports are circulated as they come in, every team having full disclosure from the others ahead of the court case, which is fast approaching.

"I didn't think it would all happen so quickly," I said to the barrister, a breath before realising that of course it has to. Our very case is built on the reasoning that it is unkind to keep Dylan alive any longer.

I switch on the light. I'm going early to the hospital today. I don't have much time left with Dylan, and there's something I want to do with him. Something I want him to see, even if only once in his short life.

My jeans smell stale, and there's a smear of dirt on the hem of one leg. I try to remember when I last washed my hair, had a shower. I have drifted from the hospital to home, from legal meetings to the hospital; self-care has been an afterthought. Dylan doesn't mind, after all, so why should I?

I'm reminded of a time when I would sit on the bed and help Max pack, when I'd pick out ties and choose a shirt that would say **I'm in control, trust me, hire me**. War paint. Armour. I can't change what's happening, or what Max is doing, but I can change how I handle it.

Twenty minutes later I stand in front of the mirror on the landing and take a deep breath. Better. I feel stronger. My face is made up—powder, mascara, lipstick—and although I'm still wearing jeans, they are at least clean. Putting on a pair of heeled boots instead of the sheepskin ones I've worn for weeks makes me not just physically taller, but mentally so. I'm holding myself straight.

Downstairs, I drink orange juice because it's quicker than waiting for tea to brew and then cool. I feel that familiar pull to be by my son's side, and I leave the glass half-drunk, and drive to the hospital. The roads are still icy, and I reluctantly temper my eagerness to be with Dylan, to ensure I reach him at all. I practise what I'm going to say to the nurses. They'll let me, I'm sure of it.

I'm sorry, Pip, it just isn't possible."

"Cheryl, please. He's been in this room for six months. He hasn't seen the sky in **six months**." The windows in Room 1 are small and high—the view the grey brick wall of the adjacent building. Like a prison. Worse than a prison. "If the judge grants the order, we might only have a few weeks left with him. I want him to feel air on his cheeks again—hear the birds singing."

Cheryl looks away. She bites her lip and I see her swallow. I hold my breath, but when she looks back she's still shaking her head. "It's too risky. We'd have to bring the monitor and—"

"It's like going to the family room. Just a little further." We used to go to the family room when the ward was quiet, and there were enough staff free to help move everything Dylan needed. We'd put cartoons on the TV and raise his pillows so he could watch, and I would choose not to see his glazed eyes, and instead gave a running commentary in the hope that he could hear my voice, and it would mean something to him.

"Cheryl, please. I'm begging you. Just a few minutes." Once the order is granted the only medication

Dylan will be given will be pain relief. If he arrests, he won't be resuscitated.

"It's too cold."

"We'll wrap him up."

"I'm sorry."

I grip the bars of Dylan's cot. I was so convinced Cheryl would say yes. "Could you at least ask Dr. Khalili?"

Cheryl sighs. "Give me a minute."

Dr. Khalili has the faintly dishevelled look of someone coming to the end of a long night shift. Her scrubs are stained and crumpled, and wisps of hair have escaped from her ponytail. She smooths a hand across Dylan's forehead, then looks at me. "Ten minutes. And we stay with you all the time."

My chest swells with relief and gratitude. "Thank you!" I look at the clock. "We need to—"

"We'll go now." She helps me wrap Dylan in open blankets, ready to cover him up as soon as we leave the warm ward. Porter Paul brings a wheelchair, and Cheryl readies the drip stand and a bag valve mask.

"Just in case," she says briskly.

"Ready?"

I nod, but Dr. Khalili is addressing the others, not me. "We treat it like any other critical care transfer, OK?"

Paul grips the wheelchair. It is too big for Dylan, too unstructured, and he leans to one side, into the pillows we have placed around him. **Easier than a**

trolley, Dr. Khalili said. Less conspicuous, too, I imagine. "Right, where to, madam?" Paul says.

"The bench by the staff accommodation block," I say at once. "Beneath the big oak tree."

And so off we set, an unlikely procession of doctor, nurse, porter, and me. And Dylan, a king held high in his sedan, an Indian prince on his elephant. Cheryl wheels the monitor, and I take the drip stand, and Dr. Khalili walks briskly in front. We take a circuitous route through the hospital, avoiding the drop in temperature for as long as we can. I don't take my eyes off Dylan; Cheryl doesn't take her eyes off his monitor. His sats wobble, but don't crash. His heart rate slows, but steadies.

And we make it.

I sit on the bench, damp seeping into my jeans, and Dr. Khalili lifts my light-as-a-feather boy and places him into my arms as though I am a new mother once more, and she the doctor who delivered him.

"Ten minutes," she reminds me, gently but firmly, and they step away. It is still not light, but the blackness of my drive here is giving way to an opaque darkness. Behind us, the hospital buildings are dressed in sodium-yellow lights and the headlamps of arriving cars, but in front of us, an expanse of lawn stretches down towards the city.

"Not long now," I whisper to Dylan, because the sky is already turning from grey to blue, and there's a hint of gold on the horizon. "I want—" I break off, but it's important he hears this. It's important I say it. "I want you to know that I have loved you since the moment I knew you existed, since the moment there was even a **chance** that you existed." I touch my fingertip to the birthmark the colour of milky tea, and I hear Max's laugh—**At least I know he's mine**—and I squeeze my eyes shut to block out the pain of the day that was so perfect.

"When you were born I promised I would keep you safe and never let anyone hurt you. And . . ." I breathe out slowly, determined to finish without crying, to show Dylan I can be brave too. "And I'm so sorry I couldn't keep you safe from illness, but I'm going to keep you safe now, baby. I'm going to take away everything that hurts, and all those wires and tubes and all the medicine. And when the court case is over, and you're allowed to go to sleep, it will all be over."

I cry silently, tears streaming down my face as I swallow the sounds that might tell Dylan I am upset. And as my son lies warm in my arms, and the cold breeze kisses our faces, pink and gold colours the skyline, bringing up the rooftops in sharp relief, and my boy sees the sun rise.

eighteen

Leila

There's a particular sort of energy in PICU when a child's condition tips from serious to critical; from stable to a state of emergency. The emergency buzzer summons at a run whoever can hear it, yet despite the extra resources that suddenly appear on the ward it will feel as though there could never be enough to catch this life that is slipping through their fingers.

Out of nowhere, Liam is crashing; his levels plummeting and a blue tinge creeping outward from his lips. The machines by his bed are playing a duet; a harsh, continuous tone peppered with insistent beeps that grow ever more prolonged as his heart rate falls.

A registrar is prepping the ventilator and suction tubes. A job performed a thousand times, yet checked and double-checked as though it were the first. Leila clears Liam's airway. She takes the bag valve mask

Cheryl hands her and presses the seal around his mouth, as Cheryl begins slow, rhythmic squeezes, pushing oxygen into Liam's empty lungs.

"Respiratory rate's forty. Sats are dropping." Leila keeps her eyes on the screen, on which Liam's oxygen levels are shown. They've been hovering around 96, but now they're free-falling, too fast to call out: 88 percent, 80, 75, 69 . . .

"We're going to have to intubate."

"What's happening? Is he dying? What can you do?" With each question, Mrs. Slater's voice rises a few notes.

"Please." Leila gestures to the side of the room, to the door, to space away from where she is trying to work. When a patient crashes on TV you see the trolley racing through corridors, the doctors shouting **Crash team**, worried relatives left helplessly behind. In theater, doctors work in private. Here, everything is exposed.

"We're not fucking going anywhere." Connor Slater's voice is gruff and angry, fear hiding beneath the surface.

Leila doesn't argue. There isn't time. No time for anything except for saving Liam's life. The registrar is ready with the ET tube, but the numbers are going down and down and the beeps are longer, longer, the space between them closing until they're hardly there at all and—

"He's arresting," Leila says, as calmly and quietly as she can. She starts chest compressions.

"Will someone tell us what the fuck is going on!" Connor Slater leaves off the question mark. He wants to stare Leila down, but he can't take his eyes off the screen where the numbers say everything, and so he shouts at her instead. "He's not fucking breathing. Do something! Fucking hell . . ." This last is directed to the ceiling, as he stands at the foot of Liam's bed, his fists clenched and his eyes squeezed shut against the threat of tears.

"Defib," Leila shouts, but it's already being pushed into her hands. Fired up. Charging. Working. Leila looks at Cheryl and nods. They place the pads on Liam's skinny chest, pause for a second's check that feels a second too long, and then Leila shouts, "Clear!" and she so badly needs to save this child's life that she's losing perspective on who she's doing it for. A safety check, then a single shock, before chest compressions again and again and—"Again!"

There's half a second of silence as the defib delivers, punctuated only by crying from Nikki, and guttural breaths from Connor. The room's full of people, it's hot and airless, and Leila's about to go again, when there's an imperceptible tremor from the boy beneath her hands. Leila's own pulse throbs in her ears.

"Heartbeat," she says, as the briefest of gaps reappear between the beeps. And gradually, the gaps become longer, and the beeps become more regular, and—"Heartbeat," Leila says again, because saying it out loud helps to get everything back to normal.

She looks at the Slaters and gives a smile that fools no one. "Giving us all a bit of a scare, there. Cheeky monkey. I bet he keeps you on your toes, this one."

"Oh, he does—he does!" Relief makes Nikki giddy. "He's always been cheeky."

"We're going to have to ventilate him," Leila tells her. "He'll be sedated—he won't feel anything—but it's tough for parents to see, and it would help us to have some space to work . . ."

"We'll wait outside, won't we, Connor?"

Liam's dad is rooted to the spot, staring at his boy with a face chalk white. Not saying a word.

It's afterward he speaks, when Liam is stable and the ward is back to normal. Leila is running on empty, returning from the canteen, where she bought a doughnut she ate in the queue, and a black coffee she drank on the way back to the ward. Connor is standing in the corridor, staring at the defibrillator. No, not at the defib, but at the piece of laminated card one of the nurses has stuck to the wall beside it, while they try to convince Finance it's worthy of something more permanent.

KINDLY DONATED BY FRIENDS OF PICU, WITH THANKS TO TOM AND ALISTAIR BRADFORD, AND THEIR DAUGHTER, DARCY.

Leila keeps her eyes on the corridor in front of her, respecting whatever moment he's having, but as she passes, he calls after her.

"Dr. Khalili?"

The pronunciation is perfect.

Leila stops. Turns. Connor Slater is waging a war with himself. His fists clench and unclench by his sides, the movement bulging his upper arms and tensing the tendons either side of his neck. His eyes are unfocused, and he blinks hard, but there's no stopping the tears, this time, and they fall onto his stomach. He makes no move to wipe them away, but scowls angrily, as though it were someone else wetting his cheeks, someone else weeping openly in a hospital corridor.

Leila waits for him to say whatever it is he's struggling so hard to put into words.

In the end, the ones he chooses are simple. And the only ones needed.

"Thank you, Doctor."

They lock eyes and his gaze tells Leila everything else he wants to say but can't. Maybe he'll find the words some other time, maybe he won't. It doesn't matter. Leila doubts there will be any more bigoted outbursts. She doubts there will be any more problems understanding her accent.

"That's what we're here for, Mr. Slater."

Leila is about to go home when the medical director calls.

"My office. Now."

Leila sighs. It has been another busy night, and she

longs for bed, and tea, and one of the Madar biscuits Habibeh brought from home. Unease pricks her spine. Has Emmett heard about yesterday's dawn excursion?

Leila left Pip and Dylan for as long as she dared, till the sky's orange flames disappeared, leaving no trace that they had ever even existed. Then, anxious to return Dylan to PICU before anyone saw them, she touched Pip gently on the shoulder.

Dylan is fine, she reminds herself now. If Emmett was going to take issue with her unorthodox decision, it would not be on the grounds that she had put a patient at risk. He had suffered no ill effects from the outing, in fact he had been stable for twenty-four hours, with no seizures and no tachycardia.

She crosses the car park toward the central building that houses the hospital's administrative and managerial functions. She thinks nothing of the first photographer she sees; it's not unusual to see journalists around the children's hospital, often here at the behest of parents campaigning to raise funds or awareness for the work done by the team here.

Occasionally, though, the press come because of a finger of suspicion—unfounded or otherwise—that points at negligence or malpractice, and so when Leila sees the second photographer, leaning against a wall, chatting idly to a puffa-jacketed companion, she changes her path and walks the other side of the paved square where they are standing. Her unease builds, and it is then that she connects the two photographers with her summons to the medical director's office.

"It's all over Twitter." Emmett swivels his screen so Leila can see the thousands of tweets that have resulted in the nationwide trending of the hashtag #DylanAdams. Other hashtags follow in its wake, delivering the public's verdict in a few cursory words. #FightForDylan, #JusticeForDylanAdams, #RightToDie. Even as Leila watches, the screen updates. **Twenty-seven new tweets. Fifty-nine new tweets. Seventy-two new tweets.** So many opinions; so few facts.

"The journalists started showing up an hour ago. There's another lot camped out at the Adamses' house."

"Are they OK?"

"Mrs. Adams is extremely upset."

Leila recalls the end of her shift yesterday morning, how peaceful Pip looked. She grabbed Leila's hands and said **Thank you, thank you so much,** then she took her seat next to Dylan's cot and gazed at him, her face more tranquil than Leila had seen it in a long time. She imagined Pip accosted by journalists, shouting for a comment, offering an exclusive.

"The poor woman."

"Her husband, on the other hand, seems to have embraced the opportunity. He's already given a statement." Emmett takes off his glasses and rubs his face. "I take it I don't need to ask whether you've spoken to the media?"

"No—of course not."

"The story would have broken eventually, but this has put us on the back foot. Any press release we put out now will look defensive, even if it's what we'd planned to say anyway." He pauses. "They knew **detail**, Leila. Not just about the court order, but about the Adamses being in dispute. Information that could only have come from the Adamses themselves— something both of them vehemently deny—or"—there's a beat—"from the hospital."

Leila feels hot. "I haven't spoken to any journalists. I wouldn't." But even as she says it she remembers her phone call to Ruby; her use of the Adamses' tragedy to explain away her rudeness. Ruby wouldn't. She wouldn't. Not intentionally. But might she have mentioned it to someone else, thinking it didn't matter?

Emmett's eyes have narrowed, and Leila feels her cheeks reddening further. "What can I do to help the situation?"

"Brief staff on their obligations in relation to data protection, and give them all the aide-mémoire on dealing with the press." Is Leila imagining it, or has Emmett's tone cooled? "And move the patient to a private room, where there's less likelihood of being overheard."

Leila does a mental audit of the space in PICU. Rather than move Dylan, she will move Liam onto the main ward, and leave the Adamses alone in Room 1. It's not ideal—two beds is a lot to lose in a department like PICU—but these are exceptional circumstances.

"I'm sorry this has happened," she says to Pip, when the beds have been moved, and the blind pulled down over the window between the corridor and Room 1. The space seems cavernous, and there's a portentous echo to Leila's words. She returned to the ward from Emmett's office to find a cardiac arrest and a doctor off sick, and so she is eight hours into her second, unscheduled shift. Tiredness has become an abstract concept, one removed from the reality of here and now. She knows she is tired, but it has no relevance. She has a job to do.

"They've got hold of my mobile number somehow." Pip is shaking. "They keep calling, again and again."

"I'm going to show you an alternative way in and out of the building." Leila unhooks Dylan's chart from the end of his cot, and puts it on the side, where it can't be seen when the door is open. "It's a little longer, but it means you can avoid any photographers waiting outside the main entrance."

Pip looks at the clock, then stands up. "Would you show me now, please?" Leila looks, too. There is another quarter of an hour until Max is due.

Leila pauses. "Things must be . . . difficult."

"It's as though I have to choose between my son and my marriage." Her words are stilted. She is trying not to cry. "I want both of them, but—" She loses the battle, and tears flow down her cheeks.

But now it feels like you might lose them both, Leila thinks. She wants to comfort Pip, to put her arms around her, but it isn't her place, isn't her job. And so she asks Paul the porter to show Pip the staff exit, and she repeats her apology to a stony-faced Max, when he arrives ten minutes later.

"They're all on Dylan's side," he says. "All the reporters, the photographers. They want him to live, too."

What they want is a story, Leila thinks, but is wise enough not to say it. That isn't her place, either. And she is relieved when she eventually finishes work. Relieved, for once, as her bike draws closer to home, that her mother doesn't read the papers, doesn't watch the news. When Leila gets home, Habibeh will be watching QVC, and Leila will sit next to her and they will discuss the relative merits of steam cleaners over elbow grease.

There is a box in the hall with contents declared by the packing tape to be fragile. Leila is wondering what her mother's latest purchase is, when she hears a voice she recognizes. In the kitchen, sitting next to Habibeh, is Leila's next-door neighbor, Wilma. In front of them are two glasses of tea, and an iPad, the screen showing the double white boxes of Google Translate.

"Hello, Leila!" Habibeh greets her daughter in English.

"Your mother was telling me how to make **kofte**." Wilma smiles.

At the mention of the meatballs, Habibeh holds up

a hand. "**Yek lahzeh lotfan.**" **Just a second . . .** She gestures to the iPad.

"Of course, go ahead." Wilma looks at Leila. "I brought it round—I thought it might help us get to know each other."

Habibeh is tapping on the screen. She stops and reads the translation, speaking slowly but perfectly, a triumphant smile emerging as she finishes. "I will give you mint." She opens a cupboard and gives their neighbor one of the bags of dried mint she brought with her from Tehran.

"**Merci**, Habibeh."

"You are welcome."

The two women beam at each other, and Leila is glad to have a neighbor who cares so much, when Leila's own heart is already too full.

nineteen

Max

Professor Greenwood has a thin wisp of white hair combed carefully across his balding pate. His elbows rest on the leather-covered arms of his chair, and he temples his fingers and looks at them thoughtfully as he speaks.

"The majority of our students have cerebral palsy, although we cater for young people with a variety of complex health needs. Many are nonverbal, and many have degenerative or life-limiting conditions."

I look at the glossy brochure in my hand, and at the eye-watering prices on the piece of paper discreetly tucked within the pages. On the cover, a girl in a wheelchair paints with her fingers, her head thrown back and her mouth open in a joyous smile.

"Our aim," Professor Greenwood says, "is to help every pupil achieve their full potential. Our therapy

team is multidisciplinary—we have speech and language therapists, physiotherapists, as well as excellent
links with feeding clinics, orthopedics, orthotics . . ."
He reels off a list of agencies, only half of which I recognize. I nod and make listening noises, and look
through the brochure at the happy, glossy faces. I
imagine Dylan in a special chair, painting, playing
music, learning to do the things Dr. Khalili claims he
won't ever do.

"The doctors at St. Elizabeth's believe my son's
needs will be profound."

Professor Greenwood looks irritated by the interruption. A sharp **tsk** escapes, disguised as a breath. He
peels his fingers apart and picks up the report I emailed
to him in advance of our meeting: an overview of
Dylan's condition, both now and predicted.

"This is worst-case scenario, of course," I add. "We
have arranged for an independent consultant to examine Dylan, and I expect his conclusions to be much
more positive."

"Indeed." Professor Greenwood puts down the
report.

"In your opinion, could my son lead a fulfilled and
enjoyable life?"

"Terms that are both subjective—"

"Could he do the things in here?" I brandish the
brochure.

"—and relative. What would be a dull and meaningless existence for one person, is gratifying and

exciting for another. Our philosophy is that every life is worth living, every achievement worth celebrating." He stands up. "Perhaps you would like to see our sensory room?"

From the outside, Oakview School has the appearance of a country hotel; from the inside it is a curious mixture of school and hospital. The hallways are wide, with ramps instead of steps, and the antiseptic tang of PICU.

"Many of our students are immune-suppressed," Professor Greenwood says, "so hygiene is paramount."

The hallways are lined with children's paintings and photographs like the ones in the brochure. We pass offices labeled with foreign acronyms—**SLT**, **SaLT**, **OT**—and a classroom where half a dozen children are banging drums. In an open-plan library area on the other side of an internal quadrangle, a child lies on a flat wheelchair. Beside her sits a woman with an ID badge pinned to her shirt.

"Genie has cerebral palsy, epilepsy, scoliosis, and profound learning difficulties," Professor Greenwood says. "She cannot walk, sit, or speak."

I notice the computer screen next to the wheelchair. "What are they doing?"

"Genie is emailing her parents to tell them what she's been doing at school." His tone, bordering on brusque when directed at me, softens as he watches his student. "They aren't able to look after her at home, and they live some distance away, so . . . That screen is an Eyegaze Edge. It can pinpoint the user's gaze to within a quarter of an inch. With its help—and a little guidance from us—Genie can control her wheelchair, play music, watch videos, generate speech, send emails, write a book, even."

"Incredible."

"She is."

Is this Dylan's future? If it is, then surely this is a life worth fighting for? I picture Genie's mother opening her emails, then showing her husband, printing out Genie's letter so it can join the others that mark their daughter's progress. They will be proud of her achievements, proud of her.

And yet Genie doesn't live at home. **Can't** live at home. Because her needs are too great? Because her parents can't cope? So Genie lives here, in this expensive, well-equipped place that is neither a hospital nor a school, yet somehow manages to be both.

I'm still thinking about Genie when we reach the sensory room, a tranquil, dimly lit space with padded floor and walls, and twinkly lights across a midnight-blue ceiling. In the corner a glass column of water sends bursts of bubbles skyward, its lights changing from green to red to purple. In the center, a glitter ball sends tiny spots of light dancing around the room. There is only one student in the sensory room, lying on the floor in the fetal position, his eyes open but his face devoid of expression. A member of the staff sits quietly nearby.

"David suffered a brain injury during a rugby match when he was fourteen," Professor Greenwood says. "He has significant cognitive impairment and limited mobility."

The young man on the mat must be as tall as I am, his limbs thin but long. "How old is he now?"

"Nineteen. He should have left us a year ago, but it's a complicated transition. David has multiple needs."

"Where will he go?" I try to imagine Dylan as an adult. "Where do they usually go?"

Professor Greenwood begins walking again, and I realize we have looped full circle, and are almost at the reception where I signed in. "We help parents find places in residential care homes, in the main, but as you can imagine, spaces are limited. There are far fewer resources for adults than for young people."

"How many students do you have here?"

"Forty-three at the moment."

I begin to try to extrapolate the figures, but Professor Greenwood cuts in gently.

"Not all of whom will reach adulthood, of course."

He continues walking, and for a second I stay behind, standing in the corridor, filled with uncertainty.

I leave with Professor Greenwood's card, and his commitment to provide evidence—should it be required by the court—of the quality of life Dylan could be expected to have, should the proton beam therapy work. Greenwood's time and expertise will cost me three thousand pounds, and I think of all the times I've billed clients three times that, and not balked at the figure.

The GoFundMe page has hit five figures and rising, but I don't yet know the full extent of what we'll need. There are witness expenses, and additional research, and the cost of flying Dr. Sanders over to examine Dylan, since the court will not accept his testimony without that. And if we succeed, I will need to find somewhere to live in Houston, and some way of paying for it. I am hanging on to my job by my fingernails, but it's only a matter of time before Chester loses patience.

Back at my hotel, I catch up on Twitter, although I have several thousand followers now, and I can no longer keep up with the hundreds of messages I receive every day.

@MaxAdams the world is fighting for your little boy—stay strong! x

@MaxAdams is an inspiration. That little boy deserves justice #DylanAdams #FightforLife

We're all behind you @MaxAdams
#DylanAdams #prolife #parentpower

I click on the hashtag of my son's name, drawing strength from the tweets that flood my screen. Many of the accounts have a flash of yellow across their avatars; a special filter added to show their support. **For my son.** I feel a rush of confidence, of vindication.

I pick up the hotel phone and dial a number I still know by heart. As I wait for my mother to pick up, I put Pip's Twitter handle into the search field. She tired of the platform a few months after she'd joined, and her feed is empty, bar a few tweets from when she was pregnant. **Can't wait to sleep on my stomach again!** she'd tweeted. Two people had "liked" it.

"It's me."

"Oh, honey . . ."

"I'm OK, Mom."

"How is he?"

"No change." I hear a sigh. I picture her in the red-brick house where I grew up, still standing in the kitchen to take the call, even though the phone that tethered her in place has long since been replaced by a cordless one. "But that's a good thing, Mom. The longer he breathes on his own, the harder it will be for them to argue against us."

I say **us** because of Laura King, witnesses like Dr.

Sanders and Professor Greenwood. I say it because of the Twitter followers, vocal in their support. I say it because it makes me feel less alone.

"And how is Pip?"

In among the few tweets in Pip's feed, the search page has brought up messages from other people. My breath catches as I read them.

Someone should switch of @
PippiLongStock's machines and see how
she likes it!

@PippiLongStock your not fit to call yourself
a mother

"Max?"

"I don't know." I feel nauseous. I hope Pip hasn't seen these messages, that she won't think to look at Twitter. "We're not talking." Silence on the line tells me my mother's views on this development. I shut the app.

"I don't want to interfere—"

"Then don't. Please."

"—but remember, that girl's hurting as much as you are. As much as we all are." There's a break in her voice and if she starts crying I know I will.

"I gotta go, Mom."

"I'm coming over," she says. "I'll book a flight tomorrow."

"Mom, please—come see us in Houston. We'll need you then. I'll need you."

She sighs an OK, and I close my eyes, wishing she weren't eight hours away. Wishing I were home with Pip, wishing Dylan were OK, wishing none of this were happening.

I only go to the GP to get Chester off my back, but the doctor listens to my myriad symptoms—the nausea, the headaches, the twisting in my gut—and concludes that I'm stressed. **No kidding**, I think.

"Is there anything going on at the moment that's worrying you?"

The GP is young and guileless. Dylan's story is in every newspaper, every day, and I wonder if she genuinely hasn't made the connection, or whether this is some kind of data protection pretense. She is, theoretically, "my" GP, although I've never met her before. In fact, I've never set foot in the doctor's office. It was Pip who brought Dylan for his shots, Pip who bagged an emergency appointment when he had a rash.

"You worry too much," I told her once. The memory brings a bitter taste to my throat. **He's fine. Nothing wrong with him. All toddlers are clumsy.**

"I'd rather see a well child a thousand times than miss a poorly child just once," the doctor told her, when Pip finally ignored me and made an appointment, only to be told that she was right to have done so; Dylan was sick.

Pip was right, and I was wrong.

What if I'm wrong now? It slides unbidden into my thoughts; a worm of doubt, burrowing into the certainty.

"My son is in intensive care at St. Elizabeth's," I say. "Next week a high court judge will decide whether the doctors can switch off his machines, or whether I can take him to Texas for treatment."

Her mouth forms a perfect O.

"Cognitive behavioral therapy can have excellent results," she says, snapping back into action, "but the waiting lists currently average six to eight weeks, so . . ." She sees my raised eyebrow, and swivels to her computer screen. "I'm going to give you something to help you sleep, and some beta blockers for the anxiety." The printer whirs into action. "This is very much a short-term solution, though—I would still like to refer you for CBT."

"Sure, whatever." In six to eight weeks Dylan and I will be in Texas. I can sleep in Texas. Eat in Texas. I just need something other than whiskey and smokes— because after eighteen years as a nonsmoker I suddenly find myself with cigarettes in my pocket again—to get me through the next week.

"Here." She hands me my prescription, a leaflet about therapy, and a sick note for my boss. She hesitates, the inside of her lip caught between her teeth. I notice the photograph on her desk: a smiling toddler with an ice-cream beard. "Good luck," she says eventually. "I hope it . . . I hope . . ."

"Thank you."

I send the sick note to Chester, then put an "out of office" on my email and turn off my work phone. My hotel room is closing in on me, the wallpaper swirling into the beginnings of a migraine. I take two of the beta blockers the GP prescribed, and go for a swim. I leave my clothes in the locker, then head through the walkway to the pool. Voices bounce off the tiles, and my feet slow down. A family. Mom, teaching a girl in floaties to swim; Dad, throwing dive sticks for two boys. Laughter taunts me from the water. I think of my Saturday mornings at the pool with Dylan, of standing arms outstretched for him to jump from the side. **Come on, Dylan, you can do it!**

My pulse pays no heed to the beta blockers, thrumming in my ears to a beat I can't breathe to. Faster, faster, faster. **Stress**, she said. I back out to the locker room and get dressed, stand for a moment in the hotel lobby—where do I go, what do I do?—then go for a run, reluctant feet finding their way on the wet tarmac. I run like I'm being chased, like I'm in a bad dream with monsters breathing down my neck, like they'll always run faster than me, no matter how hard I try. I run and I run, and then I realize my feet have brought me here. To the hospital.

It isn't "my" time. It's not yet lunchtime, and Pip

gets to be with Dylan till three. But my chest aches—Jesus, it aches so bad—and I just want to see my boy for five minutes. Five minutes, then I'll go back to my hotel, and shower and change, and I'll feel better.

The crowd outside the children's hospital is smaller today. There's a stalwart group that comes every day, and seeing them there stops me from feeling quite so alone. In the evenings, more people arrive. Often, when I leave PICU, around ten or eleven at night, the group has swollen to fifty or so people, standing in a semicircle around the candles on the ground that spell out Dylan's name. The press have been here every day, and the protestors have been quick to switch things up. New banners, new faces, new stunts. Keeping him in people's minds, in their hearts. Because if he's in their hearts, how can a court rule to let him die?

"All right, Max?" Jamie and his wife, Emma, take turns to be at the vigil. Sometimes they both come, with their little girl in her stroller. **We're sick of the system**, Jamie told me, when we first spoke. **They're trying to take away our rights as parents.**

"I'm doing OK."

"We've been talking on the Facebook group about what to do at court." Jamie has a shaved head, and a tattoo on his neck of his daughter's date of birth. He and Emma set up the Facebook group—Fighting for Dylan—which now has a hundred and forty thousand followers. "We'll be selling the T-shirts, and some of the others are working on new banners, but if there's anything specific, just let me know, all right?"

"I will." I clap my hand onto his shoulder. "I really appreciate you doing all this. It means a lot." Thanks largely to Jamie and Emma, Dylan's GoFundMe account stands at almost a quarter of a million pounds. They have mobilized supporters all over the world, sharing the link and keeping Dylan in the headlines every day. And if it's a little weird to see my boy's face on a stranger's T-shirt, well, it's a small price to pay for the money that will take us to Texas.

I nod a hello to the security staff as I go inside. Speaking to Jamie has calmed me, but as I walk down the hallway toward PICU I feel my pulse picking up, and I break into a jog, the prospect of being so close to Dylan yet not physically with him almost harder than being far apart.

If Cheryl is surprised to see me at this time, it doesn't show on her face. She buzzes me in, and I wash my hands, and she doesn't say anything. It's not a law, after all—not even something imposed by the hospital—just a suggestion we all agreed to, that Pip would take the days, and I would take the evenings. But I want to see Dylan now. And, I realize suddenly, I want to see Pip.

She's reading him a story. She sits facing him, the book resting lightly on the bed as she reads in a soft voice. "**'Chocolate mousse!' says greedy Goose.**

213

'**Don't just grab it,**' says angry **Rabbit.**" She always did do the voices so well. Rabbit's outraged squeal, Sheep's yawn, Moth's mumble through a mouthful of dishcloth.

How many times have we read that book to Dylan? How many times did he trot over to the bookcase in his room, and drag over **Chocolate Mousse for Greedy Goose?** How many times did we say **Not that again,** and Dylan bounced up and down and said **That one, that one!**

"**. . . but lazy Sheep says, 'no, let's . . . s l e e p.'**"

This is where Dylan says **Again, again!** This is where he throws his arms around Pip and kisses her mouth and laughs and says **No sleep!** and where Pip untangles herself and tells him **Bedtime now, little man. There are big adventures waiting for you tomorrow.**

But the scene in front of me won't follow the script, and my heart hurts so bad I think it might give up. I don't think I say anything, but perhaps I do, because Pip looks up, and I know she's playing the same movie in her head that I am.

"I'm sorry—I know I shouldn't be here."

"It's OK."

I walk across the room and kiss Dylan. His forehead is hot and damp, the wisps of hair clinging to his head. I sit in the chair next to Pip. I'm shocked by how thin she looks, how tired.

"What's going to happen to us, Max?" Her voice is

tremulous. She doesn't look at me but keeps her eyes fixed on Dylan, whose chest rises and falls beneath his white blanket. I think of the knitted yellow squares Pip was going to make into a throw for his room, and wonder what became of them.

I fight to keep control. "I guess we'll find out in court."

"Not Dylan." She looks at me. "Us. What's happening to **us**, Max?"

I want to hold her, to kiss her, to tell her how much I still love her, despite everything. How I'm almost as scared of losing her as I am of losing Dylan.

But I walked out on her. I'm fighting her. I'm the last person she wants holding her. So I say nothing. And eventually she turns away.

twenty

Leila

Leila can feel the tension in the air. Emmett has decreed that three nurses be kept on late, and another two brought on early, but the extra staff have added a nervousness to the ward that isn't helping. The cleaners have been briefed to be extra thorough, rightly resenting the implication they are ever anything but. Yin and Cheryl have taken down curling pieces of paper reminding people to **Wash your hands** and replaced them with laminated signs. The entire ward is standing to attention, and all for one man.

Dr. Gregory Clark Sanders Jr. is an easy decade older than the photograph on his website, which shows him as a thrusting young doctor, sitting splayed-legged in a mahogany office. Leila has looked at the photograph several times—has read the impressive list of qualifications held by the Houston specialist—and has, each time, felt a little less impressive herself, a little less qualified.

Now, as she walks up the corridor toward the glass door at the entrance to PICU, she feels her confidence coming back. Gregory Sanders is a small, slightly built man, with sandy-colored hair and a pleasant face with no sign of the smugness exhibited on his website. He extends a hand as she approaches.

"Dr. Sanders, it's a pleasure to meet you."

"Call me Greg."

Leila is not good at accents. She anticipated a stronger one from Greg—the Texan drawl she remembered from the reruns of **Dallas** Ruby loved to watch—but Greg Sanders's accent seems to her to be little different to Max's.

"And this is my barrister, Laura King." Max puts a hand on the shoulder of a woman in her midforties, with expensive caramel highlights in her shoulder-length hair. She wears a navy blazer with white tailored trousers, and looks as though she should be taking the air in Monte Carlo, not standing in the entrance of the Pediatric Intensive Care Unit at St. Elizabeth's Children's Hospital, Birmingham.

"Welcome to PICU." Leila takes them to the sink and waits while they wash their hands. Yin walks by, trying not to stare, but surely feeling the same way as the rest of the staff about this American specialist who claims he can succeed where they have failed. His visit carries implicit criticism that makes them all as defensive as they are curious. Leila is curious, too, but although she spends the next hour with Greg, he asks more than he offers, and she learns little beyond what she already knows.

"Houston ProTherapy has the highest success rates in the world," he says, as they reach Room 1. "We have state-of-the-art equipment, and our staff are outstanding."

Leila feels instantly protective of her own outstanding team. She wonders how Greg's staff would cope with NHS budget cuts and insufficient resources, whether Houston ProTherapy ever has to rely on grateful parents to buy lifesaving defibrillators.

"The main advantage of proton therapy is being able to direct the beam and have it stop where you want it to stop." Greg is answering a question from Laura King, but as he talks he makes eye contact with everyone in turn, making Leila feel as though she is back in the lecture room. "With medulloblastoma we treat the cerebral spinal fluid pathway, the whole brain, and the whole spine, but with none of the spread of radiation that occurs with conventional treatment."

He is standing next to Dylan, moving his hands to indicate where and how treatment will be administered, but he hasn't yet said hello to him. He hasn't touched the child's arm and introduced himself, explained that he'd like to take a look at his chart, and that he's here to help him. Leila knows that Dylan has little or no awareness of who is standing by his bed, but even so, she has to bite her lip. Dylan Adams is a child, not a case study. She strokes his forehead and silently tells him **It's all OK, just a lot of talking**.

Leila has read the report in the papers that came via Laura King, contesting the court order application. She has read it, and she disagrees with it. Proton beam therapy may well reduce the tumor that sits at the base of Dylan's skull, but at what cost? Another twelve weeks of treatment—of travel, scans, radiation—in the hope that Dylan will have another few months, perhaps a few years, to live within the limitations he has been left with. Little or no control over his limbs. Little or no speech. No coordination. Epilepsy, hearing loss, cognitive impairment . . .

"Dr. Sanders." Laura has a list of questions, her pen poised by each one. "The patient has posterior fossa syndrome as a result of his brain surgery, which I understand will affect executive functioning, speech, movement, and so on. Will proton beam therapy have a similar impact?"

"On the contrary, the side effects from proton beam are significantly less than from surgery." The answer is too quick, too glib, and Leila knows that they are following a script; that Laura King's questions are for Leila's benefit, not Greg's.

"If Dylan hadn't had a surgical resection," she says, sharper than she should, "he would have died."

Max looks at her. "But that's what you want now, isn't it?"

Leila feels an angry lump in her throat. "No, that isn't what I **want**. What any of us want. We all want what's best for Dylan, and in my professional opinion that isn't flying him halfway round the world and putting him through more treatment, when—"

"We'll keep this for the courts, shall we?" Laura King steps forward, her voice clear and authoritative. The two women stare at each other, and then Leila looks away. She will save her energy—and her evidence—for when it is needed.

The protesters have been at the hospital every day for two weeks. Emmett has hired security staff, who stand by the entrance to PICU in black ties and fluorescent jackets, their badges mounted on bands round their left arms. The protesters have agreed to stay within a marked-out area between the bins and the edge of the car park. There are new faces every day, but old ones, too, and Leila wonders how these people can come here, day after day. Don't they have jobs? Families? Lives? What makes them care so deeply about a child that isn't theirs?

It is raining, and there are only a handful of people in the marked-off area between the bins and the car park. The hard-core demonstrators, Leila thinks, undeterred by bad weather. She walks past them, her head down and her hood pulled up, but when she hears her name called instinct makes her look round. A woman in a red beanie begins shouting—a stream of unintelligible words—and the pack join in, baying for blood.

The next day the papers carry a picture of Leila, taken by one of the photographers who loiter by the smoking shelter in the car park, waiting for something to happen. She sees the article on the newsstand on her way to work, her bicycle wobbling as she looks a second time.

Doctor Death, reads the headline. In the accompanying image, Leila's face is set in a grim scowl, her eyes flashing at the camera.

The picture swells the crowd overnight. There are candles; music; flags strewn across the car park trees. It would be more festival than protest, were it not for the words chanted to the rhythmic beat of a small drum. **Right to life, right to life.** Leila skirts the car park, taking a more circuitous route to PICU this time. By midday, she has been summoned to the medical director's office.

"Why don't you take some time off? Just till the hearing?"

Emmett has the papers spread out in front of him.

"I can't—we're understaffed as it is, and—"

"We'll manage." Emmett is firm. "There are more protesters turning up every hour—they've laid on buses, for heaven's sake. We've had to put security on the door after one of them set up a Facebook group called Let Them Burn."

"They wouldn't actually—"

"Let's hope not," Emmett says grimly. He softens a little. "It's no reflection on you, Leila. Take a couple of weeks' holiday. Let it all blow over." Leila has no choice but to agree.

On the first day of her enforced leave, she wakes early. She hears the creak of Habibeh's bed in the room next to hers as her mother gets out to begin her prayers. Today is Norooz, the first day of the Persian year. A day supposed to symbolize new beginnings, fresh hope. Instead, Leila wakes with a feeling of dread about what is to come.

She thinks of Pip and Max, as she so often does, and she sends a silent prayer that they will find peace once they say goodbye to their son. Because Leila is quite sure that the court will grant the hospital order, despite the expensive lawyers Max has hired, despite the support he's garnered from the public, despite the attempts by protesters to discredit her testimony. The court will grant the order because it is the right thing to do.

She thinks.

Other images creep into Leila's memories, pushing logic aside. Dylan, opening his eyes at the sound of his mother's voice. His heart rate calming, as he nestles against his father's chest. Leila sits up and clicks on the bedside light. Throws her legs out of bed and stands up. Science, not emotion, she reminds herself. Facts, not supposition. A doctor, not a parent.

Downstairs, her dressing gown wrapped tightly to keep out the morning chill, she puts on the kettle and sets out two glasses. She spoons tea from the tin caddy she brought with her from Iran, and watches the dark leaves swirl around the teapot as she adds boiling water. The ritual is calming, its familiarity reassuring. She hears footsteps on the stairs as she steeps her mother's preferred tea. Not for Habibeh the rich, swirling Persian drink that makes Leila feel at home, but Marks and Spencer's finest Earl Grey, packaged in bags dangling from labeled strings. It is top of the list whenever Leila asks what her mother would like her to bring home, along with chocolate and vacuum-wrapped cheddar cheese. Leila adds milk until it's the insipid beige color Habibeh likes best. She makes **sheer berenj**, a rice pudding only ever made on the morning of Norooz, and when her mother comes downstairs, she makes herself smile.

Habibeh kisses her. "**Sad Saal be in Saal-ha**, Leila **joon**." A hundred more happy New Years. Leila would settle for one.

"I'm not working today, Maman."

Habibeh lights up. She struggled to understand that Leila could not take the day off for Norooz, that an understaffed, overstretched ward meant the consultants hadn't taken leave in months.

"Or for a while. I've taken some holiday." A little

223

white lie, settling between them. Habibeh is delighted. Leila is doubly ashamed. In honor of the occasion, Habibeh forgoes QVC in favor of BBC Persian's New Year countdown, with its array of pop stars, dances, and comedy routines. Leila forces smiles, and listens to Habibeh make plans for their time together—the dishes they will cook, the films they will watch—while inside her anxiety spirals and swoops and swirls until she's dizzy.

They snack on walnuts and dates as they prepare their Norooz meal. **Kofte**, Samanoo, a creamy dish of **must**, with its raisins and rose petals, lemon and olive oil. The table is laid with Leila's special cloth from the bazaar in Shiraz, a vase of hyacinths, the best silverware. On the television screen, Sami Beigi sings from his greatest hits.

"**Asheghetam**, Leila **joon**."

"I love you too, Maman."

The doorbell rings. Wilma, perhaps, from next door. Leila goes to answer it, while Habibeh wraps her **shall** around her head. But it isn't Wilma.

"Hey." It is Nick. It is strange to see him here, in Leila's front garden, and she feels her heart pick up its pace. She closes the door a little—she doesn't want Habibeh to hear Nick talk of Dylan's case, or of the newspapers her mother will never see.

"I wondered how you were doing."

"I'm fine."

A pause. "Can I come in?"

"It's not a good time."

Habibeh comes to the door. She waits to be introduced, but before Leila can decide what to say, Nick
coughs. "Um, **haletun chetorah**," he says, somewhat
self-consciously. "**Esm e man** Nick **ask**."

Leila is as surprised as Habibeh is. Leila looks down
at Nick's hands, which are covered in blue ink. "What
else do you have on there?"

He checks his other hand. "Er, **dashtshuee kojast?**"

There is a brief pause. Habibeh and Leila exchange
glances.

"Top of the stairs, on the left. The flush sticks a bit,"
Leila says. "If that's really what you wanted to ask."

Nick looks embarrassed. "Wrong hand, sorry. I
wrote that one down in case of emergencies."

"But why would you need any of it?" Leila is
confused.

"I didn't know if you'd be here, and I didn't want
to worry your mum by turning up and not being
able to say who I was. I took that Iranian porter for a
coffee—remember the chap who was always singing?
He wrote some phrases down for me."

"You'd better come in." Leila is glad of the narrow
hallway that means there is no room for them all to
stand; glad of the excuse to turn away and hide her
face, which flushes with sudden feeling. She makes tea
in narrow, tall glasses that slip into silver cases, and
watches Nick nod earnestly as Habibeh recites the
names of all the dishes on their Norooz table.

"Yesterday's chip papers," he says gently, when Habibeh has gone to the kitchen for more food. It takes Leila a moment to understand.

"They're calling me Doctor Death. They think I'm a monster."

"It's a game, Leila."

"It's a cruel one." Leila's eyes fill. She puts a sugar cube on her tongue, takes a sip of tea, and lets the sweet taste fill her mouth. Nick hesitates, then he takes her hand and squeezes it—just for a second—before letting it fall again. "It'll all go away after the court case." He moves away as Habibeh comes back into the room, and Leila feels too hot and too cold, all at once. "Did you hear," he says, trying to change the subject, "one of our paramedics got marched off the premises today."

"What? Why?"

"For leaking stories to the press. Do you remember that piece in the **Mirror** about surgery happening in corridors?"

Leila nods, although she doesn't really. There are so many hatchet jobs.

"Turns out, that was him. A few weeks later he went to the **Mail** with the details of an elderly patient whose wife disagreed with his DNR, and they ran a double-page spread on whether it was better or worse than euthanasia."

Do Not Resuscitate. Leila hears Jim's voice in her head. **His wife called me a murderer . . . there was a bit of me that felt like one.**

"The family lodged a formal complaint with the trust, and when Emmett went to the paper, the hack coughed his source."

"Nick . . ." Leila had felt so sorry for Jim. She thought he understood what she was going through with the Adams case, and that he would listen without judgment. She trusted him. Habibeh, lost in the conversation, excuses herself to bring in more food they won't eat. "Nick, I told him about Dylan Adams." Sickness wells in the pit of her stomach.

Only a single eyebrow, raised the smallest amount, indicates that Nick has heard at all. Leila waits for him to say something, but he takes a mouthful of tea, and his deliberate silence means Leila is the one who has to speak.

"I fell off my bike. He checked me over—Jim Laithwaite, his name's Jim Laithwaite—and gave me a lift to work. I bought him a drink to say thank you."

We should do this again. Her face burns with the memory of how stupid she was. No wonder he didn't call. He already had what he wanted. Leila imagines him picking up his mobile even as he watched her walk away.

Mate, I've got a cracking story for you . . .

"Did you realize he was fishing for information?"

Leila screws her eyes shut. "He didn't need to fish. I volunteered it." She doesn't tell Nick that she'd been crying inside, that day; that watching Pip and Max Adams's world fall apart had almost broken her.

Nick surveys Leila, thoughtfully, then his shoulders lift a fraction. "We're all on the same side, Leila. We should be able to trust each other. When that trust is broken, it hurts. But it's not your fault." He sits back in his chair, a puzzled look on his face. "Why are you taking this so hard?"

"It's a sensitive case. Dylan's parents should never have been thrust into the public eye until they were ready, until it was unavoidable."

"It was unavoidable from the outset. You know that. What aren't you telling me?"

Leila feels heat rising, creeping up her neck and across her face. "I liked him," she says eventually.

There's a long pause. Leila doesn't need to look at Nick to know he's uncomfortable; that he's wondering how he can change the subject. But he asked, and Leila is going to tell him.

She stares at the table. "I'm thirty-four, and single—as my mother regularly reminds me. And then I met Jim, and I liked him, and I thought he liked me and . . . well, anyway. That's why."

There's a long pause.

"Plenty more fish in the sea."

Leila allows the table a halfhearted smile. "I think there's a hole in my net."

And then Habibeh comes back, and Nick stands to help her with the dishes, and he asks questions about Norooz, and about Iran, and Habibeh unfurls like a flower finding sun. And it is much later, when their bellies are groaning, and their empty plates are stacked in the sink, that Nick leans toward Leila.

"That paramedic?" The corners of his mouth lift just a fraction. "He didn't deserve you."

twenty-one

Pip

Max is sitting on a red sofa. He is wearing grey suit trousers, but instead of a jacket, he has a T-shirt pulled over his long-sleeved shirt. The T-shirt has a picture of Dylan on it, and it looks as though someone handed it to Max as he walked on set, and said **Quick, put this on—it'll look great for the cameras**. It doesn't look great. It looks . . . it looks a bit pathetic, like fifty-five-year-olds in baseball caps, or mothers who borrow their teenagers' trainers. Max is clearly uncomfortable. His shoulders are slouched, and he looks older, broken. In contrast, the woman next to him— Max's barrister, Laura King—wears a suit cut like a dinner jacket, and black shoes that show red soles when she crosses her legs, which she does frequently. Occasionally, she touches Max on the arm, and I find myself talking to the television.

"Leave him alone, for God's sake."

The presenters—a man and a woman with too much chemistry to be husband and wife—are summarising the "story so far," ahead of tomorrow's court case. As the presenters talk, photographs of Dylan scroll in the top right-hand corner of the screen. They are my photo-a-day pictures—my record of his life before St. Elizabeth's—and I feel a surge of anger that Max didn't ask before sharing them.

"This must be a living nightmare for you." The female presenter tilts her head on one side. She has actual tears in her eyes.

"No," Max says. "Dylan is the one trapped in a nightmare. He's the one fighting for his life. What I'm going through is nothing compared to what he's been through over the last few months."

The male presenter leans forward. There are no tears in **his** eyes, I notice. "Sadly, this isn't the first time we've spoken to a parent who is fighting the medical team looking after their child, but there's one major difference in your case, isn't there?"

Laura King puts her hand on Max's arm again.

"He's not paying you to maul him," I mutter.

"Every case is different," Laura answers smoothly. "Our hope is that this week, justice will be done, and Max will be able to exercise his right as a parent, to give Dylan the medical care he so desperately needs."

"But there's a reason why Dylan's mum isn't with you today, isn't there?" the presenter says, terrier-like in his pursuit of something more salacious. **Old news,** I think. I want to turn it off, but missing Max has become a physical ache—like homesickness—and seeing him both hurts and heals.

"My wife and I both want the best for Dylan." Max pauses. "It happens to be that we disagree on what that means."

"I understand you're currently living in a hotel some distance away from your home." The terrier again. Nip, nip, nip.

"I wanted to be closer to the hospital. To my son."

"Is your wife staying there too?"

Max flounders. His eyes dart towards Laura King, but she doesn't see, doesn't pick up on it.

"Reports say that you've left your wife—we can only imagine the strain something like this must put on your—"

Max's fists ball by his sides. "My wife and I haven't separated, and where I'm living has nothing to do with my fight to get Dylan the treatment he deserves." He looks like he has more to say, but the camera closes on the presenters, and whatever it was is lost.

But you did leave me, I say silently.

The final days before the court case are both endless and fleeting. I spend every moment I can with Dylan, squeezing a lifetime of memories into minutes and hours. I bring in every book from his shelves at home, and read them over and over, while he lies still, drifting in and out of sleep. I sing to him, bathe him, brush his barely-there hair. I tell him stories filled with sunshine and happy endings, feeling like a liar because life doesn't have happy endings, does it?

The hearing of **St. Elizabeth Hospital Trust v. Adams** will take place in the family court at London's Royal Courts of Justice, a vast Gothic building with turreted roofs and hundreds of windows that stare down at us as I get out of the taxi arranged by my barrister.

There is no public gallery in family court, and the crowd of people outside the building have been kept on the opposite side of the road by metal barriers and fluorescent-jacketed police. They wear T-shirts emblazoned with Dylan's photo, and wave placards begging the court to **let our boy live!**

Our boy? When did he become **their boy?**

They make me want to take Dylan home and lock the doors. They make me want to take down every photo of him I've ever put on Facebook, to stop these people copying them, Photoshopping them, using them as their own profile picture. Far from drawing strength from this show of what I know is meant as solidarity, it simply serves to turn the knife.

They shout at me as I walk up the steps with Robin Shane and his two assistants.

"Murderer!"

"Don't turn round," Robin says. "Keep walking."

Inside, my shoes echo on the tiled floor as we make our way to the courtroom, where a sudden **All rise!** brings the lawyerly muttering to a sharp close.

The judge—the Hon. Mr. Justice Merritt—wears a black robe with velvet trim, the only colour two short red ribbons at the neck. He wears no wig, and his hair is grey and neatly trimmed. He looks like a grandfather. I imagine him bouncing a toddler on his knee, creaking onto all fours so the kids can play horsey.

In front of the judge's bench is a lower one, occupied—as per the plan Robin sketched for me in the back of our black cab—by the clerks. In front again, facing towards the judge, are several further rows. We are sitting on the left, behind the hospital's legal team, next to Dylan's guardian and barrister. Max's team is on the right.

"Who are all those people with him?" I whisper.

Robin raises an eyebrow. "Here to make his barrister look impressive. They'll have shoved the interns into suits, and billed your husband for the privilege."

I've seen the crowdfunding page Max started—watched it move from five figures to six. I've seen, too, the invoices from Robin's office to my father—the sums eye-wateringly large. In some unspoken agreement, neither Max nor I have touched our "rainy-day" savings account, and I wonder what it would take for either of us to do so.

"My lord," begins the hospital barrister. "The case before you concerns Dylan Adams, who is currently admitted to the paediatric intensive care unit at St. Elizabeth's Children's Hospital, Birmingham. The difficult task with which this court is charged is that of establishing whether it is in Dylan's best interests for life-sustaining treatment to continue. Discontinuing such treatment will, on the evidence before the court, sadly lead to the child's death, but it is this sad application on which this case rests—my clients seek leave of the court to end Dylan's suffering."

I stifle a cry. I have been told the case may last for several days, that I may leave whenever I want, that it may be too hard.

It is hard. Harder than I ever imagined.

But I don't leave. I listen to doctors say in calm, still voices everything Dr. Khalili said to us in the quiet room, just a few weeks ago. I listen to the judge asking **What exactly does that mean for Dylan?** and **Could you explain that in layman's terms, please?** and I try to read a face that gives nothing away.

On the second day we hear from the consultant oncologist, who speaks eloquently about Dylan's tumour and subsequent treatment, and waits in the witness box for Max's barrister to respond with more questions.

"Mr. Singh." Laura King frowns, as though she is confused. "How many children has the NHS sent abroad for proton beam therapy?"

"In the last ten years, somewhere in the region of three hundred. That's nationwide, of course. At St. Elizabeth's, we've referred eighty-seven cases."

"And how many of those patients were treated successfully?"

"Around ninety percent experienced a significant improvement following therapy." There is a shift in the room as Laura King sits down, turning to whisper something in Max's ear. Robin is on his feet instantly.

"Do you send **every** cancer patient for proton beam therapy, Mr. Singh?"

"No." The consultant appears mildly irritated by the question. "We send those patients for whom that particular therapy is considered likely to have the desired result. If we sent **all** cancer patients, the success rate would be significantly lower."

"Thank you."

Dr. Khalili is shaking slightly as she walks to the witness box, and she places both hands firmly on the wooden rail in front of her. When it is Laura King's turn to question her, her jaw tightens a little.

"In the minutes from your meeting dated tenth February—my lord, there should be a copy in your bundle—you are recorded as attesting that proton beam therapy for Dylan Adams would not be 'an appropriate use of funds.' Is that correct?"

"I did say that, yes."

I glance at Max, and see his eyes darken.

"But if I may clarify . . ." Dr. Khalili looks at the judge, who nods. "This isn't a budget issue. I don't think Dylan Adams should have proton beam therapy, full stop."

The judge leans forward. "Could you explain why, Dr. Khalili? You don't feel proton beam therapy will work in this case?"

"That depends what you mean by 'work.' Proton beam therapy won't cure Dylan's cancer, but it might buy him some time."

Laura King cuts in, softening the interruption with a deferential nod. "Which is precisely what my client is asking for, my lord. Time with his son—however long that may be."

Prompted by the judge, Dr. Khalili continues as though the other woman hasn't spoken. "Extending Dylan's life isn't the only issue, and in my view it isn't the most important one." She takes a breath. "Dylan's brain damage is irreparable. If he lives, he will not walk or talk. He will not be able to communicate his needs, or even his feelings. Those are basic human functions, and my opinion—both as a doctor and as a fellow human being—is that there is little life without those functions."

I want to catch Dr. Khalili's eye, I want to show her how grateful I am for her making our case so passionately. But she steadfastly refuses to look at me—to look at anyone—and as the judge thanks her, and she makes her way past me, and back to her seat, I see that she is shaking again.

And now I'm trembling too.

Because it is my turn.

twenty-two

Max

Pip's wearing a white shirt with thin yellow stripes. It's tucked into a fitted navy skirt and as she walks to the witness box I have a sudden image of her at work, walking down the aisle of the airplane. I think about the first time I saw her, about those impossibly long eyelashes; I think about that evening, a few hours later, in a busy bar. **I want to marry that woman**, I thought, before she'd even made the connection between the guy she'd served on the plane and this idiot, smiling gormlessly at her across the bar. I knew. You just do.

The zipper on the back of her skirt is twisted to one side, the waistband looser than it would have been a year ago. I think about how, in another life, I'd walk over and straighten it, without either of us even remarking on it, because that's what you do when you've been together for as long as we have. There's an ache inside me like homesickness, only it isn't home I miss, it's Pip. It's us.

I checked out of my hotel near the hospital and into a cheaper one a few blocks away from here. Pip's traveling from home each day—I heard her talking to her barrister as they arrived—but I need the focus of being close to court. Last night I read through the papers, calling Laura a dozen times with something else I just thought of.

"It's all under control," she said in the end. "Get some sleep."

I couldn't sleep, and by the looks of Pip, she couldn't either. Her makeup is immaculate, her hair neatly swept back, but there are dark shadows beneath her eyes and in the hollows of her cheeks.

When Dylan was around eighteen months old, he went through a phase of hitting other children when they had something he wanted. That truck you're holding? Wham! Your cookie? Wham!

"Naughty Dylan," I told him one time. Pip shook her head.

"You're supposed to separate the child from the act." The way she said it told me she'd gotten it from some parenting site. "Otherwise you're reinforcing negative self-image." She bent down real low so she could make eye contact with Dylan. "Dylan, I love you very much but I don't like what you did just now. I don't want to see you hitting anyone again, OK?"

Dylan smacked his hand against her face.

"Ow!"

"I'm not laughing," I said, laughing.

I look at Pip. I look through everything she's said and done over the last two months, and I know that I still love her. I'll always love her. And once we're in Texas, and Dylan's getting better, we'll talk. We'll get back what we had before.

"Mrs. Adams." Pip's barrister stands. "I know this is incredibly hard for you. Could you tell us, in your own words, why you support the hospital's recommendation that Dylan's treatment path should include palliative care only?"

Pip's head makes a tiny, jerky movement—more a tremor than a nod. Her lips quiver as she opens her mouth, and when she speaks it's so quietly there's a collective rustle in the court, as everyone leans forward to hear.

"I love my son. What everyone's saying in the papers, on TV, it isn't true. I'm not a monster. I would give anything to make this nightmare go away, and have Dylan back home where he belongs." She says nothing more for the longest time, her eyes tightly closed and her face tense with the effort of trying not to cry. I feel the way I did in the quiet room, when Pip was crying—like there are two of me sitting here, not one. One me fighting Pip and the hospital, and another wanting to put my arms around her and say **You're doing so well.**

240

"But that can't happen." She's louder now, her knuckles white on the rail in front of her. "I have spent every day with my son since he was admitted to hospital last autumn. I've been there when he's had seizures so bad they've had to sedate him, when they've given him morphine for the pain. I've learned how to suction his saliva, how to massage his back to loosen the secretions, how to manipulate his arms and legs so they don't waste away. It is relentless, and exhausting, and it would consume my life—our lives—if Dylan came home." Anger swells inside me but she hasn't finished. "And I would do all of it and more, if I felt that in between the drugs and the hospital appointments and the physio and the suctioning there would be a life worth living." Silence hangs over the courtroom. Pip looks at the judge. "But I don't believe there is."

I rub the back of my neck. Drop my head and screw up my face like it'll take away the noise in my head, the pictures put there by Pip. I've been there too, haven't I? I've seen those things too, I've helped with his physio, and . . . **When you're not working**, comes the tiny voice. Pip and I made our decisions based on different experiences, different realities. The realization is unsettling.

"Mrs. Adams, you understand that, if this order is granted, your son will die?"

A single word, tight and painful. "Yes."

The barrister prepares to sit, but Pip starts to talk

again. "I want to make it clear that I don't **want** Dylan to die. But I don't want him to live the way he'll live if he survives. There is . . ." She falters, and the final words trail away as though she is suddenly exhausted. "There is a difference."

I think about my own speech, prepared and ready for this afternoon, when Laura will prompt me with **Please tell the court why you oppose this application.** I think of the wealth of evidence we've put together, all focused on keeping Dylan alive. I think of the images Pip conjured for the court. And I falter.

"All the evidence has been in support of the applicant," Laura says, when court takes a short break. She takes a sip of canteen-bought coffee and makes a face. "It's bound to make you question yourself—that's its whole aim. You'll feel better once our own witnesses give evidence."

I do. Our first witness, Dr. Hans Schulz, has dark brown hair and owlish glasses, with a bearing so rigid that when he came to the hospital I half-expected him to click his heels together. He was the second independent doctor Laura found.

"I'm sorry," said the first, a French pediatrician in a Paul Smith suit. "I can't support your case." His report was brief, so similar to Dr. Khalili's they might have been written simultaneously. **No realistic possibility of a meaningful life** was his chilling conclusion.

"I spent some considerable time with the patient,"

Dr. Schulz tells the court, his English impeccable. "I noted that his pupils responded to light, and that—when I spoke—he turned his head in my direction."

The hospital's QC is making notes, leaning across to whisper something to his assistant. The room is air-conditioned, but I'm burning up, and I loosen my tie and undo my top button. I'm here and yet not here; listening to all these people talk about a nightmare that surely cannot be our life. I keep looking at Pip, but she stares at her hands, clasped in her lap like she's praying.

Dr. Schulz gives evidence for two hours. He answers questions from the judge, from the hospital's QC, from Laura, from Dylan's barrister. He has done well, I think, and with this afternoon's video evidence from Dr. Gregory Sanders, it cannot fail to make a dent in the certainty presented by St. Elizabeth's.

Laura is pleased. She thinks the judge will be swayed by Dr. Schulz, by a child who is responding to light and voice.

"The public will seize on that in particular—you'll see." We're sitting in Pret a Manger, and she dabs mayonnaise from the corner of her mouth with her napkin. "The journalists will love it."

I buy the papers every day. All of them. I spread them out on my hotel bed and cut out the pages fighting for my son's life. I highlight the quotes from campaigners, celebrities, politicians who have lent their support, and put them in a folder.

"Dylan is suffering, but his father is suffering too" reads the message from a prominent bishop, printed over and over, quoted in every paper, on every news site. "I pray that he will be permitted to exercise his right as a parent, to treat Dylan's suffering in his home country."

When Dylan is old enough, I will give him the pile of clippings that show the whole world wanted him to live.

There are problems with the video link in the afternoon. Dr. Gregory Sanders drops out twice, freezing midframe—an openmouthed gargoyle. There is frustration from the judge, and what I'm certain is deliberate eye-rolling from the hospital's QC, who sighs audibly and checks his watch, but eventually the system works.

Dr. Sanders performs well—it is obvious he has done this before. Perhaps a little **too** obvious. His confidence borders on arrogance; he has a tendency to begin talking a second before the barristers have stopped, prompting Judge Merritt to say **Please listen to the question**. But his evidence is sound.

"Proton beam therapy will reduce the tumor, and prolong Dylan's life," he concludes.

No judge in the land could rule against that.

"A good result," Laura says. We're walking from the court. Her heels are several inches high, yet she walks faster than me, like she's in a hurry, even though we're done for the day. We stop outside my hotel. It's a budget chain, all bright colors and backpackers. Laura's staying at the Four Seasons, billing it to me. "I've got some work to do on another case," she says briskly, "but I could do a late supper if you're at a loose end. Or"—there's a subtle shift in her tone—"perhaps just a nightcap?"

There's no twirl of the hair, no coquettish flutter of eyelashes, only a raised eyebrow, and a bald, no-strings offer. She looks at me, unblinking, waiting.

"I think I'll try for an early night," I manage. She gives a small smile at my unintended innuendo, and shrugs.

"Your call. See you in court."

I watch her walk away, her heels pushing her body into a Marilyn walk. I think of Pip walking down the aisle of an airplane, walking to the witness box to tell a judge why she wants her son to die. I think of the way my whole body wanted to comfort her, even while my head was filled with rage at her words. I think how she's the only person in my life I've always been able to talk to.

When this is over, I tell myself, we'll be a family again.

Pip, Dylan, and me. Just like it used to be.

twenty-three

Leila

Leila stands outside the court. Soon, she will have to go inside and take her seat in the old, quiet courtroom, and they will hear the judge's decision and know for certain what will happen to almost-three-year-old Dylan Adams.

They are all out here. Max Adams, and his legal team; Pip, with her barrister. Together, yet separate, clustered in low voices and nods on opposite sides of the court gates. Leila should join the hospital team—she is, after all, on their side—but she does not want to talk about the case. She has found it hard to hear today's evidence. She has found herself swayed by the conviction of Max's doctors, and by the evidence of Professor Greenwood and his impressively equipped establishment. She stands by her recommendation, she knows they are doing the right thing by Dylan, and yet she cannot help but wonder **what if** . . .

So she stands in the middle of the two groups, by the heavy bollards that separate the pavement from the road. She wishes Nick were here, and then, to punish herself, she pictures Nick with his family, with his grown-up children, and the wife Leila knows is a research scientist.

Max Adams is smoking. He took a cigarette offered by one of his lawyers, and now he is closing his eyes and drawing in the nicotine like it's oxygen. Leila has never seen him smoke before. She wonders what it has done to him, the last few months. If he's lost weight, if he sleeps, if he has nightmares, like she does.

They have been here for four days. Every day the newspapers have led with the story of Dylan Adams and his fight for life, his warring parents, the doctors arguing their case. Every day the photographers have followed Leila and Pip and Max and the legal teams from car to court, and from court to car. And every morning, Leila has seen the previous day's photos captioned in the tabloids.

Battling to hide his emotion, Max Adams arrives for the second day of the case.

Mum Philippa wore a fitted trouser suit and left her hair loose for the hearing.

Dr. Leila Khalili is Iranian.

They have listened to the written evidence of seventeen doctors, they have picked over every argument presented by every legal team, and still Leila has no idea what Justice Merritt will decide.

She is about to go back inside when she sees a familiar figure, hurrying along the pavement. She squints—surely not?—but her eyes are not deceiving her. Leila walks toward the figure.

"Surprise!" Habibeh is grinning broadly. She is wearing her good coat, and the head scarf Leila knows she reserves for special occasions. It is purple and green, with gold thread running through it. Her arm is tucked into Wilma's.

"Don't worry, love, we're not here to bother you. Your mother wanted to see the sights, and we thought we'd pop by to give you a bit of moral support."

"And lunch," Habibeh adds. She hands Leila a complicated arrangement of square boxes, clipped together and finished with a metal handle. "Tiffin box," she says proudly. "Dishwasher and freezer safe, and insulated for hot or cold food."

"Oh, Maman, this is exactly what I needed. Thank you." Not the food—Leila knows she couldn't eat a bite—but her mother, with her QVC English, and her squashy embrace, and her total faith that whatever Leila does will be right.

"We're going to Covent Garden first," Wilma says, "then Habibeh fancies a go on the London Eye." Leila wonders if Habibeh will think again about leaving

Iran and living with Leila, now that she can see she could have a life, have friends, here.

Habibeh is looking for someone. She scans the pavement behind Leila. "Dr. Nick?" She looks disappointed.

"He's at the hospital, Maman, he isn't giving evidence."

"Nice man," she tells Wilma. "Doctor friend. Shame he . . ." She searches for the word, her fingertips pinching together as if she might be able to pluck it from the air. She exhales sharply, irritated by her lack of language, and takes out her phone.

"**Be** Farsi **che mishaved,** Maman?"

But Habibeh refuses to take the easy route. "English," she insists, typing the word she wants into Google Translate. Leila tries to read it upside down. It's a shame Nick is . . . what? **Married,** she thinks, and flushes again at the idea her mother might have so accurately read her mind.

"Divorce!" Habibeh says, triumphantly, her disapproval tempered by delight in her linguistic achievements.

"Ah." Wilma is philosophical. "Sometimes it's for the best, though. My daughter's marriage broke up and it was terrible for a while, but now she's never been happier."

Leila is not listening to the story about Wilma's daughter. Divorced? "**Doroste?**" she asks. "Are you sure?"

249

"Aw talaq gurefth." He is getting divorced, Habibeh confirms. **He said so at Norooz, when you were making tea. It is a shame.** Like many Iranians of her generation, Habibeh disapproves of divorce. And yet there is something about the way she looks at Leila—in the fact she mentioned Nick at all—that makes Leila wonder if her instincts were right; her mother did indeed read her mind.

She cannot dwell on it. It is time to go. She kisses her mother and thanks Wilma for looking after her, and watches them head for Covent Garden, and the London Eye, and an afternoon of tourist attractions. And then she walks back into the court.

This is the final hearing of an application made by St. Elizabeth's Children's Hospital for St. Elizabeth's Hospital NHS Trust pursuant to the inherent jurisdiction of the High Court in relation to Dylan Adams, who was born on the fifth of May 2010 and is now almost three years old."

Leila watches the judge. She tries to read his expression, to find some warning of what is to come, but his poker face is well practiced.

"Where, as in this grave and difficult case, a dispute arises between parents and treating doctors regarding the proper course of treatment for a seriously ill child, the court may be asked to intervene." He pauses, and looks around the room. "By their application dated seventh March 2013 the applicants ask the court to make the following orders. One, that Dylan, by reason of his minority, lacks capacity to make decisions regarding his medical treatment. Two, that it is lawful and in Dylan's best interests for his treating clinicians to provide him with palliative care only. And three, that it is lawful and in Dylan's best interests not to undergo proton beam therapy."

Leila looks around the courtroom. Only the handful of press given permission to attend are moving, their pens making swift marks in shorthand, recording every word the judge speaks. Everyone else is quite still—watching, waiting—and Leila has the strange sensation of being frozen in time, that they might all wake, a year from now, and they will still be here in this courtroom, waiting for the ruling that will change so many lives.

"There has been much speculation about this case," the judge says, "and I would ask that those who have not listened—as we have—to the medical evidence pertaining to Dylan Adams, do not pass judgment on the decisions made in this room." There is a long pause before he speaks again, and when he does, he looks directly at Pip and Max.

"Many people believe that the courts should have no role to play in this process; that parents should be allowed to decide what is right for their child. However, when agreement cannot be reached—either between hospital and parent, or indeed between parents themselves—the court must step in."

Leila swallows. If it is this hard for her, how impossible must it be for Dylan's parents? To listen to the judge's words? To know that in a few moments they will hear their son's fate?

Before the break, Max and Pip Adams were sitting at opposite ends of the long bench seat behind their legal teams. They are still sitting on the bench, but the distance between them has contracted, and now they are sitting close enough to touch each other.

In fact, as Leila watches, and as the judge draws closer to his ruling, she sees movement. She could not say if Max moved first, or Pip. She can't be certain they even know they are doing it. But as she watches, two hands venture slowly across the no-man's-land between them, and find each other.

Dylan's parents hold hands.

The judge speaks.

And a courtroom holds its breath.

Two roads diverged in a yellow wood,
And sorry I could not travel both
And be one traveler, long I stood
And looked down one as far as I could

—ROBERT FROST

twenty-four

Pip

The judge puts on his reading glasses and picks up his notes. "It is with a heavy heart, but with total conviction for Dylan's interests, that I accede to the application made by St. Elizabeth's Children's Hospital, and rule that they may lawfully withdraw all treatment save for palliative care, and allow Dylan to die with dignity."

Instantly, Max pulls his hand from mine. I turn to look at him, but he's staring straight ahead, his head moving from side to side in small, fluid movements.

The judge's voice is neutral, his gaze fixed in the middle distance, between Max's barrister and the hospital's. He's still talking, now, but the words flow over me because all I can hear is the ruling, over and over again.

They may lawfully withdraw all treatment . . . and allow Dylan to die with dignity.

Max thrusts his hands in his pockets, out of my reach. I touch his arm, and he flinches as if he's been burned. He's still staring at the judge, still shaking his head as if he can't believe what he's heard. Relief floods through me that it's all over, that Dylan doesn't have to suffer any longer, but the relief is short-lived. I cannot celebrate a ruling that means Dylan dies, no matter how right the decision.

When Dylan was not quite a year, and crawling so fast I never stopped running after him, he was ill for a day or two. He wouldn't be put down, and we spent the hours cuddled on the sofa, watching Disney films. **He's so lovely when he's poorly.** The thought was contraband, to be kept hidden from people who would judge me. **It isn't that I** want **him to be ill**, I justified, **only that he's so cuddly when he is**.

"Max." I try to whisper, but my throat is tight and I have to force out the word, which comes out too loud, too sharp. No one turns to look at us, because they're already looking, like we're exhibits in a zoo, specimens in a lab.

Max dips his head. His eyes are closed. Perhaps he's crying or perhaps he can't bring himself to look at me. I want—no, I **need**—him to hold me, but every muscle in his body is tensing away from me. He starts to speak—too quietly for me to hear—and he's staring at the ground and I can't even be sure he's speaking to me. I lean towards him, desperate to hear his voice.

The words come slowly, a pause between each one to form the next, and I want to believe I've misheard, but even a whisper can carry betrayal. "You made this happen."

"What?" A kick to my guts, when I'm already down. "No! The hospital—"

"They took this to court, but you kept it here. You gave evidence that made up the judge's mind."

"Max, stop—"

"You signed your own son's death warrant."

My breath catches. A sharp pain pierces my chest and I put both hands on the bench in front of me and grasp it as though I'm falling.

"Court rise."

We stand. There's a rustle from the press box, and three, four, five reporters take this as their cue to leave. One of them gives a self-conscious bob of the head to the judge as he side-shuffles out, notebook clutched to his chest. The ruling will be on the internet before we leave the building, it will be in the papers tonight. The public jury will dissect the secondhand hearing as though they were standing in my shoes, and pronounce their findings as absolute. A verdict upon a verdict.

The room feels airless. The judge stands, and makes his way through a door to one side of the bench, and suddenly someone turns up the volume.

". . . statement to the press in the next few minutes."

"I've always rated him as a judge."

"Time for a quick drink?"

Every voice but Max's, whose angry hiss repeats
in my head regardless. **A death warrant.** A hand
touches my sleeve. It's Robin.

"You coped incredibly well—I know how hard that
must have been for you."

"Thank you for all your help," I say, programmed
to be polite, even though the "help" is work for which
he will shortly be sending an invoice to my father.

You signed your own son's death warrant.

I turn to Max, but he's gone, the space where he
stood already filled by the knot of people surrounding
me, their conversation a hushed murmur, like mourners gossiping at a funeral. I catch a glimpse of my
husband's jacket, the back of his head, and then the
door closes behind him.

"Excuse me." I push my way towards the exit. A
lingering journalist steps forwards, then thinks better
of it. I break into a run. Someone opens the door for
me. "Max! Max!" On the concourse people sit on rows
of plastic chairs, waiting to be called. Two women in
wigs and gowns sweep past. I stop for a second to look
for Max, and immediately two reporters flank me,
recording devices already flashing red.

"How do you feel about the judgement, Mrs.
Adams?"

Max is standing at the top of the stairs, one hand on the rail. A reporter stands two steps beneath him, not quite blocking his way, but almost.

"Max, wait!"

He looks back and this time he looks at me, only when he does it's me who can't bear it. I fell in love with these eyes, and saw that love reflected back in them. I looked into them on our wedding day, when we exchanged promises to love and honour. **Till death us do part.** I've held a hundred silent conversations with these eyes, across countless dinner tables and roomfuls of friends. **What a bore! One more drink, then let's go. I love you. I love you too.** Those eyes urged me on when Dylan was almost born and I was so tired and it hurt so much . . . **You can do it. One more push. I love you.**

I force myself to hold his gaze, but it's tearing me apart from the inside, my chest squeezed so tight I'm buckling beneath it, because it's like looking at a stranger. My husband's eyes are empty. What have I done?

There's a beat, then he leaves, pushing past the reporter, who has no choice but to step out of his way.

My own brace of journalists hasn't moved. There's a note of exasperation in their voices.

"Mrs. Adams?"

"Do you have a statement for us?"

A tiny red light blinks at me, the microphone inches from my face. My vision blurs and I blink hard, swallow. Everything I do is an effort, like I'm remembering how. Speaking seems impossible. All I want to do is get back to the hospital—get back to Dylan. Is that where Max has gone, too?

"Pip?" Dr. Khalili speaks quietly. I didn't notice her leave the courtroom, but she's standing by the door, a few yards away from me. "Did you come by train? Would you like a lift back?"

I stare at her. One of the reporters shifts his weight from one foot to the other. The red light continues to blink. It seems impossible I'll ever speak again, but if I do it won't be into this microphone. Dr. Khalili waits patiently, her face filled with the compassion that hasn't once wavered in the months I have known her. And suddenly it hits me that this isn't about a few words spoken by a judge, but about Dylan. Dr. Khalili will go back to St. Elizabeth's and update Dylan's notes, and the next time he crashes, they will let him die.

Dylan is going to die.

A wave of terror engulfs me. I look at Dr. Khalili, the horror of everything that's happened shrinking down to this one woman, to that one day she took us to the quiet room and brought our lives to an end.

"This is all your fault," I hiss. Then I walk away as fast as I can without running, Max's words still ringing in my ears. I can't be here. I can't be near this woman who has lost me not only my son but my husband, too.

Maybe I did sign Dylan's death warrant.

But Leila Khalili wrote it.

twenty-five

Max

The judge puts on his reading glasses and picks up his notes. "This has not been an easy decision. It is with some trepidation, but with complete conviction of Dylan's best interests, that I rule that Max Adams be allowed to take his son to America for treatment that may prolong his life."

Instantly, Pip takes her hand from mine. She makes a sound that's neither a word nor a cry. A single breath. And then she stands and pushes past me, running out of the courtroom. I stand too, and I'm about to go after her, but I don't know if she wants me to—if she'll even talk to me. I walked out on her when she needed me most, and I know she'll need time to understand that everything I did was for our son. For our family.

People are crowding around me, and my legal team are murmuring respectful plaudits, and my chest swells with relief and love and something that feels a lot like pride.

I rule that Max Adams be allowed to take his son to America for treatment that may prolong his life.

I fought for my son, and we won. It isn't just me who believes Dylan's life is worth saving. The court agrees. With me, with Dr. Schulz, Dr. Sanders, Laura King. The hospital can't stop treating Dylan, they have to abide by the court order. They have to allow us to take Dylan to America for proton beam therapy.

Us.

My skin still holds the memory of Pip's hand in mine, the warmth of her fingers. The reassurance brought by the presence of the one person who knows you better than you know yourself. In those few minutes, before the judge gave his ruling, Pip needed me, and I needed her. For that short time we weren't pitted against each other, but standing side by side again. Hand in hand.

Laura shakes my hand, her fingers lingering for a second longer than necessary. "They'll be expecting a statement—are you comfortable giving one, or would you prefer me to read it?"

"No. No, it should be me."

Us. It should be **us.**

I'm no longer torn in two, no longer two different men fighting different responses. Pip did what she thought was right—just as I did. The weeks spent by Dylan's bed wore her down, until she could only see the labor in looking after him, and no longer the love. But I'll help more. I'll be there more. Pip was frightened of going against the recommendations of medical staff we'd come to trust. But now she can have confidence in a new team of doctors. A team who believe they can save our son.

"I'll give a statement. But then I need to find my wife."

The pavement outside the court is thronged with people. A cheer breaks out as Laura and I step outside, and I see someone waving a flag with Dylan's photo on it. A woman I've never seen before is crying. She sees me looking and smiles through her tears, one hand on her chest. My son has touched a whole nation. A whole **world**.

A hush descends as I straighten the piece of paper in my hand, on which is scribbled my hastily drafted statement.

"A few moments ago, the Honorable Mr. Justice Merritt refused to grant a court order that would have brought about the death of an innocent child." I look up. "Justice has been done." There is another cheer. I scan the fringes of the crowd but can't see Pip. Emma and Jamie wave at me from the crowd, their banners on stakes wedged into their daughter's pushchair. "We are under no illusions that the road ahead will be easy, and we know that taking Dylan to America for treatment will not guarantee success, but we owe it to him to try."

We. Pip was torn—she said as much in her evidence—but now the decision's been made for her, all she has to do is focus on Dylan getting better.

"We are grateful for the medical care provided to Dylan by St. Elizabeth's Children's Hospital, and we will continue to work with them over the coming weeks, as we prepare to move Dylan to Houston ProTherapy. We are grateful, too, for the support shown to us by people around the world, and for the donations made to Dylan's crowdfunding page. Dr. Sanders has generously waived his charges for Dylan's proton beam therapy, but the associated costs are extremely high, and we will not be able to get there without your help." My mouth is dry; my heart pitter-patters in my chest. I want to find Pip. I want to see Dylan. I don't want to be here, outside the court, in front of a woman who is weeping for a child she's never met. I look around at the faces in the crowd, at Emma and Jamie, at the woman in the red beanie hat, at the strangers with Dylan's face on their T-shirts. I look at them all, and despite their cheers, their shouts, their cries, I see no one I know. No one I feel safe with.

Pip. I need Pip.

"Finally"—I make myself slow down—"these last few months have been incredibly stressful for us as a family, and I ask that you now give us the time and privacy we need to move forward." **Where is Pip?** Tomorrow, there will be as much speculation in the papers about our marriage as there will be about Dylan's treatment.

I look at Laura and nod, and we walk swiftly away from the court. For a few meters we are followed by reporters wanting something more, something exclusive, but we are firm with our **We have nothing further to add at this time**, and they fall away.

In the next street, we part company.

"I can't thank you enough for everything you've done." I shake Laura's hand again. She gives a crisp smile.

"Could have gone either way, to be brutally honest. I'm glad we got the result you wanted."

The result you wanted.

It's carefully phrased, a world away from yesterday's conviction, and as I walk away I wonder what she really thinks. I wonder if she would have argued just as easily on the side of the hospital. **Are you one hundred percent certain you want this to go to court?** she said, at our first meeting. **Whatever the outcome, this is going to have a lasting impact on you and your family.**

It doesn't matter what she thinks. This isn't about me. It's about Dylan. It's about getting him better, about putting my family back together. For the first time in months I feel a ray of hope pushing its way skyward.

after

twenty-six

Pip

2013

Dylan died nineteen days before his third birthday.

"But we were going to have balloons," I said stupidly. Cheryl cried as she helped me clear the locker next to Dylan's empty cot. They took him away after we'd said goodbye—**Take as much time as you need**—and I couldn't bear to think of him spending his birthday in the hospital morgue.

"I want the funeral before May fifth," I said to Max. He nodded mutely, and together we made arrangements that no parent should ever have to make.

The service lasts thirty-five minutes. One for each month of Dylan's life.

We slide into seats still warm from the previous occupants, filing out thirty-five minutes later to find reception already noisy with mourners. I hear **Haven't you grown** and **This can't be Alice**, and it might as well be a wedding, for all the hugging and shaking hands and sharing of laughter, the cheerful ties and smart heeled shoes. Someone old, I think, even before I see the **Granddad** picked out in carnations. Someone who lived enough years for sadness to become relief; for a funeral to become a celebration of their life.

Today isn't what I wanted. I wanted bright colours and songs sung tearfully but enthusiastically by everyone we knew. I wanted friends and family, work colleagues and neighbours. Standing room for the latecomers, orders of service shared three ways, soaring balloons in a cloudless sky.

"I'd suggest keeping things low-key," the police officer said, when they'd filled out the paperwork. "Less chance of the location getting out." On the table between us, a brown paper bag containing my coat.

"You'll get it back after the trial," his colleague told me. She'd written **Max Mara** as one word on the exhibit label. "You might be able to get it cleaned."

I didn't want it back. No amount of chemicals would lift that stain, or take away the metallic smell that still clung to my nostrils.

Pig's blood, she'd told the police. The woman who did it. She was still outside PICU when they arrested her, standing in her red beanie hat, with the tight knot of pro-lifers who had moved from the court to the hospital and who never seemed to go home. She seemed unfazed by the CCTV, by the handcuffs, the charges of criminal damage and common assault.

"Occupational hazard," said the police officer in my kitchen. "She should be looking at prison this time, though," he added cheerfully, as though that was what I wanted. As though that was what mattered. None of it mattered. Not the police, or the ruined coat, or the **Blood on your hands!** she'd screamed in my face. I didn't care.

But there was the dog mess through the letterbox, and the violent gouges that ran like go-faster stripes down my car, and the letters—so many letters—from people who knew so much more than I did about what was right for my son. The man who spat at my parents in the street; the journalists who wanted to **cover the event**, as though Dylan's death were a village fete.

And so the funeral was small and quiet. The crematorium, instead of my childhood church. Voices too thin to be heard. My parents, mourning as much for me as for their grandson. Everyone crying, everyone grieving. And I know it's unjust, and I know I'm not the only one with the right to feel as though her heart is torn out, but still . . . Dylan was **our son**. What right does anyone have to grieve more than us? To cry, when our eyes are dry? When we're trying so hard to keep putting one foot in front of the other?

"Come back with us." My mother's mascara is smudged beneath her eyes. She puts a hand on Max's arm. "Both of you. Stay. As long as you want." Her eyes rest lightly on Max. "You must be tired of living out of a suitcase by now."

"Karen." A warning from Dad. "Let them sort it out themselves." As though it were a teenage squabble. He gives me a smile that isn't really a smile, his lips pressed tightly together, and his brow furrowed in silent acknowledgement of the pain he would take on in a heartbeat instead of me.

"I'll come over at the weekend," I say. "I think I— I think I need to be on my own for a bit."

We watch them leave. Max's mother, Heather, comes to join us. She makes no secret of her grief, and of her resentment that Max didn't ask her to visit while Dylan was in PICU.

"Are you OK?" I ask, because that is what I seem to have done all day—comforted other people, reassured other people. **It will get easier, he's at peace now, I know it's hard. Yes, almost three. Yes, so hard. I know. I know. I'm sorry.** Handing out the words I need to hear myself.

"I'll wait in the car," Heather tells Max.

She hasn't forgiven him. I don't know if she ever will. **Come when he's better**, Max told her. **When he's home.** Such was his conviction that the court would rule in his favour. Only they didn't, and although we might have had time—we might have had months—we didn't. We had three weeks. Three weeks of sitting silently in a room with my silent son, and my equally silent husband. We weren't talking, but we weren't fighting, either. The bitter fury that inhabited Max for the weeks leading up to the hearing evaporated as quickly as it had arrived, both of us wanting nothing to sully the time we had left with our boy.

Three weeks of avoiding protestors, of saying **No comment**, of leaving the hospital together, because it meant less speculation in the papers; then driving in opposite directions, and coming home alone to an answerphone flashing red with requests for interviews.

And then, out of the blue, the call from PICU at two in the morning. **You need to come. You need to come now.**

Max was already there when I arrived, a coat pulled on over my pyjamas and no memory of the miles I'd driven. I looked at his eyes, red rimmed and swollen, and for a second I thought, **I'm too late, I'm too late**, but he reached for me and pulled me to the bed, to where our boy lay quiet but alive, and we stayed that way, the three of us, until the end.

Heather was halfway across the Atlantic when her grandson died. She heard the news in Arrivals, surrounded by joyful reunions and happy tears, and she fell against Max like she'd aged a decade right there. "Once more," she said. "I just wanted to hold him once more."

Music starts up inside the building behind us—fifty voices launching gustily into "How Great Thou Art." Tears prick my eyes. I want to leave but my feet won't move, and maybe Max feels the same, because he isn't leaving either. We stand in silence, and I look at the squares of engraved stone by the entrance and try to imagine coming here, to this conveyor belt of grief, to remember my son. I push my hands deep into my pockets.

"We could have a bench, instead," Max says.

I turn to look at him.

"Instead of a stone," Max says. "At the park, maybe, or the nature reserve. Somewhere we can sit and be with him."

On my fourth date with Max I was finishing his sentences; on our fifth he was finishing mine. By the time we got engaged we could have whole conversations without needing to speak. I remember thinking, **This is it. I've found the half to my whole.**

"We could—" The words catch in my throat as I imagine scattering Dylan's ashes somewhere beautiful, instead of burying them here.

Max nods. "Yes. They said we can collect them next week."

You cannot feel grief without first feeling love, and now my heart is filled with both. For my son, for my husband, for my marriage. Max turns to face me, lines around his eyes that weren't there a month ago. He screws up his nose, blinking away the tears that make his eyes gleam. "I'm so sorry, Pip."

I start to cry.

"I understand if you hate me. I—" He looks up at the sky. Takes a deep, slow breath. When he looks at me again he holds my gaze with fierce determination. "I just couldn't do it, Pip. I couldn't give in. I had to fight, I had to. Even though I knew what it would do to us."

"I missed you," I whisper. A convoy of cars turns into the drive and heads for the car park. Inside the crematorium they're singing the final hymn. They'll be out soon, wiping away tears and giving directions to the wake, saying what a beautiful service it was, how Granddad would have loved it. My hands creep from my pockets, just as Max's make their way to mine.

"Our boy," Max says. "Our beautiful boy." The break in his voice makes my heart hurt. I move into him, my head slotted beneath his chin in the space that must surely have been made for it, and feel his tears dampen my hair.

"Come home," I say, before I can stop myself.

He pulls away, still holding my hands. Searching my face. "Do you mean that?"

"You're the only person in the world who knows exactly how I feel right now. I can't do it without you." And I lean against his chest again and feel the thrumming of his heart, because this is what I've missed the most, that physical proof of life, proof of love. "Please, Max, come home."

twenty-seven

Max

2016

We were married in this church. Pip was baptized here. She walked through the churchyard every day on her way to school, attended Sunday service with her parents, floated sticks in the brook that runs by the lych-gate. And now here we are, saying goodbye to our son.

Today isn't a funeral. A **celebration of life**, we're calling it. **Please join us to celebrate the life of Dylan Adams**, the invitations said; **5 May 2010–1 September 2016.** In front of the congregation, on the projector screen bought for hymns and movies, a slideshow of photographs puts Dylan front and center, a two-foot smile lighting up the church. Some are of Dylan before he got sick, kicking a ball around, but most are more recent. I look at the screen just as the slideshow changes from Dylan at his music group to Dylan on the trampoline. We bought one on the suggestion of his physiotherapist, sinking it into the middle of the garden, to make it easier to transfer Dylan from his chair. He would lie on the trampoline, and we would gently bounce the edges, and Dylan would laugh because to him it must have been like flying.

That laugh filled my heart with joy. It wasn't the laugh of your average six-year-old, and if you didn't know Dylan, maybe you wouldn't even have recognized it as one; certainly there were stares from people in malls, when my boy dared to be happy in public. But it was a laugh. Webster's defines laughter as a **show of emotion with an explosive vocal sound** and I can't think of a better way to describe Dylan's laugh. It wasn't always predictable—he found joy in places I never thought to look—and it came at a volume disproportionate to his small frame. It was as though all the energy that had once powered his now-quiet limbs had instead been channeled into this one sound.

"Penny for them?" Pip's wearing a blue dress, with a lemon-colored cardigan bought especially for today.

"I was thinking about Dylan's laugh."

Her smile is brave. "Earplugs on standby."

I hold her gaze. **OK?** She nods. **No tears**, we'd agreed. **A celebration, not a wake.** Hesitantly, I take her hand and squeeze it. She returns the pressure, but a second later she slips her hand away, fiddling instead with her necklace.

There was a time when I never took Pip's hand, because it was always already there. We would fall into step together, and Pip's fingers would slide into mine, and I wouldn't have felt whole without them. Now, I see other couples walking hand in hand, and I feel . . . not jealous, but sad. Sad that we've lost that closeness. And then I think of everything we've been through, and know that it's a miracle we're walking together at all.

A woman I don't recognize walks hesitantly through the churchyard, a yellow scarf in one hand. "Cousin Ruth," Pip whispers. "She came to our wedding." We're standing in the entrance to the church, greeting guests and handing out the orders of service. On the front of each one, there's a photo of Dylan; on the back, a picture he produced on the computer at school, with the help of their eye-tracking software. It's a riot of color, but if you look carefully you can make out three shapes, distinct yet interconnected. It's called **My Family**, and the original hangs in our hall at home.

"Ruth! So good of you to come."

"I'm so sorry for your loss." She holds up the scarf, uncertain of this departure from convention. "Is this—"

"It's perfect," Pip says. "Thank you." Reassured, Ruth drapes it around her neck, and walks past us into the church.

"No black," Pip said, when we were planning today. "It isn't right. Not for a child, not for Dylan."

And so the dark pews are lifted by bursts of yellow ties, scarves, hats, dresses . . . even a mustard corduroy jacket that Pip's uncle Frank dug out of his wardrobe. Four-year-old Darcy wears a Little Miss Sunshine T-shirt, her dads sporting yellow handkerchiefs in the breast pockets of their jackets.

There are so many people here. Family we haven't seen for years; friends who stuck by us through the tough times, and others who have drifted in and out. Alison and Rupert, Phoebe and Craig, Fiona and Will. Even Emma and Jamie, the young couple whose campaigning raised so much of the money for Dylan's US trip.

There are new friends, too. Parents of Dylan's friends at school, Dylan's teachers, his occupational therapist, his speech therapist, his physio. There are wheelchairs, motorized scooters, buggies. And us. Looking at all of this, and realizing how much Dylan was loved.

I wanted to stay in the States—new starts and all that—but it was never on the table.

"I couldn't live so far away from my parents," Pip said, when I hinted at the idea we might move back to Chicago. I could have reminded her that I'd been doing exactly that for the last ten years, that my mom saw me three times a year, if that.

I didn't. Because of all that was unspoken between us, and had been unspoken since we got on the plane to Houston. Pip didn't only mean Chicago was too far from her folks; she meant **You got your way in court—you don't get to decide what happens next.** I didn't care. We were still a family, that was all that counted.

"I think we're ready to make a start, if you're ready?" The vicar is young. Instead of a surplice, she wears jeans and a yellow shirt, her clerical collar peeking out from underneath.

"Ready," we say together.

There **is** crying, of course—we were optimistic to think there wouldn't be—but for the most part there is just a gentle sadness that the life of our beautiful, brave boy has come to an end.

"We were lucky to have six and a half years with Dylan." I speak slowly, my eyes fixed on a column at the back of the church, for fear they might otherwise land on someone whose grief might spark my own. "In many ways, we were luckier than other parents. We knew our time with Dylan was limited. We have known that since he was two and a half, when we were first told about the cancer that would ultimately take his life. It was devastating. But when you know someone's life is limited, you make every single day count."

Pip didn't want to speak. She said she wouldn't be able to. I glance at her now, and her head is dipped, and I wonder if—despite her lack of faith—she is praying.

"We are grateful for the bonus years we were given with Dylan. Grateful for the friends we made in Houston, who were strong for us when we were struggling, despite the illnesses their own children were battling. Some of the children we met in Texas were not as lucky as Dylan, but many are in remission and leading vibrant, full lives. And that's what we should all do—pack our lives as full as we possibly can. Travel, visit family, make friends, eat, drink, laugh. There was a lot that Dylan wasn't able to do, but there was a heck of a lot he could."

There's more in my notes, but I find suddenly that my voice won't work, and that my legs are shaking beneath me. The vicar, who must be used to such abrupt changes of pace, nods to the organist, who launches into "Amazing Grace" as I stumble back to my seat. Pip puts her arm around me, and as everyone around us stands to sing, we cling to each other like we're drowning.

Afterward everyone takes a handful of yellow petals from the basket Pip's mum holds. We walk down the cobbled path and through the lych-gate, and as we reach the brook and follow its winding path to where our cars are parked, we drop the petals into the water, and sunshine streams downriver.

At home the silence is still too loud. Dylan died a month ago, here, at home, in the bedroom that was once a dining room. The electric bed has been returned to the hire company—collected by two respectful men in logoed polo shirts—along with the hoist, the tilt table, and the frame that held Dylan upright, so he could look out of the window. In the corner is a pile of equipment we will need to find homes for. A commode and bedpan. Packs of continence pads. Bibs. Leg supports. Harnesses. Glide sheets. Therapy wedges to support Dylan on the floor. Thousands of pounds' worth of specialist equipment.

The daybed by the window is still made up. When Dylan came home from hospital it was quickly apparent that we wouldn't hear him from our bedroom upstairs. We tried using a baby monitor, but the seconds it took to wake and get downstairs were too distressing for Dylan, waking scared and uncomfortable in the middle of the night. We put the daybed in his room, and Pip began sleeping here during the week. On Fridays I'd take over, and Pip would move back upstairs.

There comes a point when sleep deprivation becomes the new normal. When the leaden sensation in your limbs and the spacey feeling in your head become the way you live, and you can't remember a time when you bounded out of bed with more energy than you had the night before. Instead you peel yourself from the sheets, too tired even to yawn, and you drink coffee and eat peanut butter toast until you feel human again.

"There's a charity in Birmingham that'll take the lot," Pip says, looking at the pile of equipment. She sits down on the daybed.

"Great." A month since Dylan died, and Pip is still sleeping here.

"I find it comforting," she said. And so, although our nights are no longer broken, Pip remains downstairs, and I sleep upstairs, in a bed that has for a long time been half-empty.

"I wonder," I say, thinking out loud, "if we should sell up." I imagine a new start, a different town, even. I wonder if Pip will be resistant—if she will want to hang on to the memories this house has made—and even now, I can see the beginnings of tears in her eyes. But there's something like realization—or resignation—on her face, and she nods.

"Yes."

An apartment, I think. Something totally different, some modern glass loft. A city, perhaps. Still close enough for Pip's parents to visit.

"A new start," I say.

"Yes." A tear builds slowly on her lower lashes. As I watch, it tips over the edge and trickles down her cheek.

"A new house."

There's a pause. And then: "Two new houses."

I'm slow to understand. Two houses? Why do we need—

"It's over, Max."

twenty-eight

Pip

2013

Max has been back home for three months. Two months, three weeks, five days, to be precise. After the funeral he checked out of his hotel and put his bags in the hall, and stood for a moment, as though he didn't know what to say, what to do. How to **be**.

"Coffee?" I said. Because everything we should really have been saying was too hard.

"Sure."

And that was it. Max was back home, like nothing had happened, like everything was exactly the same as it was a month ago, before Dylan died.

"We don't have to do this now." Max scans my face for doubt. We're standing on the landing, my hand resting on the handle to Dylan's room. "We don't have to do it at all."

"Leave it, you mean? Like some sort of shrine?" There are times when I wake up and it's already Wednesday; others when I look at the clock and can't believe that only a few minutes have passed.

"People do."

Do they? Does clearing Dylan's room mean I love him less?

"No, we should do it now." But still I don't move, the resolve in my voice not reaching my fingertips.

Max nods. "OK." Then he puts his hand over mine and we open the door together.

It's possible to look without seeing. To act without feeling. You just have to close your heart for a while. I kneel on the floor and start sorting Dylan's clothes into piles, picking up jumpers and refolding them without letting myself think about what I'm doing. "The Red Cross will take all these," I say briskly. "Or I can pass them to Alison for the twins—they're small for their age but she could put them aside till they fit."

"I don't want anyone wearing his things." The words are curt, Max's tone harsh. He's holding a xylophone, and as he puts it in the toy box the notes make a dull clink. "The toys, yes. Not his clothes."

"We can't throw them away." I picture Alison's twins—identical, but so different already—in Dylan's T-shirts, the bright diggers and dinosaurs he loved. "I think she'd like something of Dylan's."

"No." Max goes to the window. Summer arrived without my noticing it, and the garden is overgrown and neglected. Grass grows around Dylan's football goal, loved so much for so few weeks. Perhaps we should grow vegetables instead. Create raised beds. Pave over it all. Anything that means I won't look out of the window and hear my two-and-a-half-year-old boy shouting **Go!** I watch Max's back, stiff and uncomfortable, as he looks out at the garden. I realise with a jolt that I don't know what he's thinking, and—worse—that I don't want to ask. Instead I continue sorting clothes, methodically separating what can be worn again from what has seen better days.

"I'll take them to another town," Max says, still with his back to me. "Or to a charity that'll send them overseas. But if I saw another child wearing Dylan's clothes—"

"They make a million identical shirts—"

"—I couldn't handle it."

I spread out the T-shirt I'm holding. It's white with red stripes, an appliqué shark leaping out of blue stitched waves. I mentally take myself to Alison's house, imagine Isaac running to the door in red and white and shark. It feels right. It feels comforting to imagine this scrap of cotton so full of life again.

"OK," I say, because this is how it is now. If Max doesn't want another child wearing Dylan's clothes, the clothes won't be worn. Giving Max his way is small compensation for everything he feels he has lost.

We work in silence, stacking books into boxes for Oxfam, folding sleepsuits and bedding for the NCT sale. Max finds an Allen key to undo the bolts that hold the cot together, and I hold the sections steady while he takes it apart, just as I held them steady three years ago, my bump so big I had to stand sideways.

I'm undone by a sock.

A single tiny white sock, separated from its mate and dropped between the back of the cot and the wall. The sole is grubby, the fabric still pushed into the shape of a foot, and when I pick it up I half expect it to feel warm to the touch, as though Dylan has just this moment pulled it off. I hold it to my face and breathe in the scent of my boy—a physical assault on my senses that makes me lean against the wall to keep myself from falling.

"Oh, sweetie." Max moves to put his arms around me, but I shake my head.

"I'm OK." If I cry now—even for a moment—I am lost. I have learned this the hard way. Crying is not as simple as shedding a tear, then finding a tissue and getting on with my day. Crying is an hour or more, crouched in a corner with my breath coming in hard painful lumps and my nose turning every word into a string of vowels. Crying is that first day lost, and the second lost too, to puffy eyes and a leaden, dragging sensation like waking from Valium-fuelled sleep. Crying is no longer something to be taken lightly.

"Sure?"

"Yep." I put the sock in my pocket. "But let's stop. For a bit."

A bit is a week, and then two, and then four. I
spend a few days with my parents in the autumn, and
when I return Max takes my hands and tells me he's
cleared Dylan's room.

"I put the cot in the loft," he says.

We'd always talked about a big family. Both of us
are only children. Both of us longed for siblings growing up, and yearned for them even more as adults,
with ageing parents and grown-up worries too inti-
mate for friends. Then Dylan fell ill, and now . . . now
it feels wrong. It isn't like buying a car to replace the
one scrapped. Empty arms feel empty forever, even
when they're full again.

"Just in case," Max says, and his eyes slide away
from mine. He shows me the books he's kept, and the
one-eared elephant Dylan flattened into a pillow. Then
he leads me upstairs and I find myself pulling back
slightly because I don't know if I can bear to see the
room empty.

Only it isn't empty.

The blind has been replaced by voile curtains that
pool on the floor, the walls repainted in a soft grey.

"Did you do this?"

Max nods.

"But you hate decorating!"

"It felt different," he said. "Cathartic, almost."
Against one wall, family photos sit on a writing desk
with pigeonholes already filled with notelets and
envelopes. The mug bearing Dylan's one-year-old

288

handprint holds a clutch of pens. In the opposite corner is an armchair, angled to face the window. Beside it, a reading lamp is switched on, a pile of paperbacks waiting to be read. My yarn bag is on the floor, filled with the knitted squares I haven't touched since we left the hospital.

"I thought it could be yours," Max says, as I turn slowly round, taking in all the changes. "Somewhere to knit, or read, or just to—"

"Just to **be**," I finish. "To think." And I resolve that I will not cry in this room, that it will not become a place of sadness, another quiet room. I snake my arms around Max's neck, and feel him breathe out in relief that he did the right thing. "Thank you. It's perfect."

I don't knit in my room. But I do read. I read in a way I haven't read since I was pregnant, when I'd swallow a book in one sitting. When Max is away I spend my evenings here, looking up to realise it's pitch-black outside and I'm stiff from not moving.

"How many this week?" Max asks, when he comes home. He puts his washing in the machine, but leaves his case in the hall. "Washington, DC, on Monday," he says.

"Six." I open a bottle of wine. "I'm working my way through P. D. James."

We eat on our laps in front of the television, half-watching a soap neither of us has bothered to turn off.

The camera cuts to a child in hospital, a tangle of wires across a cellular blanket. I reach for the remote, but Max gets there first, pressing a button—any button—and we finish our meal to the backdrop of a documentary about sheep farming.

"**Meet Me in Mississippi?**" I say, when we've finished eating, and I'm scrolling through channels. "It's got Bill Strachan in it. Great reviews."

Max grimaces. "Saw it on the plane. Sorry. I don't mind seeing it again, though—it's very good."

We settle on a comedy that stops being funny twenty minutes in, and when I look at Max he's fallen asleep, his head tipped back and his mouth slightly open. I slip out from his arm and he doesn't stir. Upstairs my book is waiting, the page marked with my library card, and I wrap myself in a blanket and read until I fall asleep myself.

There was no Christmas—I can't imagine there ever will be again. I wished I could sleep right through it. I took small comfort from thinking there must be others like me—other childless mothers—lying in bed with their eyes squeezed shut, thinking, **Let it be over**; others who do their shopping at midnight in near-empty 24/7 supermarkets, free from excited children tugging at their mothers' skirts and saying **When will he come, when will Santa be here?**

I stayed up, though, to see the date tip from 2013 to

2014, and I felt the beginnings of optimism at the start of a new year. I joined an online book club, spending even more time in my reading room, and tearing myself reluctantly away from my fictional worlds for mundane chores, and to put tea on the table.

I'm doing housework when my mobile rings. It's a rare occurrence nowadays, and by the time I run downstairs, the ringing has stopped and **Alison— Isaac & Toby** shows on my call log. Most of the women I met when Dylan was a baby appear in my phone suffixed by their children. As I ring Alison back I wonder if my name flashes up as **Pip—Dylan**, and whether the sight of it gives her a jolt.

"Hey, you!"

"Sorry I missed your call. I was cleaning the bathroom."

"I thought you had a woman?"

"We did. But it seemed silly keeping her on when I'm here all day, and it gives me something to do." There's a beat, just long enough for me to recognise how pathetic I sound.

"How are you doing?" I hear tapping at the other end of the phone, and I know that Alison is calling from the travel agency where she works. I picture her cradling her mobile between shoulder and ear as she completes someone's booking.

"Great." There will be a to-do list on Alison's desk. **Upgrade for Mr. & Mrs. Runcliffe, download e-learning package, see how Pip's doing.** "Tick!"

"Sorry?"

"Nothing. How are you?"

"Bit fragile, to be honest. Dinner at Phoebe and Craig's, and you know how they drink. Fiona was pissed before the starter and—" She breaks off.

They were carrying on without us. As if we'd never happened.

"It was a last-minute thing," Alison tries. "We didn't think you'd . . ."

"It's fine. I'm fine." I say an abrupt goodbye and put down the phone. I turn off the ringer, watching **Alison—Isaac & Toby** flash up silently a dozen times before it stops. It was a club, I realise. Membership cards issued along with the babies. And now our names have been taken off the list. Three years' membership invalidated by nine months without my son.

I look at my spotless kitchen, at the pile of books to be returned to the library. I think of everything I fit into my day—the cleaning, the cooking, the ten thousand steps I can do before lunch—and how empty the week still feels. How I'm simply killing time until Max comes home. And I realise it's time to go back to work.

twenty-nine

Max

2016

Y ou can't leave me." **Please don't leave me.** "Not after everything we've been through."

"You left me." Pip is still crying, but her voice is hard. She has never forgiven me.

"That was different. Dylan was . . . It was temporary." Those weeks in a hotel are a blur to me now, like a movie I watched too long ago to remember. All I know is that I never once thought that my marriage was over; just that I couldn't share a bed with someone whose decision I was fighting through the courts. I never stopped loving Pip, even when I hated her. I never thought she stopped loving me.

"Would you have come back if the court order had been granted?"

If Dylan had died? I think of the man I was four

years ago, of the precarious state of my marriage back then. "I don't know," I say honestly. It is impossible to imagine life any other way.

"We stayed together because of Dylan."

My stomach tightens. She means it. She's really leaving me.

"But Dylan's gone, and we've said goodbye to him, and now it's time to move on." Her brow is furrowed, like she's in pain, and I think, **If this is physically hurting you, why are you doing it?**

I cross the room, get down on my knees, and put my hands around hers, but she pushes me off and stands up, leaving me on the floor. "Pip, please. I love you, and I know you love me."

She looks out of the window, her back to me, and even though I can't see her face I know what she's going to say.

"It was the wrong thing to do."

After the court ruling, Pip went to the hospital. I found her outside, sitting on the bench beneath the oak tree. She started talking before I reached her, fast and loud, as though she wanted the words out of the way.

"I don't agree, I will never agree, but if you're taking Dylan to America then I'm coming too, and I don't want to ever talk about the court case, or who was right and who was wrong—I don't want to waste any more time not being with Dylan."

We flew to Houston the following week, in an eight-seater chartered air ambulance that would have felt like the height of luxury, had it not been for the medical crew, intensive care bed, and oxygen tanks required to keep Dylan alive. Dr. Sanders's team met us at the airport with an ambulance, and twenty minutes later Dylan was under the care of Houston ProTherapy. And Pip had been true to her word. No recriminations—not even when another bout of pneumonia put Dylan back on a ventilator—no what-might-have-beens. Pip and I stood shoulder-to-shoulder, for the six months we spent in Houston, and for the years since.

Until now.

It was the wrong thing to do.

I scramble to my feet. "How can you say that?" I don't mean to raise my voice, but it doesn't comply. "We had three years we would never have had. He lived for three more years!"

"On his birthday," she says, so quietly I can barely hear, "you and I ate cake and drank champagne. Dylan had synthetic milk through a feeding tube."

My hands, loose by my sides, start to tremble. I fold them into fists, and the tremor moves to my elbows.

"When other kids get colds, they get Calpol. Dylan got suction, catheters, nebulizers, inhalers, antibiotics, seizures." Her voice is rising. "Morphine when he was in pain."

"Hardly ever—"

"Too often!" Pip spins round to look at me. "He had seventeen different types of medication. Every. Single. Day."

295

"They kept him alive—"

"That wasn't a life!" She screams like she's being attacked, like there's no one for miles, like she needs the whole world to hear.

And then she leaves.

Part of me has been waiting for this day for three years. Throughout all the arguments—all the loaded looks and recriminations—I'd kidded myself that Pip stayed because, underneath it all, we had something worth fighting for. Only it wasn't about us, was it? She stayed for Dylan.

I open a bottle of whiskey.

It is six days before I'm sober again. I'm woken by the doorbell, confused by the sun streaming past the open curtains in the bedroom, when the clock on the nightstand reads two o'clock. Is it two o'clock **in the afternoon**? Where has the day gone? What time did I go to bed? Why do I hurt all over?

I open the door, blinking at the light.

"Jesus." Tom Bradford looks me up and down. He wrinkles his nose, and I realize the sour smell I detected when I heaved myself out of bed has followed me downstairs. There's a long pause, then: "It's customary to ask guests if they'd like to come in."

"Sorry." I step back, pulling the door open fully. Tom wears a pair of chinos and an artfully crumpled white linen shirt. I follow him into the house, leaving the front door ajar because I'm suddenly conscious of the stale air. When did I last open a window?

"Alistair told me to pretend I was passing. So . . ."—
he shrugs—"I was just passing, thought I'd pop in
and see how . . ." He trails off as he sees the state of the
kitchen. Crusty cereal bowls line the counter, bypass-
ing the sink, and not quite making it as far as the
dishwasher. Empty bottles circle the full recycling bin.
On the table, two flies fight over a congealed slick of
curdled milk.

"You've taken it well, then?"

I ignore the sarcasm. "Have you spoken to her? Is
she OK?" I wonder if Pip is having some sort of
breakdown.

He eyes me critically. "Better than you." He sighs,
and looks at his watch. "Right, go and have a shower,
strip your bed, and bring the laundry downstairs." He
takes out his phone, and as I'm halfway up the stairs I
hear him say, "Darling, can you do the daycare run?
It's even worse than we thought."

In the bathroom I look in the mirror. My hair is
lank, and dry patches of skin flake off my chin when
I rub it. I clean my teeth, scrubbing my tongue and
gargling Listerine until the fetid taste in my mouth
has gone, then I get in the shower and use every prod-
uct in there. I emerge fifteen minutes later, not quite a
new man, but smelling less like an old one.

"Thank God for that," Tom says when I get downstairs. The kitchen door has been flung open, and the
smell of sour milk replaced with the sharp tang of
citrus.

"Sorry. And thank you. You didn't have to do all that."

"I quite fancied having a cup of tea without contracting botulism, so . . ." Tom opens the fridge, then thinks better of it. "I'll have it black."

Pip is at her parents' house. She doesn't want to see me.

Shock, I conclude. The fallout from losing Dylan, and the memorial service . . . "She just needs time to process it all."

"Max, I don't think she's going to change her mind."

"You don't just fall out of love with someone like that. We've been through so much together, surely we can work this out—"

Tom looks at me. "Let her go, Max." He speaks softly, the words wrapped in sadness. "You can fight and fight for what you want to happen, but sometimes it's just time. Sometimes you have to know when to give up."

It's only afterward, when Tom has gone home, and I'm getting the clean washing out of the machine and hanging it on the drying rack, that it occurs to me he wasn't only talking about my marriage.

thirty

Pip

2015

"Would you like anything else, sir?"

"A beer and your phone number?" The man in seat 3F has amber eyes and an optimistic grin.

"Just a beer, then."

"You can't blame a guy for trying." He grins, and I shake my head and get him his beer, and before too long it's time to dim the lights and distribute extra blankets and pillows. This is my favourite time, when the cabin is quiet and there's nothing outside but dark sky, and nothing inside but the whisper of passengers shifting in their beds. The only seat still upright is 4B, where a woman with frizzy hair flies fingers over silent keys, her face lit up by her laptop screen. I think of Max, who works more than he sleeps, and try to remember his schedule. It's been strange, adjusting to our both working again, to being in different time zones, but I slipped back into my job a year ago like I'd never been away.

"Cuppa?" Jada already has two mugs out.

"Go on, then."

An inch off six feet tall, Jada wears her uniform like she was poured into it. I never put back the weight I lost when Dylan was ill, and on my straight-up-and-down figure the red jacket and pencil skirt look corporate; on Jada, they're undeniably sexy. Her Afro hair is relaxed and, like mine, twisted into a neat chignon.

"Ethan reckons the Ice Bar for shots, then Dusk Till Dawn. Up for it?" The Ice Bar. Airline staff's favourite Hong Kong destination, despite being essentially a walk-in freezer with a cocktail menu.

"Try stopping me."

"Party girls!" She waves her hands in the air and shimmies her hips, and I hide a smile. Jada is twenty-two to my thirty-seven, and her life so far has been such a roller coaster of fun that she assumes everyone else is a passenger on the same ride.

We hit a patch of turbulence an hour before landing, and I keep an eye on the rotund businessman in 1A, who has knocked back a bottle's worth of red and whose florid face has acquired a greenish tinge. I am as relieved as he is to land without mishap, and Jada and I stand by the exit as our passengers leave.

"Thank you, have a nice day." Jada's smile doesn't

move as she adds to me, "Skinny jeans, strapless top, killer heels. You?"

I try to remember what I threw in my case. "Black wrap dress, shoes I can dance in. Thank you, enjoy your stay." The man with the amber eyes winks a goodbye, and despite myself, I blush as he walks away.

"You're in there," Jada says. "You're welcome, goodbye, sir."

"Not my style."

"He's lush."

"Cheating, I mean. I wouldn't. Goodbye, safe travels home."

"He's a catch is he, your Max? You're welcome, have a nice day."

I smile. "I think so." Everyone has gone, and I'm about to tell Jada how generous Max is, and how thoughtful, and how he makes me laugh all the time, when I realise I'm reading from an old script. Max and I haven't laughed together for a long, long time.

The Ice Bar is busy, and Jada and I squeeze through to where the other cabin crew already have their second round of shots lined up. Ethan and Zoe count to three before knocking theirs back; Marilyn, a woman in her late forties with just as much stamina but far more decorum, drinks hers in several small sips. Like Jada and me, they're all wearing the oversized fur coats handed out in reception, looking like they've just discovered Narnia.

I'm surprised to see our pilot, Lars. I've flown with him a few times since joining the airline a year ago, but this is the first time I've seen him socialising.

"Have you been here before?" he asks me, when I've shuffled into the small space between him and the others.

"Years ago, when I was with BA. It hasn't changed." On the wall beside us is a small square hatch cut into the ice, which serves as the bar. A glamorous couple order vodka and clink their glasses together with a toast that could be Russian.

"I didn't realise you'd come from enemy lines." Lars's tone is teasing. "Why the change?"

I shrug. "I switched to short-haul for a bit, but . . ." I hold a sip of vodka in my mouth, then let it warm my throat. Stalling. "I missed the travel. And business class." In fact, it was less about missing business class, and more about avoiding economy.

"All the families," I told my HR manager, "I just don't think I could . . ."

"I understand." She'd lost a baby herself, I knew— arrived for her second scan to find silence in place of a heartbeat. She'd told me the story after Dylan died— not to compare, but to emphasise her assertion that I should take the time I needed. And even when I repaid her kindness by handing in my notice, she was unfailingly on my side.

"A new start," she said, and it felt like an order, so instead of going back to BA I launched into Virgin Atlantic's own special brand of customer service, doing a year in economy before my CV and some good timing put me into what they unashamedly call upper class. Here there are fewer families, fewer young children. It's easier.

Lars eyes me thoughtfully and I think he's going to ask more, but he smiles instead. "You get a different class of reprobate in upper class." He's tall—even taller than Jada—with thick blond hair and a square jaw, and eyebrows so fair they're almost invisible. His accent is flawless, but his surname—Van der Werf—makes my guess a confident one.

"Are you Dutch?"

"Guilty as charged." Around us there is a stirring of movement, and Jada yells across the noise.

"It's bloody freezing in here—you coming?"

"They should turn the heating up," Lars says seriously.

"They should!" Jada hugs her fur coat around her and I catch Lars's eye and grin as we follow the others out of the Ice Bar.

There's a band playing at Dusk Till Dawn, and by three a.m., when we call it a night, my feet are aching and my voice hoarse from singing. We take taxis back to the Park Lane hotel and peel from the elevators onto our respective floors. Jada throws her arms around me as she says goodbye.

"I bloody love you, Pipi-Pip. Shit, I've lost my key card."

"In your hand. I love you too. Drink some water."

She wobbles down the corridor and I hold the lift door until I see she's safely in her room.

"Kids, eh?" Lars says, with an exaggerated eye-roll. I laugh and press the button for the eighteenth floor. "Do you have any?"

"Sorry?" I stare at the lift buttons, watching them light up at each floor we pass. **Fourteen, fifteen.**

"Do you have children?"

Sixteen.

Just one. A boy. Running in the park, playing football with his dad, standing on a chair at the sink so he could help me wash dishes. Mad about diggers—his first word was "truck." Pudgy warm hands around my neck at night. **Sleep tight, Dylan, sweet dreams.**

Seventeen.

Silence stretches into rudeness. I should turn around, look at him, at least, but instead I stare at the buttons, and . . .

Eighteen. There's a ping and an imperceptible jolt, and the doors slide open.

"No," I say, as I step out. "I don't have any children."

thirty-one

Max

2016

I only brought Pip to Mom's house once, right after we got engaged. After that, Mom flew to the UK, or we met downtown, and I'm glad, now, that I didn't fill 912 North Wolcott with memories I can't shake. Instead I see my ten-year-old self, my sixteen-year-old self. I see bikes thrown on the sidewalk, Hubba Bubba and Capri Sun. I see illicit beers my folks knew about but ignored.

I drag my case up the steps, and the front door opens as though she's been waiting by the window ever since my flight landed. Like the street itself, she looks the same, yet different. Older, yet still Mom.

"Oh, my poor boy." She holds out her arms, and I smell musk and baking and the indefinable scent of home. The wind blows a clutch of burnt-orange leaves into the house.

She didn't come to England for the funeral. She visited not long before Dylan passed, hiding her shock at how much he'd deteriorated since her last visit, and by the round-the-clock care he had always needed, but which by then required a nurse as well as either Pip or me.

"We said our goodbyes," she told me, when I offered to buy her ticket. "I don't need a funeral to remember that beautiful boy—he's right here in my heart every single day."

"Pip and I will come and see you soon," I promised. **We**, not **I**.

"I never thought she was good enough for you," Mom says, when we're sitting in the living room, on the bright blue sofa she bought after Dad passed, because **I need some color back in my life.**

"Mom!" It's so outrageous a burst of laughter escapes my lips. "Pip and I have been together for thirteen years, and you have never once said anything of the sort."

"Well, I thought it." She purses her lips and sets down her mug with a clatter. I stifle a yawn, the heat and the jet lag combining to suddenly make me bonetired. "I've made up your old room. Why don't you go take a nap, and I'll fix us some dinner?"

The twin bed I slept in till I was nineteen has been replaced by a double, pushed against the wall to fit it in, and covered with a pink comforter too warm for the season. I don't need to look under the bed to remember the burn in the carpet that grounded me for a month. The walls, once a dirty cream, have long since been repainted, but if I look carefully I can see the grease spots left by the putty gluing my posters to the walls.

I'm exhausted but wired, my head full of a thousand voices, a thousand memories. Pip, when Dylan was born, her hair plastered to her face with sweat, and never looking so beautiful. Dylan playing football, arms swinging with the effort of kicking a ball without falling over. Pip knitting by Dylan's hospital bed, reading him a story. Dylan in Houston. Another scan, another shot of radiation. **Dylan, Dylan, Dylan** . . . I turn onto my side and curl into a ball, my head buried beneath my pillow to block out Pip's voice. **That wasn't a life!**

Dylan lived. He **lived**.

Hot tears push past my eyelids. I remember the way his face lit up when someone he recognized walked into the room, I hear the high-pitched, crazy sound that passed for a laugh. **Dylan lived.** Maybe it wasn't the life we wanted him to live, but it was a life. It was **his** life.

Later—it could be an hour, it could be three— I hear the door pushing open and I know Mom's standing there, trying to decide whether to wake me up or not. The thought of making conversation—the thought of just getting out of this bed—is suddenly overwhelming. I feel safe, in this bedroom that used to be mine, and so I stay here.

I stay for the rest of the day, and for the night. I hear Mom come in, before she goes to bed, and I sense her indecision as she hovers in the doorway. Should she wake me? Say good night? In the end she pads quietly across the room and closes the drapes, and I feel the bed dip as she sits on the side. She sighs, and on top of my guilt at pretending to be asleep, I add the guilt that my mother still has to worry about me, forty years after she started.

Sometime after six I get up to use the bathroom. There's a tight band across my chest, and a fluttering where my heartbeat used to be. I drink a glass of water, but the band pulls tighter. It's like indigestion, only I haven't eaten anything; like a stitch, only I haven't been running. I go back to bed, and only when I'm back in a ball, with the pink comforter pulled over my head, does the band ease enough to let me breathe.

I'm woken by a phone ringing. I feel around for my cell, pulling it into the darkness of my comforter cave. I watch my boss's name flash over and over. I put my thumb over the speaker to dull the ringing that pierces the fog and makes my head hurt, and wait for it to stop.

He calls again an hour later. And an hour after that. I switch the phone to silent, and count the calls for no discernible reason. Seven. Eight. Nine. Mom brings me chicken soup.

"You don't look well. Do you have a fever?"

"I think I might be getting something." The tightness in my chest has been joined by sticky, clammy sweats; by a stomach cramp that sends me rushing for the bathroom.

"Should I call a doctor?"

"No, it'll pass."

It doesn't pass. When I shower, Mom whips through my room, emptying the trash of tissues, and clearing half-drunk cups of water. Occasionally she'll open the window, only for me to shut it again. She brings soup, sandwiches, pieces of roast chicken. Jell-O and ice cream, like I'm nine years old. And all the time, the band in my chest wraps tighter and tighter around me, and the voices in my head grow louder.

Pip's: **That wasn't a life.**

And, louder, mine:

You're a failure.

I turn over again, screw my eyes shut, pull the comforter tight around my head.

Forty years old and you're in the same bedroom you slept in when you were a kid. Your marriage has failed. Your son died.

That wasn't a life.

The band around my chest, tighter and tighter. Sweats. Stomach cramps.

You've got no friends.

I haven't heard that voice since I was thirteen. Since a stupid argument with Danny Steinway that made

309

me hide in the basement after school, convinced he'd tell all the local kids not to speak to me. Then Danny called on me the next day to walk to school, same as he always did.

Except that now, the voice is right. I don't have friends. I have work colleagues, neighbors, people I pass the time of day with. I moved to England to be with Pip. I left my friends to have a family. Pip and Dylan were my friends, my family, my world. If we went out it was Pip who organized it; Pip who met a couple she thought I'd like, who suggested drinks, dinner, the cinema. In PICU she knew everyone's names, knew where the nurses were going on vacation, what year the other kids were in school.

You're a failure.

Why didn't I do those things? My gut twists in another wave of nausea I swallow back down. My whole body aches like I have the flu. Is that what's wrong with me? Do I have the flu?

I don't know if it's the same day, or the next day, when I get the email.

Since you're not taking my calls, I guess I'm going to have to do this by email . . .

Chester.

I know things have been difficult . . . tried to be understanding . . . there is a limit . . .

Have to let you go.

It barely registers. One more bullet point to add to the list.

Lost your wife. Lost your son. Lost your job.

Failure.

thirty-two

Pip

2015

Max kisses my neck, sweeping my hair away to find the spot behind my ear that makes my knees buckle if I'm standing. We're lying in bed, facing each other, the covers pulled up despite the warmth of the evening.

"I've missed you." The words tickle my ear.

"You've seen me for the last three days." Max worked from home on Friday, giving him a long weekend to coincide with three of my four days off. I flew in from Dubai on Friday morning and we went to the café round the corner for a greasy-spoon breakfast that beat my jet lag into submission.

"I've missed **this**."

I move my head and kiss him hard, because it's true

we don't do this as much as we used to, and because kissing is easier than talking. He moves on top of me and holds my face in two cupped hands, and I run my own hands down his smooth back. Max is in better shape than he's ever been, and I'm conscious of my soft belly and low-slung breasts. He dips his head and kisses each one in turn, and I think I should be making a sound, so I shut my eyes and moan softly as he moves down my body.

When he speaks again he's inside me, moving slowly, his whole body pressed against mine, and his lips brushing my cheeks, my nose, my lashes. I lose myself in the warmth that spreads through my body, my back arched and my eyes still closed. Max is murmuring in my ear.

"Let's have a baby."

It's the "a" that does it. As though we haven't had one before. As though we're newlyweds taking a teetering step towards parenthood.

"**Another** baby."

Max stops. He props himself up on his elbows and looks at me. "Yes," he says slowly, "another baby."

I push him off me and roll away. "It's too soon."

"It's been two years."

I go to the bathroom and shut the door. Two years. Is there a time limit on grief? Should I be ready by now? I know I appear to be functioning normally. I work, I socialise. I don't burst into tears at inopportune moments, and no one—not a single person—ever takes me to one side anymore to ask **How are you doing, Pip?**

And yet.

When I come out of the bathroom Max has put on the jogging bottoms and T-shirt that pass for his pyjamas, and is sitting on the edge of the bed. "Can we talk about this?"

I nod, although I don't know if I can, and sit next to him. He stares at the dressing table while he talks, and I'm glad of it, because although I can't explain why, it is easier to have this conversation without looking at each other.

"I'm not trying to replace Dylan."

I take a sharp intake of breath.

"I want another child because I want to be a parent."

"You are a parent," I say, but the response is hollow, and I hear the echo of my own words to Lars, as the lift door closed. **No. I don't have any children.** Max and I aren't parents. We're nothing. Childless by neither choice nor genetics. We had everything we wanted, and it was taken away, and now we're just people, sitting on the edge of a bed, trying to function as two instead of three.

"I want to kick a ball around with my son, I want to teach my daughter to play golf." He's talking quickly, his voice getting louder with each declaration. "I want to go to school plays and host Thanksgivings, and talk to other dads about what a nightmare the teenage years are. I want to give my kids advice and have them ignore it; see them grow up, make mistakes, come good." I feel him look at me. "I want to be a dad again, Pip."

There is an unspoken accusation—**You took that away from me**—and I hear again the venom in his voice that day at court. **You signed your own son's death warrant.** I don't turn my head.

"Please."

The word holds the promise of tears, and anxiety builds, ready and waiting. If Max cries, I cry. And I don't want to cry. I'm holding it together, I'm feeling as normal as it's possible for me to feel, and he's unravelling it all right before my eyes.

"I can't," I manage, staring at the dressing table. I count each object. Hair straighteners, jewellery box, basket of makeup. A trinket dish for coins and rings. An empty water glass, cloudy from the dishwasher.

"Why not?" This time he makes me look at him, pulling my shoulder round until we're facing each other. "You were such a great mom."

Were.

He's crying openly now, and no matter how hard I swallow or blink or count to ten I can't stop it happening. I'm breaking his heart all over again, and I owe him more than simply **I can't.**

I find the words. "I can't love a child all over again, only to lose them."

315

"That won't happen."

"You don't know that!" It's me who's crying now, noisy thick sobs that tear at my chest and wrack my body. "I can't do it, Max, I can't and I won't."

And for the second time in our marriage, there is no compromise to be found.

Max doesn't bring up the subject again, but I know he's thinking about it. I see it in his face when he smiles at passing children, and I feel it in the air between us when Chris Evans speaks to excited kids on his breakfast show.

"What are you doing for the first time today, Zak?"

"I'm playing the trumpet in the school concert."

I can't. I just can't.

Sometimes I dream that I'm pregnant, or I take the gurgle of an empty stomach for the quickening of early pregnancy, and my heart stops for a split second until logic takes over again. Sometimes I see a child in a wheelchair, or a specially adapted pushchair—or read an article in the paper about accomplishments **despite the odds**—and I'm overwhelmed with fear and guilt that we did the wrong thing. That **I** did the wrong thing.

I know I have a problem. I know that it is not rational to cross the street to avoid an oncoming pram, or to make excuses at work not to speak to families. I know that grief and guilt have morphed into behaviour that is far from normal, but knowing it doesn't keep it in check.

It's May when things come to a head, when I'm working one of those flights where everything goes wrong. We're delayed by fog, and when we eventually leave, even the upper-class passengers—placated with pre-takeoff champagne—are grouchy and impatient. It's seven hours to Dubai, and three hours in, the place is in chaos. After an hour held on the runway, the passengers are fidgety and out of their seats, blocking the aisles and slowing down the drinks service. The noise level is building, and the queue for the loos is spilling through the curtain separating economy from upper class.

"Pip, can you lend a hand in economy?" Derek, unflappable and with enviably groomed eyebrows, is our flight service manager today. "Things are going south fast."

There's a buzz as the cockpit door opens, and Lars emerges for his rest break, catching the last few words and looking enquiringly at Derek.

"No biggie," Derek says, "but we've had a spillage and two vomits, and there are newlyweds in row twenty-three conducting their own in-flight entertainment."

"Put the seat belt sign on for twenty minutes," Lars says.

With the aisles clear and no one queuing for the toilets, we can get the galleys straight. The vomiters are handed ice cubes to suck, and the spillage is mopped up, and Derek gives the newlyweds a blanket. I make a final check as I walk back to upper class.

"Excuse me, will the seat belt signs go off soon?" The woman in 13E is around my age. She has long dark hair in a plait over one shoulder, and a fringe that meets her top lashes. Next to her, in 13D, is a boy of around eight or nine. "He'll need the loo and he won't be able to hold it if there are lots of people waiting— I'd like to get there first if that's possible."

The boy is disabled. His head rests on his seat, but tipped to one side in a way that doesn't look comfortable. His free arm makes small jerking movements. I smile at him and he beams back.

"You can go now."

"Oh, thank you!" She unclips their seat belts and helps her son stand. He is mobile, but clumsy, each foot finding its place like a toddler's as he makes his way up the aisle ahead of her. "It's his first flight, and I've been ever so worried about how he'll cope." She lowers her voice. "The doctors said he'd never walk. Can you believe it?"

I feel suddenly cold, although the cabin is warm, and I make myself smile and say **Incredible, he's a lovely boy, you must be so proud**, and then I walk back to upper class and to the galley, where Jada is clearing away lunch and Lars is leaning against the counter, drinking coffee and getting in the way. I think about the judge's ruling, and about the evidence we heard that week; about Dr. Gregory Sanders's conviction that proton beam therapy would take away Dylan's tumour. I think about the professor, and his special school for disabled children. I picture Dylan, learning how to make sounds, to use a computer. On a plane, on holiday, in the sea. There's a buzzing in my ear and I lean against the counter, too light-headed to stand straight.

"You OK, hon?" Jada says.

There's nowhere to go, on a plane. No retreating to the ladies', or ducking out for a walk around the block. Hiding from the public, from colleagues, from yourself. "I'm fine." I smile brightly, and because Jada has never had to hide behind a smile, that's all the reassurance she needs.

It's Lars who isn't convinced, whose eyes follow me as I get myself a glass of water and drink it right down. Lars who waits until Jada is dealing with a passenger, to say, "What happened?"

And perhaps if he'd asked, as Jada had, whether I was OK, or said **Are you sure**, or **Is there anything you need?** I'd have closed him down. **I'm fine, yes I'm sure, no thank you.** But he asked the right question. He asked **What happened?**

I watch the clouds beyond the window. "My son died. The court ruled that he should be allowed to die, even though my husband disagreed."

"That was you." He says it quietly, almost to himself.

"That was me." I look at him, and I feel my face twist into tears. "And I think I got it wrong."

thirty-three

Max

2016

"Now get dressed." Mom stands outside the bathroom door, holding clothes she's taken from the suitcase I've barely touched in the two months since I arrived. Jeans, T-shirt, socks . . . all neatly folded, like she's sending me to summer camp. I guess I should feel something—shame, perhaps, that my mom's picking out my clothes—but there's nothing there. I'm numb.

"Later. I'm going to take a nap, I still don't feel well." I pull my bathrobe tighter around me, but she pushes the clothes at me, removing her hands so I have to take the pile or let it fall. I'm tired, I need to sleep. My body clock has gone crazy, with something that can't still be jet lag but may as well be. At night I lie awake, anxiety seeping like poison through my body, watching the clock mark every hour of the sleep

I won't see. In the day my body screams for rest, moving reluctantly from bed to sofa and back again, seeking the over-hot weight of the pink comforter. My eyes are hollow and I'm out of shape, with the long nails and overgrown beard of a vagrant. I look in the mirror and see a man I don't know.

I walk past Mom to my room, then stop short. I turn back and glare at her. The pink comforter is gone, the bed stripped, the mattress bare.

"Laundry day," she says brightly, like she doesn't know what it's doing to me.

"Christ, Mom, I'm sick!" I drop the pile of clothes on the floor and bang my fist against the doorjamb. She flinches, but stands her ground, and I hate myself for taking this out on her. "I just can't shift this virus, I . . ."

You're a failure.

I cover my face with my hands, my fingers splayed and my nails digging into my scalp. I hear a choking sound and realize that it's me. Mom puts a hand on my arm.

"You're not well, Max."

"I've been telling you that for weeks!" I shake her off, but she steps forward and puts her arms around me, squeezing me tight like she hasn't done in years because I'm the one who's done the squeezing. She's getting old, she should be taking it easy, not washing my sheets and getting my clothes, and holding me to stop me from breaking.

You're a failure.

The tears come from deep inside me. Hot, shameful, pathetic tears that leave me angry and exhausted. And Mom holds me till I'm done, and then she gently pulls away and I see she's crying too.

"Tell me how to help you, Max. I can't bear to see you like this."

But my throat is too tight to speak, and even if it weren't I don't have anything to say. There is nothing she can do. Nothing anyone can do. I stumble like a drunkard into the room, and fall onto the bed, curling into a ball. I hear Mom crying and I want to pull the comforter over my head, but she's taken it and I don't know if it's her I hate, or me.

"Oh, Max . . ." She's still crying, tears lacing her words. "I lost that little boy too, you know." And I want her to hold me again, I want to cry in her arms and tell her how much I miss Dylan and Pip, but I can't because I'm a failure. A screw-up. A waste of oxygen.

A week after Thanksgiving she tries again.

"The faucet's dripping—can you take a look?"

I'm on the sofa, watching **The Price Is Right**, my pajamas changed for near-identical gray sweatpants and T-shirt. "Call a plumber."

"Sonia Barking, come on down!" Drew Carey

beams from the TV like he's saying **See how much happier I am than you! How much more successful!**

"I can't get anyone. It's only a washer. Please, Max, it won't take a minute."

It takes thirty.

"I'm going back to bed."

"Since the toolbox is out anyway, how about fixing that loose carpet at the top of the stairs?"

"I know what you're trying to do, Mom." I stalk past her and up the stairs. She follows me, and I feel a sharp stab of guilt as I realize she's lugging the toolbox up with her.

"I almost tripped this morning. Gave me quite a scare—the idea of tumbling right down to the bottom."

I fix the carpet. Then I tighten the loose handrail, and replace a slipped tile on the porch roof. I move an old dresser to the basement, and fill Mom's trunk with clothes she wants to take to Goodwill. I'm clearing the yard when I hear voices.

"He's out back."

I wipe my hands on my sweatpants. Mom appears on the back steps, with a woman I've never seen before. She's about my age, with a mass of dark corkscrew curls that bob about her shoulders when she moves her head.

"Hey."

"You remember Blair, right?"

"I—" I look blankly at the pair of them. I've been awake and upright for longer than any single period since I arrived in Chicago, I'm aching for my bed, and I have no idea who this woman is.

Blair laughs. "It was a long time ago. To be honest, I don't think I'd recognize you, if I passed you in the street. Last time I saw you, you were probably on your BMX and wearing an Incredible Hulk T-shirt, or holding your breath at the Y."

It's one of those crazy Novembers where the temperature's falling but the sun won't quite give up, and I squint up at her. Who is this woman, who can take me back to 1986 in a single sentence? The corkscrew curls tug at my memory, but the recent weeks have dulled my brain and filled it with cotton.

"Blair is Bob and Linda's daughter, honey. From next door?"

And in a rush, it comes back. Ten-year-old Blair Arnold, with her boy's shorts and scraped knees, forever wanting to play with Danny and me. Tugging off her swim cap at the end of a session, releasing a mass of dark curls. I stand up. "You moved away."

"Pop got a job in Pittsburgh. It didn't work out, but when we came back they bought a place in Lincoln Park, so I stayed over that side of town."

"I'll make coffee, shall I?" Mom says. "You'll stay for some coffee, will you, Blair? So lovely of you to drop in."

There's a flicker of surprise on Blair's face, then it's

gone, and she smiles broadly at me. "Must be—what?—thirty years?"

I shrug. "An easy thirty."

Mom puts a hand on my shoulder. "Honey, Blair had a—"

"Shall I make the coffee? Do you want me to make the coffee? Or I can give you a hand here, if you like, Max?" After so much time alone in my room, Blair's sudden prattle is overwhelming. I take a step away, and she stops and gives Mom a look.

"What?" I snap. There's an awkward silence, and Mom retreats to the kitchen.

"I'll fix the coffee," Mom says. "You two stay and chat."

Chat. I have lost the ability to make small talk. No—I have lost the **desire** to make small talk. Life is bigger than that.

"Heather got you earning your keep, then?" Blair says after a while, nodding to the pile of garden waste at my feet. "I moved in with my folks for a while after my divorce and they did the same. I found my own place pretty quick." She grins. "I guess that was the idea."

The emphasis on "**my**" divorce tells me she already knows why I'm here. I wonder how much Mom's told her. Just about Pip, or about Dylan, too? Did she tell Blair I was a mess? A failure? I look at this woman, with her shiny hair and straight white teeth; her wide smile and clean, pressed clothes. I see her walking around Disney World with two perfect kids; perfect grades, perfect manners, perfect health . . .

"You got kids?"

If she finds me abrupt, it doesn't faze her. "Two. One of each."

Of course. So predictable. So perfect.

"My mom asked you to come, didn't she?"

She has the good grace to blush. "I bumped into her at a fund-raiser at Happy Village—I've still got friends in the neighborhood—and she mentioned you were back. Said you'd had a tough time." She tips her head to the side, her lips in a downturn of sympathy, and I know this is a part she's played before. Blair Arnold bakes for friends when they have babies, leaves pies on the porches of grieving neighbors. She sympathizes, empathizes, tips her head and gives that sad smile, then goes back home to her perfect kids to enjoy the warm glow of the professional do-gooder.

"Excuse me." I walk past her. "I should go **earn my keep.**" In the kitchen, Mom's fixed a tray of coffee, six cookies arranged neatly on a plate. "I'm going to bed."

"Max!"

"It's OK." I hear Blair come into the kitchen just as I leave it. "Let him go."

From my bedroom their voices drift from downstairs, punctuated by the chink of crockery.

"She just walked out on him, after everything they've been through."

"I guess she's hurting, too."

"So she, of all people, should understand!"

"That doesn't mean she can help."

I sit on the bed, wanting to bury myself beneath the comforter, but needing to hear what they're saying about me. About Pip.

"It's like when two people have the flu," Blair says. "They know how the other feels, but they're too sick to nurse each other. They both need to get better first."

I lie down on top of the comforter and close my eyes. There is no getting better. This is it—this is how I am now, how I'll always be. And for the first time ever, I understand why people decide life isn't worth living. Sometimes it isn't.

thirty-four

Pip

2015

"Thank you for seeing me. I—I wasn't sure you would."

"Why wouldn't I?"

It's been more than two years since I saw Dr. Khalili outside the courtroom. She didn't come back to work right away, and when Dylan died it was Cheryl who handed us the small box of his things, with the book of poems put together by Friends of PICU, and the leaflet on **coping with the loss of a child.**

"What I said after the ruling," I say, forcing myself to meet her gaze. "It was . . ." **This is all your fault . . .** I'm hot with shame as I remember how I hissed the words, how she recoiled as though I'd spat in her face. "It was unforgivable."

She shakes her head. "It was a stressful time." Her

fingers play with the lanyard around her neck. "I can't imagine what it must have been like for you."

I thought she would arrange a meeting at the hospital. I'd steeled myself to see the same corridors, smell the same strange mix of industrial cleaner and canteen food. But Dr. Khalili—Leila, as she prompts me to call her—suggested here, a café around the corner from the hospital. "I thought it might be easier for you to meet somewhere other than the hospital," she says now.

"It is. Thank you."

"Plus, to be honest—" She breaks off, and a faint flush creeps across her cheeks. "This isn't how it's done."

"You're not allowed to talk to me?"

There's a pause while we order two coffees, and listen to a roll call of cakes neither of us wants.

"It's not that I'm not **allowed**," Leila says, once the waitress has left. "There are protocols." The hint of an eye-roll lets me know exactly what she thinks of these protocols. "Forms to fill in, a process for patients and the families of patients to request a debrief or to make a complaint—"

"I'm not making a complaint."

"Even so. Protocols."

"And you're breaking them?"

Leila shrugs.

"Why?"

"Because I'm tired? Disillusioned? Because I don't

see how they help? Because you and your husband went through a living hell two years ago, and if talking to you in a café the day after you ask to see me means you don't have to wait six months for someone in an office to put in place the correct process, then that feels like the right thing to do." She stops suddenly, as though she's run out of steam. For the first time, it occurs to me that when a patient dies, the doctors lose someone, too, and although it can't be like losing a child, or a sister, or a father, it is nevertheless a loss. It must hurt.

Our coffee arrives and we sit in silence, me adding milk to mine, and her adding sugar and stirring longer than is necessary.

"I thought we'd have more time with him," I say eventually. I stare at my drink. "You told us we might only have a few weeks, but I thought . . . we'd been in PICU for so long already and he hadn't got better, but he hadn't got worse, and so I thought . . ." I look at her. "I felt like I was being punished."

"Punished?"

"For not sending him to America. For going against Max. For taking the easy way out."

"Easy? There's nothing easy about what you did, Pip."

We sit in silence for a while.

"I think," Leila says, after a while, "that however long Dylan had lived, you would always have hoped for more time."

"I—I keep wondering if we did the right thing." I tell her about the flight to Dubai, and the child who walked like a toddler, but nevertheless put one foot in front of the other. The child the doctors said would never walk unaided. I tell her about the articles I read, about the brain-damaged children who defy the odds. I try to put into words what I want to say, without being rude, without accusing her . . .

"What if you were wrong?" There is no other way to say it.

Leila nods slowly. She blows on her coffee and takes a sip, then sets her cup back down in its saucer and folds her hands around it. "I could have been wrong."

The breath I take pushes me backwards in my chair. Every sound is heightened—the clink of knives on plates, the hiss of the coffee machine, the scratch of the waitress's pen on her pad. I picture the boy on the plane, only now it's Dylan—the dark mop of hair replaced with my son's brown curls—and he's making his way not away up the aisle, but towards me, towards Max . . .

"But I could have been right."

The words pull me back. Back to the café around the corner from the hospital, with the doctor I once thought I never wanted to see again.

Leila sighs, and leans forwards so her forearms rest either side of her coffee, her hands clasped together. "We're used to science providing us with answers. Cures and breakthroughs and discoveries. But there are still more questions than there are answers." She closes her eyes for a fraction longer than a blink.

"None of us has a crystal ball," she says. "None of us—not you, or me, or the court—could say for certain what Dylan's future would be like. All we could do was make the best decision possible, based on the information available to us."

Frustration makes me dogged.

"But do you think it was the **right** decision?"

"All the evidence pointed towards—"

"No!" A couple on the next table look up. "What do **you** think? Was Max right? Should we have given Dylan a better chance at life?" Leila's looking down at her coffee, and I'm suddenly incensed by the lack of eye contact, the lack of compassion. I raise my voice, heedless of the other customers listening. "Maybe Dylan **would** have walked. Maybe he **would** have known who we were. Maybe he would have enjoyed music, or stories, or—" I break off, because my heart is bursting with love and guilt and loss, and I'm thinking of Max and how I almost lost him too, all because he did what he thought was right.

"Was Max right?" I finish, quiet now.

Leila looks up, and I'm horrified to see that she's crying. Tears stream down her cheeks and she wipes them away with angry hands. "I don't know. I just don't know." Not a doctor, now, but a woman haunted by a decision she had no choice but to try to make. "And,

Pip, I promise you, there isn't a day that goes by when I don't think about your boy."

We stay in the café long after our cups are empty, talking about life after Dylan. She tells me about her mother in Tehran, who refuses to consider moving to the UK to be with Leila, despite worsening health, and I tell her how I'm too scared to have another baby. We don't try to solve each other's problems, but we listen, and sympathise, and say **What will be will be**. Because the future isn't always in our control.

"I'd better go," Leila says, when her mobile has buzzed for the third time in a few minutes.

"Work?" I picture the busy PICU ward, a critical child, anxious parents.

"A friend." She hesitates. "Boyfriend, I suppose." Her cheeks colour, and she looks suddenly shy. "In fact, in a funny sort of way we're only together because of Dylan." She shakes her head at my confusion, and smiles. "It's a long story."

We stand, and it's awkward for a second, and then we both move at once, into the sort of hug that says everything and nothing.

"If you ever want to talk about it again," she says, "you've got my number."

"And you've got mine. Thank you."

Outside, we say goodbye, and as I go to my car I see

her cross the road to where an older man is leaning against a lamppost. His face lights up when he sees her. They embrace and walk away, her arm tucked through his. She will tell him, tonight, about meeting me and about what we said. She'll say how I cried, and she cried, and maybe she'll cry again and he'll hold her and say everything she said to me. That there are no right answers, no crystal balls. Only instinct, and hoping, and doing what feels right.

I envy their closeness—the way they fit seamlessly into each other, the way Max and I always used to— and I wonder how Dylan could possibly have played a part in bringing them together. I think how Max was never supposed to be on the flight I was working, the day we met, and how we found ourselves in the same bar hours later. Serendipity, Max called it. Destiny, I called it. Some things are simply meant to be.

A listair and Tom have invited us for Sunday lunch." I show Max the text. Above it, in a stream of messages that continued long after Alison, Phoebe, or Fiona stopped trying, are two years' worth of refused invitations. Dinner next weekend? Working, sorry. Walk by the river? Sorry, we're busy. At times, when it was all too much, the message thread is silent on my side, with gentle persistence—Coffee? Lunch?—and support on Tom's. Hey you. Thinking of you. Hope all's OK.

"Do you want to go?" Max looks for my lead. He hasn't avoided invitations, as I have, but then the social calendar fell to me by default, once cocktails and dinner became soft play and picnics. I realise I don't know how he feels when he sees families with children, whether he turns over the TV channel to spare his own feelings or mine. Somehow over the last two years we have stopped talking—we each have tiptoed around the very person who understands.

"I think we should. We haven't been out with anyone, since." The sentence is complete—our own shorthand for life after Dylan.

Max gives a wry smile. "We haven't been out as a couple, either."

I look away. It's not right that seeing Tom and Alistair should feel easier than going out for dinner with the man I love. It's not right that we eat on our laps in front of the TV every night we're together, or that we talk more by text, several time zones apart, than we do face-to-face. Max and I were a couple long before we became parents—surely we can get that back now we aren't?

You said you'd get horseradish."

"I said we **need** horseradish."

"You said you'd get it!"

"I didn't!"

I catch Max's eye and we both laugh.

"Glad to see it's not just us," Max says. Tom and Alistair break off from their bickering and grin good-naturedly. Alistair rolls his eyes.

"If it was down to Tom, the cupboards would be bare, and this one"—he drops a kiss on Darcy's curls—"would starve."

"If it was down to Alistair, we'd have takeaway every night, and that one would look like Buddha." Tom looks at Alistair, eyebrows raised, but he can't sustain it and they both break off, laughing. "Right, let's eat!" He takes his seat at the end of the table and waves a hand expansively. "Beef, potatoes, parsnips, peas, carrots, and some sort of cheesy thing I bought at M & S and am pretending is homemade."

"It looks amazing."

"Hungry, cherub?" Darcy's high chair is pushed up to the table next to Alistair, and she bangs a plastic spoon against her tray in anticipation, as her dad fills her plate and cuts her food into bite-size pieces. "Do you think she should have molars by now? It can't be easy, chewing beef with your gums."

"Not the way you cook it, certainly." Tom blows a kiss down the table, and Alistair pretends not to have heard.

"Dylan's were late coming through," Max says. It jolts me, not because I don't talk about him, but because other people don't. Mentioning his name prompts awkwardness and silence; embarrassed flushes and changes of subject. People shy away as though losing a child is catching, as though talking about it breaks some unwritten rule.

"That's reassuring. Hear that, cherub?"

Something brushes against my leg. Max's foot stroking mine. I look up to find him watching me. **OK?** he says silently. **OK**, I tell him. I can still read him, I realise, and he can still read me. We just haven't been listening to each other.

At close to three years old, Darcy Bradford has her fathers wrapped around her perfectly formed little finger. She was late to walk, and seems to have adopted a similar approach to talking.

"She's had lots of tests," Tom says, "and neurologically speaking, there's nothing wrong with her. She just doesn't want to speak."

"Probably can't get a word in edgeways." Alistair leans across the table and refills my wineglass.

"They all get there in their own time," I say. "Dylan said his first word really early, but it was ages before he said anything else." I look at Max. "Do you remember? Then he said 'Dada.'"

Max smiles. "To every man we met, from the postman to the supermarket cashier. Gave me quite a complex, I can tell you." We all laugh, and I feel Max's leg pressed tight against mine. I hold his gaze, and something relaxes inside me, as though I've been holding my breath. We've had two years without Dylan, but we had longer with him. We had holidays and birthday parties and cuddles—so many cuddles. We were lucky—luckier than many, many couples.

"This is lovely." I look between Tom and Alistair. "Thank you for inviting us."

"We were on the brink of sending out a search party and staging an intervention."

I flush. "It's been hard."

Alistair puts a hand over mine. When he speaks, the jesting tone has gone. "We simply can't imagine." They both look at Darcy, who is smearing cheesy leeks across her face with unqualified delight.

"It could just as easily have been us," Tom says, and there was a time when I might have thought, **Why wasn't it? Why was it us instead?** but I don't. It could have been them. It could have been the Slaters in the bed next to Dylan. It could have been—it **is**—any number of families across the world. Right this moment, two other parents are sitting in a quiet room, holding hands and listening to the words that will end their world.

I hold Max's gaze and raise my glass. "To the children."

"To the children!" the others repeat.

"Do you think you'll have any more?"

Alistair shoots Tom a glance. "Tom!"

I shake my head. "I can't go through that again." I catch Max's face harden.

"Totally understandable," Tom says. "We won't

have any more. Although there's a woman started at work with flaming-red hair. Imagine that hair, swith my bone structure and—" He's interrupted by Alistair's napkin flying across the table and landing on his plate.

"You, Thomas Bradford, are incorrigible."

Tom dips his head. "And that, Alistair Bradford, is precisely why you married me."

I move my foot to nudge Max's, but it isn't there, and when I look at him, to continue our silent conversation, he doesn't meet my eyes.

thirty-five

Max

2016

I tell Mom I don't want to do anything this Christmas. She goes to her sister's instead, where she can play with Cousin Addison's living, breathing children, and I lie on my bed and think about Dylan. I figure she'll be gone till around four, which means I have six hours to cry.

Pip used to say it made her feel better.

"I probably just need a good cry," she said once, at the end of a long week, when she was low and slightly tetchy. It was before we had anything meaningful to cry over, and she put on **Titanic**, and sobbed over Kate and Leo, and threw a cushion at me for making fun of her.

A **good cry**. The ultimate oxymoron. There is nothing good about crying—about my crying. My tears seem to come from deep inside me, ugly, noisy sobs that wrack my whole body and stop me from breathing. The more I cry, the more I cry, until it's physically hurting. And all the while the voice in my head: **You're such a failure. Real men don't cry. Look at you: bawling your eyes out in your mom's house like a lovesick teenager. Get a grip. No wonder Pip left you.**

Last Christmas Dylan was five and a half, his needs so great he couldn't stay anywhere but in his own room or at the respite center he visited three weekends a year. Pip's parents came for three days, their car groaning with food, and with presents that had been the subject of several stressful phone calls.

"You don't need to get him anything," Pip kept saying, but Karen wouldn't be dissuaded. The previous year she and Pip's dad had helped Dylan unwrap toys he wouldn't be able to play with, and I'd watched Karen's face crumple as she'd realized her mistake.

They settled on mittens—poor circulation meant Dylan's extremities were always freezing—and a lamp with streams of tiny bubbles inside. I have a sharp memory of his face when we switched on the light, the loud cry of joy, and I curl tighter into myself, the tears coming even faster.

I guess Pip'll be with her parents today. I wonder what they're doing, if they're thinking about last year, like I am. I close my fist around my cell phone—**I miss you so much**—tap her number and watch the screen as it tries to connect. Then I think about Pip's words to

341

me—**That wasn't a life**—and cancel the call. She probably isn't missing him at all. Maybe she's relieved. Happy, even. She's got her life back.

I throw the phone onto the bed beside me, but—as though prompted by the action—it starts to ring. **Pip calling.** Shit shit shit shit. I watch her name flash up, and as though it doesn't belong to me, my hand creeps out and takes the call.

For a moment I think she's rung off and there's no one there. But then I hear a choking noise and I realize that, four thousand miles away, Pip is crying too. I lie on my bed, the phone pressed to my ear, and listen to Pip try to catch her breath. When she speaks, it's a whisper.

"I miss him so much it hurts."

We cry together, the same boy in hearts either side of an ocean. The only two people in the world who know how we feel. When it's over, and my phone lies quiet again by my side, I sleep. And when I wake up, my eyes are swollen and my nose is blocked, my heart still hurts. But I feel a little better.

Mom hits the stores for the January sales. She's meeting Blair and her mother at Old Orchard mall.

"You should join us—it might do you good to get out."

"Why would I want to go shopping with some

woman I didn't even want to hang out with when I was ten?"

Mom looks like she's about to snap back, but she takes a breath and says: "I might be back by lunchtime, anyway. Linda can be awful prickly around Blair—they have a difficult relationship."

"Not so perfect after all," I say, half to myself. My mother looks at me sadly.

"When did you become so unpleasant, Max Adams?"

"Oh, I don't know," I bite back. "When I lost my son and my wife in one month, maybe?" Something shrivels inside my stomach. I loathe this man I'm trapped inside, but I don't know how else to be. I've lost count of how many times Mom's tried to get me to see a doctor, a therapist, but what would be the point? They can't change what's happened. They can't change who I am.

"Do you need me to pick you up anything?" Mom says as she's leaving. "Pants? Shirts?"

I'm forty years old, out of work, and my mother's offering to buy my clothes for me. What the fuck happened to my life?

When she's gone, I take a shower, then I wrap a towel around my waist and fill the basin with warm water. I lather up, but stop short of bringing the razor to my cheek. Do I want to see that face? I can't be that person again—why remind myself every time I look in the mirror? I wash off the soap. I neaten my beard but keep it full. My hair hasn't been cut in four months, and there's a curl in it I haven't seen since I was a kid.

Instead of the sweatpants I've lived in since September, I put on proper clothes. Jeans, a shirt, socks and shoes. They feel odd and uncomfortable, and I wonder how I wore a suit and tie every day. I open my laptop.

I joined Kucher Consulting as a business analyst, straight out of college. By rights, I should have done an MBA, but Chester liked me enough to offer me a DTA—direct to associate—testing me out with more and more client contact. I was ecstatic—I had neither the money nor the inclination to go back to school for two years—and by the time I met Pip I was an associate partner.

Where does that leave me now? Experienced but underqualified, in a field full of competition with youth on their side and letters after their name.

I start with Chester.

"I'm better." The ensuing pause isn't promising. "I'd like to come back."

"Thing is, Max, we had to restructure . . ."

"So restructure again. I'm good, Chester, you know I am. I'm back in Chicago, I can meet with clients on the ground, I—"

"You left us in the shit, Max. We lost PWK. Schulman walked out."

"My son died."

"I know." Chester sighs. "Christ, I know. I'm sorry. But . . . I'm sorry."

I hit up Google. I try three consultancies too small to have ever troubled Kucher. Two aren't hiring; the third takes my details.

"Who are you with currently?"

"I was with Kucher Consulting till last fall, then I took a break to relocate from the UK to Chicago." I sound more confident than I feel.

"We'll get back to you."

They don't. Nor does anyone else.

"The depression might be an issue," says a slick recruitment adviser with a loud tie.

"Stress," I correct, although I don't know which sounds worse. "But it wasn't work related. My son died."

"Right." He taps at his keyboard. "That might be better, I suppose. Even so, unscheduled time out is suspicious to a prospective employer, especially when you didn't leave your last job by choice."

I asked Chester if he could make it look as though I'd resigned, but it was too late.

"We had to show Schulman we meant business, that we'd taken action after you left the account hanging." I'd been sacrificed to keep a client.

I have several interviews, but nothing comes of them. As spring arrives, I drift back into my sweatpants. I get an email from Pip, and my heart leaps, but she's just telling me we finally have an offer on the house, and it's fifteen under the asking price but should we accept **so**

we can both move on. I laugh bitterly. Some of us are a long way from moving on. But I can't keep paying a mortgage on a house I don't live in.

In April I go with Mom to a fund-raiser at Happy Village, where she introduces me to new friends, and says **You remember so-and-so** about people I have no recollection of. The place hasn't changed in all the years we've been going—the black-and-white checkered floor, the stools at the dimly lit bar, where locals chew the fat over an Old Style. We sit outside, in the tent-covered garden, on white plastic chairs around white plastic tables.

Mom's invited Blair, who sits silently next to me, no doubt wishing she didn't come. She's brought her kids, Brianna and Logan, and she watches them over on the other side, leaning into the pond to count the goldfish. They're eleven and nine respectively, well mannered, well dressed. As perfect as their mom. I feel a burst of irritation.

"How are you doing?" Blair says suddenly, like she can read my mind.

I shrug. "I'm good. I'm only here for Mom—this isn't really my scene." I look around the beer garden. I loved it here, when I was a kid. Barbecues, music, begging my folks for another bag of chips. I got too cool pretty quick, of course—wanted to head to Wicker Park for more excitement, more action—but when I was Logan's age, Happy Village was where it was at.

"I don't mean now. Here. I mean: after your son.

How are you doing?" Some people ask like they don't want to know the answer. They're relieved when you say **Fine, good, yup—not bad, thanks.** Question asked, duty done. But Blair holds my gaze and I find I can't look away. Can't brush off her question.

"Pretty bad." I wonder if my honesty surprises her as much as it does me. "I wake up sometimes and I've forgotten." She nods, her face serious as she waits for me to say more. After a while, I do. "I see the sky outside and everything feels OK. Like I'm just away with work, and later I'll FaceTime Pip, and Dylan will push his face close to the camera like he can climb right into her phone. Then I remember." There's a paper cloth covering the table, and I pick at the edge, dropping crescent-shaped confetti onto the floor. "And it's a double whammy. Like I'm losing him all over again, only with a side-helping of guilt, because I forgot. Because his death wasn't the first thing in my head when I woke. And then I fall apart."

There are people coming around with trash bags, tossing in our paper plates and asking **Are you done with this?** Blair waits until they've gone before she answers. "I think it's OK to fall apart."

I think about being told to **man up** on the sports field, about the way we laughed at Corey Chambers in fourth grade because he **cried like a girl.** I think about when Dylan got sick, about the people who'd clap me on the back and tell me to **look after that poor wife of yours.** How can it be OK to fall apart?

"In fact, I think it would be really strange if you didn't." Blair's tearing the tablecloth too. Around our feet is a little circle of confetti. Across the garden, Mom's waving at me to come say hello to another neighbor I don't remember. "You've spent years being strong for other people. For your wife, for Dylan." Blair says his name without hesitation, without pity, and instead of hurting it feels good to hear it in this noisy, busy bar, full of music and chatter. "You stayed strong all that time, and then suddenly you didn't have to be strong anymore." She looks at me. "You ever get a cold the second you go on vacation? It's like that. You hold it together and you hold it together and you hold it together, and then BAM. You get sick. Our bodies are really good at working when they have to, but they need a break." She taps the side of her head. "So does this." Then she suddenly smiles. "Give yourself a break—you're not doing so bad."

"Max!" Mom gives up on the waving and hollers instead. "You remember the Nowackis?"

Blair suppresses a laugh. "I think we'd better go say hello to the Nowackis."

"Thank you."

"Don't thank me—Walt Nowacki spits when he talks."

"No, I mean—"

"I know. You're welcome. Come on. And bring a napkin."

M om can't sit still. She's cleaned the house twice, and she's standing by the living room window, twitching the drapes every time a car goes by.

"You don't need to be here, Mom." I'm as restless as she is, pacing the house, looking for things that don't need fixing, because I've fixed them all already. "I'm only signing the house papers. It'll take seconds."

I offered to meet Pip at the airport, or at her hotel. She's working again—with Virgin Atlantic, this time. **Early days, but it's good to be flying again**, her email said.

"It's OK, I'll come to the house. I'd like to see Heather."

Looking at Mom's thin lips right now, she might regret that decision.

Right at six o'clock, a cab pulls up outside. I open the door and step onto the porch, wanting to get to her before Mom does. My pulse races. I haven't seen Pip for eight months, haven't heard her voice since Christmas. I don't even know how I feel about her anymore. I miss her, I know that, but do I love her? Does she love me? Is there still a chance?

The second I see her, I know that I do. The second she sees me, I know that there isn't. The bitterness I saw in her eyes when she left me has gone, but her smile is sad. There will be no emotional reunion. This is goodbye.

"Hey."

"Hello, Max."

We hug, our bodies fitting together the way they always did, and my chest is crushed with grief that we might never do this again, that after everything we've been through, we're going to live our lives apart. I think of what I heard Blair say that day, about two people with flu, and wish I'd heard the rest. What happens when the two people aren't sick anymore? Can they look after each other then? Or is it always too late?

"I like the beard." Pip's hand moves toward it, then away again, like she was about to touch my face, before remembering we're not together anymore. "It suits you."

"How was your flight?" Mom's tone is clipped but polite. Pip hugs her, too, and some of Mom's stiffness eases.

"I'm so sorry," Pip says, holding Mom's gaze. I wait for Mom to lay into her, to share some of the things she's said about her daughter-in-law over the last few months. But although her eyes narrow, and her disapproval is evident, Pip's apology means Mom can't bring herself to be impolite.

"So am I."

There's a pause, and then Pip opens her purse. She's wearing a bright red skirt and jacket, with a crisp white shirt. I'm glad she's switched airlines, that she's not in the British Airways blue she was wearing when we met. She could almost be a different person. And then I realize that she is. That we both are.

"So, you need to sign here, and . . . here." The house chain is finally complete, and our buyers are ready to move. Once I sign the contract we can proceed with the sale, and two weeks later the final tangible link between Pip and me will be gone. Just divorce left. She hasn't said that yet, but I know it's coming.

I find a pen. Mom's looking out the window. She's jumpy again, and as we hear a car outside, she catches my eye with an expression I can't read. I sit on the sofa and find a magazine to lean on. Pip sits too, but Mom's opening the door, and I'm wondering who's there, when—

"Pip, this is Blair, an old friend of Max's from way back when." Mom won't look at me. **An old friend?** Blair was a neighbor's kid I only ever played with under duress, a girl who swam at the Y and could hold her breath as long as I could. We were never friends . . .

There's a second's silence, then Pip stands up. "Lovely to meet you." They shake hands, and I find the page I have to sign, so I can get this over with.

"Excuse us." Mom smiles. "Blair's come over to help me pick out something for Bob's seventieth." The two women disappear upstairs. Pip raises an eyebrow.

"She seems nice."

I shrug. "I barely know her."

The corners of Pip's mouth twitch, and I feel a rush of rage toward her, for not believing me, and toward my mother, for whatever game it is she's playing. Is she trying to make Pip jealous? Is that it? Is Blair in on it too? I swear, if I live to be a hundred I will never understand women.

"It says my signature needs to be witnessed."

"We'll get your mum to do it." Pip goes to the bottom of the stairs. She hesitates, then calls, "Heather!"

I sign the pages marked with yellow sticky notes, as Mom makes her way back downstairs.

"I'm sorry to disturb you—would you mind countersigning Max's signature?"

She nods stiffly and sits next to me, and I flip the pages back to the beginning.

"Oh bugger." Pip is reading the notes accompanying the contract. She holds up a hand, just as Mom takes the pen from me. "It can't be a family member." She looks up, apologetically. "Sorry, I should have read it properly. Do you think . . ." She looks up, toward the stairs.

"I'm sure she would," Mom says smoothly. "Blair, honey! Can you come down here?"

It takes an age for Blair to sign her name, and fill out her address in neat block capitals. There is much discussion about whether blue pen is OK, or whether it should have been black, and **Does this look like an "M" or an "N" to you**, but finally it's done. Mom and Blair disappear back upstairs—**It was great to meet you, Blair. And you—safe travels!**—and I go back out onto the porch with Pip. She's kept her cab running—there was never any danger of her wanting to stay longer. We hug again, and now this one really might be the last one ever. I want to hold her forever, but we both pull away because from now on that isn't how this works. There's no house anymore, no child.

There's no **us**.

thirty-six

Pip

2015

I sit on the loo and stare at the Perspex window on the test in my hand, on which my future is written in unarguable capitals.

PREGNANT.

I lean against the wall of the cubicle and let out a breath. There's no point in doing another test. My work shirt strains across my chest, and my body aches with a tiredness that's more than work fatigue and jet lag. I knew a week ago, but I didn't want to believe it. I told myself I was imagining things, that my body was translating anxiety into phantom symptoms.

Pregnant.

"Shit, shit, shit, shit, shit . . ." I moan under my

breath, my heart racing. What am I going to do? I can't have a baby—I can't risk loving a child so completely again, I can't risk losing them again. But what's the alternative? How can I end another life, after everything we've been through?

We fell the first month, with Dylan. Max pretended to be disappointed—**I thought I'd at least be able to enjoy the practice runs**—but his excitement was bolstered by that innate sense of pride men feel when they manage to achieve the very function they're biologically engineered to do. It's curious how important it is to them; how they imagine they have control over their sperm, and that, when one of their little wrigglers successfully impregnates an egg, it is entirely down to their own prowess as a man.

I did that test alone, too, already certain I was pregnant. Sore breasts, nausea, a dull ache in my abdomen. Even the fabled metallic taste, like a two-penny piece was lodged beneath my tongue. I wrapped up the test in a linen napkin and set the table for dinner à deux. Cheesy, I know. Worth it, though, for the look on his face.

Pregnant.

There's so much I need to do. I need to tell Max, of course. He'll be thrilled. He'll see it as a fresh start, a new chapter. I need to ring my mum, who grieves so much for my lost motherhood. Nothing could ever make up for losing Dylan, but a new grandchild . . . my parents will seize upon this as a sign that everything is going to be OK. I need to tell work. Airline policy says cabin crew should be grounded as soon as they know they are pregnant, to reduce the risk of anything going wrong.

I stare at the pregnancy test. I think of the linen napkin, the table laid for two, Max's naked joy as he realised what he'd unwrapped.

And then I open the sanitary bin beside me and drop the test inside.

I leave the cubicle, wash my hands, and join the rest of the crew to take the transfer bus to the car park.

"You all right? You look a bit peaky," Jada says, as we stride through Terminal One with our wheeled cases in our wake. I am both desperate to get home—to take off both my uniform and my smile—and terrified of being there.

"I think those prawns last night were a bit off."

"I did tell you."

We ate at a lobster shack last night in Vegas, and both Jada and Ethan steered clear of the prawns, which Jada had convinced herself looked "funny." They were perfectly fine—delicious, in fact—but if my current pallor can be attributed to a bad seafood meal, that suits me.

On the bus, I stare out of the window, unsettled by a sudden bout of nausea made worse by bumpy suspension, and run to my car on the pretext of wanting to get ahead of the traffic. "Text you later!" I call to Jada.

I sit in rush-hour queues regardless, my eighty-minute commute stretching to two hours. I'm glad of the delay, of the thinking time, but soon the silence becomes too much, and I flick on the radio. I have a sudden memory of my nightly drives back from PICU, and of my near-obsession with **Bringing Up B**. I feel irrationally guilty that I stopped listening, that I abandoned B and her family, and have no idea how they are, what they've been doing for the last three years. As I crawl forward I find the latest episode and connect the car Bluetooth.

For the first ten minutes, I am all at sea. Where is Bridget's dad? When did they get a dog? Who are these people? They are strange yet familiar, like the new cast members of a soap opera once watched avidly. I listen to the soft voice of Bridget's mum, and gradually I piece together the events I have missed. Eileen and B's dad have separated. I have missed the trauma, the shock, the reasons why. I have come in on act three, in a new status quo now too normal to be noteworthy, and I wonder how much blood was shed to get there. I wonder what my own normal will be, three years from now.

"B chose a cake with Dixie on it," comes the voice through my speakers. "Which is why, at eleven o'clock at night, I'm trying to cut sponge in the shape of a dachshund, and wondering why I didn't present her with easier options."

She must be tired, this mother—this **single** mother—and yet there's a smile in her voice. I picture

Eileen in her kitchen, flour in her hair and a sink full of dishes. Overworked, overwrought. But she will go to bed satisfied with her dachshund-shaped cake, in the knowledge that, tomorrow, Bridget will cry out with delight, her birthday made.

I could have that again. I could bake cakes and stay up late planning birthday surprises. I had it once, I could have it again. I press my hand against my stomach. Pregnant.

Max opens the door as I pull onto our drive. He stands, silhouetted in the light from the hall, a glass of wine in one hand.

"Traffic bad?" he says, as I emerge.

"Awful. How was work?" I follow him inside.

"Great! My client broke his leg."

I raise an eyebrow, and he grins.

"He's had to postpone our scoping visit, which means I get to stay in the office next week, instead of spending three days in Berlin. Here, take this." He hands me his wine. "Not only that, but Schulman's delighted with the project so far, so much so that Chester's dropping sizeable hints about bonuses."

"That's great, honey." I didn't drink when I was pregnant with Dylan, and although I put the glass to my lips now, I can't bring myself to take a sip.

"You look tired."

From nowhere, tears prick my eyes, and Max's face

fills with concern. "Are you OK? Did something happen?"

Now. Tell him now.

But I don't.

I don't tell him the next day, or the day after that, and as one week morphs into the next, the prospect of telling him becomes harder. Because why haven't I told him sooner? I pretend it isn't happening. I push the idea of a baby deep inside me, ignoring the waves of nausea that send me rushing to the sink, and the tiredness that sends me to bed at nine.

At work, I undo the top button of my skirt, and fight travel sickness I've never suffered with before. At home, I go through the motions of my marriage, claiming tiredness as I push Max gently away at night, so he won't feel the swell of my breasts, the thickness of my waist.

I will have to tell him soon, but telling Max— telling anyone—will make it real, and whenever I let myself think of this pregnancy, all I can see is Dylan's still body in my arms. It will happen again, I just know it. Maybe not in the same way—maybe sooner, maybe later—but it will happen. I won't be allowed to keep this child, either.

Max and I cohabit like flat sharers, polite but distant, taking turns to cook, then retreating to our separate spaces; him downstairs with the television, and me in my reading room, upstairs with a book. I wonder if he regrets making this haven for me, and then I think perhaps this is what he wanted, all along. I watch the cracks appear in our marriage, and even though I know I am the cause, and even though I love Max so much it hurts, I still pull away from him.

Work is a relief—for both of us, I suspect. Our messaging becomes more sporadic, limited to **Arrived safely x** and **Hope you had a good flight x**. I miss FaceTiming him, I miss our long text conversations. I miss **him**.

"So tell him," Jada says. We're checking the empty cabin before leaving the plane, and she's already planning which Joburg nightspot to hit first. Everything is simple, in Jada's world. You like someone? Tell them. Got a problem? Air it.

"I don't know where to start." I haven't told Jada I'm pregnant. We are friends, of a sort, but she is first and foremost a colleague, and—despite her age—a senior one; and I am four whole months into a pregnancy I haven't declared. I've attributed my sobriety to a desire to lose the extra pounds that have "crept on," and body-conscious Jada has accepted the excuse without question.

"We used to be able to talk about anything, but now it's as though the words stick in my throat." I pick up a scarf that's been left on a seat, slot an in-flight magazine back in its rack.

Jada chews the inside of her lip thoughtfully. She's wearing the airline's bespoke shade of lipstick, a deep red that looks like it was made especially for her. "My parents had couple's counselling after Mum threatened to leave Dad if he didn't stop playing golf."

"Sounds a bit extreme."

"You don't know my 'rents. Anyway, it obviously worked, because they're still together, and Dad put his clubs on eBay." We reach the end of the cabin, retrieve our cases from the hat racks, and change into our ground shoes. I can't help feeling sorry for Jada's dad. "Maybe you should give it a go."

"Maybe." My answer is noncommittal, but my mind is whirring. I think of Jada's parents—Mum no doubt as tall and glamorous as her daughter, Dad proud of his little girl—and imagine being the sort of person who goes to counselling because of an argument over golf. And yet here I am, with a problem far weightier than time spent on the golf course, and what am I doing? Ignoring it. Hoping it'll go away.

It isn't going away. I have to speak to Max.

As we stride through Johannesburg airport behind our pilot, I already feel better. A child points at us, tugging at his mother's hand. **Look!** I think about standing in my parents' garden, watching the planes, and I wonder if this little boy will grow up to be a flight attendant, a pilot, an aviation engineer. He's around the age Dylan would be now, and instead of looking away I smile at him and he beams back. **I can do this**, I think. **I can get better.**

On the transfer bus the crew are talking about hotels. Unusually, we've been split between two. Our captain, Shona, is staying in the Sandton Sun with half the team, and Jada and are I at the Palazzo Montecasino, with the rest of the crew. I tune out and turn on my phone to let Max know I've arrived safely. He flies back today, having added an extra day to his Chicago trip, so he could see his mum. Chicago is seven hours behind Joburg, and as my phone searches for a local signal I count on my fingers, too tired to do the maths in my head. Midday here, which means . . . five a.m., Max's time.

His regular good-night text comes through, incongruous against the backdrop of sunshine streaming through the transfer bus windows.

Sleep tight honey, miss you. Love you so much and feel so lucky to have you.

The South African sunshine warms my face, and Max's text warms my heart. I'm the lucky one. Max has never given up on me. He has quietly kept loving me and waited for me to come back to him.

There's more, but I have to read the rest of the text twice, because it doesn't make sense. I wonder for a second if it's me—the jet lag, the tiredness, the pregnancy.

> So good to spend the day with you today.
> Can't wait for the next time xxx

I haven't seen Max for five days.
This message wasn't meant for me.

thirty-seven

Max

2017

I stand across the street from the house.

"Looking good." A woman laden with several shopping bags stops to look with me.

"Thanks." The deep red of Mom's house is restored to its former glory, and the siding gleams white once more. My muscles ache in a way that isn't entirely unpleasant, and the June sun warms the back of my neck.

"Don't suppose you have a card, do you?"

"A card? I—oh, right. This is my mom's house—I'm not a painter."

The woman looks at my paint-covered coveralls, and the spatters of red and white on my hands. "Could have fooled me." She puts down her shopping and roots in her purse. "Listen, I'm at 1021, in a brand-new condo in need of some personality. White just isn't me, you know? Job's yours, if you want it." She scribbles a number on a piece of paper and thrusts it at me. "The name's Nancy."

I call her the next day.

She wants blue in the living room, yellow in the kitchen, green in the bedroom.

"Like I said, white's not really me." She laughs, and her earrings dance against her neck. She's maybe fifty or so, with steel-gray hair cropped closer than mine, and an armful of silver bangles that jangle when she waves her arms around, which she does frequently as she talks. I learn that she's a social worker, that she's in a relationship with a woman over in Little Italy, but they have no plans to move in together—**I'm not making** that **mistake again!**—and that she likes jazz and hates cats. She leaves me with the brushes and paint, a stepladder, and her door key.

The job takes two weeks. We settle into a routine. Nancy comes home around six, and while I'm cleaning the brushes she makes us a coffee and checks out my progress.

At the end of each week she pays me in cash, and I walk home feeling every inch like the fifteen-year-old me who got his first summer job at Eckhart pool.

Nancy sings my praises to anyone who sets foot in her apartment, and I wind up with two more condos to decorate, and the outside of a house like Mom's, only gray.

At the end of July I take Mom to Wicker Park Fest. She claims she's too old for the bands—although you'd never know it to see her toe-tapping to the beat—but she loves to wander through the food stalls. The sun beats down on us as we weave through the crowds. Everyone's eating, everyone's smiling and laughing, chatting to friends. A woman on stilts, swathes of silky fabric swirling around her, leans down to hand a balloon to a child who is gazing open-mouthed at her.

We're out back at Big Star, tucking into a plate of tacos, when Blair and the kids walk by. Blair's face breaks into a smile. "Perfect! You can settle a dispute for us." Her hair is twisted into a bun, and escaped curls tumble over the bandana that keeps them off her face. She shepherds the kids in front of her. "Say hello, guys." Logan says hello, and Brianna manages a teen-age grunt. Both look mutinous. "Kids Fest isn't for babies, is it?"

"Absolutely not!" Mom gets straight in there. "The program says they're doing balloon animals this afternoon, and I hear there's cookie decorating, too."

Brianna rolls her eyes. Blair catches my eye, and I can't help but laugh.

"I guess that settles that, then," Blair says, grinning. "No Kids Fest."

"Although," I say, "did you see they're doing karate trials?"

Logan perks up. I find the page in the program and

look at my watch. "Starts in ten minutes. You could practice kicking your sister's butt."

"Huh—I'll kick his butt before he kicks mine."

"You wanna bet?" I reach into my pocket and pull out a five-dollar bill. Brianna reaches for it and I hold my hand high. "You've gotta kick some butt first."

"Max!" My mother's disapproval is almost tangible, but Blair laughs loudly.

"Let's go!" She stops and looks at me, stricken. "You are coming with us, right?"

"I never miss a butt-kicking."

Afterward, when the kids are showing off their karate kicks—only slightly hampered by their ice creams—Blair and I sit in the shade of an ash tree, our backs leaning against its rough trunk.

"You're great with them."

"They're good kids."

Blair chases melted ice cream with her tongue. "I help out at a swim club on Thursday nights," she says, once it's back under control. "They're really short of volunteers, and I wondered if—"

"I'm really busy right now."

"Right." She leaves my lie hanging.

When Dylan left hospital I wanted to take him swimming again, like we used to on a Saturday morning, but it wasn't that easy. We were allowed to take him for hydrotherapy, to a center on the other side of Birmingham, but the public pools were no-go areas, even though they were adapted for disabled use, with hoists, ramps, and specially trained staff. Dylan's immune system was too compromised.

"Well, if you change your mind, I could really use your help."

"I won't." I don't mean to snap, and I catch a flash of hurt on her face, before the smile is back.

"No worries."

We carry on watching the kids make karate kicks, but suddenly the grass doesn't seem so green, and the sun is no longer as bright.

thirty-eight

Pip

2015

Max calls me minutes after his plane lands. I imagine him taking off his seat belt before the signs have gone off, and switching on his phone despite the announcement telling passengers not to, impatient to find out what he's missed while in the air. I picture the blood draining from his face as he realises he's sent that message—meant for another woman—to his wife.

I turn my ringer to silent and watch his name flash up again and again until it goes to voicemail. Who is she? A work colleague? Someone he met on the plane? I think of the night we met, almost fifteen years ago now, and how certain I was that he only had eyes for me. That we had eyes only for each other. Was I fooling myself? Perhaps that's what Max does, on his business trips abroad. A girl in every port. He wouldn't be the first—I've seen enough in my job to know that.

We get twenty-four hours on a Joburg stopover, and Max calls at least three times for each of them. I start listening to the voicemails but they all say the same thing. Something and nothing. **Pip, please, we need to talk. Call me. I love you.**

No explanation. No **It's not what you think, not what it looks like**. Because, of course, it **is** what I think. It is exactly what it looks like. My husband has been having an affair.

I stay in my room while the others go shopping, and cry off their evening on the town. I order room service I can't eat, and leave the tray outside my door an hour later, the food untouched. I close the curtains and lie on my bed, the only light the silent flashing of my phone's screen. **Max calling, Max calling.**

I'm woken by cramps. I lie in the dark with my eyes open, trying to stay calm, but my stomach is twisting in knots so bad my breath catches with each spasm. Gingerly, I push my legs out of bed, sit and then stand, and make my way to the toilet. I brace myself for the bloom of blood in the water.

Nothing. But my stomach still twists, and I bend double. I think of the early pain when Dylan was born—the cramps that pulled my stomach so tight I saw the outline of his feet.

And then my stomach growls. An unmistakable rumble that makes me laugh out loud, the sound echoing in the tiled room. Hunger pangs. That's all. I haven't eaten since I left the UK.

I pull up my jogging bottoms, wash my face, and stand for a moment, looking in the mirror. The drawn pallor of the first three months has gone now, replaced by clear skin and flushed cheeks, thicker and shinier hair.

You're relieved, I say silently, looking at myself. **Relieved to still be pregnant.**

"Yes," I say out loud. I splay my hands over my belly, turn to the side and stroke my hands apart until they are above and below my bump. Another rumble of hunger breaks the moment. "All right, baby, let's get you something to eat." It's the first time I've spoken to it—the first time I've acknowledged it—and the tug at my heart is both tangible and terrifying.

I open the door, but my tray is long gone, so I pull on a pair of flip-flops, and a baggy T-shirt to cover my bump, and go downstairs. Even midweek, the restaurant is busy, and I wait for the server to find space. From the corner of my eye I see someone wave. Lars Van der Werf. I raise a hand and smile politely, just as the server comes back with an apology.

"It'll be at least forty minutes. Can you wait?" She glances across to where Lars is performing an elaborate mime, rubbing his stomach and gesticulating to the empty chair at his table. "Or perhaps you'd like to join your friend?"

"He's not really a—" But Lars is coming over.

"Pip! Just arrived?"

"I was on the twenty oh five—I've been sleeping."

"Join me? I've not long ordered—I'm sure they could put a hold on mine while you choose."

"I don't want to disturb you," I say, although I'm the one wanting a quiet dinner alone. I need to get my head round Max's text; what I'm going to say to him when I get home, whether I'm going to call him before I leave Joburg.

"You'd be doing me a great favour. Left to my own devices I'll have three courses and cheese, and I won't be able to fit in the cockpit tomorrow." He pats a stomach taut enough to bounce peas off.

Lars's table is by the open doors onto the terrace, and he switches places to give me the view across the manicured lawns. A peacock struts by the side of a rectangular pool, its tail feathers sending up a thin cloud of dust in its wake. As I sit down, my phone vibrates in my hand, an insistent trill signalling yet another text from Max. I switch it to silent and turn it facedown on the table.

"Please do answer that, if you need to."

"It's OK. It's just my husband."

Love you so much and feel so lucky to have you. That isn't a message sent to a one-night stand, or to a casual pickup seen when in town on business. He loves her. He feels lucky to have her. Lucky! Because she's better than me, more attractive, more intelligent? Because she doesn't have stretch marks, yet nothing to show for them? Doesn't stare at nothing for hours at a time because she's so broken inside and—

"Pip?" Lars is looking at me, curiously.

"Sorry?"

"I was saying it's hard on relationships, being away such a lot."

"Oh. Yes, sorry, I was somewhere else for a moment." I look towards the open door, which perfectly frames a vast sky filled with orange and red. "Yes, it's tough, but you get used to it." **By sleeping with someone else, in my husband's case**, I add silently. I accept a small glass of wine, and wish I could numb my senses with alcohol. Jada and the rest of the crew will be at Club Fluid by now. I feel a brief flash of envy for their uncomplicated lives.

"Are you married?" I ask.

"Widowed." He gives a smile I know. A smile that doesn't reach the eyes, that's designed to make the questioner feel better, less awkward. A smile I recognise from the rare occasions I give a truthful answer to the question **Do you have children? I had a son**, I'll say. **He died when he was almost three years old.** And I smile and move so swiftly on to some other topic that the other person would be forgiven for thinking that I was over it.

Only you don't get over it, you simply get better at dealing with it. Better at hiding it. I hold Lars's gaze, and I ask the question I always want to hear yet never do. I hear **I'm so sorry**, and **How awful** and **That**

must have been terrible, but never something that gives Dylan **life** . . .

"What was her name?"

This time the smile reaches his eyes. "Maaike. She died when she was thirty-one. She fought cancer so many times, but the last time was too much."

"I'm so sorry." Emotion, never far from the surface, wells inside me. Thirty-one. Younger than I am now. It terrifies me to think how fragile life is, how easily our loved ones slip out of our lives. My fingertips find their way to my stomach. "Did you have children?"

Lars shakes his head. "We wanted to, but by the time we were ready, Maaike was already ill. She was a teacher, though, and she loved her children, so I think that helped a lot." He scans my face. "But how have **you** been?"

And because he has spoken so easily about loss, without looking around to see who is listening, it feels natural for me to do the same.

"Up and down. I went to see my son's doctor."

It was Lars who suggested I speak to Dr. Khalili.

"It might give you some closure," he said. Lars was a problem-solver, like Max. The comparison made me sad—I should have been talking to Max about the regret and guilt that plagues me, not a near stranger.

"Did it help?"

I think for a moment. "It was hard. I cried—we both did, actually. She said she doubted herself, too."

I see concern on Lars's face. "I know, it sounds like that would make it worse, but it helped seeing her as . . ." I grapple for the perfect word. "Fallible."

Lars is listening intently. "Will you keep talking to her?"

"No, I don't think so." I hesitate. "There's no way of knowing what Dylan's life would have been like, if we'd taken him to America. Even if there were, it's too late. I need to look forward, not back." With perfect timing, there's a bubble of movement inside me.

"We all need reminding of that, from time to time," Lars says.

The menu is Italian, and I order Caprese salad and mushroom risotto, promising a taste to Lars—who declares himself torn between the risotto and the grilled sole.

"It's the best thing about the job, don't you think? Dinner?" he says, as we tuck into our starters. I laugh, partly because there's a twinkle in his eye which suggests he's joking, but also because I've never seen someone so enthusiastic about food. He eyes up plates on other people's tables, declaring that we **chose wisely**, and insisting I try a piece of his calamari starter that is **seasoned to perfection**.

"Do you like cooking?"

"Eating. I'm ashamed to say Maaike did all the cooking—I can't make anything more complicated than a boiled egg."

"Maybe you should learn. Do a course?"

"I'd like to. Time—isn't that always the way? Maybe one day."

"One day might never come." Too late, I realise how morbid my words sound, but Lars looks at me seriously.

"You're right."

Our conversation moves quickly to work—as is often the way between colleagues—and the countries we have visited. In the middle of a discussion about the merits of Miami over Cancún, a wiry boy with a guitar arrives at our table, and launches into a rendition of Elton John's "Your Song." Lars and I exchange looks, laughing awkwardly as the musician closes his eyes, swaying slightly as he croons. He assumes we're a couple, I suppose—honeymooners, or here for an anniversary. I feel guilty, as though I'm party to a deception, and then I picture Max's text. **So good to spend the day with you today. Can't wait for the next time xxx**. Three kisses. Ridiculous though it might sound, I am as hurt by those kisses as by Max's deception. Those are **my** kisses. **Our** kisses. One for each member of our little family.

"I've kept you up too late," Lars says, when we've shared a tiramisu and a plate of cheese, and jet lag is making me yawn.

"No, it's been lovely. Thank you for letting me share your table."

We walk to the lifts, and I don't know if it's the jet lag, or the half glass of wine after three months with none, or simply a sudden, misjudged desire to get my own back on Max, but as the doors open at my floor I take a step forward, and kiss Lars on the lips. For a second he kisses me back, and lifts a hand to my shoulder, but then he pulls away, shaking his head and pushing me gently back.

"You're married, Pip."

And then the doors close and I'm left standing in the corridor on the fifth floor of my hotel, hot with shame.

thirty-nine

Max

2017

"Anything to drink, sir?"

I take a soda and some chips from a flight attendant who had to ask for my order twice because he forgot it the first time. Everyone's on edge. The flight is full, there was some mix-up over seats, and there's too much hand luggage for the overhead bins. As I put down my tray table the woman in the seat next to mine slides her elbow onto the armrest between us; the next move in the silent dispute we have had since takeoff. Cramp threatens my left calf, and I twist in my seat in an attempt to uncross my legs, but with the tray down I'm wedged in, and have to content myself with flexing them at the ankle.

Heathrow's busy, and we circle the airport for ten minutes before we're cleared to land. With my tray table stowed away I have room to get out my book, and I finish the final few pages of a Wilbur Smith I thought I remembered, but which has taken me by surprise. How long since I read a book that wasn't a business manual, or a motivational autobiography? **Feel the Fear and Let It Feed You. You Can't Fly If You Don't Jump. How to Win at Your Life.** What a load of bullshit.

After passport control I bypass the baggage carousel, and walk to Arrivals. Out of habit, I scan the waiting faces. Some have excitement written across them, others are bored, tired, and emotional, coping with delayed flights, missed flights, diverted flights. Taxi drivers and chauffeurs hold up a motley collection of signs, from hand-scrawled cardboard to fancy iPad displays.

I'm almost through the crowd when I see a familiar face. She's checking her watch—and then checking it again, as though the intervening seconds might since have become minutes. She drums her fingers on the messenger bag strung across her chest. I hesitate. Change my mind. Why would she even remember me? As I turn away I hear her voice.

"Mr. Adams!"

I turn back. Memories assault me, and I breathe slowly out.

"It is you, isn't it?" Her smile is hesitant. "I thought it was you." She's with a man I didn't notice at first glance. He's tall, and older than her, with gray hair and glasses. He gives a polite smile, then takes a few discreet steps away, leaving us to talk.

"Dr. Khalili. It's good to see you." Her hair's been cut to just below her chin, but otherwise she looks exactly the same as she did four years ago. No, not exactly the same. Dr. Leila Khalili had a face I couldn't read. A face I thought at times meant she didn't care—that Dylan was just another patient, Pip and I just another set of parents. This woman is unsure. Nervous.

She extends a tentative hand.

I take it. "Max."

"Leila."

Permission, rather than introductions. An understanding that the people we were then are perhaps not quite the people we are now.

"How are things?" The question is careful.

"Dylan passed away last September."

"I'm so sorry." And then: "Six and a half years old, though. That's wonderful."

And a half. It's important, that half. Ask anyone who's lost a child, and they'll tell you precisely how many months, how many weeks, how many **days** they lived. I'm impressed—no, I'm stunned—that Dr. Khalili remembers. How many kids has she met since Dylan?

"And how's Pip?"

"She's well. I'm meeting her in a moment, actually. She . . . we aren't together anymore."

A moment's pause. "I'm really sorry about that, too. You were such a strong couple."

There's a lump in my throat. We **were** a strong couple. The strongest. I change the subject. "Are you waiting for someone?"

"My mother." Her eyes shine. "She's moving to the UK. She's coming to live with me."

"From Tehran?" I surprise myself with the knowledge. It was Pip who held the details of everyone's lives in her head; Pip who thought to ask about relatives, and to check in after holidays.

"You've got a good memory." Leila smiles. "She's been unwell, and I've been worried for a long time—she has lots of friends in Iran but no one who could care for her on a regular basis." She sighs. "It hasn't been easy, but they're finally letting her come."

"Congratulations. She's lucky to have you."

"I'm the lucky one." There's an influx of passengers through Arrivals, and she turns, then takes a sharp intake of breath and calls to the man she's with. "Nick—there!"

"I'll leave you to it. Good to see you, Leila—I'm glad you're well."

I turn back as I reach the exit, in time to see a short, curvy woman in a midnight-blue head scarf run up to Leila as fast as her two enormous suitcases will allow. She holds Leila's face in two hands, squeezing her cheeks and kissing her forehead, before turning to the gray-haired man and doing the same to him.

"Guess who I just saw?" I'm glad to have something to launch into, to remove the awkwardness that might otherwise have fallen between Pip and me. I'm here to collect my things. At least, as many of my things as will fit in a suitcase and come in at under fifty pounds.

"Who?"

"Dr. Khalili." After the house sold, Pip had everything moved to storage. We sold the furniture neither of us wanted, and now it's just the personal stuff—the books, the vinyl, the photos. Souvenirs of a life before we got together, to take forward into the two lives we're building apart.

"I could take photos of it," Pip suggested. "Ship over the stuff you want to keep."

"I'm not sure I'll know till I see it," I told her, when really what I meant was **I want to see you again**.

Pip's hands tighten on the wheel. "Dr. Khalili was at the airport?"

I would have got the train, only Pip was working today, and it seemed churlish to refuse the offer of a lift.

"What was she doing?"

"Waiting for her mother. Doctors are allowed out of the hospital, you know."

Pip gives me a side-eye. "I know. It's always weird, though, isn't it? Like seeing teachers at the cinema, or a nun on a roller coaster." She drives in silence for a while, then says: "I wouldn't want to see her."

"No?"

Pip chews her lip. Signals, then moves into the next lane. I lean my head back and watch her reflection in the rearview mirror. I used to love watching her put on makeup before a night out, brushing color into the sockets of her eyes until they were dark and smoky. She'd meet my gaze in the mirror and poke out her tongue, or pout freshly painted lips. I swallow.

"I think I'd find it too hard," she says now, and it's a moment before I realize she's still talking about Leila Khalili. "I find it upsetting even thinking about her, to be honest."

"Sorry—"

"It's fine. Just that . . . if I saw her face, it would take me right back there, you know? Like when I—" She breaks off abruptly.

"Like when you look at me, you mean?" I say softly.

She doesn't answer. In the rearview mirror, tears find their way along the tiny lines at the corners of her eyes.

Dividing our possessions is predictably awful, but we don't argue. In fact we are bizarrely polite, each insisting the other take a vase we were given as a wedding present from someone neither of us can remember. **No, you have it. No, really, I couldn't—it's yours.**

Pip stops and looks at me, the vase in her hands. "You don't even like it, do you?"

"I hate it."

She bursts out laughing, then she weighs the vase between both hands and looks at the brick wall at the back of the storage unit. "Dare me?"

"You wouldn't."

In answer, she hurls the vase like a Russian shot-putter. It shatters instantly, and shards of shiny green porcelain ricochet in all directions.

"Better?" I ask.

She nods slowly. "Yes, actually. You try."

We look around at the remaining pile of belongings.

"The tea set?" It isn't a terrible tea set, by any means. We acquired it from Pip's parents, and in all the years we were married, we never used it once.

"Who uses a tea set, anyway?" Pip says.

I take that as a yes.

I do the first three cups slowly, the second three like machine-gun bullets. **Pow pow pow.** Then the saucers, then the plates, then finally the teapot. **Pow.**

"Wow."

"Feels good, doesn't it?"

We smash mugs too small for a decent cuppa, and glasses left over from long-gone sets. We smash a clay photo frame sporting a squirrel, and a whiskey decanter engraved with someone else's monogram, that Chester gave me one Christmas.

"Why have we kept so much crap?" Pip says, as she

jettisons an eggcup that came free with the tokens from sixteen boxes of cornflakes.

It is amazingly, absurdly, astoundingly therapeutic.

I hold up our wedding plate. A present from one of Pip's old colleagues, it was brought to our wedding reception with a pack of colored pens, and taken away afterward—replete with goodwill messages from our guests—to be glazed and fired. **May your marriage bring nothing but blue skies**, reads one of the messages.

"No." Our fingers brush against each other as Pip takes it from me. "Not that."

"Just this, then," I say softly. I pick up the framed picture. "We can't divide this in two." It's the picture Dylan made at school. **My family**. It isn't the only one—it was made on a computer and a copy emailed to us to keep—but this one was printed at school. In the bottom right-hand corner is Dylan's thumbprint, carefully helped into place by his art therapist.

"You keep it," Pip says.

I want it so badly. I hold it in two hands and think of my boy putting colors on the page until three shapes emerged, one smaller than the others. Maybe it was fanciful to imagine he knew what he was doing, but I want to believe he did. "You're his mom. You take it."

Her eyes shine as she looks at the picture, then she hands it back to me. "Take it home, Max. Take him to Chicago." I want to tell her I love her, that she's the only one I've ever loved, ever could love.

"Thank you," I say instead.

We have dinner at a restaurant around the corner from the storage lot. The place is deserted, a bored waitress perched on a stool by the bar.

"Is there any chance you could squeeze us in," Pip asks, deadpan. "We haven't booked, I'm afraid."

I stifle a laugh, but the waitress is looking around the empty room. "Um . . . yeah, I think that would be fine."

She seats us at a corner table, where we sit at right angles to each other. We work our way through the terrible menu, drink white wine that makes us grimace, and remember the awful restaurant we went to on honeymoon, when the waiter couldn't tear his eyes away from Pip's cleavage, and the steak came garnished with a hair.

"And they still asked us to leave a TripAdvisor review!"

Pip laughs, then she looks at me, suddenly serious. Something sinks inside me. We've been playacting, tonight. Remembering how things used to be. This isn't real.

"I've met someone," she says.

I swill my vinegary wine around my glass, examining it earnestly before taking a sip.

"It's early days—nothing serious—but I wanted you to know."

"Congratulations." Do I mean it? A piece of me does, I think. A small piece. A very small piece. I love her. I want her to be happy.

"His name is Lars. He's a pilot at work. I don't know if it'll go anywhere, but . . ." She trails off. We eat in silence for a while.

"If I hadn't . . ." I can hardly bear to say it, but like some kind of masochist, I have to know. "If we hadn't gone to court, do you think we'd still be together?"

I don't realize my hand is halfway across the table until I feel her fingers through mine. Our eyes lock, and our fingers intertwine, and my heart hurts so much I would give anything to turn back the clock, because she's nodding slowly, reluctantly. **Yes.**

"But it wasn't just the verdict that broke us, Max, it was everything. Dylan's treatment, the court case, the very fact we had to **choose** whether our son lived or died. It broke us."

"Afterward . . . we should have tried harder. We should have made it work."

"Afterwards, everything changed." Pip's crying, now, and I squeeze her hands in mine and wish I could take all her pain away from her. "We were carers, not parents; coworkers, not husband and wife."

I'm shaking my head, but she's right—everything she's saying is right. I wish it weren't, but it is.

"It hurts to be apart," Pip says, "but it hurts more to be together."

I'm glad we chose this godforsaken restaurant, and

that no one else wanted to eat here, because now I'm crying too. "I'm so sorry, Pip. I never thought our marriage would fail."

"Fail?" She shakes her head fiercely. "No, Max. Our marriage ended, but it didn't fail."

She leans toward me and presses her cheek against mine, and we stay like that for the longest time.

forty

Pip

2015

Aeroplanes are countries of their own, their time zones elastic. Passengers eat breakfast at supper time, crack open the G & T when the sun's still high. On aeroplanes you are oblivious to the real world, and today I wish the journey would go on forever.

I ate breakfast in my room, too worried about bumping into Lars to risk leaving. What was I thinking? What went through his head when I kissed him? **One of those**, he must have thought. **Another trolley dolly with her sights set on a pilot.** But I'm not. I wouldn't. I . . . and yet I did. At least, I tried.

What would I have done, if he hadn't stopped me? Slept with him? To get back at Max? I screw up my face, wracked with embarrassment.

"You all right, love?" A woman with severe sunburn

looks at me with concern, perfect white circles where her sunglasses have been. I'm helping out in economy, and glad of the distraction.

"Fine, sorry. A white wine, was it? And Pringles?" I put her snacks on her tray table, and pass her husband—complete with matching panda eyes—the beer and pretzels he asks for. I pin a smile to my face and continue moving slowly down the aisle. **Orange juice, no problem. I'm afraid we're out of diet. Would you like ice with that?** As I chat to passengers I wonder what Max is doing now. Whether he's still working out what to say to me, or whether he has his explanation—his excuses—all ready.

I turned off my phone, in the end. Sent a one-line text—We'll talk when I'm back—and put it in my bag.

When I switch it on in my car, in case I need it on the drive home, there's just one message from him.

Safe trip. I love you xxx

I stare at the message, unable to feel anything other than anger. Three kisses. Once so important; now so meaningless.

The roads are clear, and by nine thirty I'm pulling into our street. I should sleep after a night shift, but I'm off for three days, which means staying up so I can go to bed this evening at a normal time, in an effort to reset my clock. Johannesburg has got to be my last trip—I can't hide this pregnancy for much longer. I will call HR tomorrow. I ignore the tiny voice in my head that says it'll be easier to avoid Lars if I'm grounded.

I pause by the front door, my key in the lock, feeling like a stranger at someone else's house. In the hall it's almost a shock to find everything the same—Max's shoes by the mat, his coat on the rack—when it feels as though everything has changed.

Max is sitting at the kitchen table. Neither of us speaks. Beside him are several empty glasses and mugs, and a dirty knife resting on a plate covered with bread crumbs. His hair is unbrushed, and dark circles ring his eyes. He looks as though he's been sitting in that exact spot since he got back from Chicago.

"Who is she?" I say quietly.

He winces as though the words are physically painful, and I'm glad, because the very thought of them is hurting me.

Max addresses the empty plate. "Her name is Blair. She used to live next door . . . she went to the same swim club when we were kids. She found me on Facebook, and we . . ." He pauses. "We hung out in Chicago."

"You 'hung out'?" I make quotation marks with my fingers. "What is that? Some kind of euphemism for fucking?"

Max stands, so abruptly his chair topples backwards and crashes onto the tiled floor. He comes to stand in front of me and grips my arms fiercely, and I'm shocked to see that he's crying. "I'm so sorry, Pip, I never meant to hurt you. I never meant for any of this to happen, but you were so distant and—"

I shake him off. "Don't you **dare** put this on me!" But my anger is fuelled by the fear—the knowledge— that he's right, that I've slowly pushed him further away. Instinctively, my hand creeps to my stomach, to the secret that wasn't only mine to keep.

"No, no, of course not—that's not what I'm saying. Of course it's my fault, I'm just trying to explain that I needed—" He gives a sharp sigh of frustration, holding up his hands as if physically searching for the words, and as quickly as it came, the anger in me burns out. Exhaustion sweeps over me. I walk across the room and set right the toppled chair, then sit beside it. "You needed to be normal with someone," I say quietly.

Max nods slowly. "Yes." He hesitates, then joins me at the table. We look at each other for the longest time, and I think of everything we've shared together, all the things no one else could possibly understand.

"How long have you been seeing her?" I don't want the answer, and yet I can't not know.

"Five, six months?" His voice adds a question mark, as though he needs me to confirm it. I'm winded. I'd expected weeks, not months. She—Blair—is in Chicago, Max is in the UK, this is not about sex, at least not only about sex. This is long-distance calls, and messages and Skype, and **missing you** . . . I count five, six months backwards in my head. April. May. When Max started talking about having another child. Is that what this is about?

"Do you love her?"

He rubs his face vigorously. He looks at me—wretched, miserable. "I love **you**."

"But do you love her?" I challenge him to meet my eyes, to have the decency to look at me as he tells me the truth. The pause lasts forever.

"Yes."

I nod. And then, because things can't get any worse, I tell him about the baby. I see a shooting star of joy cross his face, before it's tempered by what's happened, by the fact I am only now telling him. He looks at me as though seeing me for the first time, taking in the changes pregnancy has brought.

"You didn't tell me."

"I'm telling you now."

"How far gone are you?"

"I don't know exactly, I haven't seen anyone. Around sixteen, seventeen weeks—"

He widens his eyes in surprise, then looks confused. "You haven't seen anyone? Shouldn't you have had a scan by now? We had one at twelve weeks with . . . before." Dylan's absence hangs between us, heavy and painful, before Max speaks again. "What if there's something wrong with the baby?"

I don't answer. What could I say? That in the

beginning I didn't care how the baby was? That at first I didn't even acknowledge I was pregnant? He must see something in my face because the colour drains from his, and he drags out the words as if each one stings.

"You were going to have an abortion."

"No!"

"How could you do that to me again?"

Again.

We have been pretending, ever since Dylan died, that we are a couple. We have limped through our separate lives, never talking about how we feel, never talking about what happened, about why we did what we did. And all the time, underneath, resentment has festered.

I speak as calmly as I can, my voice low and tense. "I would never have terminated this baby."

"Then why keep it a secret?"

"It's too hard to explain."

"Is it someone else's? Is that it?"

"Don't judge me by your own standards!" I think about kissing Lars, and fall quiet. Am I really any better than Max? "I was scared," I say eventually. "Scared of losing another child, of getting close to this baby, only to have it taken away from me." I see Max move as if planning to reach for me, then changing his mind, gripping the sides of his chair instead. "And it felt disloyal. I loved—I love—Dylan so much, and to simply replace him seemed—"

"It isn't replacing him, Pip."

"I'm not saying it made sense, I'm saying that's how I felt." **Felt.** Not **feel.**

"I can't believe you didn't tell me. All this time—"

"You're hardly in a position to judge me for keeping secrets, Max."

"Hurting you was the last thing I wanted to do, Pip, you have to believe me."

Round and round we go. I swing wildly between quiet acceptance and noisy, angry rage. Max is less erratic, steadfast in his apology, and insisting he never meant this to happen.

"But it did," I say, for what seems like the millionth time, and he asks the question we've both been wondering since I read Max's text.

"So what happens now?"

I don't answer. I'm too scared to say it, to be the one who decides.

"I'll tell Blair it's over, I won't see her again."

"You can't just stop loving her."

"I can." And this time he does reach for me, moving his chair so his knees are touching mine, and taking both my hands in his. "We can make this work, Pip. We're having a baby."

"That isn't a reason to stay together."

He squeezes my hands and rests his forehead against mine, his voice low and earnest. "I love you."

"I love you, too." I start to cry. "But I don't think that's enough."

forty-one

Max

2017

When five-year-old Darcy opens the front door, she's wearing a unicorn T-shirt and nothing else. I haven't seen her in over a year—since I moved back to Chicago—and she eyes me suspiciously. Tom appears in the hall. He scoops up his daughter.

"That's some dress code," I say.

"Sweetheart, you mustn't open the door till Daddy's here." He looks at me and grins. "Trousers are optional, in this house."

"Ah, I remember **those** sort of parties . . ." Alistair's standing in the doorway to the kitchen, a faux-wistful look on his face. "Before soft play and **Frozen** cupcakes took over."

"You love it." I shake his hand.

"How are you doing?"

I look between them, their faces near mirrors of concern. I bob my head to one side, then the other. **So-so.** "I saw Pip last night."

"Ah."

"It was . . . OK." I check myself. "Sad, but OK."

"Like Tom's fashion sense?"

"Wee-wee!" Darcy announces. Tom springs into action, racing past us and into the downstairs loo. I follow Alistair into the kitchen.

"Toilet training?"

"We thought we'd give it another go. The consultant says it'll just all click into place one day—toilet training, coordination, speech . . ." He shrugs. I search his face.

"Does it worry you?"

He pauses before he answers, holding my gaze. "She's here. That's all that matters."

"False alarm," Tom says, returning at a rather more sedate pace. "I think she just likes saying 'wee-wee.'"

"Wee-wee!" Darcy proclaims, on cue.

"See?" Tom picks up a half-full coffee mug from the counter.

"Um, Tom?"

He looks at me, questioningly, a split second before the warmth around his waist gives him the answer. "Bloody hell, Darce."

"You look well," Alistair says, when we're done laughing.

I give a self-deprecating grin. "Honest toil, I guess."

Climbing ladders all day has left me leaner; working outdoors has made me tan. My hands—once soft and manicured—are cracked and callused, but strong.

"Well, it suits you, whatever it is."

When Tom and Darcy reappear, Tom's in a fresh pair of pants; Darcy fully dressed. We sit on the sun-drenched sofa in the orangery off the kitchen, and watch Darcy totter about her pretend shop.

"So . . ." I take the plastic orange Darcy hands me, and pretend to eat it. "Pip's met someone." There's a loaded silence, and I look up sharply. "You knew."

"Lars." Tom looks awkward.

"Have you met him?" I've had fewer than twenty-four hours to adjust to the idea of Pip's having someone else—now the guy's hanging out with our friends. Maybe I should go.

I put down my mug.

But I can't help myself. "What's he like?"

"Dutch," says Tom.

Alistair rolls his eyes. "Helpful."

"Tall, blond, blue eyes," Tom adds. "Pilot. I would."

Alistair throws a cushion at him. "Your daughter is right there!"

"Hypothetically, obviously!"

They see my face and stop short. "Sorry," Tom says.

"I'm just finding this hard to process . . . It's barely been a year. I . . ." I rub my face vigorously, push my fingers through my hair. "I guess it's tough for me to realize I meant that little to her."

It hurts to be apart, she'd said. Clearly not that much.

"Ding dong!" Tom jabs at the air with his index finger. "Did someone order a pity party?"

"Fuck off." Too late, I remember Darcy. "Sorry, guys."

"That's OK," Alistair says, philosophically. "The speech and language therapist is logging all her two-word sentences, and fuck off's as good as any other."

Tom sighs, his face serious again. "You're always going to mean something to Pip, Max."

"Even now she's got the Flying Dutchman?"

There's a pause, before Tom and Alistair burst out laughing.

"Oh God," Tom says. "I'm never going to be able to call him anything else, now."

I watch Darcy transfer plastic vegetables from her kitchen cupboard to a shopping bag. "I'm being ridiculous, aren't I?"

"Yes."

Alistair is more conciliatory—but only just. "She's moving on, Max, that's all. Maybe you need to do the same."

The suitcase of belongings I bring from the storage unit stays untouched in the hallway at 912 North Wolcott. Books, clothes, a pile of records I haven't listened to in years. It's not much to show for a life.

"You could paint the basement," Mom says. "Put a sofa down there, have your things out."

She means well, I know, but it's the final straw. I am not seventeen. This is not a teenage hangout. I cannot stay here.

So what's your plan?" Blair stirs her coffee. She opens TripAdvisor on her cell and finds the restaurant we're in. "Four?"

"Get a job, I guess. Let's give them five—I like their music." Every other Saturday, when Blair's kids are with their dad, we check out some place given a shitty review in the **Tribune**, and give it our own review. It was never meant to become a regular thing. A friend of Blair's got a stinger of a write-up, and she asked if I was free to have lunch there.

"I figure she could use the business."

I read the review. **The bone-dry steak was a welcome relief after the soggy swamp of my seafood starter.** "You're not really selling it to me."

But Blair was persuasive, and I was at a loose end—hell, when was I ever anywhere but at a loose end, nowadays?—so I met her there. We had a great meal, agreed the critic had some unknown axe to grind, and that maybe we should give some of his other targets a bit of patronly love.

"Don't get excited, Mom," I said, when I told her I

was meeting Blair for a second lunch. "We're friends, that's all."

"You've already got a job," Blair says now. She types in our review.

"I paint condos."

"And you like it."

"Yes, but—"

Blair raises an eyebrow. "What am I missing?"

"I was one of the most sought-after management consultants in the country." I sound like a dick, but I can't seem to stop. "I've supported the introduction of strategic change to hundreds of companies that would have gone under without my guidance. I won the MCA project of the year in 2011 **and** 2012. I—" I stop short. It's like I'm reciting someone else's résumé. "It was a good job," I finish lamely.

"But you don't have it anymore," Blair points out, more gently than I suspect I deserve, after my verbal LinkedIn update. "So you need a new one. And right now, painting condos seems like a pretty good alternative." I open my mouth to cut in, but she doesn't let me. "Max, I get it—you miss your old job!"

"No, I—" I was going to say that I didn't feel like a management consultant anymore. That maybe it was time to try something new. Maybe painting condos was as good a job as any other. I rub the beard that feels so much a part of me now.

"Before I had kids, I was a graphic designer. I

worked on campaigns for Adidas, Coca-Cola, IBM . . ." Blair fixes me with a stare that reminds me of my eighth-grade math teacher. "Now, I file papers and make coffee for two lawyers, and help out once a week at swim club, because that's what works for me and the kids right now. Life changes. Shit happens. Get over it."

I don't speak for a second, somewhat floored by this lecture. The mention of Blair's swim club, and my pathetic excuse to avoid helping out, makes me feel even more of a dick.

Blair grins. "I know, I'm like your mom, right?"

"Oh no. You're much, much worse." I pause. "So . . . I guess I'm a decorator." I feel a tiny stab of nerves. Painting Nancy's friends' condos was something to do to fill the time, a way of putting some cash in Mom's pocket. I didn't have to rely on it for a steady income.

"I guess so."

Until now.

"I can't rely on Nancy's impressive black book forever."

"You need a plan."

"I do."

"If only you knew someone who had experience in strategic change." Blair sighs. "Someone, say, who'd won project of the year in 2011 **and** 2012 . . ."

"Touché."

"Shall we get the bill? Seems you've got work to do."

It is a hundred times easier to write a plan for someone else's business than for your own. I delete a dozen attempts, do the math a dozen more times. It takes three weeks, another lunch with Blair, a whole load of cursing, and the return of my old nemesis, Fear of Failure, but I walk into the bank with projected figures, a SWOT analysis, and evidence of demand, and walk out with a loan big enough for a van, a marketing campaign, and a new set of brushes. Max Adams Decorating Services is in business. I walk out, too, with something I've not had in a long time. Pride.

I send Blair some flowers. It feels like the least I can do, after she gave me the kick up the ass I needed. I attach a card. **One good turn deserves another. Count me in for your Thursday-night swim club.**

403

forty-two

Pip

2015

"I'm sorry, sir, there's nothing else I can do."

"But I've flown with you for more than twenty years!"

"We're grateful for your loyalty, sir, but the Met Office issued a fog warning and—"

My customer, a man in his sixties, with a loud shirt and wide lapels on his suit jacket, flings out an arm towards the exterior doors. "Fog? Does that look like fog?"

"The fog is clearing," I say patiently, "but unfortunately we now have a backlog of passengers—"

"A backlog?" The man appears to be hell-bent on repeating everything I say. He turns to the queue behind him, like a barrister addressing the jury. "Hear

that? We're a 'backlog' apparently. That's great customer service."

"I can offer you these refreshment vouchers with our
compliments—"

"Vouchers!"

I just stop myself rolling my eyes, instead keeping
a neutral expression on my face until the loud-shirted
man eventually runs out of steam. He takes the vouchers and goes off to grumble somewhere else for the
six-hour predicted delay before his rescheduled flight.

Not everyone takes the news so badly.

"More time for Christmas shopping," says one passenger with a grin.

"We can't control the weather," says another.

I check in a heavily pregnant woman and her partner, scanning the doctor's letter to make sure the dates
fit. "I'll move you to an aisle seat," I tell her. "Make
sure you walk around at least every thirty minutes,
and drink lots of water."

"Told you." Her partner nudges her.

"She doesn't think I should fly at all," the pregnant
woman says to me, "but it's my brother's wedding, and
it's Antigua, for God's sake—this might be my last
proper holiday for years."

I laugh. "It might well be." I tap my keyboard,
checking availability on their flight. "Look, I can't do
anything in upper class, but if I bump you up to pre-
mium you'll have a bit more leg room."

"Thank you!" They grin like kids let out of school early, their joy infectious.

"Have a great time." I print their boarding passes and hand back their passports. "And good luck with the birth."

"And you!" The pregnant woman nods towards my bump, which—at twenty weeks—is now unmistakable, as though my coming clean about the pregnancy were permission enough to balloon.

My shift is coming to an end, when I see Lars standing nearby. He checks his watch—he's waiting for someone. I feel my cheeks colouring, and I hide them in conversation with the girl taking over from me, but he's still there when I slide out of my seat and pick up my bag. I'm conscious of my bump, feeling more ashamed than ever of the last time we met. **Yes, I tried to kiss you. Yes, I'm married. Yes, I'm pregnant as well. Surprise!**

"Hi!" Lars walks towards me and drops an air kiss by one cheek. "Your friend Jada told me your news. I thought I'd drop by to say congratulations."

"Oh! Thanks." He was waiting for **me**.

"I wondered if you had time for a coffee."

"I have a hospital appointment." I point to my bump, abdicating responsibility for my availability, and thus avoiding the risk of an awkward conversation about what happened in Johannesburg.

"Nothing wrong, I hope?"

"Just a routine scan. I should have had one at twelve

weeks, only I—" I break off. "Anyway, my twenty-week scan is this afternoon, so . . ." I gesture vaguely in the direction of the exit.

"You're anxious, perhaps?" Lars scrutinises my face. "After losing your son? It must be . . . bittersweet—is that the word?"

Bittersweet. It is exactly right.

"Yes, that's the word."

"Perhaps we may talk as we walk?" He speaks English in a correct, almost old-fashioned way that makes me smile. We fall into step together, occasionally breaking apart to circumnavigate a stranded suitcase or a throng of passengers.

"So . . . what have you been up to?" I jump in with the small talk—anything to avoid talking about Joburg . . .

"Actually, I've been learning to cook."

I stop walking and look at him. "Really?"

"Like you said—one day might never come. It's two hours once a week, and I keep missing them because of work, so I can tell you how to make pastry, but not what to do with it, or how to make gravy, but not how to roast a chicken to go with it."

I laugh. "Who else is on the course?"

"There are six of us. Four men and two women. One of the women thinks she's a Cordon Bleu chef, and keeps telling the tutor how **she** does it."

"Bet that goes down well." We've reached the exit, and I stop walking. Lars turns to face me.

407

"Last time we met . . ."

Oh God, last time.

". . . we talked about the countries we'd been to, how much we loved to see the world. When Jada said you were grounded, I thought you must be missing the travel." He takes something from his pocket, and hands it to me.

It's a postcard. A sunset, like the one we saw from the hotel restaurant in Joburg, only reflected in open water instead of a formal garden pool. Reds and oranges shimmer across a lagoon on which is moored a flat-bottomed boat with a tall mast.

"Thailand?"

"Cambodia."

"It's beautiful." I turn to look at him. "Thank you. For this, and"—I hesitate—"for thinking of me." We reach the exit and stop, awkward again. "Things are a bit . . . difficult at the moment." I hope he won't ask me to elaborate. He doesn't. Instead he reaches again into his jacket pocket and pulls out a business card.

"My number. If you feel like a coffee, or a walk, or . . ." He shrugs. "Sometimes it's easier to talk to someone you hardly know, isn't it?"

I watch him walk back the way we came, his long legs making short work of the return journey. I think about how being at work is often more straightforward than being at home, and how much easier it can be to share confidences with hairdressers, dentists, taxi drivers, than with our loved ones. I think of Max meeting up with Blair after a lifetime in different countries—the years making them strangers—and how easy it must have been to fall into a friendship that quickly became more.

I think about all these things as I walk to the car park, and it's only when I'm looking for my keys that I realise there's writing on the other side of the post-card. In thick, confident strokes Lars has written:

Cambodia, December 2015
Wish you were here.

I meet Max in the hospital car park.

"It'll be easier," I said, although we both knew that wasn't the real reason. The maternity unit is next to the children's hospital—I wasn't sure I'd even be able to walk up to the door.

"You look great." Max kisses my cheek. He holds my gaze for a second, and I feel so suddenly sad that we couldn't make this work, and yet at the same time so certain that it's over. "How are you feeling?"

"OK. Good." I stop. "Nervous."

"About the scan?"

"About . . ." I wave an arm towards the hospital. Max takes my hand.

"Me too. Come on." We walk together, our eyes

dead ahead, and we don't stop until the doors slide open and we're in the entrance to the maternity unit. I let out a breath. That was easier than I thought.

It is nothing like PICU. There are rows of women, stroking enormous bellies and—for the most part—looking perfectly content to be doing so. A heavily pregnant girl runs after an errant toddler, catching him by the play area and tickling him till he squeals with laughter. He'll adore that new baby, I think. And then she'll start crawling, and wanting big brother's toys, and . . . I feel a tight pain in my chest.

"OK?" Max searches my face for concern.

"OK." **Stop doing that, Pip. It's like picking a scab, or throwing stones at a bear. You know what's going to happen, how it's going to make you feel.** I stop it. At the far end a nurse with a clipboard calls someone's name. "Let's sit over there." I find a magazine and flick idly through the pages.

Max leans forward on his knees, picking at his fingers, working up to something that doesn't surprise me when it comes. "I miss you."

What can I say? What **should** I say? I miss him too, but that doesn't change anything.

"You can't have us both," I say softly. If there are two paths, two choices, you have to pick one. We, of all people, know that.

"Philippa Adams?"

"Saved by the bell," Max says, with a wry smile. He

holds out a hand and I take it and squeeze it as we follow the woman with the clipboard.

"First baby?" the sonographer says. The pain in my chest returns, and I look at Max, but before either of us can speak, she finishes reading our notes. She looks up. "No, I see it isn't. I'm so sorry for your loss." There's a tiny pause, and I wonder if I can deal with this, but then she picks up a pen and asks, "Any complications in that first pregnancy. With . . ."—she checks the notes again—"Dylan?"

"None." It feels good to hear his name. To confirm that he came from me, that he existed. "It was a textbook pregnancy." I put a hand on my stomach. "And no problems with this one, either."

"Excellent." She beams at me as though I've passed a test. "Hop onto the bed, then."

I should be anxious. What if there's no heartbeat? I try to remember when I last felt movement. What if there's something wrong? I finally give shape to the fear that has plagued me since I fell pregnant—since Max and I first talked about having more children. What if this baby is already sick? What if he has disabilities incompatible with life?

What if that's my punishment?

I close my eyes as the sonographer smears cold gel across my stomach, and only as the whoomph whoomph whoomph of a heartbeat echoes around the room do I turn my head and look at our baby.

"Do you want to know the sex?"

"Yes." Max and I speak at the same time. We've had enough unknowns to last a lifetime. I feel his hand slip into mine as the sonographer slides the probe across my stomach and the funny bean-shaped baby on the screen slips in and out of focus.

"Congratulations," she says at last, pressing a key to print a copy of the scan. "You're having a little girl, and she looks absolutely perfect."

forty-three

Max

2017

In the few days between Christmas and New Year, I finally get my own place.

"You know you could have stayed here as long as you wanted to," Mom says, as she helps me pack my things. Now that I no longer spend my days curled beneath the pink comforter, I think she quite likes having me around.

"I'll come over all the time."

Before my parents bought their house here in East Village, it wasn't even called East Village. It was a few streets between Ukrainian Village and Noble Square; an area where more people spoke Polish than English, and it was easier to buy kielbasa than hot dogs. The year I was born the arson rate generated its own task force. My parents stayed because it was where Dad's family had always been—way back when they were Adamczyk instead of Adams. I looked at a couple of apartments close by, but settled on a studio at 555 Arlington, Lincoln Park. It's tiny, but it's not far from the lake and it comes with parking. I signed a twelve-month lease.

"You better."

When I came back to Chicago I thought Mom's world was small, her social life limited. Now she's out every day, and busy with meetings and coffee mornings, and I realize she was staying home for me. That she put her life on hold while her adult son had a breakdown.

I do what I can to say thank you. I cook most evenings—although never as well as she does—and I look for movies I think she'll enjoy. I drive her in my new van to the t'ai chi class at her senior fitness group.

I think of Leila Khalili, and her excitement at the prospect of her mother's moving in with her. **I'm the lucky one**, she said. I've been lucky, too. Lucky to have another opportunity to spend time with my own mom, to live together as adults, not parent and son.

Blair helps me get settled. "Where do you want these books?"

I look around the tiny space, smaller than the sitting room of the house Pip and I have not long since sold. "Over there. I'll need to put the bookcase together."

The studio isn't furnished, but since there's little

room for much more than a bed, a small sofa, and a bookcase, my trip to IKEA hasn't broken the bank. I'll eat on the sofa, and, well, if there's ever any call for a dinner for two, it'll be side by side at the breakfast bar that separates off the kitchen area.

It's a weird feeling, starting over. Weird having just two of everything in the cabinets—two cups, two plates, two bowls—when for years you've had dinner sets and extra flatware for Thanksgiving. Weird, too, to make decisions without checking. Putting the pans—one big, one small—in whatever cabinet you want. I feel the beginnings of sadness but don't let it take root. Instead I think of the spiffy writing on my van, of the logo that Blair has designed, with its cheerful brush like an exclamation mark after my initials. I think of the place I'm in right now, and how different it is from the place I was in last year. And I count my blessings.

When we've finished, we fall onto the sofa and survey our work.

"Very comfy," I conclude. I rest my head back against the pink comforter I took from Mom's.

"I've got a gray one somewhere, I think," she said, when I asked if I could have it.

"I'd like this one—if you don't mind."

She held my gaze and I guess she understood, because she smiled and didn't ask why, just took it off the bed and gave it to me.

"Oh, I got you something!" Blair picks up her keys

and disappears. She's back in two minutes, carrying a big bag containing a plant and a handful of other things I can't make out. "OK, so this is a bit cheesy, but . . ." She flushes, and instead of watching her unpack the bag, I find myself watching the color on her cheeks—the way her eyes are half excited, half apprehensive.

"May your new home be full of life." She takes out the plant, a fern with light green fronds that dance in the breeze from the open window, and hands it to me.

"Thank you—it's lovely."

"There's more." Another blush, half-hidden by her hair, this time, as she leans forward to look into the bag. "OK. May you live in light and happiness." She sits back on her heels and presents me with the next present, a Moroccan-style lantern with crescent-moon cutouts revealing the candle inside.

"This is amazing." I look at her. "You're amazing."

The next gift is a saltshaker. I raise an eyebrow.

"So that life will never be bland." Blair grins.

"Brilliant."

A loaf of bread is given with the hope that my new home will never know hunger; a jar of honey to add sweetness to the hours spent here. Blair's awkwardness fades, the color in her cheeks returning to normal.

"Last, but not least," she says, producing the final gift. "May you never go thirsty."

We drink the champagne out of highballs—I add wineglasses to the list of things I still need—and toast to **new beginnings**.

"To friendship," Blair adds, raising her glass. We lock eyes for a second and now it's me who colors, because the feeling that rose up inside me as she said it seemed a lot like disappointment.

"To friendship," I echo. That's all I want. I love Pip, and that's not going to change. "Hey, I got my police checks back," I add, as though I just remembered.

"Oh, great!"

"So I can help out with swim club this week, if you still want me to."

"You bet we do."

I follow Blair's directions to the sports club on Sheffield and give my name to the woman on reception, who tells me the Challenge Swim Club runs in the smaller of the two pools. **Mixed ability**, Blair said. I wonder how much of my own training I'll remember, and how easy I'll find it to share that knowledge with others.

In the locker room I keep my T-shirt but change my jeans for swim shorts. I leave my shoes in a locker and head for the pool.

A sound stops me in my tracks, even before I see the water. A high-pitched cry you might take for distress, but which hollows my chest and makes me look to the wall for support. There's another high-pitched cry, only it isn't a cry at all, but a laugh. Another, and another.

Dylan.

The thought is there before logic can take over. I take a few steps more and come out poolside, and then my feet won't move anymore. I expected a line of kids in matching suits, perched on the pool edge, waiting for their turn. I expected tumble turns and freestyle, butterfly and backstroke. Stopwatches and races.

Not this.

There are around a dozen kids in the pool, and at least as many adults. The children sit, or lie, in floating pillows, their heads pushed carefully out of the water. Some are motionless, their only movement the rise and fall of the water; others thrash their limbs wildly, splashing everyone in their orbit. By the side of the pool is a hydraulic hoist, there to help the children in and out.

Blair is in the pool. She sees me, and says something to another volunteer, before swimming to the steps. She's wearing a blue Challenge Swim Club T-shirt over a one-piece swimsuit.

"You should have said," I say, as soon as she reaches me. A tremor runs through my body.

"I didn't think you'd come."

"I wouldn't have done." My heart feels like it might stop, or explode, or . . . **Dylan, Dylan, Dylan.**

"I can't do this. I'm sorry." I start walking toward the locker room.

"This was my daughter's club."

I stop. Turn back.

"My eldest child, Alexis. She was born with cerebral palsy and a ton of other challenges." She gives a gentle smile, holding my gaze and stopping me from leaving. "She died the year Brianna was born. She was four years old."

There's a scream of delight from the pool. A teenage boy in a float jacket is being spun round and round by two volunteers.

"You never said."

"I didn't want it to seem like I was preaching. In grief, I've found you have to make your own journey."

I wonder if Mom knows, and if Blair told her not to say anything.

"Alexis loved the water—it was her happy place. I started helping out when they were short of volunteers, and I never stopped."

"Don't you—" I stop.

"Find it hard?" She thinks about it for a moment, then shakes her head. "Not in the way you mean." She looks at the pool and then at me. "Having kids isn't a zero-sum game, Max."

"I look at these children and I—" I swallow. "I see Dylan."

Blair's eyes soften, but when she speaks again, she's firm. "Then you're not looking hard enough."

forty-four

Pip

2016

The sky is the cloudless kind of blue that looks like a summer's day, until you step outside and see your breath misting before you. The washing line flutters with tiny onesies, softened by a wash, and pegged out to profit from a rare dry day. I wedge my basket against my hip, awkward against my vast bump, and with my free hand unclip each garment and drop it inside. My baby will bring the spring with her, and we will spend the summer months lying on the grass in the sunshine.

As I work, an aeroplane passes overhead and I wave, still the eight-year-old child who would lie in her parents' garden watching planes, wishing for adventures. I didn't fly until I was seventeen, but I knew the name of every plane leaving Birmingham airport, and how many staff would be on board. When I was fourteen my father arranged for me to visit the airport. I was treated like royalty, allowed to press the button to start the baggage belt, sit in the cockpit of a Boeing 747, and demonstrate the safety jacket and emergency exits to rows of imaginary passengers. My parents have the photograph on their mantelpiece. When I joined British Airways, eight years later, Dad sent it to the weekly paper, who ran a cheesy piece headlined **Local girl's career takes off**.

I reach the end of the line and take my full washing basket inside. What will I do, once the baby is born? I stopped working long-haul when we had Dylan, but I missed it, and it's taken years to get my career back to where it was. Maybe I could manage part-time long-haul if Max weren't away so much, but . . .

"I'll still be there for you," he said, as he packed the last few things into his car. "Now, and when the baby comes. Just like before." A box of vinyl leaned drunkenly against the passenger window, wedged on top of a bag of clothes.

"I know." Only of course it wouldn't be like before. Max wasn't going to rub my feet after a long day at work, or lay his head by my bump at night to sing tuneless lullabies to our unborn child. He wouldn't be there at three in the morning, with a baby who won't sleep.

"We don't have to do this." Max paused by the open car door. "It's not too late."

It would be so easy to tell him to unpack, to tell Blair he doesn't love her, to move back in and wait for the baby to be born and then . . . what? Be unhappy? Look at each other and think of what might have been? What could still be?

When people talk about riding out the ups and downs of marriage, they mean the usual stresses of life. Redundancies and money worries, health scares and recovery. My relationship with Max was played out in the national papers. In court. The nuances of our body language were captured by paparazzi and discussed across the kitchen tables of houses in which we never set foot. These are not normal circumstances. We are not the same people we were when Dylan was alive.

"It is." We kissed, then, a slow, lingering kiss I felt in every part of my body.

A sad kiss, a goodbye kiss, is quite a different kind of kiss. Just as new lovers, too nervous still to say the words, thread their embraces with silent **I love you**s, so a goodbye kiss hides words beneath its surface. **I'm so sorry**, ours said, **so sorry it happened this way**. And more than that: **I still love you, I will always love you**.

My parents don't understand it.

"But if you still love each other . . ." Mum looked for support from my father, whose discomfort was clear.

"It's their decision, Karen."

"They're having a **baby**."

"I'm right here," I reminded them. "And well aware we're having a baby, as is Max. But that isn't a reason to stay together." Mum's pursed lips suggested otherwise.

Any shred of doubt she might have had that our separation was permanent was destroyed when I told her we'd filed for divorce.

"But that's so . . . so final."

"That's sort of the idea, Mum." We needed the closure. Both needed it, although Max more than me, I suspected. He remained wracked with guilt over cheating on me, prepared to finish things with Blair and make a go of our marriage. But our marriage was a ruin; his relationship with Blair a clean plot, foundations laid, ready for a new start. I owed him that new start.

Inside, I put the washing basket on the table, and hear the drop of letters on the mat. I am so large, now, that I can't bend to pick up the post, but have to spread my legs wide and crouch, one hand pushed against the door for balance. Two utility bills, a letter from my solicitor, and a postcard from Johannesburg.

It isn't the same without you! says the card, on the back of a picture of the Palazzo Montecasino. It's been taken from the end of the garden, looking across the pool to the restaurant terrace. A hand-drawn arrow points to one of the tables—to **our** table.

I put the card on the fridge, where it joins the cards from Barbados, St. Lucia, Shanghai, Boston, Vegas,

Seattle, and more. My virtual round-the-world trip, courtesy of Lars. **Sometimes it's easier to talk to someone you hardly know.** Maybe I **will** call him, sometime. After the baby's born.

Upstairs I put away the clean onesies in the chest of drawers on the landing. She—we haven't yet found a name on which we both agree—will be next to my bed for the first few months, and this delay gives me justification for not yet having created a nursery for her. We have four rooms upstairs. The master suite I still think of as "ours," despite having slept alone there now for almost three months; the guest room; Max's study—now empty of books and computer; and Dylan's room, now my reading room. I wander into all of them, now, and imagine the cot in each one, a little girl bouncing on the mattress, impatient to get up. Will I see that? Will this baby inside me grow to Dylan's age? Beyond? **Of course she will**, I tell myself sternly, but still I can't bring myself to fetch the cot from the loft, to paint a room in cheerful colours. **Small steps**, I think.

I sit in the armchair by the window in the room Max made for me, and look out across the rooftops. I pull my aching feet up beneath me, and rest my head against the side of the chair. My book lies on the table next to me, a folded hospital appointment letter marking my page, but for once I don't feel like reading.

Beside my chair, where it has stayed untouched for the last three years, is my bag of knitting. I reach for it and pull it onto my lap, pausing a moment before I open it. When I do, I have to close my eyes and focus on breathing in and then out, in and then out. The smell of the hospital, real or imagined—I can't tell; of antibac gel, and rubber-soled shoes, and laundered nurse's scrubs. The beep beep beep of Dylan's machines, the sticky feeling on my fingers from the electrodes on his chest. My eyes still shut, I put my hand in the bag and feel the soft knitted squares. I imagine the finished blanket draped across the end of the "big-boy bed" we'd planned for when Dylan was three. I feel the pain in my chest and instead of fighting it I let it bud and bloom and die back, and when it is gone I open my eyes, and I feel lighter. I watch the birds on the rooftops for a while, and then I take out my knitting needles, with the half-finished square dangling midrow, and I start to knit.

forty-five

Max

2018

"Hey, big man, how's it going? Missed you last week."

Eight-year-old Michael is lying outstretched in the water, float rings around his neck, pelvis, arms, and legs. His therapist is gently guiding Michael's limbs through a range of movements designed to improve his muscle and joint function, the water providing natural resistance.

"He had a cold, so he stayed in school. Better safe than sorry, right?"

Like several others in the Challenge Swim Club, Michael lives in a residential school in Chicago, and is brought to the pool once a week in a specially adapted minibus. Some of the kids—including Madison, who is right now splashing her mother with unbridled glee on her face—live at home, and come with their parents. In addition to the volunteers, like Blair and me, there are physical therapists and specialist water therapists, and sports club staff to operate the hoists. The place is packed, and the noise level extraordinary—like a kiddie play center with the volume turned up.

I talk to Michael so his therapist can focus on the exercises. Although Michael loves being in the water, he hates being splashed on his face, and will respond by holding his breath until his lips turn blue. My job is to watch out for the splashers and steer them gently away, which is easier said than done in a pool full of excited kids.

After the session I hang around for Blair, who emerges with hair still wet from the shower. She pulls on a purple bobble hat as we walk to the car park together. "Did you see the **Tribune**'s write-up of the new pizzeria at Clark and Diversey?" I say. "Might be one for Saturday's lunch?" Our last lunch, a fortnight ago, was at a Latin fusion bar in the West Loop that had more than deserved the scathing review dished out by the newspaper's restaurant critic. We were as kind as we could be with our TripAdvisor review.

"I was gonna talk to you about that, as it happens."

"Will you have the kids? Bring them too, if you want."

"No, they're still going to their dad's, but . . ." She takes her keys from her purse. "I wondered if you wanted to have dinner instead of lunch." She looks at me and lifts her chin slightly. "Someplace nice."

"Someplace nice," I echo, taking a moment to catch up. I take in her raised chin, the color in her cheeks. "Oh. You mean . . . like a date?"

Blair laughs. "Yes, Max. Like a date. An actual date. You and me. What do you say?"

Despite the biting March winds, I feel suddenly too hot. I want to try to explain, but all I can think of is **It's not you, it's me**, and even I'm not enough of a dick to say that.

"Gotcha." Blair drops her head and holds up a hand, flat palm toward me. "No need to spell it out." Then she looks back up, and she laughs again, and maybe she really doesn't care, or perhaps she's a great actress, but either way there's nothing in her expression that suggests it matters.

"Pizza, then?" I raise my voice as she walks to her car. "Apparently 'the menu is as uninspired as the setting' so it should be a blast."

"I'll let you know!" She waves a cheery goodbye and drives off, and I stand for a second, wishing I could have the last two minutes again, then realizing I still wouldn't know what to say.

Blair's busy on Saturday. She lets me know via text, complete with kisses and a smiley face that tell me she's not mad at me. I go to the pizza place with Mom, who is bemused by the dull menu and by the brick walls the owners have inexplicably painted brown. I think how Blair and I would have laughed about it, how we would have ordered different things, so we could experience the full range of terribleness. I feel in limbo Saturday night, and wake up the next day leaden and unsettled, wanting the day over, the week over. I go for a run, crossing the park on Fullerton, then swinging right to head south on the lakefront, million-dollar penthouses on my right-hand side, and the lake as big as an ocean to my left. The wind's up and the water's gray, waves hitting the jetties and crashing over the beach to where the lifeguards stand. I drop down to the trail and find my rhythm, still restless when I hit the Loop.

Blair doesn't suggest another lunch. I think that perhaps I should message her, but days go by, and then two weeks, and then it feels awkward that it's been so long. I take a job out of town, sending apologies to the swim club secretary, but not to Blair, and spending the evenings alone in my studio, the walls closing in on me. A familiar weight presses on my chest, and as spring arrives in Chicago, a black cloud dogs me. I stop chasing new clients, only working when it falls in my lap, and when Blair texts—Hey, stranger, what's new?—I leave the message unanswered.

So." Mom surveys the empty bottles of wine on the kitchen counter, then eyes me with a critical gaze. "I've not been feeling great," I mutter.

She drags me out, ordering coffee and making me eat breakfast. "Blair said you're ignoring her calls."

"One or two, maybe." Three, four, five . . .

"She's a nice girl, Max." Mom hesitates. "You've got a lot in common, as it happens—"

"I know about Alexis."

Mom breathes out. "I would have told you, but . . ."

"It's OK." A lump forms in my throat even as I think about what I'm trying to say. I fold my napkin in half, then half again. "Dylan would have been eight next week." I blink at my napkin, knowing without looking that Mom's fighting tears, just as I am. "I should be out buying him a present."

There's a moment of silence, then she reaches out and puts a hand over mine. "Make him proud of you, Max. That's the best present you could give him." And I realize she isn't crying for Dylan, but for me.

I call back a guy with a ten-day job in a new development on Milwaukee, and agree to start right away. The building's empty and I'm glad of the solitude. I focus on my brushstrokes, on the cutting-in, the neat line where paint meets glass. I breathe with my strokes. Up, down; in, out. I empty my head, pushing out the thoughts that threaten to engulf me, and by the end of the first week I feel the black cloud starting to lift.

At five o'clock on the Saturday, I take a break. I sit

on the floor with my back to the wall beneath my freshly painted window, and I rest my forearms on my thighs, my cell phone in my hands between them. I watch the clock tip from minute to minute.

At five ten precisely Pip rings. I wondered if she might. I hoped she would.

"And just like that," she says, "we became parents. Ten past eleven, on the fifth of May 2010."

"You were amazing."

"You never left my side."

"Remember that brilliant midwife?"

"'Put those away, Dr. McNab—I've been delivering babies since before you qualified, and we are a long way from forceps time.'"

Pip laughs, and I close my eyes, leaning my head against the wall and wishing so much she were here, by my side. "How are things with the—" I stop myself just before I say **Flying Dutchman**. "With Lars?"

"OK." It's a cautious answer, and my heart leaps, but she hasn't finished. "Good, actually. Great."

"I'm glad." **I'm not.**

"Have you . . . have you met anyone?"

I think of Blair. About the dinner date that didn't happen, and the way she didn't seem to care. I think of the flush of color her cheeks take when she feels awkward, and the Cheshire Cat grin, when she doesn't. I think of shiny brown corkscrew curls.

"No. There's no one."

After Pip's gone—after we've said **Happy birthday,**

Dylan, and I've bitten back tears and heard Pip do the same—I call Blair to see if she's free this weekend.

"I wondered if I could take you out to dinner. Someplace nice."

T he someplace nice ends up being Roister in the West Loop, on seats around the open kitchen, where we have beef broth with bucatini noodles, and chicken cooked three ways—every one of them delicious. Blair's wearing a dress made from some stretchy material that clings to her hips, and ties in a complicated fashion twice around her waist. Her hair is loose and smells of something I recognize but would never in a million years be able to name. Pip would know.

"How long did it take you to get over losing your daughter?"

Blair's eyes widen slightly. **Way to go, Max. As first-date conversation starters go, that one's a blinder.** I shake my head. "Christ, sorry, that came out without—"

"No, it's fine. I don't mind talking about her. But what makes you think I'm over it?"

"Because you're . . . you're so . . ." I wave a hand around, encompassing her hair, her outfit, her . . . "You're so **together**."

She laughs, then. It's different to Pip's. Pip's laugh is high and light—like the top notes of a musical score. Blair's is a bark—a loud snort of amusement that makes people look, makes people smile. "I'm fifteen years down a freeway you've only just joined, Max."

"Tell me it gets easier."

She hesitates, like she's considering a lie, then she shakes her head. "No, it doesn't get easier. But you get better at it. Like you got better at riding that BMX of yours when we were kids. You had wobbles, you fell off from time to time, but mostly you didn't have to think about it. You knew you were riding a bike—you knew your legs were pumping those pedals, and your hands were gripping that handlebar—but you didn't **think** about it. You just did it."

I have a sudden memory of Blair at ten years old, hair flying out behind her as she bumped up the curb on the bike she'd borrowed from her brother. So much has happened in both our lives—would we be the same people if we hadn't lost our children?

After dinner we walk to the El and my hand finds Blair's. It's soft and warm, but it feels strange in mine, it doesn't find its place instinctively. I feel as though I'm playing a part—**Look how much better I am, see how I'm over Pip!**—and I listen to Blair talk and feel myself pulling away, retreating into myself.

As we round the corner onto Sangamon, Blair stops walking. "What's wrong?"

"Nothing," I say automatically. I keep walking, because sometimes it's easier to talk when you don't have to look at someone. I sigh. "Your hand feels wrong."

"I've got another one." She jazz-hands them both at me, then stops when I don't laugh. "Max, I'm not chasing you down the aisle. We're on a date. We've had a nice evening, a lovely evening—at least **I've** had a lovely evening—and now we're walking to the El. That's it."

"Being with someone else . . . I feel like I'm cheating on her."

"Even though she's seeing someone?"

"How do you know that?" The line for the El crosses the end of the street, and I can hear the rumble of a train approaching.

Blair looks uncomfortable. "Your mom told me, I guess. Sorry. We weren't talking about you. Much." She tries for a grin, but it doesn't quite happen.

"I feel like such a shit, Blair."

"Because you're out with me? Because I honestly don't think Pip would mind. If anything, I think she'd be—"

"No, this isn't about Pip—I feel like I'm being a shit to **you**." I stop walking and turn to her, my hands on her shoulders. "I really like you. I really, really like you. I'd like to see where this goes. But however much I try, I still love Pip."

"Of course you still love Pip. I'd be worried if you didn't." She smiles. "When Alexis was born, I thought I'd never have a second child. How could I, when I'd already poured all my love into my first? But then

434

I had Brianna, and then Logan, and I realized something they don't teach you in biology." The train thunders above our head, a blur of light and noise and screeching brakes. Blair takes my hand and places my palm flat against my chest. "The heart stretches."

forty-six

Pip

2016

I press the button and wait for the lift. The Clubhouse is only one floor up, but the last few weeks of my pregnancy have been blighted by pelvic pain, forcing me to bring forward my maternity leave by a fortnight. Today is my last day at work, and any hope of knocking off early disappeared when my supervisor appeared, carrying a large cake box and looking harassed.

"Can you take this up to the Clubhouse? God knows how it ended up down here, but there's a private party missing their cake, and somehow I'm the one getting it in the neck."

No doubt everyone else had suddenly been "too busy," I think now, shifting uncomfortably from one foot to the other. The smell of sugary icing from the box in my hands makes my mouth water. If the

Clubhouse isn't busy, sometimes they'll let us grab something to eat when they refresh the buffet. My stomach rumbles at the thought, but when I reach the lounge I don't recognise the girl on reception. She smiles with relief, no doubt having got it in the neck herself for the missing cake. I go to leave it on her desk.

"Sorry, would you mind taking it through? I can't leave reception."

I am fast losing patience. There must be a hundred people on duty today, yet somehow the massively pregnant one ends up running errands. I am definitely not leaving here without a sandwich for the drive home.

The Clubhouse has different zones, separated by partitions that give the illusion of privacy. At the back of the room I hear a buzz of conversation, and I make my way through the rest of the lounge, where couples and solo travellers sit in relative silence, reading, working, eating.

What am I supposed to do with this cake, anyway? They better not be expecting me to serve it, as well. But when I walk behind the partition the first person I see is Jada, still in her uniform, but holding a glass of champagne.

"Oh!" I hold the box in front of me. "Do you know anything about this cake?"

She grins. "I do, as it happens. I ordered it."

I'm slow to catch on—too busy thinking that if she

ordered the bloody thing, the least she could have done was get it to the right place herself—so that when I see Ethan, and Marilyn, and then—the cheek of it!—the very supervisor who sent me up here in the first place, I still don't realise what's going on, until . . .

"Surprise!" Everyone holds up their glasses, and I look up to see a banner strung along the partition, saying **Congratulations!** Jada takes the box from me, and opens it, and I gaze down at the most beautiful cake with pink frosted roses and **It's a girl!** iced around the edge.

"It's **my** cake?"

"It's your baby shower!"

Everyone laughs, and someone hands me a glass of sparkling elderflower, and then it's all kisses and hand-shakes and **Hope it all goes well.**

They all know, these people, they know what happened to Dylan. It passed from one person to another—not gossip, exactly, but a quiet explanation I found I didn't mind. And now, here they all are—people I have worked with both airside and landside—wishing me well, not only because that's what you do when people have babies, but because they really mean it.

"Nice party." Like at least half the people here, Lars is on the orange juice. He tips his glass towards mine and we clink a toast.

"If I'd known, I'd have dressed up." I give a rueful smile and sweep my free hand along my outfit and out to the side. **Ta-da!** I'm wearing Virgin's answer to maternity wear: a black top and trousers, with my red crew cardigan. Hardly glamorous.

"You're . . . what is it they say?" Lars finds the word. "Blooming."

"And I thought pilots had to have perfect eyesight . . ."

He opens his mouth to protest, before realising I'm joking. "So," he says instead. "Now that you're on maternity leave, perhaps we could have that coffee?"

Y ou're going on a date with Lars Van der Werf?"
"It's not a date." The party is over, and Jada and I are sitting in neighbouring loungers in the corner of the Clubhouse. "It's a cup of coffee." On the floor next to me is a hamper of goodies, stuffed with onesies, chocolates, nappies, a mountain of toiletries, and a miniature bottle of champagne from Marilyn— **to sneak into your hospital bag.**

Jada pinches a piece of icing from the plate resting on my bump, weighed down with my second enormous slice of cake. Eating for two, and all that. "You might get carried away and shag him over the fondant fancies."

I laugh, and my plate wobbles.

"You do fancy him, though, don't you?"

"Don't be ridiculous."

She raises one perfectly arched eyebrow.

"Oh OK, maybe a little bit."

She holds her hands aloft, claiming victory.

"But in a purely objective way." I ignore Jada's pointed stare. "I'm about to have a baby with a husband I'm divorcing—it's a bit early to be shopping around for a replacement, don't you think?"

"You're being proactive."

"It's purely platonic, I promise you. Not least because, as far as he's concerned, I'm still married." Thankfully, Lars has never mentioned my clumsy attempt to seduce him.

"Oh no, he knows you're separated." She stands up. "Come on, I promised we'd be out of here by five."

"What? How does he know that?"

Jada grins and holds out a hand to heave me up. "Because I told him."

I meet Lars a few days later, at the end of March. He lives in St. Albans, and so we meet halfway, at a pub just outside of Milton Keynes, where we end up having lunch, instead of coffee.

It's not a date, I remind myself, as he helps me out of my coat, and pulls out my chair for me to sit down. **It's not a date**, I repeat, as I feel my skin warming under his gaze, and the jolt of my nerve endings as my arm brushes against his. **It's not a date.**

"What's the one place you'd like to go, that you've

never visited?" Lars leans back in his chair, waiting for my answer.

I think for a moment. I've flown every week—discounting my time off with Dylan—since I was twenty-two. There aren't many places I haven't been. Suddenly I have it. "The Lake District."

"Really?" Lars laughs.

"Really. I've never been, and it looks beautiful. I'd like to go camping by the lakes, and sit by a fire toasting marshmallows and telling stories. How about you?"

But I never do get to hear where Lars would like to go, because just at that moment there's a rush of wetness down my legs, and my first thought is how glad I am that this is my second baby, because if I hadn't given birth before I might have thought that my bladder had let me down. My second thought is that I have no idea where Max is.

"I'm so sorry," I say, absurdly British, "but I'm having a baby."

To his credit, Lars simply smiles. "I had noticed." For a moment I think he's referring to what feels like a tsunami of amniotic fluid beneath our table, but then I realise he thinks I'm apologising simply for being pregnant. I open my mouth to explain, just as the first contraction hits me, and a low moan escapes me, like a cow coming in for milking. I double over, gripping the table with both hands.

"Oh my God, you mean you're having a baby now!"

I nod, unable to speak until the pain recedes, and the tightness across my bump passes. "I'd better go home and get my notes ready." I still haven't packed a bag, and despite my midwives' advice to keep my notes in the car, they are sitting on the kitchen table.

"I'll drive you."

"It's fine, it'll be ages yet. With Dylan I was in labour for—" Pain punches me in the stomach. "Oh God!" I'm vaguely aware of people rushing around us, of Lars asking staff to call an ambulance, and me saying **It's fine, let's drive**. I hear him telling them **It's too early—she's not due for another month**, and I think suddenly that yes, I would like an ambulance, because it **is** too early, and what if . . . what if . . .

"Max—" I manage.

"I'll call him."

I reach for my bag, where somewhere, I know there is a tatty business card. I fish erratically for it, and someone takes it from me and retrieves the card. I feel a sudden urge to be on all fours, and I half move, half fall onto the floor, crying out as another contraction seizes me. It's happening too fast. Too early, and too fast. If the baby's in distress I can't be here, can't give birth on the floor of a restaurant . . .

And then I hear the distant sounds of a siren, and they get louder and louder, and Lars is rubbing my back and saying **You're doing so well**, and then someone says **She's in here**, and there's a wheelchair, and paramedics, and gas and air—oh, glorious gas and air!

I deliver my daughter in the back of an ambulance, halfway between the pub and the maternity unit at Milton Keynes hospital. I deliver my daughter with Lars's hand crushed in mine, and with a paramedic at the business end. And despite being three weeks and four days early, and despite her weighing just five pounds one ounce, she is absolutely perfect.

At the hospital they take her away. I beg them not to, but the midwife—though kind—is firm.

"She's early and a bit grunty. I'd feel happier if NICU check her over. I'm going to get you a cup of tea with lots of sugar, and before you know it she'll be back with you where she belongs."

My chest tightens, my breasts tingling with the promise of milk that has nowhere to go. I'm supposed to be at Warwick maternity unit. I'm supposed to give them my notes, which say in big letters that we've lost a child, that we might be worried, we might be scared. They take me onto the ward, and I keep asking **When will she be back? Can you see if she's OK?** but they're busy, and they don't understand—they don't understand what we've been through.

"It'll be OK," Lars says, and although he can't possibly know that, I am reassured by his calm presence, by the fact that he seems utterly unfazed by what has happened. My arms ache with the weight of the empty space between them. I try not to—I try so hard not to—but I start crying. **I just want my daughter. Please, give me my daughter.**

"Pip!" A door swings shut with a loud bang, and Max rushes onto the ward, jacketless and with his tie hanging crooked, loose around his neck. He looks wildly around, sees me, and crosses to my bed. Then he sees me crying, he sees the empty Perspex crib next to me.

"No." He shakes his head and takes a step back. "No, no, no . . ."

"Here she is!" The midwife walks briskly towards us, pushing a cot. "Here's Mummy." She's talking to the bundle of blanket she now lifts and places in my arms. She's talking to my daughter.

"She's absolutely fine. A tiny bit jaundiced, which is quite normal for a preemie, but nothing we're concerned about. Congratulations, Mum and . . ." The midwife looks between Max and Lars. Lars coughs awkwardly.

"I'm just a friend."

"We were having lunch when I went into labour."

Max doesn't seem to be listening. He's gazing at the scrap in my arms, and reaching to stroke a single finger across her forehead. "Can I hold her?"

"Of course." I open my arms and let him take his daughter, and he walks over to the window and holds her up to kiss her face and whisper words I only hear in my heart. The midwife leaves, and Lars stands up.

"Thank you so much," I say. "I don't know what I would have done if you hadn't been there."

Max seems to see Lars for the first time. I wonder what's in his head—if he's wondering who Lars is, what he means to me—but he shifts our daughter to the crook of his left arm, and extends his right to Lars. "Max."

"Lars. I work with Pip."

The two men look at each other for a moment, and then Max smiles.

"Thank you."

"It was nothing," Lars says, which makes us all laugh, because it was everything. "Look after her," he says to Max, as he leaves, and I don't know if he means the baby or me.

forty-seven

Max

2018

At Kucher Consulting, life revolved around problems. I was a problem-solver, a troubleshooter, the guy who could see what no one else could. The fixer. I could identify the barriers to a successful merger, or set the strategy for a new market entry. I could find the weak spots in a company's organizational structure, and make it stronger. There wasn't a problem I couldn't solve.

None of those problems involved a teenage girl who doesn't want me dating her mother.

I like Brianna. I thought we got on well. We chat about music—we found unlikely common ground in Eminem—and I gave her a tin of paint and some brushes so she could upcycle a desk Blair had given her for her bedroom. She'd smile and say hello when

I came to see Blair, and show me YouTube clips of orangutans being reunited with their keepers.

So it's somewhat of a shock when I turn up to collect Blair a couple weeks after we went to Roisters, to be left standing in the doorway as Brianna turns on her heel and stalks away.

"You told the kids, then?" I say, when Blair's briefed the babysitter and we're walking to the cinema.

"I thought they'd be pleased." Blair looks pained. "They like spending time with you—I didn't think it was a big deal. But Brianna went batshit." She groans and puts her head in her hands. "She said she hates me."

"She doesn't hate you." **Although she might hate me**, I think, remembering the cold look on her face when she opened the door.

"I know that. I do. But . . ." Blair's voice wobbles and I reach for her hand. "I'm so stupid. I thought they'd be happy we were dating."

"They'll come round. What did Logan say?"

Blair makes a sound that's half laugh, half sob. "He shrugged and said, 'I thought you already were.'"

"Hey, that's a fifty percent hit rate—that's not too bad."

The evening goes from bad to worse. The film, billed as a comedy, has about as much punch as an Amish disco, and twice Blair gets her cell from her bag to check for messages from home. The restaurant, for once not picked from the **Tribune**'s don't-risk-it range, more than merits a place there. We sit in near silence, pushing bland noodles around our plates.

"Maybe this was a mistake."

"The restaurant? It was definitely—" I see Blair's face. "Oh. You mean the whole thing. You and me. Right." An attempt to be casual comes out as curt and uncaring. My head hurts and I don't know what to say to make it better. Does Brianna not want her mom dating at all, or is it just that she doesn't want her dating **me**? A tiny voice whispers **Failure** in my ear and I shake it away. **No, you don't get to talk to me like that. Not anymore.**

"Let's just go, shall we?" Blair's cell has been on the table beside her for the whole meal, on the off chance that Brianna might message her. As she picks it up the screen lights up.

When you're a management consultant you spend a lot of time waiting at reception to be collected. You go to the desk and give your name, and wait while they run a finger down a list of expected visitors. **I can't see it**, they say, and you lean over and point at your name, which jumps out at you even though it's upside down. Because it's your name.

Or, in this case, Pip's name.

Pip Adams.

I blink. "Why is Pip texting you?"

Blair puts the cell in her bag. "What?"

"That was Pip's name on your screen."

She stands up. "No—it was a different Pip." She's flustered, making a meal of putting on her jacket, hiding her discomfort.

"A different Pip Adams?" I give a hollow laugh and throw bills on the table. I follow Blair out of the restaurant. "How does she have your number? Why do you have her name stored in your cell? What the hell is going on, Blair?"

"We talk, all right!" Blair stops short, five yards from the restaurant, spinning round to face me. Her eyes are wide, her jaw defiant.

"You . . . talk?" It's like two separate worlds have collided. "How?"

"Well, **she** says something, then **I** say something, then **she** goes, then—"

"No, I mean **how**? **Why**?" I run my fingers through my hair. "For how long?"

Blair sighs. "Since she came to your mom's house for you to sign the house papers. She had my address from my countersignature, and she wrote me."

"She **wrote** you?"

"She was worried about you, Max." Blair's shoulders drop, and she starts walking. "She said she thought you looked sick, that she didn't know what to do, she felt so far away . . ."

I hear Pip's voice in her words, imagine her finding paper and an envelope, sitting at the kitchen table and writing to a woman she'd only just met.

"Your mom had been a little . . ." Blair searches for something diplomatic. We wait for the lights at Belmont and Broadway; cross as soon as the traffic stops. "Prickly toward her—understandably, I guess—and she wanted someone to keep an eye on you and . . . report back." She trails off, the final words a reluctant admission.

"You agreed to . . ." Anger closes my throat, and I have to force out the words. "Spy on me?"

"It wasn't spying! I promised I'd look out for you, that's all. Let her know how you were, try and get you out of the house a bit—"

I think of the times Blair would come around to see my mom. I think of the way we bumped into her "by coincidence" at the Wicker Park Fest, and ended up spending the day together. I think of her suggestion that we give her friend's restaurant some support after the terrible **Tribune** review.

"So all this"—I wave my arms in an ineffectual sign language meaning **you, me, us**—"it was because you felt sorry for me? Pity dates?"

You're such a failure . . .

"No!" Blair tries to take my arm, but I snatch it away. "Max, no. I **like** you. God, I might even—"

"Don't." I look at her. "Just don't."

Back home I ring Pip and leave an angry voicemail. I pace my studio, resenting the tiny space that seemed cozy when I left, and now feels pathetic—a measure of how far I've fallen. I open a bottle of wine, and I'm halfway through it when my gaze falls on the comforter over the back of the sofa.

Isn't this what happened before? When Pip left me? The angry drinking, the bitter resentment? I remember Tom's face when he took in the filthy kitchen, his nose wrinkled at my unwashed odor. I think of the months spent curled beneath the pink comforter at Mom's house, of the crushing failure that weighed so heavy I couldn't get up even if I wanted to.

Isn't it what happened? And, before then, wasn't it always what I did? Back off, run away, keep my distance. I think of the night Pip and I argued, and I packed my bags. I think of the weeks I lived in a hotel by the hospital, communicating with Pip through lawyer's letters and terse notes left by Dylan's bed. She came back to me for his sake, but is it any wonder she didn't stay?

I look at the wall, to where Dylan's picture hangs. **My Family.**

No. I say it again, out loud, this time. "No." I screw the lid back on the bottle, then take it off again and pour the contents down the sink. I run the faucet and watch the red fade to pink and then disappear altogether. **No.** No more running away. No more shutting myself off.

I text Blair. I overreacted. I'm sorry. Can we talk tomorrow? And Pip. That voicemail was out of order, I'm sorry. But can we talk? And then I go to bed.

I don't normally work weekends, but the last couple Sundays I've been at the Dearborn Institute—one of the schools that brings kids to the swim club. I did a few small jobs for them, just to help out, and I said I'd paint a wall on the outside of the residential unit. I'm on edge in the morning, waiting for either Blair or Pip—or both—to call, but I soon get into the zone. I guess some people feel like this about ironing, or running—that chilled-out state you get in when you're making the same movement over and over.

"I can help." It's delivered as a statement, not a question. I straighten. A boy of eighteen or so is standing by my brushes. Thick brown hair almost hides heavy eyebrows that run in a straight line and meet above the bridge of his nose. He wears glasses, and a broad smile I can't help but return.

"Sure." I find a decent-sized brush. "I've done the edges, so we're just coloring now."

He puts too much paint on his brush—everyone does—and I show him how to wipe the brush on the string I've tied across the top of the paint pot, to stop the tin getting covered in paint. He watches me apply the paint to the wall—stippling it into the mortar lines, angling the brush on the smoother bricks—and copies me perfectly.

"Hey, that's pretty good. You'll be taking my job, if I'm not careful."

I introduce myself, and learn that his name is Glen, and that he's eighteen and in his last semester at Dearborn. He tells me his favorite food (cheese), what color his best shirt is (green), and what baseball team he supports (Cubs). We've almost finished the wall when Jessica Miller, one of the residential teachers, comes by. "Great job! You been helping out, Glen?"

"He's been brilliant."

"I need to go now," Glen says. "I need to see Martha Stewart."

"Thanks for your help," I say, but Glen has hurried off. I raise an eyebrow at Jessica. "Martha Stewart?"

"Glen's an avid baker. He likes her cooking program." She admires the finished wall. "He's done a good job. Maybe we should add painting to his résumé."

"Is he looking for a job?"

"He will be. A lot of the kids here will move from school to some sort of residential home, but some of them—Glen included—will be supported into independent living, which could include getting a job." She looks at me, and I see the thought forming.

"Look, I don't have enough clients to start taking on staff," I say, before she can ask, "but if it would be useful to do some shadowing . . ."

"Really?"

My phone rings and I check the screen. "Would you excuse me? I need to take this."

"I'll be in touch." Jessica starts walking away. "I'm going to hold you to that offer, Max Adams!"

"Hey."

I can't read Blair's voice. She sounds wary, like she's keeping something back. **I like you**, she said last night. **I might even . . .**

"I'm an idiot," I tell her.

"So, what's new?"

I can hear her smiling, and I breathe out slowly. I think I'm getting a second chance.

forty-eight

Pip

2016

The noise is incredible. Like standing on the runway at Heathrow as a plane takes off, only with no ear defenders, and with children instead of planes.

"God, I hate soft play." Kat looks around and grimaces. "Heaven knows what's in that ball pit." We're sitting on wipe-clean leather-look sofas in the "baby zone" corner of a giant warehouse on the outskirts of Leamington.

"They love it, though—look at them." Grace is eight months old, and bottom-shuffling at an impressive speed around an obstacle course made from a series of colourful padded blocks, doing her best to keep up with Kat's son, Thomas, all of a week older than Grace, but already a confident crawler. She has the fair curls Dylan had as a baby, and I wonder if they'll darken, as his did. Sometimes I see him so clearly in her face that it takes my breath away, but mostly I just see Grace. My little girl. As Kat and I watch our children play, Grace traps herself in a corner and forgets how to turn around, and Thomas crawls on top of another child.

"It's like an episode of **Robot Wars**, isn't it?" I say, as we rescue them. "You half expect them to spontaneously combust." We lift the children over the low picket fence that encloses the baby zone, and I'm settling Grace for a feed when Priya arrives with Aeesha, her shock of black shiny hair already long enough for two pink hair bobbles on top of her head.

"Sorry I'm late." Priya looks around. "No Charlotte?"

"She's gone back to work," I remind her.

We move up and Priya squeezes onto the sofa. "Ugh. It's like the summer holidays are ending and now term's starting."

"Not for me," Kat says. "I'm going to be broke but happy, staying home, getting fat and making cakes and babies." She grins, and looks at me. "Has work approved your hours yet?"

"Yes, I can go back part-time next month. But that only works if Max can convince his boss to give him some flexibility." Grace pulls away from me, too distracted by the noise and colour around her to feed properly. I rearrange my T-shirt and root in my bag for a bread stick for her. "I can do one five-day trip each fortnight, but only if Max can guarantee to work from the UK office on those days, so he can do the daycare runs."

"And his boss won't let him?"

"It's a work in progress. Chester's not big on family." I stand up. "Right, I need coffee—anyone else?"

I'm standing in the queue at the café, when a familiar voice calls my name.

"I thought it was you!"

I turn round to see Alison, a sticky-fingered toddler on her hip, and a broad smile on her face.

"You look amazing. Gosh, how long's it been?"

Since you stopped including me in invitations? "Must be three years," I say lightly.

"Must be." She pulls a face. "Isn't that terrible? Isaac and Toby are in year two now, can you believe that?"

Can she really be that crass? That insensitive? Doesn't she think I know full well what year her children are in at school, what year Dylan would have been in? Doesn't she imagine how it feels, each September, to see the barrage of photos on Facebook of uniformed children clutching oversized book bags?

"A little bird told me you'd had a baby. A boy, wasn't it?"

"A girl. Grace." No doubt the same little bird told her that Max and I have split up.

"Lovely name. This is Mabel." Alison presents the sticky-fingered toddler to me, and I notice the stickiness extends to her face. Mabel was clearly mid–jam sandwich when Alison spotted me. "Say hello, Mabel."

Mabel buries her face in her mother's chest, and I take comfort from knowing that Alison's light grey angora cardigan is now smeared with raspberry jam. I move forward in the queue.

"She's a bit shy. Fiona's over there—she's had another little girl, too. Why don't you join us? It would be lovely to catch up. So lovely to see you looking so well, after all that awful business."

All that awful business. All that time in hospital. All that devastating news, the terminal diagnosis, the decision no parent should ever have to make. All that media intrusion, all that time in court. All that awful business of your son dying . . .

I take a long hard look at Alison, who has discovered the jam on her cardigan, and is trying in vain to wipe it off with a tissue. "I don't think so, thank you. I'm here with some friends." I reach the front of the queue and turn my back on Alison. "Two flat whites and a tea, please."

What a bitch." Lars is sitting on the floor of my sitting room with Grace, stacking plastic blocks on top of one another. Each time he completes the tower Grace pushes them over and laughs hysterically, and Lars rebuilds it. Again and again and again.

"She always was, I think, I just hadn't noticed it." Or perhaps, I think guiltily, Alison's bitchiness simply hadn't ever been directed at me. I look at the clock. I need to get Grace into the bath.

"I'm not working tomorrow." Lars continues stacking blocks, with a focus that far outweighs the task at hand. He leaves a silence I think I'm supposed to fill.

"So . . ."

Grace swipes obediently at the finished tower, and Lars holds his hands over his face in mock dismay. My daughter laughs and laughs, and Lars smiles at her as he carries on speaking to me. "I could stay. After dinner. I could stay the night. You know, if . . ." He stacks the blocks, his eyes resolutely on the brightly coloured plastic.

We are, it seems, in a relationship, of sorts. It is not a conventional relationship—it certainly did not have a conventional beginning, but then, for the past four years, little about my life has been conventional.

"I'd like to take you for dinner," Lars said, when Grace was six weeks old. "But because that's logistically a little difficult for you, right now, I wondered if it would be OK to bring dinner to you?"

If I had any doubt that this was to be a Proper Date, it vanished when I opened the door to find Lars in a beautiful navy suit, with a pale pink shirt and navy tie. He had a large bag in each hand.

"I'm not quite ready yet—sorry. Would you mind watching Grace, while I get changed?" I had already changed—into a clean pair of jeans, and a top that didn't have baby sick on it—but it would take moments to change again. I hated the thought that Lars might feel overdressed, and as I pulled from the wardrobe a dress in which I would still be able to breastfeed, I felt a spark of excitement I hadn't felt for a while. I was going on a date! And I didn't even have to leave the house for it.

Lars didn't only bring dinner. He brought the tablecloth and place mats, crockery and cutlery. He brought flowers and a vase to put them in, and a candle that sat in the centre of my table, on a little silver stand.

I stood in the doorway to the kitchen, suddenly shy, watching Lars put the finishing touches to the table, and chatting to Grace in her bouncy chair. As if he could feel me watching, he turned round, and for a second we just looked at each other. Something shifted in the air, and suddenly I really did feel as though I was on a date.

"You look lovely."

I blushed. "I do have plates of my own, you know."

"Ah, but this way I can whisk them away at the end of the evening, and we can pretend we're in a restaurant, and someone else is doing the washing up for us."

I laughed. "I suppose you'll be expecting a ten percent tip for your trouble . . ."

"At least. I do need some wineglasses, though—I didn't think they'd survive the shopping bag experience."

"Here." I crossed the room and took two glasses from the cupboard.

"I wasn't sure if you'd be drinking." Lars held up two bottles—one of wine, and one of something fizzy and nonalcoholic.

"One won't hurt."

We clinked glasses, and I tried to think who else I knew who would go to this much trouble to give me a lovely evening. I came up blank. "This is really, truly lovely," I tell him. "Thank you."

Lars had cooked. Chilli con carne, with paprika rice, and the lightest lemon sponge, served with a spoonful of vanilla ice cream.

"I didn't make the ice cream, I'm afraid."

"I'm impressed you made any of it—I feel I should email your cookery teacher with a testimonial."

"I've signed up for the intermediate sessions," Lars says, a slight blush to his cheeks.

Afterwards, we retired to the sitting room with our coffee. It was strange to see another man sitting where Max used to sit, and I felt a wave of sadness that life had not worked out the way either of us expected. But then, I suppose life rarely does.

We talked about Grace, and about travel—of course—but so much more besides. We talked books, and politics, and feminism, and although my eyelids were dropping I didn't want the evening to end.

I woke, groggy and confused, to the sound of Grace crying. The lights were dimmed and I was lying on the sofa, still dressed. Pulled over me was the blanket from the back of the sofa, made from the yellow squares I'd started by Dylan's bedside and finished in my reading room, three years later.

Where was Grace? Where was Lars?

I was seized by panic, tangling myself in the blanket as I got up, and tearing it off me, leaving it lying on the floor. I rushed to the kitchen, where a light shone around the slightly open door.

"Grace!"

Lars stood and handed me my daughter. He looked relieved, as well he might have done, given that I had literally left him holding the baby for—I checked my watch—**three hours**.

"I thought you could probably use the rest."

"I'm so sorry, Lars." I turned away so Grace could latch on, and checked my dress for modesty, wondering if I was the only woman to have ever breastfed on a first date. "You must think me so rude."

"I think you're a new mother, coping brilliantly. And I think I should leave the two of you in peace now."

We didn't kiss, not on that first date. But we did kiss on the second, a fortnight later, when Grace and I met Lars at the butterfly house, and it just . . . happened.

"You could stay," I say now, as though I'm testing out the idea. Repeating his words, not giving an answer.

"Only if you want me to."

My heart pitter-patters, because I **do** want him to, but—God, this is complicated—I have an eight-month-old baby, the skin on my stomach is stretched and silvered, and as for **down there** . . . I remember when Max and I had sex after Dylan was born—the tentative, sometimes painful forays back into a physical relationship. And that was a man who knew me before, who'd watched my body change into pregnancy and beyond. I move to sit on the floor next to Lars. He puts his arm around me, and I nestle into him. "I'm not young anymore," I say hesitantly.

"Nor am I."

"Having a baby has . . . my body is . . ." I stumble on, and eventually Lars twists to face me.

"You're beautiful. I have thought you were beautiful since the first time we met, and if you only knew how hard I found it to walk away from you, that night in Johannesburg . . ."

He moves forward to kiss me, and I let myself melt into his body. He has seen me give birth, this man. He has watched me sleep, and breastfeed, and he has looked after my child while I have a bath, and handed her to me while I've been wrapped in a towel. He wants this. And I do, too.

forty-nine

Max

2018

Glen sits on the floor and strokes his brush carefully along the baseboard. His tongue pokes from the corner of his mouth, the way Blair's does when she puts on mascara in the morning. He's spent six months with me, on what started as a week's shadowing and ended up as a paid apprenticeship. That Jessica Miller sure knows how to work a favor.

At the end of today Glen will put down his brushes for the last time—I'm letting him keep the coveralls— and tomorrow Mikayla will pick them up. Like Glen, Mikayla has Down syndrome, and like him, her fine motor skills are good, and she's interested in the work. It remains to be seen whether my clients will appreciate her renditions of songs from **High School Musical** as much as I do.

I stop by Blair's on my way back from work, peeling off my coveralls and leaving them in the van. My hands are covered in tiny dots of paint that disappear in the shower each night, only to be replaced the next day. I like them. I like the tangible proof that I've done a hard day's work—so much more satisfying than a printed report or a page of meeting notes.

I ring the bell. I have a key, but I don't use it when the kids are home. Blair's decorated the flat, and a festive wreath hangs on the door, tiny silver bells tied on with red ribbons. The bells jangle as Logan opens the door. He high-fives me. "Down below," he says, moving his hand to somewhere near his thigh, and then swiping it away before my own hand meets it. "Too slow!" He grins. "Can we play Fortnite?"

"Sure. Where's Mom?"

"Cooking." Blair comes into the hall. She's wearing an apron, and as I kiss her I feel an inappropriate stirring in my jeans. Presumably she feels it, too, because she grins and says the shower's free if I need it. "Maybe a cold one," she adds, sotto voce. I laugh.

"What's funny?" Logan says.

"Nothing. Right, **Battle Royale** or **Save the World**?" I follow Logan to the living room.

"We need the TV," he announces to his sister, who grabs the remote and hugs it to her.

"Hey, Brianna." I keep it light, but she doesn't even acknowledge my presence.

"I'm watching something."

"You've been watching it for ages—it's my turn. Max, tell her."

I hold up my hands like my back's against a wall. "Not my house, not my rules, pal. We can play another time." Logan aims a halfhearted kick at the sofa, then leaves the room, no doubt to moan to Blair about his sister. I sit on the sofa. Brianna stares fiercely at the TV. "How was school?"

Nothing.

"That interesting, huh?" On the TV, a girl with an extraordinarily short skirt is standing on a table in a school cafeteria and shouting something about respect. "This looks good," I lie. Brianna sighs loudly. She picks up the remote and changes the channel.

"Right, that's it." It seems I have reached the end of a tolerance zone I didn't even know I had. I stand up and switch off the TV. "We're going out."

"Have a good time," she says, in a tone that suggests entirely the opposite.

"No. You and me. We're going out for waffles. We're going to talk about this on neutral territory, because it's making your mom miserable." Brianna wavers, then. She might not like me dating her mom, but she's a good kid.

"Fine." She heaves herself off the sofa. "But I'm not eating anything."

"Honey." I pop my head round the kitchen door. "Brianna and I are going for waffles. We won't be long."

"You're—" Blair checks herself. "OK then! Great!"

We go to Butcher & the Burger on Armitage, where the temptation of the custard cart means Brianna can't stick to her threat. She mutters a **thank you** because even she isn't rude enough to ignore the heaped plate I just bought her. We sit on chrome stools, and I try to work out what I'm going to say to this angry teen, now that I have her here. As it turns out, she gets there first.

"I don't want another dad. I've already got one."

It's hardly a surprise—those teenage angst films are clichéd for a reason, after all—but even so, I'm glad it's out in the open.

"I get that." I take a spoonful of custard, and let it melt in my mouth. "The thing is, Brianna, I kinda like being around you and Logan. Not just because you're great kids, but because . . . because my own son isn't here anymore."

Brianna's eyes widen slightly. She knows about Dylan, but I don't talk about him much in front of the kids. I guess I don't talk about him much at all, because now that I've started, I can't seem to stop.

"He loved being outside. Even when it was really cold, or raining hard. When he started walking he'd never pass a puddle without jumping in it—we used to have to carry a spare set of clothes with us, just in case." I smile at the memory. "Even after he got sick, when he was in a wheelchair, he wanted to be outside. When it rained he'd throw back his head and open his mouth."

Brianna stares at her waffles, heaped with ice cream and hot-chocolate sauce. "Mom used to push my sister in a wheelchair."

"I know." **Slowly. Don't fuck this up, Max.** "We've got a lot in common, your mom and me." I eat my custard, trying not to show how much I want to make this work. She doesn't say anything for the longest while, and I run through a million things I could say, rejecting them all. I want to tell her that her mom saved me. That she made me smile again, that without her I might still be hiding under a pink comforter. I want to tell her that Blair makes me laugh the way no one else has since Pip left; that she understands me like no one else but Pip does. Only Brianna's still a kid. So I eat my custard, and she eats her ice cream, and I guess we're both thinking our own thoughts for a while.

"We did English," she says, after a full five minutes with nothing but the sound of our spoons. She glances up at me. "In school."

"Cool."

"And Maria Perez hurt her ankle in phys ed and had to go to the ER."

"That's not so cool."

Brianna shrugs. "No one likes Maria Perez."

I do, I think.

fifty

Pip

2017

The bench is on a hill overlooking the park where Max and I used to bring Dylan. We were playing there when everything went wrong; me, sitting with Dylan in the sandpit, my phone ringing with a call I didn't yet know was urgent, walking a few feet away from the playing children, one eye still on Dylan, one finger pressed to my free ear so I could hear.

We've had the results of Dylan's blood tests. The consultant would like to speak to you. When could you come in? No, not tomorrow. Today, if possible.

The bench is made from teak. It has a curved back, and smooth arms, and a silver plaque I polish with my sleeve every time I come.

DYLAN ADAMS, 05/05/10–16/04/13

We scattered Dylan's ashes along with handfuls of meadow seed. Now, wildflowers abound on either side of the bench, filling the air with their scent, and with the buzz of honeybees. Buttercups and yellow rattle colour the ground with sunshine.

"Mummy!" Grace is fourteen months, at that stage where every day brings new discoveries.

"I see! Clever girl."

Today's finding is that, if she faces away from me, and bends to look between her legs, I will appear upside down, and that, if she leans forward from this position, she will tumble over and end up sitting on the ground. This she does, over and over, until she is dizzy.

I look down the hill to the playground, where a woman is attempting to round up several small children. As soon as she has one of them standing by the gate, a second one breaks for the seesaw, and a third makes a bid for freedom. The fourth takes off the coat his mother has just this moment put on him. It is like watching a particularly unsuccessful sheepdog trial, and I can't help but smile. Beyond her, a man walks from the car park. He passes the play area and continues up the hill.

"Gracie, Daddy's coming."

She stops, mid-forward-roll, and untangles herself, pushing herself up on all fours before getting to her feet. She is still unsteady, with more purpose than direction. "Dada!" She runs to meet him, and I wince as she careers down the path, waiting for the trip, for the skinned knees, for the tears.

But Max thinks the same, and he runs to meet her, scooping her up before she falls, and giving her a great bear hug, before setting her down again. They walk up, hand in hand, and I hear Grace chattering to him in her own peculiar brand of English and Grace-language.

"Hey," he says to me, and he kisses me on the cheek. The logistics of divorce take some working out, and I'm grateful for the fact that Max and I remain not just on speaking terms, but good friends. Best friends, I suppose, with the caveat that I don't want to know the details of his relationship with Blair, and I imagine he would prefer not to think too deeply about me and Lars. They have met, of course, not just when Grace was born, but several times since. They are polite to each other but unlikely to ever reach the going-for-a-drink stage, which I think is reasonable. Max still lives in the UK, but he spends increasingly more time in Chicago. Blair and I are Facebook friends, which is terribly modern and civilised, and means I am forever untagging myself from photos in which I'm not wearing makeup, or where I have hair that looks like it belongs to one of Grace's matted dolls.

"Hungry?" I open the hamper I've lugged up the hill, and spread out the picnic blanket. "Grace, can you help me unpack the picnic?" She takes out a stick of bread and the hummus, olives, pâté, and cheese I packed this morning, sticking her fingers into each one in turn to taste it, before finding a place for it on the rug.

Max kneels next to Grace, and opens his rucksack. He takes out three plastic mugs, a half bottle of champagne, and a carton of apple juice, and lines the mugs up on the bench to pour the drinks.

He has a flat, with a pink-painted room full of Grace's toys and clothes, about half an hour from the house that remains in both our names. Once a fortnight, when I go to work, Max stays in the guest room at mine. He takes Grace to daycare, and goes on to the UK office, thanks to Chester's finally agreeing to Max's not unreasonable request to spend more time in the UK. It is an unusual arrangement, but it works. Occasionally, I will get back home to find Max has made supper, and we eat it together, and I think how strange it is that we get on so much better now. We separated just in time, I often think, as though someone took the lid off the pan right before it boiled over.

"Cheers," Max says softly, touching his plastic cup to mine. "Happy birthday, Dylan."

"Happy birthday, Dylan." I can't help it, my eyes still fill with tears, but I smile and blink them away, and look at our amazing daughter, who has a fistful of olives in one hand and a mug of juice in the other.

"Gracie!" She bangs her juice against my cup, and then Max's.

Max shakes his head. "Not Gracie's birthday—your

brother Dylan's. It's his seventh birthday." He looks at me, and his tone changes. "Seven."

"I know."

We eat our picnic, then Grace becomes restless, and I send her with Max to run down the hill to the playground. I put away the food, and tip out Grace's leftover juice, and when everything is tidy, and I've checked the ground for rubbish, I sit on Dylan's bench. A butterfly flits across the top of a cowslip.

"I took your trike out of the loft for Gracie. Do you remember it? It had a handle on the back, so we could push you around when your legs got tired. Grace loves it. I told her it was yours. I talk to her about you all the time, you know. She doesn't understand—not yet—but she will." I look down the hill to the playground, where Grace is perched on the roundabout. Max is pushing her slowly round, one hand on her shoulder. I imagine her telling him **More, Dada, more!**

"I wish . . ." I rub my thumb across the grain of the bench. "I wish I knew for certain what would have happened." I think of Dr. Leila Khalili, sitting in the café around the corner from the hospital. **I could have been wrong . . . But I could have been right.** "Should we have taken you to America?" My voice rises a notch. "Would the treatment have worked? Would I be buying you a new bike for your birthday, instead of—"

I break off. This isn't what I want this place to be.

I want this bench to be a happy place, where Max and I—and Grace, when she's older—can come alone, or together, and think about the happy times we had with our beautiful boy. I want people to pause awhile, resting their legs after the climb from the park, enjoying the flowers that wouldn't be here if Dylan had lived. And if they notice the silver plaque, and if they take in the dates, and realise our boy was little more than a baby, then I hope it reminds them that life is short, and that tonight they will hug their own children a little tighter. Because I would give anything for one more cuddle with my boy.

In the playground Grace has made a friend—a boy a little younger than her—whose mother stands nearby, talking on her phone. They dig in the bark chippings, making piles and then running around them until they fall over. Max and I lean on the railings and watch.

"All this play equipment, and she wants to play in the dirt," he says, secretly delighted. And then, from nowhere, "Chester wants me to head up the US office. It's a promotion, of sorts. Less travelling, more strategy."

I'm silent for a while. "What will you say?"

"No, of course. Grace is here." But he answered too fast, too unequivocally, and if he had no doubt, then why tell me at all?

"What does Blair think?"

Max digs the tip of his shoe into the bark chippings. "I spend as much time with her as I can, but she finds it hard, not living together all the time. It's . . ." He looks for the word that will explain the situation to me without being disloyal. "It puts a strain on our relationship."

"Do you want the job?" I see Max about to speak, and I hold up my hand. "Ignoring the location, is the actual job something you want to do?"

"Hell yes. It's perfect. I'm sick of travelling, Pip, sick of living out of a suitcase. I want to wake up in the same place every day, play soccer . . ."

I look at Grace. She already talks to Max on Skype when he's away, or at his flat. Would it be any different if Max were in Chicago? "You should take it."

"No. It wouldn't be fair."

"It's where you're from, Max. Where your parents are. You moved to England because you married me, but . . ." **But we're not married any more.** "Grace and I could visit all the time—I can use my staff travel passes." I touch his arm and he looks at me. "Don't say no just because of us. You need to live your own life, too."

"What about you, then? How's Lars?" As always, it sounds strange to hear Max say his name.

"He's fine. We just booked a holiday, actually. We're going camping in the Lake District."

"We never did do that, did we?" There's a touch of

bitterness in Max's voice, and I feel like a bitch. I didn't need to tell him where we were going—didn't need to remind him he'd promised to take me. I cast around for something to say to level the scales.

"He wants us to get married, but I don't want to." I'm stretching the truth. Lars has talked about marriage, on several occasions, but he's never put pressure on me, and I've never given a definitive no. I suppose I just want to show Max that not everything is green on my side of the fence, either.

"Why not?"

I shrug. If I haven't been able to give Lars a convincing reason, I doubt I can give Max one.

"You need to live your own life, too." He gives me a lopsided grin.

"Touché." I laugh. "Look at us, being all grown-up. Like the poster couple for amicable divorce."

Max doesn't join in. He turns away and looks at Grace, playing so nicely with her new friend, and I know that in his head it isn't a stranger's son playing with her, but **our** son. Our Dylan. Because that's what I'm seeing, too.

"I wish things had been different."

"The doctors did what they thought—"

Max turns. "No, not Dylan. You and me." He looks away again. "I wish things had been different for us."

fifty-one

Max

2019

Blair is dozing in her seat. She's pulled her sweater over her like a blanket, and her head is inches from mine, her eyelashes resting on her cheeks. Ten days in Florida has made her tan, and the color suits her.

"Stop watching me," she says, without opening her eyes.

I drop a kiss on the end of her nose, and she smiles. In seats across the aisle, Brianna and Logan are watching movies—**The Rosie Project** and **Hobbs & Shaw** respectively. They lack their mom's sixth sense, and don't feel me watching them. Logan is still wearing the Black Panther hat we bought on our first day in Disney World, the peak pulled so low I'm amazed he can see the TV screen. For ten days Brianna has worn a glittery rose-gold Alice band complete with Minnie Mouse ears, but as we reached the airport she pulled it off and shoved it into her case. It's a tricky age, on the cusp between childhood and adulthood, and she and I are still working out where we stand.

They bicker at the airport, the postholiday comedown exacerbated by delayed baggage. When the belt finally creaks into action it produces Logan's small case, and the larger one I shared with Blair, but no pink carryall with **Brianna Arnold** on the luggage label.

"It's caused a security scare," Logan says.

"Shut up."

"They'll have to search it."

"Shut up!"

"They're probably going through your underwear right now." Logan holds up an imaginary bra to his scrawny chest. He assumes the deep voice of a fictitious security guard. "Gentlemen, there's no room for explosives in here—we can move on."

"Mom!" Brianna swipes at Logan's head, knocking his cap to the floor.

"Ow! Mom!"

"Cut it **out**, you two! You're worse than toddlers."

"Shall we order in tonight?" I say to Blair. "Give real life a miss till tomorrow?" She nods gratefully, and I spot Brianna's pink bag finally emerging onto the conveyor belt.

We're walking to the parking lot when I see Pip

and her colleagues. They're walking in formation, like flightless tropical birds—ten cabin crew, in their red coats, and two pilots, rings of gold around their sleeves. They pull their wheeled cases behind them, and I have a sudden memory of taking Pip's case out of the boot of her car, of carrying it upstairs and putting it on the bed.

"Can I catch you up?" I give Blair the car keys. "I just want to—"

But she's seen, too. She smiles. "Go. I'll take the suitcase."

Pip's talking to a tall black girl who walks like a model. They'll be discussing last night, I guess. The bar they went to, the meal they had. The shopping, the sightseeing, the socializing.

"Pip!"

She turns instantly, a smile on her face as though she half-expected me. "Two minutes," she tells her colleague. She hugs me, squeezing me hard. "Where have you been?"

"Disney World."

"With Blair and the children? Did you have a good time?"

"It was great." I hesitate. "It's good to see you. I wanted . . . I wanted to tell you in person." There's a flicker of alarm in Pip's face—the legacy of a time when all news was bad news—and I don't leave her hanging. "Blair and I are getting married." Her mouth opens slightly but she doesn't say anything right away, and I search her face for disapproval, regret, concern . . . anything. "You think it's too soon. You think we're rushing things."

And then her eyes widen, and she breaks into a smile. "No, I think it's wonderful. I'm so glad for you, Max. I'm so glad you're happy again."

"We'd like you to be there—if that's not too weird."

"I wouldn't miss it." Her eyes are shining. Behind her, a hundred yards away, the formation of red and blue has stopped. They are waiting for her. Pip follows my gaze. A male pilot stands slightly apart from the rest.

"Is that Lars?"

She nods. Flushes slightly, the way you do when you hear the name of someone you're in love with. We lock eyes for a second. "I could—"

"Introduce us?" When you've finished someone's sentences—and they've finished yours—for so many years, it's a hard habit to break. "Sure."

Lars is tall, with blond hair and blue eyes. He's older than me—it is pitiful of me to care, or even notice, but there you go—and he shakes my hand with just the right grip. Not weak, but not aggressive— no unnecessary marking of territory.

"Pip talks about you all the time," he says, right off the bat. "It's good to finally meet you."

"And you." They look good together. Is that a strange thing to think about your ex-wife? They look right. Happy. Pip looks happy. And that's all I want for her.

I watch them rejoin the others, slotting into place like they were never away. I see the girl with the model walk look back at me—**So that's your ex-husband?**—and I smile to myself as I turn, and head for the car park.

It is a curious thing, when you fall in love for a second time. I would do anything to be able to turn back time to that summer before Dylan went into hospital. Before we knew he was sick, before we were asked to choose, before Pip and I slowly fell apart.

And yet, if Pip and I were still together, I wouldn't be marrying Blair. I wouldn't wake every day with hope in my heart and a mass of corkscrew curls on the pillow beside me. I wouldn't be running a business I love, in a city I love, with trainees who have made me see the world a different way.

I can't have both lives, I can only live this one.

fifty-two

Pip

2019

Weddings are different, second time around. Quieter, more cautious.

No less exciting, no less nerve-wracking.

Butterflies swoop in my stomach as Mum walks around me with a critical eye, picking invisible bits of lint from my dress, and stroking a stray hair into place.

"Perfect." There are tears in her eyes. "You look perfect, Pip."

I'm wearing a wedding dress. I was hesitant, but everyone encouraged me. Mum, Jada, even Lars.

"You're the one everyone will be looking at," he said. "You should buy the biggest, most beautiful dress you can find."

It isn't big, but it is beautiful. A satin sheath skims

my hips and narrows to my knees, before kicking out into the hint of a train. The top is strapless, but antique lace covers my arms, and ties in a loose bow in the small of my back, before trailing down the back of the dress. Even Jada, who had been trying to persuade me into a Vivienne Westwood number three sizes too small, was convinced.

"That's the one!" She clasped her hands together, pressing her thumbs to her lips.

I twisted round to see the label. "It's horribly expensive."

"You only get married—" Jada bit off her sentence, and I finished it for her with a wry smile.

"Twice?" I looked in the mirror. The lace was pale gold, and even without makeup, it made my skin glow. This was indeed the one.

"Pretty Mummy!" Grace reaches for me, and I pick her up and twirl her around.

"Pretty Grace." She's wearing a white dress dotted with buttercups, with a net petticoat she has so far showed to everyone at the registry office, and several people in the car park. I have a sudden memory of Dylan at eighteen months, and the time he became obsessed with tutus, wearing a pink one from breakfast till bedtime. I squeeze Grace until she wriggles free, then kiss her on the nose. She is three—older now than Dylan was when he died. We are in uncharted territory, no longer drawing comparisons. Grace is her own little person, different in so many ways to her big brother, and finding her way in the world with energy and confidence.

"Careful of Mummy's dress." My mother holds Grace's shoes—white Converse with yellow ribbon laces—away from my side.

"It's fine." I rearrange her on my hip, remembering how precious I was about my first wedding dress, how Mum brought an iron to the church for last-minute pressing in the vestry. The door opens, and Dad appears.

"Ready?"

I feel a sudden swell of nerves. Mum kisses me and goes to take her seat, and Jada, who chose a simple shift dress as her bridesmaid's outfit, takes one last check in the mirror before taking Grace from me.

"Come on, princess, let's help Mummy get married, shall we?" She gives Grace her posy of yellow flowers, and picks up her own, and they wait by the door of the anteroom we were given, in which to get ready. Dad stands next to me, and I tuck my arm in his.

"Well, I never thought I'd be doing this again," he says.

"You don't think I'm doing the wrong thing, do you?" I search his face for what he's really thinking. Last time he took me to one side as the guests were sliding into pews and picking up hymn sheets, and said that if I changed my mind—**even if we're half-way down the aisle, even if you're standing at the**

blooming altar, Pip—I only had to say. It didn't matter, no one would think less of me.

"Didn't you like Max?" I asked him, years later.

"Of course I did," came the response. "But I liked you more."

Now, I wait for him to tell me I'm making a mistake, and I wonder what I'll do if he does. But he just smiles, and pulls my arm close to his.

"None of us knows what's going to happen in the future, love. The only thing we can do is make our choices on the way we feel right here, right now."

"I love him," I say simply, and my dad nods.

"Well, then."

A fresh start, I think. **For me, and for Grace.**

She steals the show instantly, an **aah** travelling across the room like a Mexican wave. There's a shuffling of feet as everyone stands to watch my little girl walk slowly down the aisle, the way Jada showed her, her chin held high like a three-foot catwalk model. I can't see her face, but I know she'll be looking serious, her brow furrowed as it always is when she's concentrating.

There's nothing serious, nothing stately about my own face, which sports a smile that makes my cheeks ache. Dad's keeping the pace, but I want to run, because I'm suddenly so desperate to be married, to feel by my side the other half that makes me whole again. I see Tom and Alistair, and seven-year-old Darcy, and then, from the front of the room, Lars turns to look at me. I feel a skip in my heart. He dips his head in an old-fashioned, gentlemanly bow, taking in my dress and nodding in silent admiration. **You're the one everyone will be looking at.**

Although really, it's Grace, who spots Max and breaks away from Jada, scattering petals from her posy as she thunders into him and demands to be picked up. There are more **aah**s, and a ripple of laughter, and before I know it Dad is slipping my arm from his, and kissing me on the cheek and whispering **Proud of you, love,** in my ear.

And then the registrar is asking if we're ready, and could everyone please take their seats now? Jada finds a spot next to Lars, and I stand next to Max, who has Grace wrapped round his neck like a monkey. And as the service begins, the room disappears and it's just me, Max and Grace, and the registrar, making us all a family again.

before

Two roads diverged in a wood, and I—
I took the one less traveled by,
And that has made all the difference.

—ROBERT FROST

fifty-three

Leila

Leila wonders if the judge has a family. She wonders if they visited at the weekend, if Justice Merritt played with his grandchildren and thought about the week ahead, about the decision that lay before him. She wonders if he'll go home this evening and eat dinner with his wife, and talk about the neighbors, the rubbish collection, a theater trip; or if he'll sit in his study, the door closed, hoping he made the right choice. She knows he will think about this case for the rest of his life, just as she will.

Justice Merritt has heard all the evidence. He will have done as Leila did, as Pip and Max Adams did—he will have tried to imagine the future. What will life be like if Dylan has treatment in America? What will it be like if his care is palliative only? Which is better? Which is kinder? Which is right? He will have asked himself question after question, and searched for the answers in the evidence put before him.

And now he has decided.

Leila feels light-headed, as though she's been sprinting and has stopped, suddenly, at the finish line. Her body is still, but her pulse is still racing, the adrenaline still fizzing, nowhere to go.

She looks around the courtroom and sees not people, but feelings. Anticipation. Fear. Sorrow. Regret. Determination. Pip and Max stare straight ahead, their hands clasped tightly together. Leila has never known a couple so well suited. She grieves for what this has done to them, and she hopes they will stay strong. They will need each other, no matter what the outcome of today.

"I would like to thank the medical team at St. Elizabeth's Children's Hospital, and the numerous experts who have given evidence over the last three days." Justice Merritt speaks slowly and clearly. "You have treated Dylan with the dignity and compassion he deserves, and you should be commended for such. Most importantly, I thank Dylan's parents, Max and Philippa Adams, who have conducted themselves in this uniquely difficult situation with bravery and dignity, and with nothing but their son's interests at heart."

Dylan's parents are hollowed out with grief. Leila tries to imagine what it must feel like to have your own private hell made public, and finds that she cannot. She feels a flash of anger toward paramedic Jim, and his disregard for the Adamses' feelings.

"My judgment today is incredibly difficult, but the parameters of my decision-making are simple. I must decide what is in Dylan's best interests. I must consider his emotional needs, as well as his medical ones."

It is hard enough to have a child in intensive care, Leila knows. It is harder to know that they may not survive, harder still to be asked to take their life in your own two hands, and then decide where to place it.

"The question on which this sad case hinges," says the judge, "is not only will proton beam therapy extend Dylan's life, but what is the quality of that life? Indeed, what **is** a life?"

How much harder must it be, Leila wonders, to face all of this with the world watching? To walk past a newsstand filled with your photographs, to turn on a radio and hear your own name? To read tabloid columns and broadsheet think pieces that lay bare the fears that plague you at night?

Leila feels suddenly nauseous.

"My decision is not based on what **I** would do, but on what I believe is right for **this** child, in **this** circumstance. It is made on the basis of the laws that govern us and protect us."

Leila stands up. She fights the urge to run, and instead walks as fast as she can across the courtroom. Her shoes echo in a void where a dropped pin would clang like an iron bar. There is no break in Justice

Merritt's speech, and Leila does not look back to see if he disapproves of her abrupt departure. His words are swallowed by the soft shush of the courtroom door as it closes, and Leila walks out onto the concourse.

She is momentarily thrown by the realization that life is still proceeding at the same pace. There are people moving about in this limbo between courtrooms, between opening and closing speeches. There are barristers and witnesses, applicants and respondents. Journalists. Somewhere outside are Habibeh and Wilma. Life continues.

But for Pip and Max Adams—for Dylan Adams—life will never be the same again. And Leila feels suddenly that it is wrong to share this pivotal moment with them—to take for entertainment something as life-altering as this. She cannot stop the newspapers printing their stories, or the chat show hosts planning their debates. She cannot tell the millions of people on Twitter to stop passing judgment, to stop this invasion of privacy. She cannot tell the crowds outside the court to go home. But she can close her own ears, for just a little longer. She can give Max and Pip this tiny piece of privacy, of respect.

And so Leila waits outside the court. She thinks about the little boy with a halo of soft brown curls, and the empty nursery at home, and the parents who love each other, but love their son more.

In a few moments, the doors will open, and the next act of Dylan's story will begin. No matter what the judge's ruling, Max's and Pip's lives will be irreversibly changed today, and Leila knows they will forever question the choices they made in the weeks leading up to the hearing. But when you stand at a crossroad you cannot see each destination, only the beginnings of the paths that will lead you there. All you can do is choose one, and walk, and hope that someone will walk with you.

There is a burst of activity behind her. Leila turns. Through the open door of the courtroom she sees Pip and Max, the distance between them seeming to grow even as she watches.

It is over. And it is only just beginning, too.

acknowledgments

With sincere thanks to Robin Shane and Baljinder Bath for legal detail; to Cheryl Payne, Bryony Gamble, and Sarah Hawthorne for advice about medical matters and overseas treatment; to Maryam Ozlati for her insights into Iranian food, culture, and language; to Nina Smith, for information about private air ambulances; to Shona Bowman, Nicola Boddy, and the Virgin Atlantic Twitter team, for answering my questions on flight attendants and airline policies; to Robert France, for solving a time difference conundrum; and to Toni Hargis, for helping me with Max's American English. All mistakes are mine, and detours from reality generally made for considered reasons. Thank you to Alan Donnachie, for making a generous charitable donation in exchange for naming a character in this book. I hope your mother, Wilma, would have liked her namesake. I am enormously grateful to

acknowledgments

Claire Zion, who showed me around her hometown of Chicago. Her insights have made all the difference to this book.

Thank you, too, to everyone who has backed this story behind the scenes, who understood what I wanted to do, and supported me when I didn't know if I could do it. To my agent, Sheila Crowley, and to Abbie Greaves and the whole Curtis Brown team; to my editors, Lucy Malagoni and Cath Burke, and the entire Little, Brown office—too many to name. In the US, thank you to Tara Singh Carlson and the Putnam team.

Thank you to all the book bloggers, reviewers, booksellers, and librarians who have shared their love for my books, and to all the readers who have championed them.

Thank you to Kim Allen for keeping me organized, and to the MOB for keeping me sane. And finally, thank you to Rob, Josh, Evie, and George, for filling my empty arms again.

from the author

In 2006, my husband and I were faced with an impossible decision: to keep our critically ill son alive, or to remove his life support and let him die. It was a decision that needed to be made swiftly, and by both of us. I asked the consultant what would happen if we wanted different outcomes, if we couldn't agree. "You have to," she said. The NHS was incredible; the doctors sensitive and compassionate. I owe a great debt to them, and also to our families, who loved and supported us, and never once questioned our decision.

There have been many tragic cases, in recent years, where parents have disagreed with the recommendations given by their children's care providers. In every case I have had the utmost admiration for the medical teams and for the parents, who have had to live out their worst nightmare in the public eye. Everyone has an opinion, yet the truth is that no one can really know what is right. No one can predict the future, and so all we can do is make a decision based on the facts we have, and—sometimes—on what our heart tells us.

I doubt my judgment every single day. I miss my son every single day. This has been an incredibly difficult book to write, but one that has also brought me great joy. I know that for many people it will have been a difficult book to read, and I will understand if you have put it down before reaching this page. But this is a story not about loss, but about hope. Hope for the future, for a life beyond an unavoidable tragedy. We cannot predict the future when we make difficult choices in life, but we can shape the years that follow. We can choose to live again.

Clare Mackintosh